Then We Die

Also by James Craig

London Calling

Buckingham Palace Blues

Time of Death

The Criminals We Deserve

A Man of Sorrows

Then We Die

An Inspector Carlyle Mystery

JAMES CRAIG

WITNESS
IMPULSE
An Imprint of HarperCollins*Publishers*

This book was previously published by Constable & Robinson in 2013.

EPub Edition FEBRUARY 2015 ISBN: 9780062365378

Print Edition ISBN: 9780062365385

10 9 8 7 6 5 4 3 2 1

Acknowledgements

THIS IS THE fifth John Carlyle novel, and thanks for getting it over the line go to: Polly James, Gillian McNeill, Paul Ridley, Michael Doggart, Luke Speed and Peter Lavery, as well as to Mary Dubberly and all the staff at Waterstones in Covent Garden.

Particular mention has to go to Chris McVeigh and Beth McFarland at 451 for all their help in promoting John Carlyle online, and to Donald Leggatt and Anthony Willis at Wildflower for producing the video promos for the series.

I also thank Richard Lewis, Simon Beckett, Ryszard Bublik, Michael Webster and William Baldwin-Charles for their enthusiasm and encouragement, without which this latest effort might well not have seen the light of day.

Of course, nothing would have come of any of this without the efforts of Krystyna Green, Rob Nichols, Martin Palmer, Colette Whitehouse, Saskia Angenent, Joan Deitch, Clive Hebard and all of the team at Constable.

I should add a particular thanks to my parents for helping me get this far. They didn't get me to London, but they set me on the right road. This year they celebrate fifty years of marriage, which makes me smile, particularly given the storyline in this book!

As always, the greatest thanks are reserved for Catherine and Cate. This book, like all the others, is for them.

James Craig
London, 2013

Death never takes the wise man by surprise. He is always ready to go.

JEAN DE LA FONTAINE (1621–95)

Chapter One

'I NEED TO talk to you . . . about your father.'

Plucking a French Fancy from the three-tiered cake stand, Carlyle carefully nibbled at the pink icing skin before attacking the exposed sponge underneath.

She shot him a sharp look, knowing that he wanted to ignore the subject at hand and was simply playing for time in the hope that it would go away of its own accord. 'John . . .'

'Mm.' With his free hand Carlyle pulled at the collar of his shirt, wondering what was coming next. The hotel's formal dress code required him to wear a jacket and tie and he had felt somewhat uncomfortable even before the conversation had changed tack. Fumbling with the top button of his shirt, he tried to think of something to say, but nothing sprang to mind. The only thing he knew was that he really didn't want to talk about his dad.

Not with his mum, anyway.

Refusing to make eye-contact, he played for time by scrutinizing a sculptured female figure crafted in gilded lead, flanked by a pair of floor-to-ceiling mirrors. Tea at the Ritz with his mother always felt a little surreal. God knows why she liked it so. The whole place looked like a Gianni Versace wet dream.

Afternoon tea had been a special treat for almost twenty years now, something that they had first stumbled upon by accident. Like the Changing of the Guard at Buckingham Palace or a trip to the Tower of London, it wasn't the kind of thing you thought of doing if you ever actually lived in the city. However, he had brought his mother here for her birthday one year, and thereafter it had become an annual event. It was the one occasion during the year when they did something together as mother and son. It had thus taken on a kind of timeless quality that allowed both of them the pretence that their relationship was immutable.

Located at number 150 Piccadilly, César Ritz's hotel had first opened in 1906. The only hotel awarded a Royal Warrant by HRH The Prince of Wales for services to Banqueting and Catering, it was a London landmark, a staple of the city's tourist trade. These days, in order to get a table in the famous Palm Court, you had to book at least three months in advance. At more than forty pounds a head, it wasn't cheap either, but it was *an event*.

Today, as always, both mother and son were determined to get their money's worth. For Carlyle, that meant seeing how many French Fancies and cupcakes he could devour in just forty-five minutes (his record was nine). For his mother, it meant savouring her brief escape from the city outside. Amidst the over-the-top Louis XVI style decor – where Winston Churchill, Charles de Gaulle, Charlie Chaplin and Evelyn Waugh had all sipped and nibbled before them – it was hard to imagine that London was still going about its never-ending business outside.

For Carlyle too, the ritual offered a rare chance to escape from the real world. As such, it was not a place to discuss serious family business. Today, however, he knew from his mother's firm tone – her Scottish accent still clearly detectable after all the decades in sensible exile – that she definitely wanted to talk about something serious.

Being a policeman, dealing with 'serious' issues was Carlyle's job. Disasters were a daily occurrence, but they were a purely professional rather than a personal concern. Anything closer to home was primarily his wife's concern. Carlyle would meet his domestic responsibilities, but only from the back seat. Wasn't that what most men did? Whatever, that was the way things worked in his family. He liked it that way. And he wanted to keep it that way for as long as possible.

What could his mother want to talk about? He could only assume that there was something wrong with his old man's health. And why not? His dad was only human. Carlyle double-checked the maths in his head. His parents were both in their seventies now. Life expectancy in the UK was around seventy-eight for a man and eighty-two for a woman. They were getting old.

Obviously, the clock was ticking louder and louder for both of them, but Carlyle wanted to ignore it for as long as possible. Apart from anything else, he wasn't sure how well he would rise to the occasion. If nothing else, John Carlyle was aware of his own limitations, or rather his own selfishness. He was already responsible for a wife and child. He had his own life to lead, just as his parents had lived theirs.

By and large, Lorna Gordon (she had never abandoned her maiden name) and Alexander John Carlyle had been blessed with good health and an extended period of active retirement. That was all anyone could ask for, was it not? Now, however, it was clear that these golden years would soon be coming to an end, in all likelihood to be replaced with something rather grim.

Carlyle thought back to the last time he had set eyes on his father. They had been to see a Fulham game at Craven Cottage a few weeks earlier – an entertaining 0-0 draw with Spurs – and he recalled the older man struggling up the steps of the Johnny Haynes Stand. At one point, his dad had slipped, falling awkwardly, and Carlyle had to lift him up. It was clear that his father had become less agile over recent years, but he was far from being an invalid. They were still very much father and son, so it was not something that either of them had been prepared to discuss further.

How bad would it get, though? His mind had started galloping ahead now and nothing could stop it. Would his father need to go into a home? His mother was by no means frail, but acting as a carer was extremely tough going, even for someone much younger. And then there would be the emotional strain . . .

He sneaked a glance at his mother as she poured some more tea into her cup. Something would have to give, sooner or later. Maybe something had given already. Would he himself have noticed? Quite possibly not.

His mind now in overdrive, Carlyle desperately wished that his wife was here. Helen was so much better at handling this type of situation than he was. Unlike him, she wasn't thinking about herself all the time.

An incredibly fat woman wearing a floral print dress lowered herself into a chair at a nearby table. Carlyle idly wondered if it would be able to support her weight. Grabbing a menu from the waiter, she devoured its contents with ravenous eyes. You should get your stomach stapled, he thought nastily.

Tearing his gaze away from the human whale, he scanned the room, suddenly conscious of the hum of conversation as tourists and day-trippers up from the Home Counties struggled to make themselves heard over the clink of cutlery against fine bone china. At least the surrounding noise meant that he could slurp his Jasmine tea without causing offence. Raising his cup towards his lips, he took a sip and looked over the rim expectantly, waiting for his mother to continue with her chosen topic of conversation.

Taking a modest bite from her smoked salmon sandwich, Lorna looked at him with sharp blue eyes. They were rather watery nowadays, but they still showed the steely determination that had taken the young Ms Gordon from the Fife backwater of Kirkcaldy to post-war Glasgow and, with her new husband in tow, on to London by the time she was barely eighteen. They had settled in Fulham, where she had become a schoolteacher while he had taken on a variety of jobs, some more menial than others. Their only son had been born there and grown up to become a policeman. A commendable family, committed to honest endeavour, they had modestly prospered for more than half a century.

A considerable achievement.

Something to be proud of.

'John . . .' his mother repeated.

'Yes?' Carlyle forced himself to meet his mother's gaze.

'Your father and I,' she said, with only the slightest of tremors evident in her voice, 'are getting a divorce.'

'*What?*'

Almost falling off his chair, Carlyle stared at her in absolute astonishment. Tea dribbled down his shirt and on to his lap. A waiter in bow-tie and waistcoat appeared by the table to offer him a napkin. Feeling flustered, he took it and waved the man away.

His mother watched impassively, finishing her sandwich as he mopped himself up.

'What do you mean,' he asked finally, dropping the tea-stained napkin on the table, his appetite well and truly gone, 'you're getting a divorce?'

She looked back at him sternly. 'I would have thought, Inspector John Carlyle, that the meaning of what I am saying is perfectly clear.'

'Yes,' he said, looking down at his plate. 'But – why?'

His mother narrowed her eyes and gave him another stare that made Carlyle feel as if he was eight years old. He had a flashback to some time around 1970, sitting in Macari's Café Bar off the Fulham Palace Road with a large glass of milk, reading the *Beano* and munching on a Tunnock's Caramel Wafer while his mum puffed away on an Embassy Regal and raced through the *Daily Mirror* crossword. She had given up both vices not long after. He tried to remember the last time he had seen a Caramel Wafer. Did they even still make them? Would they still taste so good?

Questions, questions – anything to avoid the matter in hand.

After dabbing at the corner of her mouth, his mother put down her napkin and stood up. 'Excuse me for a moment,' she said, before hurrying off in the direction of the Ladies. Watching her go, Carlyle pulled his mobile out of his jacket pocket. He was about to call and ask Helen for some advice when the waiter suddenly reappeared.

'I'm sorry, sir,' he declared officiously, 'but the use of mobile phones is not allowed in the Palm Court.'

Carlyle felt the panic rising in his chest. 'But—'

'I'm sorry, sir,' the waiter said firmly, standing his ground.

Reluctantly, Carlyle placed the mobile on the table. As he did so, the handset started vibrating, indicating that he had received a message. Waiting for the waiter to turn away, he opened it up.

On my way, pick you up outside the hotel in 15 minutes.

'Fuck!' Cursing a little too loudly, given his surroundings, Carlyle glanced at his watch. Surely that wasn't the time already? He had told his sergeant, Joe Szyszkowski, to come and collect him from the hotel at five o'clock. The pair of them had business to attend to this evening. The inspector was hoping that it would lead to a breakthrough in what had become a troublesome case. There would be arrests, followed by stories in the papers, personal glory and the admiration and respect of their colleagues – the kind of thing that was supposed to get you out of bed in the morning. Carlyle sighed. On the one hand, the call of duty was his *Get Out of Jail Free* card; on the other, much as he might wish to ignore what his mother had just said, he knew that he would have to deal with it at some stage, and the sooner the better.

Sticking the remains of the French Fancy in his mouth, he made a decision. His domestic dramas would have to wait, at least until tomorrow. Would his mother understand? Like her son, Lorna Gordon was an arch pragmatist, so he decided that she would allow herself to be usurped by The Job.

Washing down the mouthful with the last of his tea, Carlyle picked up the silver teapot and glanced inside. Empty. He looked around for a waiter who could bring them some more hot water. The guy who had stopped him using his mobile phone was hovering beside a table ten feet away, where a couple of men were perusing the menu. After a short discussion, the pair made their choices and the waiter bustled off, walking straight past Carlyle without acknowledging his signal.

The two men looked to be around forty, give or take. One of them said something and the other laughed loudly. It struck the inspector that they looked rather out of place here in the Palm

Court. Apart from Carlyle himself, most of the other customers were women, mainly fifteen or twenty years older. The men were dressed like American tourists: chinos and loafers with striped shirts and horribly clashing ties, tweed jackets and wraparound sunglasses. *Sunglasses?* London hadn't seen any sun worth talking about for more than six months. Carlyle listened to his brain taking notes. Both men had severe crew cuts which hardly complemented their attire, and both were wearing Bluetooth headsets, which did not sit well with the Palm Court's no-phones policy.

Picking a cupcake off the stand, Carlyle took a bite and slowly scanned the rest of the room. When he looked back at the duo, he could see they were peering through the arches of the Palm Court, past the Long Gallery beyond, and into the lobby. Following their gaze, he spotted a third man who seemed to be the focus of their interest. This one was dressed more like a proper businessman, in an expensive-looking navy suit, white shirt and red tie. Talking into a mobile, he used his free hand to cover his mouth while keeping his eyes on the revolving doors at the hotel entrance.

Three men on a mission. *So where was number four?*

Carlyle recalled an operational note that he had read the week before. It concerned a gang – believed to be of four men – who had been targeting the hotel rooms of rich visitors. There had been three incidents over a period of two months, with the last one almost a fortnight ago. The story had been kept out of the papers for fear of scaring away the top-end tourist trade.

Each robbery had been at a different hotel. The Ritz, so far, had not been one of those hit. The group's MO was the same in each case: follow the target up to his or her room, burst in as they are opening the door, force them to unlock the room safe, then drug them and grab whatever is to hand. Not very subtle, but effective. The crew's total estimated haul to date was almost half a million pounds in currency and valuables.

It had all been very professionally handled. On the way out, the gang had put *Do Not Disturb* signs on the door – a nice touch, Carlyle had to concede. In each case, no victim had been able to raise the alarm until several hours after the robbers had left the hotel. The gossip at Carlyle's police station was that the team from West End Central investigating the case had nothing to go on apart from a couple of security camera images that may or may not have caught the four unknown males thought to be involved.

Trying to appear as casual as possible, Carlyle looked around slowly for the CCTV. From where he was sitting, he could see three cameras fixed to the columns in the Palm Court. There were bound to be more in the lobby, so there would be plenty of images of all three of these guys. Maybe they were getting sloppy. He reached for his phone and, watching out for officious waiters, began surreptitiously typing a text to Joe under the table.

Possible situation here. Wait for me in lobby. Check availability of back-up.

After pressing Send, he looked back towards the lobby in time to see a middle-aged couple, laden with shopping bags covered in designer logos, coming in through the entrance. The businessman type said something further on his mobile, ended the call and fell in behind them. The two men sitting in the Palm Court got up from their table and headed for the lobby. One of them was still holding his napkin, and Carlyle thought he detected something black wrapped inside it. *Could it be a handgun?* He frowned. As far as he could remember, no weapons had featured in the earlier robberies. *Then again*, he reminded himself, *things change.*

Standing up, he let the men disappear through the intervening arches and counted to three. Then he followed.

'Sir?'

Carlyle had barely gone two steps when he was stopped by his ever-so-friendly waiter.

'Is everything all right? Are you finished with your table?'

'No,' said Carlyle hurriedly. 'My mother will be back in a second.' He pulled a business card out of his pocket and thrust it into the man's hand. 'Police,' he said quietly. 'Is Edwin around?'

Edwin Nyc was the hotel's Head of Security. Carlyle had met him a couple of times over the years. Presumably he would have been briefed about those recent robberies, along with his equivalents at the other big hotels.

The man looked at the card and nodded. 'Yes, I think so.'

'Good. Get him to meet me by the concierge's desk in ten minutes.' He gestured back to his table. 'And tell my mother I won't be long.'

'What's going on?' the waiter asked, not sure whether he should feel excited or worried.

'I don't know,' replied Carlyle, striding away.

Chapter Two

MAKING HIS WAY out of the Palm Court, Carlyle forced himself to slow down and stick his hands casually in his pockets. Eyes to the floor, he took a left and headed towards the bank of three lifts at the rear of the hotel lobby. As he approached, he heard a bell signal that one had arrived. Looking up, he saw the doors of the middle lift open and the couple with the shopping get in, followed by a large guy wearing jeans and a pink shirt, open at the neck, and a navy blazer with gold buttons. Was this the fourth member of the crew?

The man had his back to Carlyle, who therefore couldn't get a proper look at him. He peered around for the other three, but they had disappeared. He wondered if he was letting his imagination get the better of him. 'Bollocks,' he muttered. 'In for a penny, in for a pound.' Jogging forward, he stepped into the lift just before the doors closed, lifting his gaze to the ceiling.

The guy in the blazer pressed the button for the third level and then looked at Carlyle.

'Which floor?'

Carlyle checked the panel, noting that five was also lit up. He smiled at the man. 'Five's fine, thanks.'

The other man nodded, silently. He looked to be in his fifties, balding, overweight, of Middle Eastern appearance. *Maybe*, the inspector thought, *a rich Arab with a taste for losing ridiculous amounts of money in London casinos*. Carlyle again wondered about the scenario that he'd been so quick to pull together in his head. This guy just didn't look like he belonged with the other three.

The lift shuddered into motion and began its slow journey upward. When they reached the third floor, the Arab type got out, leaving Carlyle alone with the shoppers. In the silence, Carlyle eyed the pair's reflection in the lift doors. The husband was wearing a Dallas Cowboys jacket, so presumably they were American. He thought back to the operations note: in the previous robberies, two of the victims had been Chinese couples, the other a French businessman. All the victims had been super-rich. The couple in the lift looked well off – maybe the guy was a dentist from Texas or something – but not the kind of folk who would have a hundred grand or more in cash lying about in their hotel room.

Sighing, he felt his analysis completely unravelling before his eyes. He shook his head. *John bloody Carlyle! All this running around just to get out of having a difficult conversation with your mum!*

On the fifth floor, Carlyle stepped out onto the landing. Feeling rather embarrassed, he fiddled with his BlackBerry while he watched the middle-aged couple make it safely to their room.

Waiting for the lift to take him back down to the lobby, he sent Joe another text: *False alarm. See you in a minute.*

Heading down, the lift stopped again at the third floor. Carlyle stood aside to let a couple of Japanese girls enter. Both of them were dressed like faux punk rockers with spiky hair and purple eyeliner. *It's like the bloody United Nations*, he thought. Distracted by their giggling, not to mention their short skirts, he didn't see the man with the tweed jacket and crew cut hovering outside until the doors had almost shut.

'Shit!'

The girls looked at each other and giggled some more.

Reaching across them, Carlyle hit the button for 2.

The lift slowly trundled away from where he wanted to be.

'*C'mon! C'mon!*'

It took maybe twenty seconds for the lift to move down one floor and the doors to open. Jumping out, Carlyle took a left, following the signs for the emergency exit, cursing until he found a small door leading to the stairs.

Bounding up two steps at a time, his heart was racing by the time he reached the third floor. Taking a moment to calm himself, he stepped as casually as he could into the corridor and headed back in the direction of the lifts, adopting the air of a guest having difficulty in locating his room.

When he reached the lifts, the man in the tweed jacket was still standing there, staring aimlessly at a print hanging on the wall. There was no sign of his twin or of the third man, the one in the suit.

As he approached, Carlyle could see that this guy was at least six inches taller – and probably a good 20 kilos heavier – than himself.

What are you going to do now, genius? he wondered, now bitterly regretting his rather premature text to his sergeant.

The man turned to face Carlyle, his expression hidden by the sunglasses. Carlyle nodded politely and made to walk past.

'Excuse me, sir,' the man said, 'do you have the time?'

His English had a slight accent, but Carlyle couldn't place it. He checked his watch and smiled. 'Almost exactly five.'

'Thanks.' The man gestured towards the print. 'Nice picture, don't you think?'

'Very nice,' said Carlyle, quickening his pace in order to avoid being caught up in any more chit-chat. 'Very nice indeed.'

He sensed the man hesitate, before making a decision not to follow. As he turned the corner, the inspector heard the guy say something in a language that certainly wasn't English. Carlyle continued walking down a long, gloomy, curving corridor, with doors on either side, but empty of any other people. Gritting his teeth, he hoped this didn't lead to a dead end. Pulling out his mobile, he again called his sergeant. When the call didn't go through, he studied the screen and was dismayed to realize that he had no signal. 'Fucking hell!' he hissed. 'The middle of London and there's no bloody signal. How the hell can that be possible?'

Ten yards along the corridor, Carlyle came to a room-service tray deposited outside one of the guest rooms. On it stood an empty bottle of Cuvée Dom Perignon 2000. Might be handy, he thought, picking it up by the neck and weighing it in his hand. Looking up again, he spotted the second tweed-jacketed jerk from the Palm Court coming out of a room ahead of him. *Game on!* With one guy in front and one behind, there was no chance of backing down now. Carlyle strode forward, smiling inanely.

Tweed jacket number two was also clearly bigger and heavier than Carlyle himself. Still wearing his sunglasses in the semidarkness, he held up a hand, like a traffic cop directing traffic.

'Hotel Security.'

Carlyle nodded politely, but said nothing. The man in front of him was wearing surgical rubber gloves, of the kind doctors used. Carlyle felt a wave of relief pass over him, mingling with the adrenalin that was coursing nicely through his veins. This must definitely be the crew that was hitting London hotels. He might be about to get his head kicked in, but at least he wasn't going to end up looking like a paranoid idiot.

The man frowned when he realized that Carlyle wasn't backing off. 'Can I help you, sir?'

Another accent he couldn't place.

'No, I'm fine, thank you,' said Carlyle, moving closer.

'I'm sorry, sir,' the man smiled malevolently, 'but I'm going to have to ask you to return to the lobby.'

'Uh-huh.'

Carlyle kept coming.

The man nonchalantly moved his feet apart, adopting a lower centre of gravity. 'We have a small issue here that we need to deal with,' he said flatly. 'It is nothing serious and you will be able to access your room very shortly.'

'I understand,' Carlyle nodded. 'Edwin Nyc is on his way up.'

The name of the hotel's Head of Security garnered no response from behind the sunglasses.

Big surprise.

Carlyle tightened his grip on the neck of the champagne bottle. For a split second he considered smashing it against the wall and glassing the overgrown shithead in front of him. He discarded the idea immediately. Too messy, and it would raise the stakes too high. No one needed to get seriously hurt here.

Carlyle kept advancing, speeding up slightly to gain the extra momentum. He was almost on top of the bastard now.

'Sir!' The man's voice jumped an octave. He looked past Carlyle, clearly wondering where his back-up was. 'I have to insist that you go back downstairs. Now!'

'Like fuck,' Carlyle grinned. With a skip in his step, he lifted himself a couple of inches off the ground, took the bottle in both hands, and in one smooth arc, smashed it as hard as he could into the guy's face.

There was a dull thud and the crack of plastic as the sunglasses disintegrated and the man crumpled to the carpet. Surprised that the bottle didn't break, Carlyle tossed it further down the corridor and moved quickly to the door of the room from which the fellow had recently emerged.

In the comparative gloom, it was only when he pressed the handle that he realized that the lock had been forced. Pushing open the door, he stepped inside.

'Police!'

He was standing in a small sitting room. It was empty. On first glance, the room hadn't been tossed and nothing seemed out of place. To his left was a half-open door leading to a bedroom. Behind it he could see signs of movement. Carlyle stepped over and kicked the door open wider.

'*Police!*' The shout died in his throat as Carlyle took a moment to process what he was seeing. The Arab guy from the lift was lying face down on the bed, out for the count. His blazer had been tossed on the floor and his right shirt-sleeve rolled up past his elbow. There was a large hypodermic needle sticking out of his arm. Pressing down on the plunger was the 'businessman' from the lobby. His red tie loosened, sweat beading on his brow, he too was wearing a pair of surgical gloves. He carefully finished administering the injection and looked up at the inspector.

This guy is more my size, Carlyle decided, licking his lips. His blood was up now and he had a taste for action. 'Step away from the bed!'

The man frowned but did not move.

'I said—'

'I heard you,' the man smiled.

What's he got to smile about? Carlyle wondered.

Then he heard the sound of a safety-catch being released behind his ear.

Oh, shit.

Everything was happening too fast.

Far too fast.

Out of the corner of his eye he could just make out the muzzle of a semi-automatic with a silencer attached. There was a whiff of body odour and a malicious whisper in his ear: 'On your fucking knees, copper. Hands behind your head.'

Slowly, Carlyle did as he was told. Lifting his eyes to the ceiling, he thought of Lorna Gordon abandoned downstairs and cursed himself. Maybe there were worse things than discussing your mum's divorce, after all.

He took a couple of quick slaps to the back of his head; nothing serious. Hands went through his pockets until they found his warrant card.

'Metropolitan Police,' announced the voice behind him – one of the tweed jackets, he assumed. 'What are you doing here?'

'My colleagues are on the way,' Carlyle said quickly. It was worth a try.

'Unlucky for them if they are,' the voice behind him laughed. 'Unlucky for you, my friend, either way. You are playing with the big boys now.'

'What shall we do with this one?' the businessman asked, pulling the needle out of the Arab's arm.

Carlyle looked over at the man lying on the bed, his eyes half-closed, his breathing laboured. The guy in the tweed jacket stepped past Carlyle and prodded the body on the bed with the silencer of his semi-automatic. Without his sunglasses, Carlyle could make out the dark rings under his brown eyes. He had a large bruise rapidly developing on the side of his face. Carlyle wished he'd kept hold of the champagne bottle, so that he could at least fight back; try and give him another whack, put him down properly this time.

The gunman gave the body on the bed another prod. There was no response. 'How long?'

The businessman type dropped the syringe into a small holdall and shrugged. 'I have given him the full 100 millilitres,' he said, doing up his tie, 'so twenty minutes. Maybe twenty-five.'

'Too long.' The man with the gun looked at Carlyle and shook his head. 'Anyway, we don't have to worry about an autopsy any more. No one's going to write this off as natural causes.' He took a pillow and carefully placed it over the comatose man's head. Then he shot twice into the pillow, sending down feathers flying into the air.

Carlyle winced as a feather landed on his head.

'Like I said, Officer,' the gunman said grimly, 'you're playing with the big boys now.' Stepping back from the bed, he raised the pistol and aimed it at Carlyle.

Closing his eyes, Carlyle mumbled something that even he didn't understand.

'Are you sure we want to . . . ?' The businessman's voice trailed off into nothingness.

There was the click of the safety going back on.

Carlyle opened his eyes, relieved that he hadn't voided his bowels – so far, at least.

The gunman laughed. Then he stepped closer to the kneeling policeman. 'Luckily for you,' he said quietly, 'the big boys have fucked up more than enough for one day.'

Carlyle's eyes widened as the gunman stepped forward and smashed the pistol down on his skull.

'That's for hitting me with the bottle, copper!'

There was a second blow. And a third. Carlyle swayed on his knees, and then pitched sideways into blackness.

Chapter Three

WHEN HE CAME to, it took Carlyle several moments to remember where he was. The man on the bed brought it all back very quickly. The remains of his French Fancy reappeared as he vomited his Palm Court tea on to the carpet. Forcing himself into a sitting position, he put a hand to his right temple where the skin had been broken. He rubbed the blood between his fingers – sticky, but nothing too serious. The stitches could wait.

'Oh fuck!' His nose crinkled at a whiff of excrement mingling with the smell of vomit. He put a hand to his crotch, but there was no sign of any accident. A dark stain on the dead man's jeans confirmed the source of the odour. Carlyle let out a relieved sigh. 'Thank You, God,' he said out loud. In the Met, no one could ever recover from getting a reputation for having shat themselves in the line of duty.

Standing up, he felt his headache spreading effortlessly to all parts of his body. Gazing at the destroyed pillow, he didn't even bother checking the body for a pulse. He peered groggily around the room. The alarm clock on the bedside table said 5.09. Maybe he'd been out cold for only a couple of minutes. His warrant card lay on the carpet by his feet. Picking it up, he placed it back in his pocket and staggered to the door.

The sitting room of the suite was empty. Gingerly, Carlyle stuck his head out of the busted door and looked up and down the corridor. Empty.

Right, you bastards, let's be having you! A surge of anger and adrenalin sent him running back towards the lifts.

THE FIRST PERSON he saw as he reached the lobby was his sergeant, Joe Szyszkowski. Ignoring the look of surprise on Joe's face, Carlyle hissed: 'Three men, two of them with crew cuts. Wearing tweed jackets. Armed and dangerous. Call for back-up . . .'

Even as the words were coming out, he spotted the same trio casually hailing a taxi on the street outside.

'There they are! Come on!'

Carlyle rushed across the lobby, searching in vain for Edwin Nyc as he went. He burst through the revolving doors and past a startled doorman, just as a cab pulled up at the kerb.

'Stop!' he yelled. 'Police!'

The three turned to face him with the weary look of executives whose bad day at the office showed no sign of abating.

'Police!' Carlyle repeated, waving his warrant card above his head.

The cabbie took one look at what was transpiring and promptly switched his light back on, squeezing in front of a coach and into the middle lane as he went in search of a less troublesome fare. Disgusted, two of the men turned their backs on Carlyle and stepped out into the road to begin crossing the four lanes of slow-moving traffic on Piccadilly. The third man opened his jacket, as if to remind Carlyle that he was carrying a weapon.

The sound of sirens in the distance made Carlyle feel a little better. He just hoped that they were coming to help him. 'Put the gun on the pavement!'

The man shook his head. 'Is this how you repay me for saving your life?' He frowned. 'Don't be stupid. I am going to walk away now. If you take one step further, I will shoot you in the head.' He grinned. 'Maybe in the balls first.'

The sirens were getting louder.

'Where are you going to go?' Carlyle asked. 'There's nowhere to hide.'

'Home.' The man shrugged. 'My job is done. Now I'm going home.'

Carlyle felt someone at his shoulder.

'The cavalry will be here in about one minute.' His sergeant stepped past him, brandishing a pair of plastic handcuffs.

'Joe . . .'

'What the fuck *is* this?' The man pulled the gun from the waistband of his trousers and shot twice.

Joe Szyszkowski hit the ground before Carlyle had a chance to move.

Chapter Four

'ARE YOU GOING with him?' Ashen-faced, Edwin Nyc scanned the lobby. The guests had been evacuated, to be replaced by a growing number of emergency services personnel methodically going about their business. Perched on the arm of a chair, Carlyle watched as Joe was carefully stretchered into the back of the ambulance outside. He knew that he should be out there with his friend and colleague, but an overwhelming sense of uselessness washed over him. He tried to stand up but found that he lacked the energy to move.

'Where are they taking him?'

'St Thomas', I think.'

'I'll make my own way over there.'

'How bad is it?'

'No idea,' Carlyle said listlessly. 'Pretty bad, I suppose.' A reasonable assumption, given the two bullets lodged in his sergeant's chest.

In silence, they watched Joe disappear inside the ambulance. The doors closed and the vehicle edged out into the traffic, its siren blaring. After watching it depart, the technicians quickly got back down to business. All around them, life was effortlessly returning to normal. Few people in the city had time to stop and gawp.

Nyc disappeared into the Rivoli Bar, returning almost immediately with a bottle of whisky and two glasses. He handed Carlyle one empty glass and poured him a triple measure. Then he poured an equally large one for himself.

Gesturing for Nyc to hand it over, Carlyle inspected the bottle: Caol Ila, an eighteen-year-old Islay malt. Nice. He studied the label:

> *Caol Ila (Gaelic for 'the Sound of Islay', which separates the island from Jura in one of the most remote and beautiful parts of Scotland's West Coast) was built in 1846 by Glasgow businessman Hector Henderson. The barley used is still malted locally at Port Ellen and the pure spring water it contains still rises from limestone in nearby Loch nam Ban, then falls to the sea at Caol Ila in a clear crystal stream, just as it always has. Their offspring is a fine-ageing malt reserved in oak casks for up to eighteen years.*

And, best of all, it was 43 per cent proof. *I'll drink to that*, Carlyle thought grimly. Taking a small mouthful, he let the golden liquid soothe his throat if not his soul. Placing the bottle carefully on the floor, he slithered into the armchair. Nyc plonked himself down in the one opposite. Both men drank steadily, in silence, for several minutes.

Still without saying anything, Nyc disappeared for a second time. When he came back, he was carrying a damp hand towel in one hand and a clean white shirt in the other.

He handed Carlyle the towel. 'Here, tidy yourself up.'

'Thanks.' Getting to his feet, Carlyle walked across the lobby, positioning himself in front of a full-length mirror next to the concierge's desk. Tentatively dabbing at the cut above his eye, he winced.

Arriving at his shoulder, Nyc held up a large fabric plaster. 'Use this.'

'Thanks.'

His wound now bandaged, Carlyle tossed his jacket onto the chair and pulled off his tie. As he began undoing his shirt, he realized it was splattered with Joe's blood. He instantly felt woozy and began to sway.

Nyc placed a hand on his elbow. 'Are you all right?'

'I'm fine.' Carlyle took off the ruined shirt and bundled it into a ball, tossing it onto the floor. 'Bin that for me, will you?'

'Of course,' Nyc nodded.

After putting on the fresh shirt, Carlyle rang home. To his relief, the call went straight to voicemail. After the beep, he gave the briefest summary of what had happened, stressing that he himself was completely okay but explaining that he might not get back to the flat until well into the wee small hours. With that minor but important task achieved, he went back to his whisky.

The more he drank, the more he thought about his responsibility for what had happened. And the more he thought about it, the clearer it became to him that he had fucked up big time.

Fucked up – and maybe got Joe killed.

As Carlyle brooded, the silence grew poisonous.

'Has someone informed his wife yet?' Nyc asked eventually.

'Yes,' said Carlyle. 'They'll be taking her straight to the hospital.' He had no idea if that was true or not, but there was no way that he was volunteering for the job himself. He knew Anita

Szyszkowski well enough, but they had never really established any kind of close relationship. To the inspector's mind, Anita was always too ready to blame him for Joe's late nights and missed family gatherings. If she got wind of what had happened here, she'd probably try and eviscerate him with her bare hands.

Above all, however, he didn't want to have to face the kids. William and Sarah Szyszkowski were only slightly older than Carlyle's own daughter Alice. The idea of having to tell them that their dad had been shot in the street did his head in. Someone else could take care of that.

After a while, Chief Inspector Chris French, officer in charge of the crime scene, strode through the lobby. He saw the glass in Carlyle's hand and frowned.

Fuck off, you prick, Carlyle thought. French worked out of West End Central, on Savile Row. Carlyle knew French by sight, but otherwise wasn't aware of much about him. He couldn't recall having seen the chief inspector's name mentioned on the report about the robbery crew, and he certainly hadn't ever worked with him before. Sitting in the lobby of the Ritz, however, it took him less than ten minutes to take a profound dislike to the guy as French fussed about, wasting time on irrelevant details when he should have been out searching for the gunman and his colleagues.

Edwin Nyc cleared his throat. 'Look, apologies for being so callous, Chief Inspector,' he said, eyeing Carlyle, 'but how long will it be until we can re-open the hotel lobby? We have guests using a side entrance but there are still some diners waiting outside, I believe.'

French nodded thoughtfully, like he was being asked to answer a riddle or a complicated maths puzzle. 'I understand, Mr Nic . . .'

It's pronounced 'nike', you dick, like in the shoe, Carlyle groused to himself as he guzzled some more scotch.

'. . . I will make sure we get things up and running again as quickly as possible. However, I'm sure that you understand the seriousness of the situation.'

'Of course. Thank you.' Nyc gave Carlyle a pleading look and stalked off in the direction of the bar.

Carlyle watched the man go, taking the rest of the eighteen-year-old single malt with him. *You could at least have left me the bottle*, he thought mournfully.

French turned to Carlyle. 'I need you to go to West End Central to make a formal statement.'

Carlyle drained his glass and stood up rather unsteadily. 'Of course,' he said. 'I was going to head over to the hospital first, and then I need to speak to my commanding officer.'

French thought about that for a moment. He clearly wasn't happy with this plan, but at the same time he knew that he couldn't object without coming across as a total arse. 'Who's your CO?' he asked finally.

'Simpson – Commander Carole Simpson.' Carlyle made a vague gesture in a northwards direction. 'She's based up in Paddington.'

'Don't know her.' French yawned. 'Any good?'

I bloody hope so, thought Carlyle. He would need all of Simpson's political skills to help pull him out of the shit this time. 'Yes, not bad.'

'Okay,' French sighed. 'Take your time. It's clearly going to be a long night.'

Carlyle nodded. 'Yes, it certainly is.' His mobile started vibrating in his pocket. Pulling it out, he checked the screen. No number. Hoping that it wasn't the Commander, he hit the receive button.

'Hello?'

'Do you know what time it is?' Despite the background noise on the other end of the line, the inspector recognized the voice immediately. It certainly wasn't Carole Simpson. And it certainly wasn't happy. 'Where the hell are you?'

Shit. Walking away from French, Carlyle took a deep breath, followed by another. His headache had returned with a vengeance and he wondered if he might be about to puke. He had completely forgotten about the evening's planned business. Thoughts of arrests, newspaper ink and glory seemed, at best, totally irrelevant now.

'John?'

'Piccadilly,' he said wearily. 'I'm in Piccadilly.'

'What the hell are you doing there?'

'Sorry, Dom,' he mumbled, trying to keep his voice even. 'Something came up. Tough day.'

'I don't give a monkey's about that,' Dominic Silver snapped. 'This is your window of opportunity here, sunshine. We are good to go. You need to get your arse over here *tonto bloody pronto*.'

'But—'

'No buts – I've laid out everything on a plate here for you. Not for the first time, I might add. So get your arse in a cab and get over here. Right now.'

Still holding the phone to his ear, Carlyle stepped out of the lobby and onto the pavement. Right in front of him, a cab pulled up at the kerb, disgorging a couple of hotel guests who were immediately swept up by one of the liveried doormen and shepherded to the side entrance. Grabbing the door before it slammed shut, Carlyle slid onto the back seat of the taxi and barked an address at the driver. 'Okay,' he said into the handset. 'I'm on my way.'

Ending the call, he tossed the phone onto the seat, closed his eyes to stem the tears and rested his head on the cool leather. Blocking out the sounds of the city, he said a silent prayer. It was time to go to the show.

Chapter Five

Just how surreal could this day get? All the background noise and bustle gradually faded to the point where he was aware of nothing beyond the fantastically pretty girl standing five feet in front of him, without a scrap of clothing on. Ignoring the swaying inspector, she idly scratched her left breast, just beneath the erect nipple, as she sucked on a cigarette. Blowing smoke into the air, her eyes locked on Carlyle's. Feeling himself redden, the inspector nervously fingered the plaster over his left eye and tried not to lower his gaze. Making no effort to cover herself, the girl took another drag on her cigarette, her grin effortlessly mutating into a sneer. 'Rollo!' she shouted. 'Pervert alert! . . . Rollo!'

A small, fat, bald man of indeterminate age waddled over. Beside him was Dominic Silver. Wearing an expensive-looking navy suit with a black shirt, Silver looked like he owned the place, which, in effect, he did. The fat man, by contrast, looked like an extra from *Pirates of the Caribbean*, in black leather jeans and a ruffled white shirt that was unbuttoned almost to his waist. All that was missing was a parrot on his shoulder.

'You finally made it then?' Silver asked.

'Yes,' Carlyle coughed.

'Good.' Copper turned drug dealer, turned entrepreneur, Dominic Silver had known the inspector for something like thirty years, give or take. They had a good, if occasionally fractious relationship, which they both knew would survive this latest blip.

'Charlotte,' Silver's sidekick hissed, 'get dressed! We are starting in ten minutes.'

Rolling her eyes to the ceiling, the girl handed the fat man the cigarette, then turned and flounced off in the direction of a stylist waiting beside a long rail of clothes. Despite everything, Carlyle couldn't help but be transfixed by the sight of her perfect buttocks as they retreated across the dressing area. He let out a deep, deep sigh.

'And who are you?' The fat man broke the angel's spell by prodding Carlyle in the ribs.

'He's my guy,' Dom said hastily, shooting Carlyle a look that said: *be cool, stop embarrassing yourself.*

'Oh, I see.' If anything, this news made the fat man even less happy about Carlyle's presence.

'Rollo Kasabian, fashion designer,' Silver kept his voice low, trying to play the peacemaker, 'meet Inspector John Carlyle, policeman.'

Without offering a hand, Kasabian grunted something that could not easily have been translated as *Pleased to meet you.*

Carlyle didn't even bother with a response. Kasabian was Dom's bunny, so Carlyle knew that the man would do what he was damn well told.

Another babe walked by, this one naked only from the waist down. His embarrassment waning, Carlyle smiled at Dom. 'Are we ready to go?'

Silver looked at Kasabian, who nodded.

'Good,' said Silver, slapping Kasabian on the back.

The designer mumbled something about 'last-minute arrangements' and sloped off.

Silver took Carlyle by the arm and led him towards the curtain leading to the runway. 'Let's go and get our seats.'

ROLLO KASABIAN'S COLLECTION for London Fashion Week was being showcased on the ground floor of an empty office block in Knights-bridge, close to the Royal Albert Hall. The seats surrounding the runway were six rows deep – enough, Carlyle calculated, to accommodate maybe 200 people. As they stepped out from behind the curtain, he was pleased to see that the lighting made it impossible to see the audience from the runway. That would make his job easier when it came to effecting an arrest. Two uniforms were parked in a car outside, ready to take the suspect back to Charing Cross police station. After everything that had happened during the last few hours, Carlyle seriously doubted he would have the energy to conduct an interview this evening.

Dom led him to a pair of seats at the back, to the side of the runway. After they took their places, he pointed out a couple of celebrities and fashion editors, stern women with oversized sunglasses perched on their heads, who were sitting in the front row on the opposite side.

Carlyle grunted, unimpressed as he hadn't heard of any of them. He jerked a thumb at a gaggle of snappers at the end of the runway, saying, 'I don't want any of those buggers getting a picture when I slap the cuffs on the lovely young drug-dealing model.'

'Don't worry,' said Dom. 'It will all be done backstage after this has finished.'

'The show must go on.'

'Of course. But it makes sense for you, too. There's half a kilo of coke in the girl's bag.'

'That's handy.'

Silver ignored the insinuation.

'How much is it worth?' Carlyle wondered.

'It varies,' said Dom casually. 'The middle-class clientele she serves more or less demand to get ripped off. Maybe quarter of a mil, give or take.'

Carlyle let out a low whistle.

'Want to rip it off?' Dom grinned. 'Get me to sell it for you?'

'Yeah, right.' Carlyle shifted uneasily in his seat. After all these years, Dominic Silver's willingness to dangle temptation in front of him continued to annoy and make him feel uncomfortable in equal measure.

Dom gave him a reassuring pat on the arm. 'Don't worry. There will be no cameras, no drama. Plenty of opportunity for you to make the collar with a minimum of fuss.'

'No drama!' Carlyle snorted. 'Is that possible? With this lot?'

'Rollo knows what he has to do. Anyway, I know that you've had quite your fill of excitement for one day.'

'I certainly have,' Carlyle replied.

'It was all over the news. How is Joe? What's the latest?'

'No news yet,' Carlyle mumbled. The truth was that he hadn't yet spoken to the hospital. Having allowed himself to be diverted to the fashion show, the inspector was too scared to give the doctors a call. No news, he believed, really was good news. Bad news would find him soon enough.

Dom gestured to the plaster on Carlyle's forehead. 'Are you sure you're okay?'

'I'm fine.'

'I'm sorry I was so bolshie on the phone earlier. I didn't realize . . .'

'It doesn't matter.' Carlyle looked over at the runway. 'You were right – we have to move on this now. Apart from anything else, Joe did a lot of work on this case.'

Dom nodded. 'He'd want you to get the result.'

Carlyle made a face. 'Right now, I don't imagine he could give a toss. But *I* want to get a result.' He gestured towards the empty runway. 'This is the girl's last show in London this week?'

'Yeah. Then she's booked on the lunchtime BA flight to Rio tomorrow.'

I wish I was flying down to fucking Rio, Carlyle thought sourly. He looked at his watch. 'Shouldn't this shebang have started by now?'

Dominic shrugged. 'They're always running late.'

'Great.' Carlyle looked at his shoes, knowing that he really should call the hospital.

He really should *be* at the fucking hospital.

'How are the family?' he enquired.

Dom turned and gave him a pained look. 'Not great, to be honest.'

'Oh.' Carlyle was already wishing that he hadn't asked that question.

'You know we've had some problems with Marina?'

'Er . . . yes.' Carlyle vaguely remembered Helen telling him, a while back, something about Dom's youngest child needing to go into hospital for some tests.

Dom let out a long sigh. 'The doctors think it's something called Cockayne Syndrome.'

'Uh-huh?' Carlyle murmured, clueless.

'Type One,' Dom continued, sounding as if the words were seared into his brain. 'The classic form: impairment of vision, of hearing, and the central and peripheral nervous systems progressively degenerate, until death occurs in the first or second decade of life.'

'How old is she now?'

'She was five only a month ago.'

'Fu-uck.'

'I know.' Silver shook his head. 'It's a complete and utter fucker, a genetic disorder so rare that less than twenty other children in Britain have it. Just one in 186,000 people carry the gene. Both partners need to have the gene, and then there's a one-in-four chance of them passing it on to the kid.'

You've beaten the odds big time, then, Carlyle thought, keeping his mouth firmly clamped shut. Silver and his partner Eva Hollander had five kids.

'There's talk of her taking part in a new drugs trial which could slow down her deterioration, but there's no cure and, so far, there's no treatment. All anyone can offer her is palliative care.'

'That's terrible,' said Carlyle, wishing desperately that this bloody fashion show would start.

'Eva's in bits about it.'

'I can imagine.'

'I'm cutting back on my schedule, to spend more time at home.'

'Of course.'

'It's lucky that I'm able to do that, I suppose.'

'Yes,' Carlyle nodded as the lights finally went down and the first model appeared on the runway wearing something that looked like a plastic bag, accompanied by the opening strains of U2's 'Beautiful Day'.

Charlotte Gondomar – 'Lottie' to her friends – had a perfectly symmetrical face, long black hair, cynical lips and honey-coloured eyes. From the photo on her agency calling card, she looked like the kind of girl who could have anything, or anyone, she wanted. The promo blurb on the back said that she liked Spiderman, Guinness and the poetry of Pablo Neruda. Now twenty-one years old, she had been a beauty queen back home in Brazil when she was only fourteen. A lingerie model since she was sixteen, she had been working the runways of Europe and North America for almost four years. According to Dominic Silver, she had been transporting cocaine from Rio de Janeiro into London, Paris, Milan and various other European cities for the last two.

Dom was a perfectly reasonable man, but he didn't like someone else doing *his* job. He had acquired Rollo Kasabian's fashion house as part of the ongoing diversification of his business interests. 'This is definitely *not* a money-laundering ruse,' he harrumphed when Carlyle had raised an eyebrow. 'We have a five-year business plan, break-even targets, brand extension aspirations, the lot.'

While Dom was busy diversifying into legitimate areas of business, Lottie was going the other way. Using her fashion contacts, she had put together a small team of pretty and discreet girls to transport the product across the Atlantic. Almost every week, one or two of the crew would travel from Brazil to Spain, via Cancún. Each girl would have a small amount of drugs hidden in their luggage . . . or somewhere more intimate. In one case, a make-up girl had apparently swanned through customs at Barcelona airport with 1.29 kilos of coke inside a pair of fake breast implants.

It was not so much the competition that annoyed Dominic Silver as the threat that Lottie presented to his business overall. He knew that the girl would come a cropper sooner rather than later. When she did, the subsequent spotlight on his operations could be uncomfortable, to say the least. Especially at a time when he had to focus on the needs of his family and let business largely take care of itself. After some deliberation, he had decided that the best course of action would be to pre-empt the situation. So he had called in his friend, Inspector Carlyle, to do something about Lottie's little sideline.

'NARCO-TRAFFICKING IS ONE area where women have definitely broken through the glass ceiling,' Dom said with a smirk, when they had first discussed the matter a few weeks earlier, in a bar in Soho. 'It started in Colombia in the 1980s with two high-flyers – can't remember their names. One was known as *La Viuda Negra* – the Black Widow. She was a woman who gave her children the names of characters in *The Godfather* as a joke.'

'Better that than calling your sprog something like Kylie or Jason,' Carlyle mused, taking a sip of his Jameson Redbreast twelve-year-old Irish whiskey.

'The other was called *La Mariposa*, the Butterfly,' Dom continued.

'Do you have a nickname yourself?'

'What?' Dom took a sip of his Château La Fleur de Gay 2005, irritated at Carlyle's repeated interruptions.

'You could be, like . . . I dunno – *the Professor* . . . or *the Scorpion*.'

'Fuck off,' Dom scowled. 'I'm a serious businessman.'

'Maybe *the Cobra*?'

'Fuck *off*!'

'It might be a good idea. It's all about marketing, after all.'

'Anyway,' Dom sighed theatrically, keen to get his story back on track, 'the Black Widow and the Butterfly were on the Drug

Enforcement Administration's Most Wanted list back in the 1980s. One of them – I can't remember which – was captured in Venezuela and sent back to America naked, in chains, in a dog cage.'

'Nice,' Carlyle grinned. 'You'd better hope the Americans never get hold of you.'

'They don't care about me,' Dom sniffed. 'I am a very small-scale, local operator. And I am very careful to have no dealings with anyone who does anything at all in the US.'

'You wouldn't go on holiday there, though, would you?'

'No,' Dom admitted. 'Why take the risk? Anyway, we prefer Tuscany.'

'In terms of the women?' Carlyle prompted, glancing at his watch.

'Yes . . . right, there are some women at high levels in the Mexican cartels; other women who are awaiting trial on charges of trafficking large quantities of cocaine into the US. And why not? The drugs business is the same as any other. It reflects the wider trends in society. And it is more meritocratic than most. If a woman has the necessary skills to do the job, she can get on.'

'And this model?'

'Lottie seems very good at organizing people and handling money. She's wasted as a model, in fact.'

'So why not give her a job?' Carlyle asked. 'Rather than dragging me into it.'

'I did try and broach the subject, but she's a bit . . . headstrong. And I think she thought that I was just trying to get into her knickers.' Dom raised his eyes to the ceiling. 'People management is a really shit part of the job. I don't really want any more high-maintenance employees if I can possibly help it. Anyway, I don't have a vacancy. The boys of Class A Company are doing a really good job.'

As it happened, the boys of Class A Company – named after the UK's A, B, C classification system for illegal drugs – came from A Company, the Ninth Battalion Royal Regiment of Fusiliers. Over the last few years, they had divided their time between ceremonial duties, guarding Buckingham Palace and the Tower of London, and conducting rather more stressful tours in Afghanistan. They were famous for spending 107 consecutive days fighting the Taliban at Now Zad in a single summer.

They were also famous, in some quarters, for their recreational activities. Four Fusiliers had been caught taking cocaine on a rifle range during a live firing exercise. Others had tested positive for cocaine or cannabis in compulsory drug tests. When the young culprits were unceremoniously thrown back on to Civvie Street, Dominic Silver was waiting for them with the offer of a new job, and a new 'family' to go with it.

'The Ninth Battalion is getting the chop, you know.'

'Eh?'

'It's being disbanded as part of the latest defence review.'

'Bummer.'

'Bad news for the Army,' Dom said, 'but good news for me. Plenty of fresh talent coming onto the market.'

'I suppose.'

'It's just one more reason why I don't need Lottie,' Dom explained. 'I can't see any way round it – she has to go.'

'If you say so.'

Dom clapped him on the back. 'Think of it as one small victory in the never-ending war against drugs.'

'Right.'

'Seriously, this is one of these classic win-win situations.'

Carlyle placed his glass back on the table. Whenever Dom used the phrase 'win-win', he knew that trouble lay ahead.

WITH THE SHOW finally over, the multi-talented Lottie was pulling on a pair of skinny jeans as Carlyle approached her.

'Ms Gondomar?'

Zipping up her trousers, a look of recognition mixed with disgust crept across the girl's face. 'Rollo!'

But the fat man was nowhere to be seen.

'*Rollo!*'

'I'm police,' Carlyle said quietly, brandishing a warrant card in one hand and a pair of speedcuffs in the other. He gestured towards the shoulder bag sitting on the floor by the girl's feet, as if that was the only explanation necessary for his presence here. 'Please put on a shirt, before we head to the station.'

Chapter Six

After almost four hours of emergency surgery, Joe Szyszkowski had been placed in a private room at one end of the Sarah Swift Ward, the short-stay acute medical admissions unit at St Thomas' Hospital. Standing guard outside was his wife Anita, flanked by two of her brothers.

Skulking round the corner was John Carlyle.

After dropping off an outraged but clearly guilty Lottie Gondomar in a holding cell at Charing Cross, he had grabbed a sandwich from a newsagent's just off Trafalgar Square and headed straight down to Westminster Bridge Road. Not wishing to face his sergeant's family, he had slumped on a sofa in a nearby waiting room and promptly fallen asleep.

'John?'

Waking with a jerk, he found his boss, Commander Carole Simpson, standing over him.

'Was I snoring?' he asked, embarrassed.

'I don't think so,' she smiled, handing him a coffee. 'Here.'

'Thanks.'

Taking the lid off the cardboard cup, he took a sip before looking her up and down. Out of uniform, in jeans and a fleece, with no make-up, she looked tired and frail. Just about as tired and frail as Carlyle himself felt.

God, he thought, *is this what The Job does to us?*

Simpson was five or six years younger than Carlyle. They had worked together for almost fifteen years now. Unlike Carlyle, she had spent most of that time on the fast track to success. But any aspirations Simpson might have had of a Deputy Commissioner's job had been derailed when her husband, Joshua Hunt, had been jailed for financial fraud. Simpson had kept her head down, refused to resign, and taken whatever solace that her work could offer. But she knew that she was considered damaged goods. There would be no more promotions. Now, like the inspector himself, she was basically doing her job because she didn't know how to do anything else.

Ironically, the collapse of Simpson's own career had paved the way for a much improved relationship with her troublesome inspector. Whereas Carlyle had been deeply suspicious of her on the way up, he felt far more sympathetic to her current plight. For her part, Simpson had responded to Carlyle's belated ability to show some empathy at a time when others were all too ready to keep their distance from her.

'Did you speak to Anita?'

Carlyle put the lid back on his coffee. 'No, I don't think she'd be too happy to see me right now.'

Simpson gazed out of the window. 'So what's the latest news?'

'Dunno . . . I'm still waiting for a doctor to show up.'

Simpson sat down glumly. 'I hate hospitals.'

'Me too,' Carlyle yawned, wishing he could just go back to sleep.

'Joshua's been in and out of here God knows how many times in the last six months. It's been horrible.'

'I can imagine,' Carlyle lied. No chance now of nodding back off, so he pushed himself upright. While he was in prison, Joshua Hunt had been diagnosed with cancer of the colon. Karma, or just shit bad luck? Either way, he had been released on compassionate grounds on the expectation that his illness would prove terminal in fairly short order. 'How's that going?'

Simpson stared at her sensible shoes for a long time. 'Well,' she said finally, 'he's lasted longer than they thought he would.'

'That's good.'

She looked at him defiantly. It was the kind of *Don't patronize me, John Carlyle* expression that he was more than familiar with from receiving it regularly at home.

'The end result is always going to be the same, though, isn't it?'

Mumbling something meaningless, he quickly retreated back into his own thoughts and fears.

From the corridor outside came a woman's scream. It was soon followed by a generalized commotion. The inspector knew only too well what that meant.

For as long as he dared, he sat still, staring vacantly into space at the floor, refusing to move. Finally he got to his feet. As he did so, the door opened and a small, dark-haired woman in a white coat stepped into the waiting room. Turning to Simpson, she offered her hand. 'I'm Dr Victoria Taylor, one of the consultants in Emergency Medicine.'

Simpson stood up sharply and shook her hand, gesturing in the direction of her subordinate as she did so. 'Commander Carole

Simpson and this is Inspector John Carlyle. We're colleagues of Sergeant Szyszkowski.'

Carlyle knew what was coming but held his breath anyway. He had been on the other side of this conversation many times before, and knew that there was no point in messing around.

Taylor nodded. 'I'm sorry to have to inform you that Joseph Szyszkowski died approximately ten minutes ago. He went into cardiac arrest after suffering considerable blood loss.'

Staring at the floor, Carlyle kept his jaw clamped firmly shut as he again tried to fight back the tears.

'Thank you, Doctor,' Simpson said. 'How are the family?'

'The wife has been sedated,' Taylor said matter-of-factly. 'She was in quite a state.'

Carlyle needed to get out of there. Bringing his emotions under control, he thanked the doctor and walked out.

In the corridor, he walked straight into a large Asian bloke, six-foot-plus, with the over-developed torso of a bodybuilder. He had clearly been crying, and a flash of anger sparked in his eyes when he saw Carlyle.

'You're the bastard who got Joe killed!'

Before Carlyle could say or do anything, the guy took half a step backwards and unleashed a thunderbolt left hook that hit Carlyle squarely on the chin. For the second time that day, the inspector's lights were well and truly extinguished.

Carlyle pushed away the smelling salts that Dr Taylor held under his nose. *I'm far too old for this*, he thought unhappily. Getting beaten up once was unfortunate – but twice in the same bloody day! His headache was now so bad that he could barely open his eyes under the harsh strip-lighting. Forcing himself to his feet, it took him a moment to realize that Simpson was still beside him in the corridor, while his assailant, staring defiantly into space as if he had nothing to do with any of this, was in handcuffs.

'How did you manage that?' Carlyle asked groggily, gesturing at the cuffs.

Simpson shrugged.

As the nausea passed, Taylor handed him a small bottle of Scottish spring mineral water and he took a large gulp. Screwing the lid back on the bottle, he turned again to Simpson. 'Let him go.'

She gave him a frown. 'There's a van on the way to pick him up.'

Carlyle shook his head. 'Stand them down.'

'But—'

'Let him go. It's been an unbelievably shit day . . . for everyone.' He gingerly felt his jaw. 'It's not a big deal. No one wants any more hassle. And he needs to help look after his sister and the kids.'

Sighing, Simpson did as he requested. After the cuffs were removed, the big guy glared at Carlyle before walking off slowly down the corridor without saying a word.

Carlyle watched him disappear round a corner.

'Time to go home,' he said.

'Are you feeling okay?' Taylor asked.

'Yeah, fine.' He turned to Simpson. 'Let's speak tomorrow. I need to go up to West End Central first, to give Chief Inspector French my statement, so I'll swing over by Paddington after that.'

'Fine,' she said. 'Meantime, I'll make sure all the necessary arrangements are being taken care of regarding the family.'

'Thanks,' said Carlyle, already turning away and heading off in search of an exit and some cold, fresh air.

Chapter Seven

HE WAS VAGUELY aware of a phone vibrating somewhere in the bedroom.

'Yes?' Helen enquired. 'Hold on.' She bowled the phone underarm onto the duvet, where it landed next to his head. 'It's for you.' It was an accusation rather than an observation.

You didn't need to answer it, he thought grumpily. Slowly, he opened his eyes to acknowledge another grey London morning. He looked at the alarm clock: 8.05 a.m. He had been asleep for barely two hours.

He picked up the phone. 'Carlyle.'

'Inspector, it's Kevin Price from the station.'

Carlyle grunted. Price was the third desk sergeant they'd had working at Charing Cross police station in less than nine months. That kind of staff turnover was a real pain; it meant you never really got to know who you were dealing with. When Carlyle had first arrived at Charing Cross, Dave Prentice was the main man working the desk. He had been doing the job for ever, but once he'd retired, they couldn't get anyone else to stay for more than two bloody minutes. All in all, Prentice had been a lazy so-and-so, but even Carlyle was beginning to miss him.

'We've found a body.'

Fuck me, Carlyle thought, *what is this? Wild West Week?* He pushed himself up into a sitting position. 'Where?'

'Are you still in bed?' Price asked.

'Where's the fucking body?' Carlyle said irritably, ignoring the question.

'Lincoln's Inn Fields,' Price replied.

Lincoln's Inn was one of the Inns of Court where barristers worked. The 'fields' referred to the park next door. 'Maybe it's a lawyer,' the inspector quipped, 'if we're lucky.'

'Huh?'

'Never mind.'

'They need you over there,' Price persisted.

'Okay.' Carlyle jumped out of bed, scratching his balls with his free hand. He looked at Helen, who was in the middle of applying some lipstick, and realized that she was considering his naked form with something that seemed closer to amusement than admiration. 'I'll be there in ten minutes.'

The park was a short walk away from Carlyle's flat in Covent Garden. After pulling on some jeans and a sweatshirt, he kissed his wife goodbye, grabbed his North Face Lightspeed jacket, and headed outside. Picking up a latte and an outsized raisin Danish from Marcello in Il Buffone, the tiny 1950s-style Italian café situated opposite his block of flats, he walked on down Macklin Street, eating his breakfast and wondering why he still couldn't feel anything about Joe's death. They had worked together for more than eight years. Standing in the middle of the roadway, he lifted his polystyrene coffee cup in a mock toast.

'God bless you, Joe Szyszkowski,' he roared, 'you stupid bastard!'

A woman walking past gave him a concerned look.

Carlyle sucked down more coffee and walked on.

THE CHILL WIND helped bring him back to the land of the living. It was the kind of unpleasant, all too bloody common London day that made you fantasize about emigrating to Australia. Pulling up the hood on his jacket, he dropped into Parker Street, and then on to Kingsway. Waiting to cross the road, he attacked the remains of his pastry with gusto, relying on the trusty mix of sugar and caffeine to get him properly going.

London's largest public square, Lincoln's Inn Fields, wasn't much of a park but it was the only green space near where he lived, and so Carlyle liked it well enough. Allegedly the inspiration for New York's Central Park, it consisted merely of a couple of scruffy patches of grass, a decaying bandstand and some tennis courts. In the 1990s, a group of homeless people set up home there, leading the council to close it for the best part of a year. These days, the vagrants only appeared in ones and twos to sit on the park benches, congregating en masse only at dusk, when a mobile soup kitchen made its nightly appearance.

Tossing his breakfast rubbish in a bin, Carlyle entered by the north-west corner of the park just after eight-thirty. A couple of joggers were moving slowly around the path that followed the perimeter fence while a handful of workers went scurrying, heads down, to their nearby offices. A few familiar faces from the halfway house on Parker Street already occupied various benches. Otherwise, the space was almost deserted.

The small white tent set up by a tree at the far end, next to a small digger, showed him where he was going. A group of technicians were working behind a blue tape, while a uniform chatted to a gaunt-looking woman out walking her dog. Another day at the office beckoned. Carlyle's bones ached with fatigue, and he felt a sudden keen desire for a second cup of coffee. Ignoring the craving, he thrust his hands into his pockets and marched on.

Approaching the blue and white police tape, he was stopped by a woman in her thirties. She was almost as tall as him, a tired-looking redhead enveloped in an outsize puffa jacket.

She gave him the once-over with her dull green eyes. 'Inspector Carlyle?'

'Yes,' he admitted, without any enthusiasm.

She held out a hand. He shook it limply.

'Alison Roche. They've sent me over from the Leyton station to stand in for Joseph Siz . . .'

'Joe – Joe Szyszkowski.'

'Yes.' Roche blushed, gazing down at the grey mud under her feet. 'How's he doing?'

Carlyle looked at his own shoes sinking into the mush. 'Didn't make it. Heart attack.'

'Oh – I'm sorry.'

Carlyle nodded towards the tent. 'What have we got here?'

'Man shot in the head.'

Carlyle let out a deep breath. 'Have you spoken to the other people in the park yet?'

'No.'

'Why not?' Carlyle snapped, getting ready to take an instant dislike to Ms Roche.

'Because all we've got back there is a skeleton. The man – or woman – has been dead for maybe fifty years.'

Fifty years? How could you leave a body in a park in the middle of London for fifty bloody years? Only if no one cared about the poor bugger who had died, for a start. Even then, wouldn't some sodding dog have started digging up the bones?

This wasn't a case; this was just paperwork. Carlyle's interest level went straight down to zero. Mentally, he was already back in bed. 'Who's the pathologist?'

'Phillips.'

Ah! Some good news at last. He perked up imperceptibly.

'Excellent,' he said cheerlessly. 'I'd better go and have a word with her.'

Susan Phillips worked out of Holborn police station on Lamb's Conduit Street, less than ten minutes' walk from the park. She had been a staff pathologist with the Met for the best part of twenty years. Slim, blonde, with a healthy glow and a cheery smile, she brought a smidgen of much-needed glamour to The Job. More to the point, she was quick, no-nonsense and dependable – just what Carlyle liked in a colleague. They had worked together many times and he was always pleased to see her present at a crime scene.

Carlyle strode away from Roche, stepped under the tape and walked over to the small white tent, which stood about eight foot tall and six foot wide, barely bigger than two large wardrobes placed back to back.

He stuck his head inside and clocked Phillips on her knees, holding a skull up to the light.

'"Alas, poor John Doe,"' he quipped.

She turned to face him and smiled. '"Where be your gibes now? Your gambols? Your songs? Your flashes of merriment?"'

Touché, thought Carlyle. Having already exhausted his knowledge of the Bard, he stepped halfway inside the tent.

Phillips' smile faded. 'I'm sorry about Joe.'

Carlyle grunted.

'He was a good guy.'

Not wanting to talk about it, Carlyle gestured towards the skull. 'I hear that we're dealing with ancient history. Do I really need to bother with this one?'

'That's up to you, good Inspector,' Phillips replied evenly, sticking the index finger of her right hand into a perfectly circular hole in the back of the skull. 'But I would say fairly conclusively that death here was not by natural causes. This guy was obviously shot in the back of the head.'

'How do you know it's a bloke?'

'Fifty-fifty chance.' Then, seeing his expression: 'No, not really. I do this for a living, so I know it's male. The skull has three points in determining gender – the ridges located above the eyes, the bone situated just below the ear, and the occiput, the bone located at the lower back of the skull.' For the benefit of her colleague, Simpson pointed out each in turn. 'The occiput has been badly damaged, but the bone below the ear is a muscle attachment site, more prominent in men and indicating greater physical strength.'

'I see,' said Carlyle, enjoying this quick reminder of why he'd never had any interest in O-level Biology at school.

Phillips nodded in the direction of the plaster over his eye. 'How's your head?'

'It's fine.' Carlyle gestured towards the skull. 'Better than his, anyway.'

'He was found by some council workmen who were digging up this corner of the park to build a kiddies' playground.'

Carlyle didn't remember seeing any workmen hanging around outside. 'Where are they now?'

'Roche took their statements while she was waiting for you, and then she let them go home. One of them seemed quite upset.'

'Upset?' Carlyle scoffed. 'It's only the bloody skeleton of some poor sod who's been dead for fifty years. What is there to get upset about?'

Phillips ignored his little outburst. 'He may well have been buried here for *more* than fifty years,' she observed.

Carlyle wished more than ever that he had stayed at home in bed. Why did Helen decide to answer his damn phone?

'I need to get him back to the lab to do some proper tests,' Phillips continued.

'No need to go all trainspotter-ish on me,' Carlyle grunted.

'You are in *such* a good mood this morning,' Phillips teased, bouncing the skull gently in her hand. 'No wonder they call you the rudest cop in Westminster.'

'Do they fuck,' Carlyle retorted, not even stopping to consider who, in this instance, 'they' might be.

'If you say so,' Phillips teased. 'Anyway, this guy could have been buried here for seventy or eighty years, maybe more.'

'Excellent,' Carlyle sighed. 'Just what I need – a fucking historical murder mystery.'

'It makes an interesting change,' Phillips mused, 'from teenagers knifing each other, or husbands trying to batter their wives.'

'I don't know about that.'

'Come on, John,' she chided. 'Aren't you even a little curious about how this guy got here? He must have an interesting story to tell.'

Her forced good humour was making him feel grumpier by the second. 'I'm a copper,' he complained, 'not a sodding archaeologist.'

'But still—'

'I bet you love that show on the telly . . .' He struggled to think of the name but couldn't dredge it up from the back of his mind. Helen watched it sometimes; she would watch any old crap.

'*Time Team*? I watch it now and again,' Phillips admitted.

'Gripping stuff,' Carlyle said sarkily. 'Anyway, I need to speak to those workers from the council.'

Getting to her feet, Phillips placed her hand on his forearm and said gently, 'You should relax a bit. It's not a big deal. What are they going to tell you that they didn't already tell Roche? They came in, started digging up the grass – and found some bones.'

'Yeah, yeah, yeah.' Carlyle held up a hand, finally conceding defeat. 'Okay, Tony bloody Robinson, let me have the report when you're done.'

'Of course,' Phillips smiled. 'It may take a little while, though.'

'No rush,' said Carlyle, exiting the tent. 'No rush at all.'

Chapter Eight

'HEY, MARCELLO! WHERE have Trapattoni and Platini gone?'

Carlyle returned to Il Buffone just as the breakfast rush hour was coming to a close, allowing him and Alison Roche to grab the tatty booth at the back, next to the counter. Looking up, he realized that the crumbling poster of the 1984 Juventus scudetto winning squad had disappeared, leaving a lighter patch on the back wall. Torn and faded, curling at the edges and only held together with Sellotape, it had enjoyed pride of place in the café for as long as he could remember. Over the years, Marcello had tried to replace Juve on several occasions, most recently with the Italian World Cup winning team of 2006. Always, however, the protests of Carlyle and of a few other regulars who knew their football forced him to return the team of Trapattoni and Platini to their rightful place. A few moments spent contemplating their achievements were, to Carlyle's way of thinking, always time well spent. Apart from anything else, that team would have beaten Marcello Lippi's Azzurri hands down.

'I threw it out.' Marcello appeared from behind the counter, wiping his hands on a tea towel. 'It finally disintegrated.'

'Jesus!' Carlyle felt a stab of genuine upset. 'Everything's fucking collapsing about my ears,' he grumbled to himself. Taking a large bite out of his raisin Danish – his second of the morning, so far – he waited for the sugar rush to mingle with the double espresso already spreading through his bloodstream. When it had done so, his sense of well-being improved enough for him to ask: 'What are you going to replace it with?'

Marcello studied the empty space on the wall for a moment, then said, 'Dunno. I'm open to suggestions.' A thought crossed his mind and his face broke into a broad grin. 'Not Fulham, though.'

Suitably unfashionable, Fulham had always been Carlyle's team. The thing he liked about them most as he got older was that they never got you too excited. 'No, of course not.' He nodded in agreement. 'Got to be Italian.'

'*Sí, italiano – certo!*' Marcello cranked the Gaggia into action and before long dropped a fresh demitasse in front of his appreciative customer. 'Inter are the team at the moment,' he suggested doubtfully.

Carlyle held up his hands in mock horror. 'Noooo . . .'

Stifling a yawn, Alison Roche looked up from her mug of tea. 'Milan's 94 Champions League winning team,' she said quietly. 'Albertini, Donadoni, Maldini, Desailly . . .'

Marcello nodded enthusiastically. 'Good choice! Fabio Capello's team. Beat Barcelona four-nil to win the European Cup!'

'Yes,' Carlyle assented. 'I think we have a winner.'

'I'll find you a poster, Marcello,' Roche promised.

'Thank you. That would be perfect.' Marcello gave Carlyle a playful punch on the shoulder. 'You're a very lucky man, Inspector. The signora, she is pretty, she's smart *and* she knows her football.'

'Just don't tell the wife, Marcello,' Carlyle mumbled, before taking another massive bite out of his pastry.

'So, SERGEANT ROCHE, what's your story?' Marcello had retreated into his store room to check on the stock. Carlyle drained the last of his coffee from the cup and made a show of giving the sergeant a careful once-over. He didn't know how long she was going to be around, but he might as well exhibit a degree of interest.

Roche considered her answer carefully. 'Well,' she said finally, 'I've been at Leyton for two years, and been a sergeant for almost five now . . .' She came to a halt.

Surprised at how quickly she had run out of steam, Carlyle bowled her another one. 'Did you always want to be a copper?'

'Not really,' she shrugged. 'I kind of drifted into it, I suppose.'

God Almighty, Carlyle thought, *you're not giving much away, are you?* On the other hand, however, he could empathize with people who kept their cards close to their chest. In his experience, there were far too few of them around.

'I almost packed it in before I became a sergeant,' Roche continued suddenly, sensing his dissatisfaction at her monochrome answers, so finally offering up a bit of colour.

'Oh?'

'Yes,' she said and laughed. 'When I was a WPC, I did a stint as a dog-handler. I was paired with a German Shepherd called Robbie. Bloody psycho, that dog! We were chasing this armed robber one day, but instead of jumping on the robber, Robbie bit me on the arm as the bloke ran off with the eight grand he'd just stolen from a pub landlord.'

'Christ!' Carlyle chuckled despite himself.

'That was the whole point. Everyone else thought it was hilarious. I was at Ealing station at the time and everyone took the piss out of me for ages.'

'You can see the funny side . . .'

'I can *now*. At the time I was bloody furious. It was really painful too, and I had to have rabies shots.'

'What happened to Robbie?' Carlyle asked, trying to suppress his laughter.

'He was decommissioned after that. The last I heard, he was working for a security company, protecting building sites.'

'Ah, well, at least you lived to tell the tale.'

'Yeah, yeah. I refused to work with any more dogs after that, but I got over it fairly quickly once I got back on the beat.'

'Thanks for helping me out today,' said Carlyle, changing the subject. Having ticked the touchy-feely box, he now had to get on.

'No problem.' She smiled sadly. 'I'm just sorry about the circumstances.'

'Quite.' Carlyle looked towards the store room. He wondered if he should tell Marcello the bad news about Joe, before deciding it could wait.

'Round here is a bit more glamorous than Leyton.'

'*Most* places are more glamorous than East London,' Carlyle joked.

'I suppose so,' she agreed.

'Look,' he said, clasping his hands together and resting them on the table, 'I don't know what's going to happen next. Obviously, we will be needing to get a full-time replacement for Joe . . .'

Roche gave him a look that suggested he was being a bit, well, emotionless about the whole thing.

He ignored that, ploughing on.

'But that will doubtless take time. I don't know whether you are going to be here for a day, a week or whatever, but like I said, I'm very grateful that you are here, so if you want to stick around, let me know.'

'Thank you,' she replied, still giving him a rather curious look. 'I will check in with Leyton this afternoon and see what they say. In the meantime, what should we do about that guy in the park?'

'The guy in the park?' Carlyle had forgotten about him already. 'Well, let's see what Phillips can tell us. The more she can narrow it down, the easier it will be for us i.e. *you* to chase down any relevant files from the time it occurred.'

Roche emitted a mock groan. 'Great! Maybe East London isn't so bad after all.'

'Now, now,' Carlyle grinned, 'we could be looking at some genuinely interesting detective work here.'

'Yeah, if you're a historian!'

'I'm sure we can wrap it up quickly,' he said, getting to his feet. 'Phillips has already said he's an adult male. She should be able to make a reasonable guess at his age, and hopefully give us a better steer as to when he died. Then you need just take a quick look at any unsolved murders from around then, or people reported missing. If anything interesting comes up, let me know. Otherwise, we can just drop it into the bottomless pit of cases that will remain open forever.'

Carlyle fished a fiver out of his wallet and dropped it on the counter. '*Arrivederci*, Marcello! See you later.'

An indistinct reply issued from the store room.

He looked again at Roche, who seemed in no hurry to leave. 'I'll meet you back at the station. I need to go and see some people first.'

Chapter Nine

'INSPECTOR CARLYLE? I'M Adam Hall.'

Carlyle looked up at the fresh-faced young man and scowled. He'd now been sitting in a windowless interview room for almost forty-five minutes, without even the offer of a cup of crap police coffee. West End Central's hospitality left a lot to be desired. 'Where's French?'

'Chief Inspector French is no longer involved in this investigation,' Hall said, trying – and failing – to keep the smirk out of his voice.

Bloody hell, Carlyle thought. *He didn't last long.*

'I will be conducting your interview,' Hall explained, taking a seat at the table opposite the inspector.

'And who are you?'

In a cheap suit and wearing a blue and white checked shirt open at the neck, the little scrote only looked about thirteen. Carlyle couldn't believe he could be anything higher than a constable, so what the hell was going on here?

The youngster leaned back in his chair, while assessing the situation. 'This,' he said finally, sitting back up straight, 'is all highly confidential.'

Yeah, yeah, whatever. 'Of course,' Carlyle replied solemnly.

'Nothing said in this room can be repeated to anyone – *anyone at all* – outside.'

Get on with it, you little twat.

'Of course,' Carlyle repeated. For emphasis, he nodded and smiled a fake modest smile.

'Good,' Hall said slowly. 'For your information only, I work for MI6. We are now handling this investigation.'

MI6, technically known as SIS, meaning the Secret Intelligence Service, was the UK's external intelligence agency. It was famous for being the home of James Bond and, more recently, for spending £150 million on its not very secret HQ on the southern bank of the Thames in that no-man's land called Vauxhall.

Carlyle took a moment to show the boy that he was digesting this *bombshell* news. 'I take it,' he said finally, 'that this means that we don't think this was the same gang who were taking down rich folk in their hotel rooms.'

Hall put on his best approximation of a poker face. 'I am not at liberty to discuss anything relating to the matter.'

Carlyle held up a hand. 'Fine, fine, I understand.' He gave Hall a hard stare. 'Just remember, though, it was *my* partner who was killed by those cocksuckers. I will not just walk away from this.'

The kid blushed, saying nothing.

'So do not fuck this up.'

'Rest assured, Inspector,' Hall stammered, 'that will not happen.'

Sorry, Joe, Carlyle thought. *It looks like things are moving away from us. But I promise I will do what I can to stop these spook bastards letting you down.* 'Okay,' he said, nodding towards the tape recorder on the table. 'Let's get started.'

TWENTY-FIVE MINUTES AFTER completing his interview with the junior spy, Carlyle emerged from Edgware Road tube station, heading towards Paddington Green police station, a brutalist Sixties cube straight out of the *couldn't-give-a-fuck* school of architecture that had been fashionable at the time. Ten minutes later, he was sitting in Simpson's office, waiting politely for her to finish off a phone call. Her desk was bare save for a copy of the *British Medical Journal.* Carlyle tried to read the contents of the cover page, but it was upside down and the text was too small.

Simpson finished her call and put down the phone. 'How are you, John?'

'Fine,' he replied. 'A few aches and pains but basically okay.'

She nodded. 'Good.'

'I've just been to West End Central . . .'

'Oh yes?'

'. . . and MI6 have taken over the investigation into Joe's death.'

'Have they indeed.'

Simpson's smile suggested that she already knew what was going on, and that she was not going to share.

Deeply annoyed, Carlyle went on: 'That tells me two things.'

'Does it, Inspector?' Simpson's eyes positively sparkled with amusement. 'And what would they be?'

'First, this is something political. The guy shot in his hotel room must have been someone important.'

'Someone dangerous.'

'Whatever.'

'And the second point?'

'The second point is that if our little spook pals are primarily investigating this bloke, then they won't much care about what happened to Joe.'

'But the same man was responsible for both deaths, was he not?'

'Yes.'

'So the Security Services can kill two birds with one stone, as it were.'

'Let's hope so.'

'I am sure they will do what they can.'

'Will you keep me informed?'

'To the extent that I can.' Simpson's eyes lost their sparkle. 'The quid pro quo here is that you leave well alone.'

'Of course.'

'This is a dangerous game, John,' she added firmly, 'one for the big boys. You have to accept that it is no longer a police matter. That has come down from the top. The very top.'

Carlyle stiffened. 'That's what the guy said as well.'

'What?' Simpson frowned. This part of their conversation had already gone on far too long.

What the hell, Carlyle thought. *I might as well go for the sympathy vote*, and he launched into his mini-monologue. 'When I was on my knees in that hotel room, looking down the barrel of his semi-automatic, waiting for him to pull the trigger,' he stole a quick glance at Simpson, not wanting to overdo it, 'he said, "You're playing with the big boys now". I still don't understand why he didn't pull the trigger.'

Simpson gave him a sceptical look. She knew Carlyle was no delicate flower, but she didn't want to call his bluff. 'If you need to see a psychologist . . .'

Carlyle dropped his gaze to his lap. 'No, no.'

'Okay,' Simpson said primly, 'but don't rule it out. Anyway, that's not what we really need to talk about.'

Carlyle looked up. 'Oh?'

'Charlotte Gondomar.'

Carlyle held up a hand. 'Don't applaud, as they say – just throw money.'

'Now is no time for one of your lame jokes.' Simpson gave him a stern look. 'She was found hanged in her prison cell this morning.'

Fucking great. 'Ah . . .'

Simpson's mobile started ringing. She looked at the number on the screen, and cut it off. 'So – we have a problem.'

'We do?'

'Don't mess me about, John,' Simpson hissed. 'First, we have to explain why we didn't show proper care and attention to a vulnerable girl in custody. Initial indications are that she died around five a.m. It seems that she wasn't checked after one a.m.'

'Someone fucked up.'

'Too bloody right,' Simpson snorted. 'And there will be hell to pay over that. And with hindsight . . .'

'Hindsight,' Carlyle scoffed.

'I know, I know,' Simpson sighed. 'But that won't stop the press and the politicians from coming on board and giving us a good kicking. Did you really have to stick her in that cell?'

'She was a drug-trafficker,' he protested. 'What was I supposed to do?'

'She was a vulnerable young girl who you picked up with a large quantity of cocaine about her person.'

His patience snapped. 'Don't start trying to spin it.'

'Plenty of other people will. Then there's the question of why you didn't hand this over to the Drugs Squad?'

'It was my tip,' he explained. 'I was supposed to go to that fashion show with Joe.' Carlyle sat back in his chair and folded his arms. Almost immediately, he decided that gesture could be interpreted as defensive body language, so he unfolded them again. All of a sudden, he didn't know what to do with his bloody limbs. Finally, he clasped his hands as if in prayer and forced them down into his lap. He looked up, to give Simpson some good eye-contact: 'My tip, my arrest.'

Simpson sniffed. 'Never were much of a team player, were you, John?'

Knowing she was right, Carlyle shrugged.

'Anyway, you will be contacted about the IPCC investigation within the next couple of days.'

'That's fine.' Carlyle knew he had done everything by the book. The Independent Police Complaints Commission investigated deaths that occurred in custody as a matter of routine.

'You might want to speak to your Union rep.'

Carlyle shook his head. 'No need.'

Simpson looked at him. 'It would be a good idea – if not for the IPCC, then maybe for the Middle Market Drugs Project investigation.'

Carlyle made a face. 'What the hell's that?'

'It's a new joint venture between the Met and Customs and Excise, aimed at targeting dealers acting as the link between smugglers and street-sellers. After a successful trial, it has been given a mandate by the Home Office to disrupt criminal networks, stifle supply, arrest traffickers and seize their assets.'

Fuck, thought Carlyle. *I don't like the sound of that. I don't like the sound of that at all.* He had a big problem when it came to any kind of internal police investigation – and that problem was called

Dominic Silver. How do you explain your thirty-year relationship with a successful drug dealer to someone trying to winkle out even the merest whiff of corruption on the police force? The simple answer was that you can't. Hell, most of the time, he couldn't even explain it to himself. Did Simpson know about Silver? He had no reason to believe so; certainly he had never discussed his contact with her. And, despite the fact that his relationship with his boss had improved significantly over the last few years, he wasn't going to start now.

'Apparently,' Simpson continued, 'they had Charlotte Gondomar already under surveillance when you arrested her.'

Ignoring the sick feeling in his stomach, Carlyle smiled blandly. 'I'm perfectly happy to talk to them at any time.'

'Good.' Simpson looked down at her desk, as if surprised to see it bare of paperwork. 'Anything else?'

'The usual.' Running through the list of his current cases, it took a moment for Carlyle to recall the skeleton in the park. After his run-in with Spy Boy and now Simpson's unwelcome news, that discovery seemed years ago now. 'The council dug up a skeleton in Lincoln's Inn Fields this morning,' he said flatly. 'An adult male, shot in the head.'

He paused to let Simpson give him a funny look.

'Susan Phillips reckons that the victim has been in the ground for more than fifty years.'

'That's a bit of a turn-up for the books,' Simpson observed. 'Okay. Make sure the paperwork is dealt with, and then move on to more pressing matters.' She lifted a large shoulder bag onto her desk and started rummaging inside. 'And ask my PA to come in on your way out, will you?'

Chapter Ten

HELEN HAD SPENT the early part of the evening working herself into a state. 'You don't mess with bloody Mossad!' were the first words out of her mouth as Carlyle stuck his head through the living-room door.

Alice wandered in from the kitchen, a glass of orange juice in one hand and a sandwich in the other. 'Mum says you'd better be careful or they're going to kick your arse,' she said cheerily, before stuffing half of the sandwich into her mouth and flopping down on the sofa beside her mother.

'What the hell are you two talking about?' he asked, stepping into the middle of the room.

'It's all over the bloody television!' Helen replied angrily, waving the remote control at the screen.

The television was tuned to News 24, with the sound muted. The anchor, a middle-aged Irishwoman with big hair who always looked like she was reading someone's obituary, was talking to some politician about tax rises. What's that got to do with me? Carlyle thought irritably. Then his eye caught the ticker running across the bottom of the screen.

BREAKING NEWS: *Intelligence sources have told the BBC that Israeli Secret Service Agents are suspected of being behind the double murder at a top London hotel.*

That's great, Carlyle thought. *Just fucking great! Can no one in this country keep their bloody mouth shut for more than two minutes?*

He sat down on the sofa, prompting Alice to jump up and head for her room, mumbling something about 'homework'. Careful not to make eye-contact with his wife, he stared intently at the screen.

'Well, John Carlyle,' she said finally, once it was clear that he wasn't going to volunteer any information unprompted, 'have you not got something to tell me?'

Sighing, he braced himself for another political lecture. Helen worked for an international medical charity called Avalon. After several years as a senior administrative manager, she had recently been promoted to the role of Chief Operating Officer. That meant she was directly responsible for a budget of almost £40 million and a team of 200 people working in 30 countries, including the Palestinian Territories. Carlyle was well aware of her views on the Israeli checkpoints, roadblocks and border closures that made it difficult for ordinary people to access healthcare. He knew her mantra off by heart, how the recent violence in the Gaza Strip had left more than 1,300 people dead and over 5,000 people wounded. The safety of Avalon health educators, nurses and volunteers was a constant source of concern to his wife.

She looked at him with fury in her eyes. 'It could have been you.'

'What?'

'It could have been you, bleeding to death on that dirty pavement.'

'Joe didn't bleed to death.'

'You know what I mean, you stupid man.'

Clumsily, he reached out to hug her but she shied away and punched him hard on the arm.

'Hey! That hurt!'

'You bloody deserve it,' she sniffed, half-crying, half-laughing, then hitting him again, not quite as hard this time.

'Look,' he said, finally getting close enough to slide his arm round her. 'It was a very strange situation. Maybe it could have been me. But it wasn't. I'm okay.'

The expression of anguish on her face almost broke his heart.

'Look,' he repeated gently, 'I've been a cop now for – what? Almost thirty years. Nothing like that has ever happened before. Nothing like it will ever happen again. It was a once-in-a-lifetime event, at the very most.'

Helen blew her nose on her sleeve, desperately wanting to be convinced.

However, they both knew, deep down, that such assertions were all just talk.

As husband and wife they didn't do awkward silences. Holding his breath, Carlyle felt a tension such as he hadn't experienced since their early courting days, those agonizing times when he worried that she might pack him in.

'Poor Anita,' she said finally.

Breathing out at last, Carlyle felt himself relax slightly. 'I know,' he murmured. 'I know.'

'Poor Anita,' Helen repeated.

Poor Anita? She would have quite happily let one of her brothers beat me to a pulp. 'She is being well looked after,' he said.

'And the kids?'

'Yes, them too,' Carlyle nodded solemnly, happy to give any reassurance now that they were over the worst of their conversation.

'And,' Helen jabbed a gentle finger into his chest, 'I had your bloody mother on the phone, moaning that she went to the loo at the Ritz and came back to find that you'd done a runner.'

His mother! Carlyle suddenly realized that he'd forgotten all about her. 'Oh fuck.' He remembered the conversation they'd been having at the time, but decided not to get into that with Helen right at this moment. 'I'll give her a call. Did she see all the fuss?'

'I don't think so. Anyway, she didn't mention it.' Helen pushed herself away from him. 'She said how she told you that she was divorcing your dad.'

'Er . . . yeah.'

Helen gave him one of her *Why didn't you tell me this?* stares. 'And?'

Carlyle shrugged. 'Well, we didn't really get into the details. She just dropped her little bombshell and then went off to the Ladies. Everything kicked off while she was still in there.'

'You must have sensed something before.'

'No.' Carlyle shook his head. 'Everything seemed pretty much normal to me. When she said she wanted to talk about my father, I assumed she was about to tell me that he had developed cancer or something.'

'John . . .' They both knew how he paid minimal attention to wider family issues beyond the walls of their own flat.

'Come on!+-' Carlyle allowed himself the smallest of smiles. 'How could I have suspected anything? They've been married for almost fifty years! What's the point of getting a divorce now?'

Helen gave him a sly look, one that he interpreted as saying: *Why not? You should never rule anything out.* He felt his balls shrink up inside him. Message received and understood.

'Maybe she's found someone else.'

'Mum? Nah.' Carlyle felt funny just thinking about the possibility.

'Maybe *he's* found someone else.'

'I got the impression that this is all her initiative,' Carlyle said. 'I can't see either of them ever playing away from home. So, I suppose that she's just decided she needs a change – or something.'

'Well, anyway, you need to talk to her about it. And to your dad, as well.'

'Yes, yes – in a minute.'

Helen unmuted the television. A reporter was standing on the north side of the Thames, with MI6's lego-like headquarters clearly identifiable on the other side. He was saying, '*It is very unusual for MI6 to become involved in this type of investigation. Sources have told the BBC that this is because the man killed in the Ritz Hotel . . .*'

One of the men, Carlyle thought sourly.

'*. . . is thought to have been a certain*,' the reporter glanced down at his notes, '*. . . Omid Jarragh Ajab. Now, Mr Ajab is believed to have been one of the founders of the military wing of the Hamas militant movement which had control of the Gaza Strip. One line of thinking is that he was visiting London in order to buy weapons for Hamas. If this information is correct . . .*'

Not that you really have a clue whether it is true or not, Carlyle thought.

'*. . . then the prime suspects in his assassination will inevitably include Israel's secret service, Mossad. Which, of course, is where MI6 comes in.*'

Carlyle had heard enough. He grabbed the remote from Helen and switched over to Sky Sports News.

'Hey!' Helen complained. 'Don't you want to hear more?'

'No, I bloody don't,' Carlyle grumbled, taking solace in the latest football trivia. 'I've heard more than enough already.'

'I thought you were going to phone your parents,' she reminded him.

'I am,' he lied.

'It's already late.'

'I know. By the way, who is the best person at your place to talk to about Gaza?'

'Fucking *hell*, John.'

'What?'

'I thought you said it was all over. There is no way that this can still be your case.'

'No, no, of course not,' he said quickly. 'This is not even a police inquiry any more. It's being handled by MI6.' He recounted his meeting with Adam Hall, the youthful SIS guy, earlier in the day.

'MI6?' Helen snorted. 'That's great. That lot couldn't find their way out of a paper bag.'

'It doesn't matter, anyway. If it is Mossad behind it, the guys who did this are probably safely back in Tel Aviv by now. The Israelis will tell anyone who complains to fuck right off while they smile smugly and do their usual "*We never confirm or deny anything*" routine.'

'So why do you want to speak to someone at Avalon?'

'You could say I've recently developed an interest in the subject.'

Helen let out the longest of sighs. 'Well, our Gaza co-ordinator is a woman called Louisa Arbillot. She's French and worked for Médecins Sans Frontières for years. She joined us about nine months ago.'

'Can you get her to give me a call?'

'She's over there at the moment,' Helen said, the lack of enthusiasm in her voice obvious, 'but I'll see what I can do. It might have to wait until she gets back next week.'

'Thanks.'

'I'm going for a bath,' Helen yawned. 'Remember to call your mother . . .'

Chapter Eleven

A COUPLE OF Ibuprofen and a large glass of Jameson whiskey ensured that Carlyle slept soundly. By the time he reached the office the next day it was after eleven. Roche was sitting at Joe's desk when he arrived, staring intently at the computer screen. Carlyle paused a moment to check her out. She was dressed in washed-out grey jeans, Gola trainers and a blue, long-sleeved T-shirt. Her hair was pulled back and she wasn't wearing any make-up. As her fingers danced across the keyboard, he idly noticed that she wasn't wearing any wedding or engagement ring.

'How's it going?' he asked, flopping into his chair.

'Not bad,' Roche replied, not looking up. 'Got some interesting stuff back from Phillips.'

Carlyle leaned back in his chair and yawned. 'About the skeleton, you mean?'

'No, that will still take a while. But she found a cartridge in the grave. Presumably the bullet that killed our victim.' She swivelled in her seat to face Carlyle directly, a big grin on her face. 'And she found the gun too.'

Carlyle sat up.

'Presumably what happened was that the guy was shot and dumped in the shallow grave. The killer couldn't keep the weapon about his person so he tossed it in too.'

'Thank you, Sherlock Holmes.'

Carlyle saw her face darken and he quickly held up a hand. 'Sorry, my sense of humour.'

She gave him a sharp look.

'Not always to everyone's taste,' he admitted. 'Anyway, what else do we have?'

'The gun is a . . .' Roche looked back at the notes on the screen '. . . Walther P38.'

'Never heard of it,' Carlyle said.

Roche squinted at the screen and read out: '"It's a nine-millimetre weapon that was developed as the service pistol of the Wehrmacht at the beginning of World War Two.' She shrugged. 'Dunno who the Wehrmacht are.'

'The German army.'

'Okay. So someone used a German pistol to shoot this man and bury him in a park in Central London.'

'If it was during the war,' Carlyle mused, 'in a blackout, during the Blitz, that might explain how someone could easily get away with it. Bloody long time ago, though. How the hell are we going to find out who this guy was? It'll be like looking for a needle in a haystack.'

Roche tapped the keyboard on her desk with an index finger. 'I've been taking a look through the Zella-Mehlis database.'

'Have you indeed?' Carlyle replied, not having the remotest clue what she was talking about.

'Basically, in 2009, the Met digitized all of its still open Missing Person cases.' She gave the keyboard another tap and a new screen popped up. To Carlyle it looked like just an endless list of words. Roche clicked on a name and a man's photograph appeared. 'This is just some guy I picked out at random, but you can do a search by various characteristics, date of birth, date reported missing and so on.'

'Sounds good. Have you found any possibles yet?'

Roche shook her head. 'I've only just started. What I thought I would do is first search for anyone who went missing near Lincoln's Inn Fields during the war.'

'Won't there be a lot of them?'

'I'll start off by looking for men between eighteen and thirty. Most of those otherwise would have been off fighting at that time.'

'I suppose,' said Carlyle vaguely. As far as he knew, no one in the Carlyle family had fought during the war, apart from some distant cousin of his grandfather, who had never come back from a prisoner-of-war camp in Burma. Not one to daydream, he pulled himself back into the present. All of this was basically of historical interest only, and he had work to do.

And he needed another coffee.

And he still had to phone his mother.

He pushed himself out of the chair and headed for the door. 'It's all sounding very interesting,' he said over his shoulder, leaving Roche to her databases. 'Keep me posted.'

AT THE FRONT desk, Carlyle waited for Kevin Price to finish talking to a geography teacher from Doncaster who'd been relieved of £150 in a Soho clip joint. Carlyle watched the man slouch out of the station clutching a piece of paper containing his crime-identification number.

'Will he be able to claim on his insurance?' he asked.

'He probably won't even dare try,' Price laughed, 'in case his wife finds out what he's been up to.'

Price was a tall, thin man, with plenty of grey in his black hair and also in his badly groomed beard. He had recently started wearing reading glasses, and these, Carlyle thought, made him look like a psycho librarian.

'Dirty little bugger,' Price snorted. 'Don't they have any tarts up north?' Without waiting for an answer, he pointed to a round tin at the far end of the desk. It was slightly taller than a soup can, and maybe twice as wide. On it, someone had stuck a label that simply said *Joe S.*

Carlyle fished out his wallet and looked inside. He was rather surprised to see that it contained a twenty-pound note, along with a ten and a five. He pulled out the twenty and the ten, folding them twice before placing them carefully in the tin, which was already almost full.

'Thank you,' said Price stiffly. 'The funeral has been arranged for a week from today, but I expect that you already knew that.'

'No,' Carlyle said quietly, 'I didn't. Thanks.'

'No problem. Apparently it's going to be a small family affair, but no doubt you'll be going along.'

'Of course.'

'And the boss.'

'Simpson? I suppose so.'

Price shook his head. 'It's a terrible thing. Especially with him having young kids.'

'What's the gossip in the station about it?' Carlyle asked, as casually as he could manage.

'You tell me.' Price scratched his beard. 'I haven't heard anything at all.'

Don't be a sod, Carlyle thought. *Desk sergeants hear everything. Just tell me what people are saying. Do they think that Joe's death was my fault?* He waited for Price to say more, but the sergeant kept his counsel.

'I haven't heard anything either,' Carlyle said finally. 'I haven't been around much.'

'But you were there,' Price was obviously keen to probe but didn't want to be seen to be too interested in the juicy details, 'when it happened.'

Now it was Carlyle's turn to remain unforthcoming. 'It's still all a bit of a blur really.'

'I suppose it must be.' Unhappy at being fobbed off, Price picked up some papers from the desk and stuffed them into a box-file. Wedging the file under his arm he then wandered off, leaving Carlyle none the wiser.

SITTING IN VISCONTI'S café on Maiden Lane, Carlyle sucked down a double espresso and pulled up the number for his parents on his mobile. Taking a deep breath, he hit the call button and waited to be connected.

After the third ring, he relaxed slightly, thinking that it would now go to voicemail.

'Hello?'

Shit.

'Ma? It's John.'

'Master John Carlyle,' his mother replied, 'how good of you to call. I assumed that you had simply vanished off the face of the earth.'

In his mind's eye, he could see her standing by the phone in the hallway of the Fulham flat that he'd grown up in, the same flat she had lived in for so many years. Pursing her lips, she would be wondering what she'd done to deserve such an errant son. He forced himself into grovelling mode. 'I'm really sorry, Ma.'

Lorna Gordon wasn't one to acknowledge apologies. 'Running off on me like that,' she said, her disappointed tone rolling back the years, 'and leaving me to pay the bill.'

Carlyle had paid the bill himself, in advance over the internet, but he let that matter slide. 'I know, I know. But there was a serious problem and I had to try and deal with it. It was all in the news.'

'Nasty business,' his mother mused. 'The poor policeman . . . getting killed like that. What a terrible thing to happen!'

'Yes,' Carlyle agreed, his desire to talk about it rapidly evaporating. 'It certainly was.'

'I hope they catch the people who did it.'

'So do I.'

'Isn't that *your* job?' she scolded.

'It isn't my investigation.'

'It might not be your *investigation*, John,' she said, her voice rising slightly, 'but surely it is still your responsibility?'

You're right about that, Carlyle thought. He caught sight of his reflection in the café window. Despite everything, he was smiling. His mother could always cut straight to the heart of an issue. Pissing about around the edges of any problem was not Lorna Gordon's style. It was one of the things he loved about his mother, that same characteristic he was glad to have inherited from her.

'Well?'

'We should meet up again,' he said, getting back to the point of his phone call, 'and finish our discussion.'

'You're the one with the busy schedule,' she groused.

Carlyle shook his head, but, once again, didn't rise to the bait. Once they had agreed a time and a place, he said goodbye and hung up, relieved that the conversation was over.

As soon as he put the mobile on the table, it started vibrating again. Noting that the call was from Simpson, he picked it up.

'Commander?'

'Inspector,' she said evenly. 'How are you?'

'I'm fine.'

'Have you spoken to the IPCC yet?'

'No.' Carlyle had forgotten all about the Independent Police Complaints Commission. 'Not heard a dicky-bird. Nothing from those other guys either.'

Whatever they were called.

'That's a bit surprising. You would have expected them to have been in touch by now.'

'They know where to find me.'

'Let me know how things go.'

'Of course.' Carlyle signalled to the girl behind the counter for another double espresso. 'Any news from Joe's family?'

'No. I expect that it is very hard for them,' Simpson sighed. 'Things are bound to be tough.'

'I hear that the funeral is next week.'

'Yes – that's what I wanted to speak to you about. Look, John, there's no easy way to say this, but they don't want you to attend.'

The girl placed a fresh demitasse in front of him, scooped up the empty cup and went scuttling back behind the counter.

'I know that must be difficult news for you to hear.'

Carlyle took a sip of the fresh coffee. 'No, no.' He shook his head. 'That's fine. I understand. It's got to be Anita's decision. I don't want to cause any problems.'

The man who dodged the bullet that killed her husband.

'That's good of you, John,' said Simpson. 'Thank you.' He could hear the tension ebbing from her voice as, for once, a tricky conversation went better than might have been expected.

'Will you be going?'

'Yes. I will represent the Force at the service. But it will be family only at the graveside.'

'Okay.' Thinking about it, Carlyle was really quite relieved. He had been to more than his share of funerals over the years. He certainly didn't need any more.

'There will, of course, be a memorial service at a later date.'

'Yes.'

There was a pause.

'How are things going with your skeleton?' Simpson asked finally.

'Roche is making some progress,' Carlyle said. 'We think it might be some bloke who died during the Blitz.'

'Interesting.'

'Not really,' Carlyle laughed, 'but we'll see what else we can find out. By the way, am I getting Roche for long?'

'I don't know,' Simpson said evenly. 'Do you want her?'

'She seems okay.'

'Fine. I'll speak to her CO at . . .'

'Leyton.'

'. . . and see what I can do.'

'Can't say fairer than that.' Ending the call, Carlyle finished his coffee, paid the girl behind the counter and headed back outside.

Chapter Twelve

THE WOMAN SENT by the Independent Police Complaints Commission was a doddle. The kind of bored bureaucrat who gave box-ticking a bad name, she skipped through the necessary forms with a minimum of fuss. Keen to get out of the interview room as quickly as possible, she gave no indication that she was in the least bit interested in what had happened to Lottie Gondomar. As she flitted from one form to another, Carlyle looked her up and down: colourless hair, featureless face, indeterminate age, dressed by Marks & Spencer; a mere cipher of an individual. He couldn't even remember what she'd said her name was. He watched her sign the bottom of the last form with a flourish and scrawl a large X next to the line below.

'Sign here,' she mumbled, shovelling the paper across the desk, without even looking up.

Carlyle accepted the pen she offered and obediently made his scrawl.

Grabbing the form back, the woman gave a thin smile. 'Thank you,' she said, her voice still completely lacking in any conviction. 'We'll be in touch with you.'

Carlyle forced a smile in response. 'No problem. I'm sure it's all completely straightforward – as far as I'm concerned, at least.'

Mistaking his small talk for real interest, the woman's smile widened. 'We'll see what happens next.'

'After all,' Carlyle said cheerily, 'it's not like this is another Jean Charles de Menezes, is it?'

It was a deliberately low blow, and delivered with a modicum of relish. Jean Charles de Menezes was the innocent Brazilian shot seven times in the head by police marksmen while sitting on a tube train at Stockwell station. It was two weeks after the London bombings of 7 July 2005, which had cost fifty-six lives. Apparently, the police had mistaken de Menezes for a suicide bomber.

The woman stuffed her documents back into a plastic bag and stood up.

'I mean,' Carlyle continued, 'how badly can you fuck this one up?'

Looking like she was going to be sick over the desk, the woman fled without saying another word.

Folding his arms, Carlyle sat back in his chair. 'One down,' he said to himself, 'one to go.'

IF THE WOMAN from the IPCC had been instantly banished from his thoughts, Inspector Sam Hooper was another matter entirely. Sitting in the same interview room in Charing Cross police station, Carlyle was this time on high alert. The man from the Middle Market Drugs Project could pose a serious threat to his career. Every word had to be weighed carefully, but uttered instantly, particularly if the conversation turned to Dominic Silver.

As far as he could tell, the interview was not being recorded. And Hooper had said nothing about the basis of the conversation – whether it was on the record or not. On balance, Carlyle took comfort from the vague nature of the conversation: it was shaping up to be a glorified fishing exercise. *Take control from the outset*, he told himself as he watched Hooper take out a file of papers and a notepad from his briefcase. *Make the other man do the talking.* It was a simple rule. The less you said, the less likely you were to trip yourself up.

'So,' he asked, 'what exactly is the Middle Market Drugs Project?'

Hooper looked at him blankly. 'I thought Commander Simpson would have told you about that.'

Carlyle shrugged. 'Not really.'

Hooper pulled a pen from the pocket of his jacket. 'We are looking at bringing down drug dealers of significance across the capital. That way, we can make seizures of a decent size and also disrupt supplies to the sellers out on the street.'

'And have you uncovered much?' Carlyle asked, in a tone that suggested a casual yet professional interest.

Hooper made a show of trying to size him up.

Carlyle made sure he kept their eye-contact until the man across the table was forced to break it off.

'Has it been successful?' Carlyle asked again.

'Very.' Hooper bowed his head slightly, and Carlyle felt irritated by his false modesty.

'But now we are moving out of the trial phase. The Home Office is throwing money at us. The Project is due to grow from eight officers to twenty-five in the next three months.'

A thought suddenly flashed across Carlyle's brain: *maybe he wants to recruit me?*

Hooper opened his notepad. 'How did you know about Charlotte Gondomar?'

Show-time. Carlyle sat up slightly in his chair. 'It was a tip-off.'

Hooper nodded as he wrote down the words. 'From whom?'

'From a confidential informant.' He had already thought about what he would say next; the trick was not to make it sound too rehearsed. 'Ms Gondomar came onto my radar in the course of an investigation we were doing into complaints that a couple of models had been abused by a local photographer.' This last was a total fabrication, but the paperwork existed to back it up. 'I would have handed the matter on, but it became apparent that my sources would only deal with me.'

He paused, checking how this was going down, but Hooper, still busy scribbling, was not giving anything away.

'There was also the time issue,' Carlyle continued. 'I was aware that Ms Gondomar had a significant amount of Class A in her possession on the night in question.'

The night in question. Classic police-speak from a humble plod. Carlyle, amused by the shit coming out of his own mouth, fought back a smile.

'Also, she was due to return to Brazil the following morning. Therefore I acted in an expeditious manner, by taking advantage of the limited window of opportunity available to me.'

Despite having seen my sergeant shot down in the street only a few hours earlier.

Hooper finished his note-taking and dropped his pen on the desk. 'And how did you get to know all about that?'

'Like I said,' Carlyle repeated, 'I was fortunate enough to have my source.'

'One you are not prepared to share?'

Carlyle made a face that suggested that the question was a long way past unreasonable. 'No, of course not,' he said. 'I have to protect my sources, just like you do. Just like everyone does.'

Hooper looked doubtful.

'Anyway,' Carlyle continued, 'we got a result – a good result. If you're feeling pissed off that it doesn't go down on your Project's scorecard, I'm sure we can arrange to sort that out.'

A cunning light appeared in Hooper's eyes. 'You think we should fiddle the stats?'

'No,' Carlyle said firmly, 'I'm not saying that.' He cursed himself for having given Hooper something to work with. 'What I *am* saying is that it was a successful arrest, and you should be pleased about that.'

'The girl subsequently died.'

'The IPCC investigation into that is well underway. I have already spoken to them.'

Hooper scratched his head. 'Don't you feel responsible for what happened to her?'

Carlyle thought about that for a moment. He knew nothing about Lottie Gondomar, other than the fact that she trafficked drugs and had truly wonderful breasts. He did not know why she was smuggling drugs (for the money, he presumed) nor had he any idea why she'd decide to kill herself in one of his prison cells. He had stuck her in that cell, it was true, but it wasn't his job to check on her during the night and make sure she was okay. Ultimately, however you looked at it, he had only been doing his job. Lottie Gondomar's fate was one of the few things in recent days for which he *didn't* feel responsible. 'Everything was done properly. Everything was recorded properly. I left the girl in the care of the duty officer. So, no, Inspector, I don't feel responsible.'

'That's handy,' Hooper smirked.

Fuck off, thought Carlyle.

'What about Rollo Kasabian?' Hooper asked.

'What about him?'

'Was he your informant?'

'No, he wasn't. I'd never even met him before the other night.' Carlyle was happy to talk about Rollo. Maybe getting some accurate facts into the conversation now would help him later on.

Hooper picked up the pen and started doodling on his pad.

'No?'

'No,' Carlyle said, 'Rollo was not the source of my information. I will give you that, but I'm not going to play Twenty Bloody Questions about who it was.'

'Interesting.' Hooper thought about his next move. 'We have had him under investigation for some time.'

'Rollo?'

'Yes.'

You're bluffing, thought Carlyle. *You haven't been watching him. You don't have shit.* 'Based on what information?'

Hooper smiled. 'We have our sources too, Inspector.'

'I'm sure that you do,' Carlyle smiled back. 'Just not as good as mine.'

Chapter Thirteen

CARLYLE WALKED INTO Il Buffone still deep in thought. In some ways, the fact that Hooper *hadn't* mentioned Dominic Silver was even more troubling than if he had. At least, that way Carlyle would have had a better idea of what the Middle Market Drugs Project knew. If they didn't know about Silver they should do, since he was exactly the type of dealer that they were trying to target. And if they did know about him, they clearly didn't trust Carlyle enough to tell him the whole story. What was it some politician had said about *known unknowns*? Well, he would just have to wait and see – keeping his guard up in the meantime. Sighing, he slipped onto a stool at the counter and stared vacantly out of the window.

After a minute or so, Marcello appeared at his shoulder and placed a double macchiato on the counter. 'We're out of pastries,' he said. 'Do you want anything else to eat?'

Having been looking forward to the sugar rush, Carlyle felt a pang of annoyance. He carefully considered his options: he didn't really care for croissants and the only other cakes on offer – stodgy

Bakewell tarts wrapped in plastic with sell-by dates well into next year – were only to be resorted to in times of emergency. 'No,' he said finally, 'it's okay, Marcello. Coffee's fine.'

Nodding, Marcello pulled a copy of the *Evening Standard* from under his arm, unfolded it and placed it carefully on the counter, in front of Carlyle.

'Why didn't you tell me?' he asked quietly.

Carlyle took a sip of his coffee and glanced at the front page. The headline screamed *THE FACE OF A KILLER* above a grainy black and white picture taken from a CCTV camera. The image showed the pavement outside the front entrance to the Ritz, moments after Joe Szyszkowski had been shot. Joe himself already lay on the pavement, while Carlyle, turning away from the camera, was looking towards his fallen colleague. The gunman, his face blurry and indistinguishable, appeared to be staring right into the lens.

Carlyle took a deep breath, then let it out slowly. Avoiding Marcello's gaze, he scanned the text: *The murdered officer was last night named as Sergeant Joseph Szyszkowski . . . wife and two children . . . the authorities say that they are pursuing several leads . . .*

At least there was no mention of Carlyle's name. He handed the newspaper back to Marcello.

'I'm sorry. It's been a tough time.'

'Sure, sure.' Marcello gave him a comforting pat on the shoulder. 'It's a terrible thing to happen.'

'Yes, it is,' Carlyle nodded, finishing his coffee.

Marcello lowered his voice. 'It could have been you.'

'That's what Helen said.' Carlyle smiled weakly. 'What can you do? It's a bit like the lottery in reverse.'

Marcello poked him gently in the chest. 'You have to be careful.'

'Marcello,' said Carlyle, more tired than peeved, 'I get more than enough of this type of talk at home. I *am* careful. And, by and large, London is a very safe city.'

'Not for Joe, it wasn't,' said Marcello, crossing himself. 'God rest his soul.'

'Yes, well . . .'

Marcello took the empty cup and waved aside Carlyle's offer of payment. 'I'll see you tomorrow. I'll make sure to keep some Danish pastries for you, even if you don't deserve them.'

'Thanks,' said Carlyle, heartened by this use of the plural.

'And give his family my condolences.'

'I will,' said Carlyle. *Assuming that they ever speak to me again.*

Chapter Fourteen

Tapping his hands on the steering wheel, Ryan Goya sat gazing at the long line of vehicles leading up to the traffic-lights on Lisson Grove. Heading north into St John's Wood, he was singing along quietly to Rihanna's 'Rude Boy' on the radio.

For the hundredth time that afternoon, Goya glanced down at the newspaper folded on his lap, then looked up to check his reflection in the cab's wing mirror. Yet again, he concluded that it was impossible to identify him as the man pictured in the paper. A fresh number-one buzz cut under his beanie hat, and several days' worth of stubble had changed his appearance well enough. Anyway, given the extremely poor quality of the CCTV image, it was going to be impossible to identify *anyone* as the man in the picture.

Ryan smiled to himself: he was in the clear. This was just as well, given that the work assigned to his team here in London was far from finished.

The man sitting in the back of his cab was Noor Gyula Teleki, a known associate of Omid Jarragh Ajab. Both men were important members of Hamas's military wing, the Izz al-Din al-Qassam Brigades, and part of a four-strong cell that Mossad had been tracking through Europe for the last six months. Reliable intelligence from an informer inside the Palestinian Authority in Gaza had told them that the Hamas crew were presently in London to buy a cache of Chinese QBZ-95 rifles from an Armenian arms dealer. The guns were thought to be intended for Hamas's Executive Support Forces in their ongoing squabble with the Preventive Security Force of the rival faction, Fatah. Palestinians shooting each other seemed like a good idea to Goya; he often wondered why his bosses didn't just let them get on with it. But he knew that was considered an exotic notion. Anything that put arms into the hands of the Palestinians was to be stopped – by any means possible.

The other reason why Noor Gyula Teleki had to be killed was Itay Kayal. Kayal had been an eighteen-year-old conscript in the Israeli army who, ten years earlier, was standing, dressed in his uniform, at a bus stop near the southern Israeli town of Ashkelon when a battered white Mercedes drove past. Inside the car were Omid Jarragh Ajab, Noor Gyula Teleki and a third man, Karrar Shawqi Aboud. Turning the car around, they drove up to the bus stop, shot the boy in the legs, then bundled him into the boot and drove off.

Three weeks later, the Ha-Televizia Ha-israelit television channel had received a video of Itay Kayal's execution. On his knees, bound and gagged, he had been decapitated with a sword. Itay's body was only recovered seven years after the kidnapping, buried under a road near the border with Gaza.

Before leaving for London, Goya and his team had met with Itay's sister, Tal. She told them how her parents had died brokenhearted soon after their son's death. She told them how she herself had hosted a party to celebrate the death of Karrar Shawqi Aboud, after he had been killed three years later, shot by troops from the Israeli Defence Force, the Border Guard and the security service Shin Bet. And she told them how she prayed every night that Mossad would now step forward to complete the job and fully avenge her brother's death by killing the other men responsible.

'The memories continue to haunt us,' Tal Kayal had said, holding Goya's gaze with eyes devoid of any light. 'We will always remember Itay, so I very much hope that you can find these terrorists and kill them.'

'We will,' affirmed Goya, bowing his head.

'Kill them like dogs,' she pleaded, her eyes welling up, 'just like they killed my brother.'

By the end of that meeting, everyone present had been in tears. Goya was relieved when they were finally able to leave the room after faithfully promising Tal that they would bring about the answer to her prayers.

LONDON WAS AN extremely suitable place for the Mossad operation to take place. The risks were negligible here: even if they fucked up – which they already had – the British would do nothing. The Israeli Ambassador might get a talking-to, some minor 'diplomat' might get expelled, but that would be it. No one in Israel would admit to anything, and that would be all. It was because the British were such pussies that they'd been kicked out of the Middle East in the first place. Nowadays . . . well, if they allowed arms dealers and terrorists to operate out of their capital, they deserved everything they got.

Goya stole a quick glance in the rear-view mirror. He was amazed that Teleki hadn't run straight for the airport once his brother-in-arms had been eliminated. Hamas must need those weapons badly – or maybe he just had balls of steel. He was a big man, much stronger than Ryan, and doubtless felt that he could look after himself.

Whatever, he had taken a big risk there, and now he was going to pay the price.

Teleki was still talking away on his mobile phone. Ryan's Arabic wasn't up to much but he realized this was not a business conversation. Teleki was laughing and joking, talking about a couple of 'English whores' he had ordered for later in the evening. *Ain't life funny*, Ryan grinned to himself. *You're lining yourself up a threesome and I'm sitting here safe in the knowledge that you'll never get to shoot your load again.* There was the sound of a horn behind him; the car in front had advanced about three feet. Releasing the handbrake, he let the cab roll slowly forward.

The car in front was some kind of Toyota mini-SUV. A young girl, maybe nine or ten, bored with being stuck in the traffic, was staring out of the back window. Catching Ryan's eye, she pulled a face. Keeping eye-contact, he casually flipped the kid the finger. Laughing, she copied the gesture with both hands, before slipping back into her seat. *Watch out for ricochets, little bitch*, Ryan hissed silently.

He watched the clock on the dashboard tick round another thirty seconds. His mouth was dry and his heart-rate elevated. Licking his lips, he again flicked his eyes to the rear-view mirror. Teleki was still gabbling away about the hookers, oblivious to the fact that they had been heading away from his intended destination for the last ten minutes. Not that they had managed to get very far. When they'd decided to steal a taxi, Goya reflected with a sigh, they should have factored in more time to get to *their* intended location, a lock-up garage in the expensive neighbourhood behind Lord's Cricket Ground. The clock on the dashboard told him that it was now almost three hours since they'd picked up this cab from outside a café in Victoria while the cabbie – a guy called Allan Johnstone according to the licence Ryan had removed from the glass partition between the front and back seats – was munching on a bacon roll and watching a Chelsea game on television.

Ryan knew that the cab must have been reported stolen by now. However, they had been careful to target an independent cabbie; Johnstone was not part of a collective like Radio Taxis or Dial-a-Cab, so there would be no one tracking the vehicle's whereabouts in an office somewhere. Moreover, with hundreds if not thousands of black cabs on the roads of Central London at any one time, the chance of their being stopped by the police was statistically zero. Still, to be on the safe side, they'd changed the licence-plates and stuck on some decals advertising holidays in Malaysia. If he saw it driving past right now, Allan Johnstone himself wouldn't recognize it.

Acquiring the cab was the easy bit. The biggest challenge in the whole operation was making sure that Teleki got into the right taxi as he left his hotel. As he came through the lobby of his Park Lane hotel, one of the Mossad team masquerading as a member of the hotel staff ushered him away from the official taxi rank and into the back of Ryan Goya's vehicle. The click of the door locks confirmed that they had their man safe and secure. Pulling quickly away, Ryan nodded when Teleki gave him an address in Notting Hill. Cutting across a couple of lines of traffic, he skipped through a red light heading north. In less than a minute, he was past Marble Arch and heading up the Edgware Road. Passing a massive police station on his right, he smiled, before turning east onto Frampton Street. Almost immediately, however, he hit the traffic caused by the roadworks on Lisson Grove itself. Since then, they'd taken almost fifteen minutes to crawl barely 500 yards.

In the back of the cab, Teleki ended his call and sat forward. Peering through the windscreen at the stationary traffic outside, he cursed loudly in Arabic. 'Faster!'

Ryan looked at him in the rear-view mirror, gestured at the cars in front of them and shrugged.

'Faster!' the man repeated. It was just about the only English that the bastard seemed to know.

Ryan shrugged again.

Teleki tried to open the door, yanking on the handle, oblivious to the small red light signalling that it was locked. Cursing more quietly this time, he pulled his wallet out of the back pocket of his trousers and thrust a twenty-pound note through the small gap in the partition.

'Stop now,' he instructed.

Ignoring the money, Ryan put a confused look on his face. 'We *are* stopped.'

'I get out.' Teleki pushed the note through the gap in the partition.

Ryan let the money fall to the floor.

'Money,' Teleki grunted. 'Is enough?'

Ryan glanced at the twenty. His pulse was racing now; he was sweating heavily despite the cold, and he felt a migraine brewing at the base of his spine.

'How much?'

Ryan looked at the meter and realized that he hadn't switched it on.

'Hey!' Teleki banged on the partition with the palm of his hand. Twisting in his seat, he pulled at the door handle again, more vigorously this time.

'Damn!' Ryan felt that his heart was about to burst out of his chest. He fumbled under his seat for his SP-21 'Barak' semi-automatic. Sliding his fingers round the grip, he flicked off the safety catch and pushed the silencer through the partition, pulling the trigger twice.

The first round shattered the cab's rear window, missing the target completely.

The second shot hit Teleki in the neck, sending a spray of arterial blood right across the glass partition. Clutching his neck, Teleki fell across the back seat, screaming and gurgling at the same time.

Taking careful aim this time, Ryan put two shots in his chest and then another two in his head.

Teleki's last living act was to void his bowels. The smell of shit and death immediately permeated the cab.

'That is for Itay Kayal,' Ryan shouted. He wanted the young soldier's name to be the last words that this murdering terrorist bastard heard on this earth.

Teleki gazed at him blankly, the light fading from his eyes.

'Itay Kayal!'

Teleki's mouth opened but all that came out was a bloody bubble of air. His body twitched one final time and was still.

For the briefest moment, there was silence. It was followed by the angry sound of horns from the vehicles behind him. Ryan turned to see that the traffic in front of him was finally moving. Sticking the Barak into the waistband of his jeans, and concealing it under his Bon Jovi T-shirt, he pushed open the door of the cab and jumped out. Slamming the door behind him, he ignored the growing cacophony of horns and the shouts of angry drivers questioning his parentage, and jogged quickly away down a side street.

After he had travelled four blocks, Ryan Goya slowed to a walking pace. Pulling a mobile out of the back pocket of his jeans, he dialled the only number stored in its memory.

Someone picked up immediately.

'Job done,' he said breathlessly. 'Two down, two to go.'

Ending the call, he stepped into the gutter and dropped the handset down the grate of a nearby drain. Upping his pace again, he headed further into the London night.

Chapter Fifteen

'I DON'T CARE if I am causing the biggest traffic jam in the whole of bloody London, nothing is being moved from here until this scene has been processed properly.'

Adam Hall stood in the middle of Lisson Grove and watched the DCI from Traffic Police scuttle off, shaking his head in disgust. Hall knew that the frisson of satisfaction he felt was a pyrrhic victory. He might be new to this game, but even he knew that the bloody corpse found in the back of the black cab meant only one thing: Mossad were still in town, and furthermore, they had unfinished business.

Hall's phone started ringing – the *Looney Tunes* theme – and he checked the screen. There was no number indicated but he took the call anyway. 'Hello?'

'Adam? This is John Carlyle.'

Carlyle? It took Hall a moment to place the name. Then he cursed. How did the stupid bloody plod get his number?

'I'm kind of busy right now,' he hissed.

'I can imagine,' Carlyle said evenly, ignoring the younger man's frosty tone.

'Can you now?' Hall sneered.

'Yes,' Carlyle told him, 'I can. Because I'm sitting at home on my sofa, watching you right now. Sky News are broadcasting live pictures from the scene of the shooting.'

'Shit!' Hall looked around. When he spotted the camera, he skulked out of the picture.

'Relax,' Carlyle laughed. 'No one ever watches rolling news.'

My bosses do, Hall thought.

'And even if they did, they still wouldn't know who you are.'

You may have got that bit right, the junior spook reflected sullenly. 'I can't tell you anything,' he said.

'You don't have to. The sexy blonde reporter with the big hair is giving me a full update every fifteen minutes.'

Hall located the blonde woman standing in the middle of a small group of reporters beside the police tape. 'Hell!' he groaned.

'Don't worry,' Carlyle said soothingly. 'I know you're having a tough time at the moment. I have no intention of adding to your problems.'

'Thank you,' Hall replied, clearly unconvinced.

'But presumably,' Carlyle continued, 'this latest shooting confirms that Sergeant Szyszkowski's killer is still in town.'

'Is that what Sky is saying?'

'No,' Carlyle sighed. 'They're not talking about him at all. As far as the media is concerned, Joe is ancient history already. They're only focused on the guy in the cab.'

Hall lowered his voice: 'It certainly looks like a Mossad hit squad is in London to take out some Hamas bigwigs.'

Bigwigs? That's a rather archaic use of language, Carlyle thought. Presumably this boy went to a very expensive school. But Hall had at least started talking, so he waited silently for him to continue.

'Your own guy was just unlucky to be in the wrong place at the wrong time.'

Tell me something I don't know, Carlyle thought. 'Why are these people bringing all their shit here to London?' he asked.

Hall coughed. 'We don't know.'

'And why haven't they slithered back under their respective rocks after the first shooting?'

'Things are just not clear,' Hall replied limply.

'It's just as well that I'm here to help then,' Carlyle said cheerily,

There was a pause while Hall stepped straight back into shot. Behind the tape, ten yards or so from the Sky camera, he stared towards the lens. '*Can* you help?' he asked.

'Yes,' Carlyle nodded at the screen. 'I think I can.'

Chapter Sixteen

He found Alison Roche standing in the internal courtyard at Charing Cross police station. It was a grey day with more than a hint of rain in the air. Aside from a mechanic working under the hood of a police Skoda in the far corner, the place was empty. Wearing a thin navy cardigan over a black T-shirt, she shivered as she watched Carlyle approach.

'Those things are bad for your health,' he began, nodding at the cigarette in her hand. He hadn't realized that she was a smoker. Smoking was a major character defect in Carlyle's book, so he wondered if he'd been rather too hasty in trying to get her transferred. After all, he knew next to nothing about this woman – other than she was no good with dogs but she did know a bit about Italian football. And now, it appeared that she was stupid enough to smoke.

'That's what my boyfriend tells me,' Roche grinned, taking a deep drag with relish.

She registered the curious look on Carlyle's face as she slowly exhaled.

'David Ronan,' she added, taking another puff. 'He's a DI in SO15. We met when we were both working at Shoreditch. We've been going out for . . .' she thought about it for a moment '. . . almost four years now.'

Too much information, Carlyle decided. If you'd been having this conversation with Helen, before you knew it she'd be on to wedding plans, thoughts on children and, most importantly, Ronan's doubtless long list of bad habits. He sometimes suspected that his wife would have made the best copper in the Carlyle family; she was interested in people, whereas he was primarily interested in facts.

Fact: SO15 was the Met's Counter Terrorism Command Unit.

Facts like that could be very useful.

'How long has Dave—'

'David,' she corrected him, before taking one last lungful of poison and flicking the stub of her cigarette into the gutter.

'I beg his pardon,' Carlyle smiled. 'How long has *David* been in CTC?'

'Over a year now,' she replied slowly, as if checking through the dates in her head. 'Since February of last year.'

Carlyle squinted up at the sky as he felt the gentlest of raindrops land on his forehead. 'And would he happen to know anything about Middle Eastern terrorism?'

'I suppose he knows the basics,' Roche shrugged. 'Why?'

Carlyle felt a larger raindrop hit his head. And another. 'Let's go inside,' he suggested.

CARLYLE USHERED HER into one of the third-floor meeting rooms, before closing the door behind them. Placing her cigarettes and lighter on the table, Roche took a seat and looked up at him expectantly.

'I want you to talk to David for me,' Carlyle began, 'but you both have to be extremely discreet.'

'Sure,' she said.

'I mean it,' he said, knowing he was sounding like an overbearing teacher. 'This is a very delicate situation.'

Sitting up straighter in her chair, Roche cleared her throat. 'I understand, Inspector.'

'With a bit of luck, we might be working together for a while . . .'

'It looks like it,' she said. 'Leyton told me this morning that I was to report here until further notice.'

'Good,' he nodded. 'That's good. But what I'm now going to tell you about is not a Charing Cross investigation.'

'Joe Szyszkowski?'

'Yes. It's not even a police investigation.'

'Oh?'

Pulling out a chair, Carlyle sat down opposite her. For the next ten minutes, he quietly went through what had happened on the afternoon Joe was shot, then his interview with Adam Hall of MI6, and the subsequent murder of Noor Gyula Teleki in the back of a London taxi.

Once he had finished, Roche stared at the table for five or six seconds.

'How do you think David can help?' she asked, looking up.

Good question, thought Carlyle, but now was not the time to let on that he was clutching at straws.

'The murder of a London policeman is incidental to the MI6 investigation,' he continued, wondering how he was going to finish this sentence, 'but . . .'

She watched him carefully. 'Yes?'

'I think that there is some reason why these guys are shitting on our doorstep. If we can discover exactly why they are here, then we might be able to track them down.' As the words finally tumbled out, he wondered if they made any sense at all.

Roche's expression suggested she wasn't convinced.

Carlyle made a vague gesture with his hands. 'MI6 can do the big picture, international stuff,' he burbled, 'but we have the local knowledge. There must be something very important happening in London, otherwise everyone would have split right after the first shootings at the Ritz.'

'And they have asked for your help?'

Carlyle looked her straight in the eye and smiled. 'Yes.'

Roche frowned. 'Isn't that what the security services are for? Surely that's their job?'

For fuck's sake, Carlyle thought, *give me a break here*. He forced his smile to widen. 'They're too busy trying to keep tabs on all the would-be suicide bombers in Bradford, apparently.'

Roche let out a long sigh. 'Okay,' she said, 'I'll speak to David.'

'Discreetly.'

'Of course.' She flashed him a cheeky grin. 'It will be strictly pillow-talk, Inspector.'

Carlyle felt himself blush.

'Don't worry,' Roche laughed. 'We are both thoroughly professional. And anyway, it is the death of a policeman we are talking about here. I will find out what he says and report back.'

'Thank you,' said Carlyle, getting quickly to his feet.

'Inspector?'

Carlyle, already at the door, turned back to face her. 'Yes?'

'The skeleton . . .'

'Huh?'

'The skeleton that was dug up in Lincoln's Inn Fields.'

'Oh, yes, yes . . .'

'We're still waiting for the forensic but, based on the criteria that we already set . . .'

'Yes?' Carlyle tried to remember what those criteria were, but his mind came up with a complete blank.

'. . . I have come up with records for twenty-two men aged eighteen to thirty who were reported missing in that area during the Blitz i.e. September 1940 to May 1941 and never accounted for.'

'Er . . . good.' Carlyle pulled the door open. 'Talk to Phillips about it. See if you can narrow it down a bit further, and then we can review where we are.' Without waiting for a reply, he slipped out into the corridor and away.

Chapter Seventeen

IT WASN'T THE Ritz, but at least he didn't have to worry about an Israeli hit squad bursting through the door before his mother could finish her first scone. Working himself up to restart their earlier conversation, Carlyle watched a bored-looking yummy mummy pushing a pram down the Fulham Road. The look on the woman's face suggested that she harboured more than a few regrets at having washed up on the dreary shores of SW6.

In the nondescript café, they had the place to themselves, apart from a pale kid in the back tapping away on his laptop. 'Brown Eyed Girl' was playing at a low volume through a couple of tinny speakers above the counter, to the irritation of Carlyle, who felt offended on Van Morrison's behalf. The great man's songs deserved a better environment than this. He took another sip of his coffee and grimaced. It was too weak and too cold. 'Almost three quid and it is utter crap,' he grumbled to himself. He thought about taking it back to the girl behind the counter and asking for a fresh cup, but somehow lacked the energy.

Lorna Gordon ignored her son's incoherent mumbling. After carefully cutting the scone in half, she buttered each section and applied a modest amount of raspberry jam. Lifting the first piece to her mouth, she took a dainty nibble and began chewing it slowly.

Carlyle waited for her to swallow. 'So,' he said, conscious of the nervousness in his voice. 'You were talking about Dad.'

Lorna gave him a careful look. 'The divorce, you mean?'

Carlyle glanced back towards the street, but the yummy mummy was gone. 'Well, yes,' he stammered.

'You are not going to change my mind, John,' she said firmly, wiping an imaginary crumb from one side of her mouth before picking up another piece of scone.

'No, no.' He held up his hands in mock surrender. 'I'm not trying to do that. I just want to understand the reason.'

Lorna next took a sip of her tea. Placing the cup back on the saucer, she gazed directly at her son. 'Your father,' she said quietly, 'has had an affair.'

'Ah.' Carlyle lifted his cup to his lips but didn't drink. His mother had given him more than enough information already, and his only concern now was to end this conversation as quickly as possible.

Looking embarrassed but determined, his mother gazed at a spot somewhere above his head. 'I was visiting your gran when she was ill.'

'Gran's ill?' Carlyle frowned. He hadn't seen his grandmother – now well into her nineties and living in sheltered accommodation in the Partick district of Glasgow – for almost a year, and he wasn't even aware that she had been unwell.

'This was a while ago,' his mother explained.

Carlyle suddenly felt a strong urge for a glass of Jameson Irish whiskey. A double; served straight, with no ice and no water. He looked longingly over at the Three Monkeys pub on the other side of the road.

'You had only just qualified as a policeman at that time.'

'But,' Carlyle did the maths, 'that's almost thirty years ago!'

'As far as I'm concerned,' Lorna Gordon said tartly, 'there is no statute of limitations on infidelity.'

Scratching his neck, Carlyle shifted uneasily in his seat.

'Do you remember a woman called Maureen Sullivan?'

Carlyle thought about it for a few moments and was relieved to come up blank. 'No,' he said. 'The name's not ringing any bells.'

'Well,' his mother mused, 'maybe she only arrived on the scene after you had left home. She was a downstairs neighbour for a while. Anyway, I was up in Scotland, looking after Gran when she broke her arm . . .'

'I remember that,' Carlyle chipped in, happy that not every detail of their family life at the time had passed him by.

'I ended up staying in Scotland for a month. Your father huffed and puffed, claimed he wasn't at all happy about it but that it was the right thing for me to do.'

'Why has this become an issue now?' Carlyle asked, keen to skip over further historical detail.

His mother sighed and took another sip of tea. 'We had a big argument a fortnight ago. About nothing particularly important, but things got heated and he dropped that bombshell on me. I've thought about it a lot since, and I can only assume that he *wanted* to tell me. He was always rather boastful, and this was his way of putting me in my place.'

Looking Lorna Gordon up and down, Carlyle resisted the urge to smile. His mother would never let anyone put her down. She was the first in a long line of strong women who had kept him in his place all his life, and he realized that it had been the same for his father too. He knew that he had to talk to his dad – there always being two sides to every story – but he didn't think it would have any impact on the outcome. 'So what happens now?' he asked.

'I've spoken to a lawyer. As long as your father doesn't contest it, the divorce should be sorted out fairly quickly.'

'And will he?'

'Will he what?'

'Contest it.'

She gave him a look that reminded Carlyle of his days as a naughty eight year old, caught stealing wine gums from the corner shop. 'I would have thought that would be very difficult, given that he has already confessed to being an adulterer.'

Staring out of the window, Carlyle tried to make some sense of this mess. It was typical of his parents that, with divorce rates at a thirty-year low, they had nevertheless found a way to tear their marriage apart over some long-past misdemeanour. Ever the pragmatist, he knew that he should really try to help them patch things up. However many years of active retirement each of them had left, divorce would not make things any happier or more comfortable. Ever the pragmatist, however, he also knew that this was ultimately not his fight. 'Okay,' he said finally, 'what do you want me to do?'

'Do? I don't want you to *do* anything, John. I just wanted to make sure that you understood what was going on between your father and me.'

'Helen is really quite worried about you,' he said. *I, on the other hand*, he thought, *am just totally bemused by the whole business.*

'Well, tell her that there's absolutely nothing to worry about,' his mother said sharply. 'I'm fine.'

'And what about Dad?'

'He can speak for himself,' she harrumphed.

'What will happen if – once the divorce goes through?'

'He'll have to find somewhere else to live,' she said. 'At the moment, he's sleeping in your old room, but that is only temporary.'

'Where? How will he be able to afford somewhere else in London?'

'That's his problem,' she said calmly, turning her attention back to the remains of her scone.

Chapter Eighteen

THE CLOCK ON the dashboard said 2.37 a.m. Adam Hall yawned and squirmed uncomfortably in his seat, wondering when he was going to get the chance to relieve himself. His bladder had been uncomfortably full for over an hour, and he cursed himself for not nipping round the corner earlier. There was absolutely no way he was going to try and piss into his empty Starbucks cup, not with his boss, Gillian Strauss, sitting in the passenger seat next to him.

Gritting his teeth, Adam tried to grin and bear it. He knew that sod's law meant that, the moment he went off for a piss, the subject would walk out of the door of number 17 Peel Street, twenty yards up on the other side of the road from where they were sitting. It stood in the middle of a row of expensive houses just south of Notting Hill Gate, a few blocks to the west of Hyde Park and Kensington Palace.

He glanced over at Strauss and felt the discomfort in his crotch increase further. With her head in the confidential reports on Al-Amour that he had lovingly collated for her, Strauss studiously ignored him, so Adam allowed his gaze to linger on her.

Mid-thirties, short blonde hair, ultra-fit, she was a Home Counties beauty who, even in jeans and a fleece, was more glamorous than anyone else in MI6 by a factor of at least 100. The monster rock on her wedding finger, courtesy of the stereotypically wretched merchant banker husband, did not make her any less of a young spook's wet dream. Hall had been assigned to work with her in his first week on the job and he now lived in mortal terror of being moved on to another boss. When he realized that they would be spending the night together, even if it was only in the confines of a grubby Ford Focus, Adam had initially found some difficulty in breathing.

Underneath the fleece, Strauss was wearing a white blouse with the top two buttons undone. As she shifted in her seat, Adam caught the merest glimpse of décolletage, and had to stifle a low groan in his throat.

Strauss gave him a quizzical look over the top of her papers. 'Are you okay?'

Adam pushed open the door. 'Sorry,' he said, swinging his feet onto the tarmac, 'I need a comfort break. Won't be a sec.'

Without waiting for a response, he stepped out of the car, closed the door, without letting it click shut, and began jogging down the street.

Halfway down the road he found an alley. It was a ten-foot-wide gap between two houses, and ran into Campden Street to the south. The place was well-lit but there was no sign of any CCTV and anyway Adam was by now in a major hurry. Stepping into the alley, he unzipped his trousers just at the moment where his bladder was about to give out. Picking his spot on the wall in front of him, he let fly.

'Aaahhh!!'

A sense of immense satisfaction and well-being pervaded his whole body, followed by the thought that his bladder capacity must be greater than he had previously thought. The flow was just starting to weaken when Adam became conscious of movement at the far end of the alley. He looked up to see that a man had entered from Campden Street, and was walking towards him with a big smile on his face.

Pushing hard, Adam tried to hurry things up, but his bladder decidedly wasn't finished yet.

'I bet that feels good!' the man laughed. His English was good, but he clearly wasn't a native. Adam couldn't identify the accent.

The young spook grunted in acknowledgement as the stream of piss finally subsided to a dribble and died. With a sigh of relief, Adam gave himself a final shake.

RYAN GOYA WAITED for the young guy to put his pathetic-looking tool back in his trousers before he pulled the Barak from the back of his jeans. He watched him fiddle with his zip, head lowered.

'Hey!'

Adam Hall looked up, and barely had time to register the gun before the first .40 S&W round shattered his breastbone and sent him sprawling back on the pavement. He was dead by the time Goya stepped across and put a second cartridge between his eyes – just to be sure – before heading out of the alley to deal with the boy's good looking colleague.

Chapter Nineteen

THE MI6 WOMAN didn't even realize that Goya was standing there next to the car, before he sent a bullet into the side of her skull. Sticking the Barak through the shattered window, he fired a second one into her head as a matter of routine, although it was clear that she was already dead. Looking swiftly up and down the street, he confirmed that no one was watching, then jogged quickly across the road, heading for the house where the man travelling under the name of Lefter Sporel would be waiting.

Using a key that had been stolen from the cleaning firm which looked after the house for its peripatetic owner, he opened the door and slipped inside. Keeping the semi-automatic out of sight behind him, he walked carefully down the hallway towards the kitchen, the only light source in the house.

Seated at the kitchen table, Sporel looked up as Goya appeared in the doorway. He smiled nervously. 'Are you with Sol?' he asked, in heavily accented English.

'Yes,' Goya nodded.

'Where is he?'

'He will be here very soon,' Goya replied, glancing back down the hall. 'Where are the others?'

'It is just me,' the man shrugged, 'but I can still do the necessary business with Sol.'

'What happened?'

'We have had some problems . . . with the Israelis.'

'Tsk,' Goya hissed, 'those bastards never let go.' Lifting the Barak to chest level, he gave Sporel a moment to understand what was going on before he jerked the trigger, sending him on the way to his heaven . . . or his hell.

CONSCIOUS THAT TIME was not on his side, Goya scurried round the house, looking for cash, documents or anything else that might be of use. Finding nothing, he was just about to leave when he heard a key in the lock. Not waiting to see who was coming through, he squeezed off a couple of rounds into the front door.

There was a pause. Then the door swung slowly open, and the wall above Goya's head exploded as someone returned fire. 'Damn!' he grunted, quickly dropping into a crouch and then backtracking down the hallway. In the kitchen, he skipped over the pool of congealing blood on the floor, wrenched open the back door and rushed outside.

The garden looked about thirty feet long. At the bottom was a stone wall, maybe eight feet tall. Next to the wall was a small white plastic stool. Slipping the Barak into the back of his jeans, Goya jumped onto the stool and began hauling himself up. He was just about to swing a leg over the top of the wall when he felt a hand seize him by the collar and pull him backwards. Goya tried to grab for his gun but it was gone. Once, twice, his face was unceremoniously slammed into the brickwork. Dazed, with blood filling his mouth, he offered little resistance as he was flipped round and a massive fist smashed into his stomach. Collapsing, he tried to cover his head as a succession of well-controlled blows rained down on his body.

'Up!'

Struggling to breathe, Goya looked at the hulking figure in front of him. He was a brute of a man, maybe six foot three and weighing maybe 110 kilos. In the giant's hand the Barak, now pointed at Goya's nose, looked like a child's toy.

'Up!'

'Who are you?' Goya panted, reluctantly struggling to his feet.

Saying nothing, the man simply flicked the barrel of the gun in the direction of the house. With his free hand, he hoisted Goya up by his shirt and began dragging him back inside.

Chapter Twenty

MOVING SLOWLY ALONG the South Bank, Carlyle felt a sharp wind blowing off the Thames. He knew that this was as close to fresh air as he would ever get in London, so he was determined to make the most of it. It was not quite 6.15 a.m. and he was feeling pleased with himself for getting out of bed and going for a run. A combination of endorphins from the exercise and listening to The Clash, Stiff Little Fingers and a selection of other Punk tunes on his iPod further added to his good mood.

Even at this early hour, there were plenty of other joggers about, eyes glazed, headphones on, enjoying having the city to themselves. Occasionally, Carlyle waved to those passing him while heading in the opposite direction. Invariably, they ignored him. As 'Safe European Home' gave way to 'Nobody's Hero', he kicked on. Heading through the tunnel under Southwark Bridge, while taking a swig from the small bottle of water he carried in his hand, he trundled past the rows of dossers sleeping underneath their cardboard boxes. He was approaching Tate Modern, an old power station alongside the Thames which had been converted into an art gallery. Here he could take the Millennium Bridge back across the river, and then be home in twenty minutes or so. The alternative would be to keep heading east towards Tower Bridge. His head said 'yes', but his legs were not so sure.

Carlyle was still undecided about his route as he reached the Tate, and just then his mobile started vibrating in the back pocket of his shorts. Pulling it out, he slowed to a walk.

Number withheld.

Carlyle thought about it for a moment before deciding he'd rather take the call than persevere with his run.

'Hello?'

'Inspector Carlyle?'

A man's voice he didn't recognize. Sirens in the background. Carlyle knew the signs: something had happened.

Something bad.

'Yes, speaking,' he admitted with some reluctance. He started up the ramp of the footbridge, stopping in the shelter of a wall so as to complete this call out of the wind.

'This is Detective Inspector David Ronan from SO15.'

Roche's boyfriend. Carlyle wiped his nose on his sleeve.

'Alison told me about your dealings with Adam Hall.'

'Ah, yes,' Carlyle grinned, 'pillow-talk.'

There was a short pause on the line. 'What?'

'Nothing,' Carlyle said quickly. 'What can I do for you?'

'I'm on Peel Street, just off Kensington Church Street,' Ronan continued, in a matter-of-fact manner.

Carlyle quickly scanned the A–Z in his head. 'I know it.' It was vaguely true.

'Someone executed Hall here a few hours ago.'

RIP, young Adam, Carlyle thought ruefully, his heart still beating rapidly in his chest. *James Bond you were not.*

'And he wasn't the only one.'

'Is this related to the killing of my sergeant?' Carlyle asked.

'Looks like it.'

'Thanks for the heads-up. How long are you going to be at the scene?'

Ronan sighed. 'There are multiple scenes. It is quite a mess, so it looks like I will be here for a considerable while.'

'Okay, I'll be there within the hour.' Ending the call, Carlyle moved up onto the bridge and began slowly jogging towards home. Feeling the wind full in his face, he let all thoughts of spies and murder fall from his mind as he upped his pace and ran on towards St Paul's Cathedral.

Chapter Twenty-one

STUDIOUSLY IGNORING THE television cameras hovering just outside the police tape, the crews now taking a break from providing live reports to the early breakfast news bulletins, Carlyle ducked into Peel Street. It was a fresh, bright day and the morning rush hour had not yet started. After the carnage of the night before, comparative peace reigned in the vicinity.

Peel Street, with its expensively renovated four-storey Georgian townhouses, was the kind of exclusive London street that only bankers, arms traders and drug dealers could afford to live in. For now, it was empty, apart from a couple of uniforms mooching about and a gaggle of techies buzzing around a vehicle parked halfway along on the south side of the street. The car itself had been screened off to stop any journalists, residents or gawpers taking any pictures. Carlyle guessed that the one guy not in a white body suit was DCI Ronan.

Although dressed like a rich teenager – in blue Adidas Forest Hills Originals, carefully distressed jeans and an expensive-looking black leather biker jacket – David Ronan looked rather old and careworn. Worse, it looked like his raven-black hair had been dyed. Certainly, Carlyle thought with a stab of jealousy, the man looked a bit past it to be going out with the rather fragrant Alison Roche. Even allowing for the fact that he had the haggard look of someone who had been up all night, Ronan had to be at least ten years her senior, therefore almost as old as Carlyle himself.

'Here.' Carlyle had taken the precaution of bringing along a couple of lattes from the Caffè Nero round the corner. Extra hot, and with two extra shots each.

'Excellent,' Ronan said gratefully, taking one of the twelve-ounce cups. 'You must be Carlyle?' He extended his free hand and they shook. 'Got any sugar?'

Carlyle dug into his jacket pocket and pulled out a couple of small white sachets. 'There you go.'

'Thanks.'

Ronan peeled the plastic lid off his latte, tore open each of the sachets in turn with his teeth, and dumped the sugar into the froth. Putting the lid back on, he gave the cup a gentle shake before taking a mouthful.

Stepping towards a narrow gap in the screens, Carlyle peered through. Still in the front passenger seat of a red Ford Focus was the body of a woman. It looked like she had been shot multiple times.

Squeamish at the best of times, Carlyle moved away quickly. Taking a couple of deep breaths, he waited for that familiar feeling of his breakfast coming back up his throat. Then he remembered that he hadn't actually had any breakfast, and for that gave silent thanks. Turning back to face Ronan, he exhaled deeply and lifted his gaze to the heavens.

'A right old mess,' Ronan observed quietly, 'isn't it?'

'Who is she?'

'Gillian Strauss. MI6. Adam Hall's boss.'

The female spook and her little apprentice. Carlyle let out another long sigh. 'And where is Hall?'

Ronan finished his coffee and looked around, wondering what to do with the cup. 'We found him in the alley over there,' he said, gesturing over his shoulder. 'Looks like he was shot first, and then her. Then they shot the third guy.'

The third guy? Carlyle wondered. *This just gets better and fucking better.*

The SO15 man saw the sickly look on his face and said, 'Come on, I'll show you.'

RONAN NODDED TO the uniform standing outside number 17 Peel Street and jogged up the three steps leading to the open front door. Carlyle followed him inside and down a hallway that ran the entire length of the west side of the house, to reach a large kitchen at the back. In the middle of the room stood a rectangular wooden table, with two chairs on either side. One of the chairs had been pulled out, as if someone had recently been sitting on it. The whole scene was unremarkable, apart from the large pool of congealed blood covering most of the table-top. At the far end, blood had dripped onto the floor, forming a pool leading towards the back door that opened onto the garden.

One of the technicians, wearing a white body suit, appeared in the doorway and said to Ronan, 'We're done here.' He began stripping off a pair of protective gloves. 'For now, at least.'

'Thanks,' Ronan replied. 'Let's touch base back at the station.'

'Will do,' said the man, turning to head out of the house.

Ronan explained to Carlyle, 'The body's gone to the morgue.'

'Who was it?'

'Middle-aged guy. He was carrying a German passport under the name of Lefter Sporel.' Ronan looked at Carlyle. 'Not a very German name, is it?'

Carlyle thought about that for a moment. 'Germany has a large Turkish population,' he reflected.

'Probably a fake ID anyway,' Ronan said. 'If Mossad were after him, it's very unlikely that he was Turkish.'

'Unless he's some random Mujahideen nutter,' Carlyle ventured, keen to show his impressive grasp of international affairs. 'They can come from anywhere.'

'I would be very surprised, though. Maybe if he came from Blackburn, or Birmingham, but not from Berlin. We'll just have to see if we can work out his real identity.' Ronan pulled a packet of Marlboro out of his jacket pocket and stuck a cigarette in his mouth without lighting it. 'What I assume happened is that this guy here was the target, and the MI6 bods outside just got in the way.'

'Presumably MI6 may be able to tell us who he really was?' Carlyle said.

Ronan made a face. 'You would hope so.'

'You don't sound too convinced.'

'They're not known for sharing information at the best of times, and right now they will be busy trying to work out how to spin the fact that two of their agents got whacked in the middle of London.'

'The body count is piling up a bit.'

Ronan grinned. 'Alison told me you were a master of understatement.'

Me? Carlyle thought.

The DI's grin grew wider. 'Or rather, if I recall rightly, her exact words were "sarcastic old bastard". Anyway, six murders, including a police officer and two spooks, is a genuine, bona-fide shit storm.'

'Good job MI6 are handling it, then,' Carlyle said.

'Not any more.' Ronan gave him a stern look. 'SO15 are not going to just sit by while all this crap is dumped on their doorstep.'

Great, Carlyle thought. *A bit of inter-agency politics is just what we need right now.*

'MI6 have blown it big-time,' Ronan continued. 'Now it's up to the Met to get a grip on things.'

Carlyle shrugged.

'This has come right from the top. The Commissioner has given CTC the green light to deal with the problem.'

Carlyle wondered whether that also chimed with the Secret Intelligence Service's understanding of this situation. He very much doubted whether the Metropolitan Police Commissioner could ever win a pissing contest with the head of MI6. On the other hand, he really couldn't give a toss about who did what, as long as Joe's interests were properly looked after.

'Okay,' he said finally, 'how can I help?'

Chapter Twenty-two

ARRIVING AT CHARING Cross police station, Carlyle made his way through the usual flotsam and jetsam gathered in the waiting room and headed on past the front desk. Looking up from his copy of the *Sun*, Kevin Price gave him a quizzical stare.

'What are you doing here?'

Carlyle frowned. 'What do you mean?'

Price closed his paper, folded it and stuck it under the desk. 'I thought you'd be at Joe's funeral.'

Carlyle glanced at his watch. The funeral was due to start in twenty minutes and he felt hugely relieved that he didn't have to go. He held Price's gaze. 'It's a small family-only affair,' he said, keeping any suggestion of emotion out of his voice. 'Simpson is representing the Met.'

'I assumed you would have gone as well,' Price persisted.

'It's a family decision,' Carlyle said brusquely, heading quickly down the corridor to bring this conversation to an end.

Back at his desk, he was surprised to see the third floor almost empty. He tried calling Roche, but the call went to voicemail and he couldn't be bothered leaving her a message. His legs still ached from the early-morning run, and a wave of tiredness washed over him. Dropping his mobile on the desk, he stretched out in his chair and yawned widely. Almost immediately, the phone began to ring. He looked at it for a minute then picked it up cautiously. Despite not recognizing the number on the screen, he answered.

'Carlyle.'

'Mr Carlyle, this is Louisa Arbillot.'

Who?

'I work with your wife.' The voice was heavily accented, almost like a comedy French accent. Traffic noise in the background suggested she was standing somewhere out on the street.

'Ah yes, thank you for giving me a call.'

'Helen explained your situation to me. I think we should meet.'

'OK.' Carlyle was caught off-guard by the woman's ready offer. He wasn't used to Helen's leftie friends being in any way co-operative. Simply because he was a policeman, they usually treated him with a mixture of contempt and distrust.

'I happen to be in Soho at the moment. Could you do it sometime round about now?'

'Sure.' Mentioning the name of a coffee bar on Berwick Street, he said he'd meet her there in twenty minutes. Forgetting all thoughts of tiredness, he jumped to his feet and headed for the stairs.

SITUATED AT THE northern end of Berwick Street's fruit and veg market, the Flat White café was one of the most celebrated coffee shops in Soho. Inside, the place was crammed, as usual. Even so, Louisa Arbillot was easy to spot in her Avalon T-shirt. They exchanged nods as he stood at the counter and ordered his drink.

Sitting underneath a small poster advertising a Grace Jones concert, she sipped daintily on her latte and waited patiently for him to collect his double espresso and take the spare seat at her table.

'Very nice to meet you, John.' She offered him a moist hand and, rather reluctantly, he shook it.

'Thank you for agreeing to see me.'

Louisa studied him closely through dull grey eyes. Draining the last of her coffee, she placed the cup back on the saucer with a flourish. 'When Helen told me what you were interested in,' she said, 'I didn't think I could help at first.' Her French accent seemed less obvious now than over the phone, but it was still clearly detectable. Carlyle took a taste of his own coffee and waited for her to get to a point.

'After all, Avalon is a purely independent charity.'

'Of course.'

'And anything that could compromise our integrity' – she gave him an arch look – 'such as, for example, informing on behalf of the police, could prove to be very damaging to us.'

Carlyle said nothing. He had little time for people who used words like 'informing' or 'informer' so readily. In his view, that kind of language was just an excuse adopted when they wanted to look the other way. Being honest with the police was just like being honest full stop. Surely that was a good thing for normal people to aspire to. No one should ever consider themselves above the law.

'We have to be very . . . proper in the way that we conduct ourselves.'

'Nothing you say to me will go any further,' he replied, taking care over the words. 'This is not any kind of interview. I simply wondered if I might have the benefit of your professional opinion.'

Arbillot placed her hands in her lap. 'Go ahead.'

'Well, I'm sure Helen has explained the general situation that I'm dealing with here.'

'She outlined the general situation, yes,' Arbillot said. 'You seem to have got yourself caught up in a very dangerous set of events, Inspector. Helen is very worried. She is really quite angry about it.'

Carlyle shrugged. 'Our big concern is that there will be more killings. What I was hoping is that you might be able to give me some insights into the, er . . .' he wondered how he should put it '. . . the Arab side of the problem.'

Arbillot leaned forward in her chair and suddenly her eyes were very much alive. 'I have spent the last six months in Gaza, trying to provide basic medical care – the type of things people here would have taken for granted even fifty years ago, never mind now – while being constantly bombed and shot at by the Israelis.'

Folding his arms, Carlyle sat back in his chair with a carefully neutral expression on his face. He didn't come here for a political lecture, but was prepared to put up with one for a while.

'Working for Helen,' Arbillot went on, 'you have to be doctor, diplomat and accountant, all in one. She is a tough boss.'

'I'm sure she is.' Carlyle smiled.

'Anyway, I don't pass any judgements. I am not in any way political, but I understand what motivates these people.'

'To be honest,' Carlyle kept his voice even, though he was beginning to run out of patience with this lady, 'I'm not so much interested in anyone's motivation. What I am trying to find out is why these Hamas guys were in London and whether some of them are still here. I do not want to see any more officers of the law getting killed.'

Arbillot nodded. 'Or innocent members of the public, for that matter.'

'Quite.'

'Which is why Helen was able to persuade me to meet with you.'

'Helen?' Carlyle asked, surprised. Down the years, on the handful of occasions that he'd asked for her help, his ultra-liberal wife was always adamant that she would never try to convince anyone to talk to her copper husband.

'She said you were a very fair man, especially for a policeman.'

Suddenly embarrassed, Carlyle lowered his gaze to his knees.

'And she said you genuinely wanted to stop more bloodshed.'

'I do.'

'Then go and speak to a man called Fadi Kashkesh.'

Carlyle pulled a pen out of his pocket and cadged a slip of paper from a passing waitress. 'How do you spell that name?'

Arbillot had to repeat it three times before he got it right.

'What's Mr Kashkesh's story?' he asked, looking up.

'A familiar one,' Arbillot sighed. 'Intelligent young man with nothing to do and no prospects, moving steadily downwards on a path to destruction. First they throw stones, then they are given guns and sent out to fight the IDF, who make short work of them.'

'The IDF?'

'The Israeli Defence Force – part of the army. Fadi would have been dead by now, but he got lucky. I took a bullet out of his abdomen four years ago, and we got him out alive.'

'We?'

'The staff at Avalon paid for him to come over to London. He's found it a bit of a struggle here, but things are now getting better. He's studying politics and working as an administration assistant for a road-haulage business.'

'As an illegal?' Carlyle enquired, already wondering what leverage he might be able to exercise over the guy. 'He must have a pretty precarious existence.'

'No,' Arbillot stated. 'He's here legally.'

'How so?' Carlyle frowned. 'Did he get asylum?'

'No.' Arbillot smiled sadly. 'I married him.'

Blimey, Carlyle thought. *That's a bit above and beyond the call of duty.*

'We're separated now,' she continued, 'which I suppose is not really that surprising, given all the difficulties we faced.'

'No,' he mumbled, 'I can see how it would have been . . . tricky.'

She shot Carlyle a defiant look. 'But you never know – I still see Fadi when I am in London. And there is no plan for us to divorce.'

'Where will I find him, then?' Carlyle asked, keen to move the conversation on to less personal matters.

'You don't,' Arbillot said. 'I will speak to him and he will get in touch with you.'

'Okay.' Carlyle wasn't happy with that arrangement, but knew that he couldn't really force the issue.

'Fadi says that he has no contact with anyone from the old days, but you know what men,' she corrected herself, 'what boys are like.'

Carlyle nodded.

'There is quite a big Palestinian community here, and others are passing through London all the time. He will be able to help you find the right people. Or, at least, point you in the right direction.'

'Good.'

'And in return,' she said, a nervousness in her voice now as she got round to naming her price, 'you will make sure that he doesn't become the next victim of the Israelis here, in London.'

'I will do what I can,' Carlyle said. He sucked the last drops of coffee from his demitasse and stood up. 'Thank you for your help with this.'

'You shouldn't be thanking me,' Arbillot replied. 'You should thank your wife. She is the one who got me to understand why we should talk. She is a good woman and a good colleague; a great asset to us and a great asset to you.'

Don't I know it, Carlyle thought as he headed out into the hustle and bustle of the street.

Chapter Twenty-three

'WHOSE HOUSE WAS it?'

Sitting on a bench on the first floor of the British Museum, Carlyle gazed at a small group of kids clustered round a table, chatting away happily as they painted their decorative tiles. They were coming to the end of an Islamic tile-painting workshop that had been inspired by the museum's Middle Eastern ceramics collection. It had been Helen's idea to get Alice together with Marina Silver for a play date. Even though the museum was literally five minutes' walk from the Carlyle home in Covent Garden, Alice had seemed none too keen. She clearly objected to the idea of hanging out with a younger girl. Once she was actually there, however, she quickly got into the spirit of things and had then taken good care of Marina, even telling her father to go away when he once tried to lend a hand. Carlyle couldn't have felt prouder of his daughter if she'd been appointed Prime Minister.

The tile painting provided a welcome distraction from certain other matters. He had arrived at the museum undecided about what – if anything – to say to Dom about Sam Hooper and the Middle Market Drugs Project. While trying to make up his mind, he had instead filled him in on the situation with Joe's killers, and their subsequent murder spree.

The fact that Dom had gone on to ask a very relevant question, one that the inspector should have asked himself, irked Carlyle intensely. Now that this question had been raised, it seemed obvious that he should have given more thought to the very desirable number 17 Peel Street. What was a suspected Hamas terrorist doing in a multi-million-pound townhouse in one of the smartest areas of the city? Now that he belatedly considered it, the place had looked as pristine and unlived-in as a designer hotel. Apart from the blood and brains splattered about the kitchen, of course. 'We are looking into it,' he said blandly, unwilling to admit his own oversight.

Sitting next to him on the bench, Dom turned and gave Carlyle one of his famous shit-eating grins. 'Well, look no more, my friend,' he said. 'Dominic has the answer.'

Carlyle was so shocked he almost missed noticing Alice wave at him from across the room. Smiling, he waved back. She held up her tile to show him the result, and he gave her a thumbs-up.

'You're joking,' he hissed out of one side of his mouth.

Dom lifted his gaze to the heavens and lowered it with a more modest smile. 'No, I'm not. I've been there myself a few times.'

Jesus fucking Christ, Carlyle thought. 'Not the other night, I hope.'

'No, no, no. The last time was about eight months ago. The place belongs to a guy called Sol Abramyan, although I'd be amazed if that name showed up on any search. The lease will doubtless be registered to some holding company with a PO Box in the Cayman

Islands. Twenty-five middle-men later, you might find Sol's name crop up, just maybe. Even then you'd have to know who you were looking for. More likely, you could have a dozen accountants on it for twenty years and still get nowhere.'

'And who is Sol fucking Abramyan?' Carlyle asked, taking on the familiar role of the slow plod for Dom's amusement.

'Sol,' Dom explained, 'is an Armenian arms dealer.' He glanced over at the kids, who were still painting away, and lowered his voice. 'And an occasional customer of mine. He's a very quiet, low-key bloke who I don't suppose will be coming back to London for a while.'

'Is he here now?'

Dom shook his head. 'No. Even if he was staying at Peel Street when this shit was going down, he will have vamoosed.'

'Maybe the Israelis have him.'

'Hah!' Dom laughed. 'More likely the other way round.'

'No one fucks with Mossad,' Carlyle said, 'that's what they all say.'

Dom gave him a searching look. 'So why are you trying then, you fucking muppet?'

Carlyle looked away, saying nothing.

'How many gunmen were there?' Dom asked quietly.

'We don't know. One, maybe two – but not many. All three victims were shot by the same gun.'

'In that case,' Dom said, 'I very much doubt that Sol was there. We can assume that he wasn't the target.'

'We don't know that.'

Dom scratched the back of his neck and stretched out his legs. 'Well, if he was, and if Mossad are as bloody good as everyone says they are – although all this carnage suggests that they might not be – they wouldn't have started the shooting without knowing for sure that he was home. They would also have known that it would take at least a dozen of their top guys to take Sol Abramyan down. He always travels with at least two very large Somalian bodyguards, who carry enough weaponry between them to start a small war.' He grinned like the big kid that he still was at heart. 'And also to finish it.'

Carlyle made to open his mouth.

'Before you ask,' Dom said quickly, 'I don't know their names. I only know that they're Somalian because Solly made a joke one time about their previous career as pirates.'

'Oh, so it's *Solly* now, is it?'

'Hey,' Dom shrugged, 'I take people as I find them. He was always an okay guy as far as his dealings with me were concerned. Yes, so he sells guns; it's not exactly social work, but I'm not judgemental.'

'That's handy,' said Carlyle sarkily.

Dominic tutted. 'Don't try and wind me up, John. I'm a drugs dealer, so what gives me the right to get up on my high horse? More to the point, who do you think the biggest arms dealer in this country is?'

Why don't you tell me? Carlyle thought, giving him a blank look.

'Her Majesty's Government,' Dom said forcefully. 'In other words, your employer. So you are in no position either to claim the moral high ground.'

Here we go, Carlyle thought wearily: *the philosopher coke dealer takes to the stage.*

'Anyway, it's not like Sol sells to any UK customers. After all, Britain is his home – well, one of them at least.'

'Good for him,' Carlyle quipped. 'It's good to know that he has standards. But he wasn't above conducting a bit of business here, was he?'

'You don't know that.'

'No – but why else would he have some senior Hamas guy sitting in his kitchen?'

'That's a fair point,' Dom conceded.

'Can you get me in front of him?' Carlyle asked.

'No.' Dom shook his head. 'And even if I could, why in God's name would you want to do that?'

'Maybe,' Carlyle laughed, 'he could help the police with their enquiries.'

'Yeah, right.'

'I'm serious,' Carlyle persisted. 'You of all people know that I am pragmatism personified when it comes to dealing with gentlemen criminals.'

'A gentleman criminal?' Dom put on a hurt face. 'So that's what I am?'

'You could vouch for me.'

'John, be serious. Sol is way out of my league. Which means that he is way, way, way out of *your* league. He once told me that there are almost a hundred warrants out for his arrest in various countries. For all I know, some of those may have been issued by the Met. I don't think you can go anywhere near him, even if he were to agree to see you – which he won't.'

'Let me do the worrying about that.'

'Our relationship is a one-off,' Dom said quietly. 'You can't hope to replicate it with other people.'

Carlyle frowned. 'You're not feeling jealous, are you?'

'Don't be silly.' Dom looked embarrassed. 'Look, he's a customer, I only ever see him once in a blue moon. He always contacts me, never the other way round.'

The workshop was coming to a close. Chatting away happily, the girls were bringing over their tiles for inspection.

'Just see what you can do,' Carlyle said, standing up to admire their daughters' handiwork.

Chapter Twenty-four

DESPERATE FOR A cigarette, Hilary Waxman paced a corridor deep inside the Foreign and Commonwealth Office on King Charles Street, just off Whitehall. The Israeli Ambassador hated this fey Italianate building. Previously the home of the India Office and the Colonial Office, a seventeen-year, £100 million renovation had done little to drag the place into the twenty-first century. The edifice simply had no character and, like the organization it housed, it had no balls.

It was almost 11 a.m., and Waxman had been summoned to see the Foreign Secretary at ten-thirty in order to 'share information' on the spate of killings that had rocked genteel British sensitivities. It was unusual for her to be kept waiting like this. Whatever else you could say about the British, they were usually punctual.

Waxman checked her watch for the sixth time in two minutes and cursed under her breath. She glared at the young staffer hovering at her elbow. 'Go and find out what's going on,' she hissed.

As the young woman jogged off down the corridor, the Ambassador now at least felt the minor solace of being alone. With her mobile and her BlackBerry switched off inside her bag, she could enjoy the rare pleasure of being almost incommunicado. After all the shit she had been receiving from Jerusalem over the last few days, that was, Waxman decided, the very least she deserved.

The prospect of another dressing-down from the British Government did not bother her in the least. It was, in the famous words of some long-forgotten English politician, like being savaged by a dead sheep. Waxman, who was considered a bit of a liberal back home, knew that she had bigger balls than all of them here put together.

In fact, there wasn't a single British politician that Waxman didn't feel she could have for breakfast. The Foreign Secretary himself was a particularly ineffectual young man, promoted too far, too fast, by a weak Prime Minister. Waxman herself wouldn't have given him a job as a junior ADC on her staff.

After growing up on a kibbutz on the West Bank, then ten years in the army and almost another ten in the snake-pit of Israeli politics, Waxman at first had found London a real shock to the system. Britain was obviously the most complacent country on earth and the British political classes appeared truly spineless. As far as she could see, all they ever did was cheat on their expenses and wail about their 'broken' society. Meantime, the place had become a haven for criminals and terrorists. God knows, if they were better able to keep their own house in order, there wouldn't be any need to send Mossad in to do their dirty work for them.

On the other hand, Mossad wasn't exactly covering itself in glory either. Six deaths, three of them 'collaterals', i.e. innocent bystanders, was the kind of thing you could get away with in Beirut, but not here. What really annoyed the Ambassador was that she had demanded that the mission be abandoned after the débâcle at the Ritz Hotel. Overruled by her military attaché, she now had to face the uncomfortable truth that she was stuck in the middle of an increasingly acrimonious dispute between London and Jerusalem, with her only role in this tawdry little drama to take a kicking from both sides.

Worst of all, while the mission had yet to be completed, the lead Mossad operative had gone missing. Three of the four Hamas targets had been taken out, but they had meanwhile lost a man of their own.

Losing a man was one thing but, at the very least, you needed a body. Or, at the very, very least, some body parts. Something to take back to his family.

They had *nothing.*

Ryan Goya had executed his orders and taken out his target. Then he had just disappeared off the face of the planet. Jerusalem was going crazy. They were talking about sending in another assassination squad to try and rescue him. But, as Waxman had pointed out, no one knew if Goya – or his corpse – was even still in London.

It was just the biggest mess imaginable.

The Ambassador checked her watch again: it was now five past eleven. What could the Foreign Secretary be doing that was so bloody important that she had to stand about in a corridor for all this time? The little bastard was punishing her. It was so childish. How dare the little shit treat her like this?

How dare he?

Six minutes past eleven.

The staffer had completely disappeared.

Waxman paced the length of the corridor. She had half a mind just to walk out. In fact, she had more than half a mind to walk out, and then issue her immediate resignation. Maybe now was the time to take up the directorship she had been offered by a company that specialized in security software, utilizing technology developed by the Israeli army.

Rummaging in her bag, she pulled out her BlackBerry. A few quick keystrokes and she could put all this shit behind her. A quick email to Jerusalem announcing that she was resigning would do the trick. Or, even better, just a quick line to the London correspondent of Jerusalem Newswire. The news would be out in minutes. It would give the Foreign Affairs Ministry a hell of a shock.

The more Waxman thought about it, the wider her smile grew. Why wait minutes? She could just send a Tweet. Being *au fait* with all the craziness of the internet, she could have the news all the way around the world and back again before Jerusalem even knew what was going on. Her youngest son had set her up with a Twitter account a few months ago. After getting her PA to post a few bland observations, Waxman was amazed to find that she had almost 1,000 followers, including the London bureau chiefs of the Israeli newspapers *Haaretz* and the *Jerusalem Post*. Maybe she could be the first-ever diplomat to resign via Twitter. God knows, it was maybe the only way she could ever hope to make it into the history books.

She was interrupted in her reverie by a pallid figure ghosting down the corridor towards her. As he approached, Waxman noticed the unpleasant grin on the man's face.

The flunky stopped about five feet from the Ambassador. 'The Secretary of State will see you now,' he said solemnly.

Even at that distance, his foul breath made her want to breathe through her mouth. She struggled to keep a look of disgust off her face.

'Follow me.' Oblivious to her discomfort, the man then turned and walked back the way he had come.

Chapter Twenty-five

WITH HER PORTFOLIO under her arm, Emma Trimingham came out of the model agency, glanced up and down the street, and then headed off in the direction of the tube.

'About fucking time,' Sam Hooper said to himself, tossing his empty coffee cup into the gutter and starting after her. Half a dozen underground stops and twenty minutes later, he watched her skip up the steps of a warehouse building near Tower Hill. Strolling into the reception, he flashed his ID at the security guard and then scanned the company names listed on a board behind his head. Buzz Photography Services was on the third floor. He opted for the stairs and was more than a little out of breath by the time he got there.

Going through a set of double doors, Hooper found himself in a large open-plan space with floor-to-ceiling windows on one side, overlooking the street. At the far end, a young bloke was setting up an expensive-looking camera in front of what looked like a life-size model of an Aberdeen Angus cow. Only as he moved closer, did Hooper realize it was a bucking bronco machine.

'Cowboy theme today, is it?'

The photographer's assistant turned to face Hooper. 'Who are you?' he asked. Unshaven and bleary-eyed, he looked like he hadn't slept lately. With a sigh, Hooper got out his ID again. *Any shit from you*, he thought, *and we can always go for the full-cavity body search*.

'Is that genuine?'

Hooper threw it at the kid's head, missing by maybe six inches. 'Of course it's fucking genuine.'

After wiping his hands on his New Order T-shirt, the kid slowly bent down and picked up Hooper's warrant card. After careful inspection, he stepped over and handed it back. 'We're shooting an advert for tampons,' he announced matter-of-factly. ' "Don't let your time of the month stop you from riding a bull" type of thing.'

'Outstanding,' observed Hooper sarcastically, stuffing the warrant card into the back pocket of his jeans.

The kid scratched his head vigorously.

I wonder if he's got head lice, Hooper wondered idly.

'Yeah,' the kid yawned, 'the photographer's Paul Urbandale.'

'Uh-huh,' Hooper nodded. He didn't have a fucking clue who the boy was talking about.

The other registered Hooper's blank expression. 'He's famous for his war photographs in Iraq and Afghanistan.'

'Okay.'

'He did that one of the little girl with her legs blown off.'

'Lovely.'

'Such beautiful composition,' the kid added wistfully.

'And now he's doing tampon adverts?'

'Yeah,' the kid shrugged.

'Where's the girl?'

The kid nodded towards another door in the far corner of the room. 'She's getting changed. Up the stairs, first door on the right.'

'Thanks,' said Hooper, already heading for the door indicated.

'Tell her that we're due to start in fifteen minutes.'

'No problem,' Hooper smiled. 'I'll be done with her by then.'

SITTING IN HER dressing room smoking a cigarette, wearing jeans with a check flannel shirt, Emma Trimingham looked pretty but nothing special. Fresh-faced, with her hair pulled back in a ponytail, he would have put her age at about thirteen or fourteen. On a table behind her, a large cowboy hat sat next to a make-up bag and an open packet of Royals.

'Who are you?' She frowned, blowing a stream of smoke towards his head.

'I'm Inspector Sam Hooper,' he said, leaning against the doorframe.

'A copper?'

'Yes.'

Shrugging, she took another drag on her cigarette.

'Want to see some ID?' he asked.

'Why would you lie?' The girl gestured to the Royals. 'Want a cig?'

Hooper shook his head. 'Nah, not my kind of thing.'

'So,' she smiled coquettishly, 'what do you want?'

'I want to talk to you about your friend, Charlotte Gondomar.'

The smile vanished as quickly as it had appeared. 'God! What a nightmare. What's to say?' She lifted the make-up bag from the desk and pulled out an eyebrow pencil and a mirror. 'That girl always was highly strung.'

Hooper watched her begin to make up her face. 'It seems she was a fancy drugs mule.'

'It's that kind of business.' Emma started applying some lipstick. She seemed to have aged ten years in barely ten seconds.

'She wasn't the only one.'

The girl stiffened slightly but kept her gaze firmly on the mirror. 'I wouldn't know about that.'

'Are you absolutely sure?'

She glanced up from her handiwork and gave him the briefest of smiles. 'Very sure.'

'How old are you?'

'Nineteen,' she said, without missing a beat.

Hooper crossed the room in one and a half paces. Taking the mirror from her hand, he tossed it onto the table. Bending down, he took her chin in his hand. 'How old are you?'

'Okay,' she snapped, 'so I'm only sixteen. But my parents know what I'm doing. They're cool about me missing school.'

Bloody parents, Hooper thought, *they don't know shit*. Happily, he himself was never going to bother with kids. 'Stick to the truth,' he advised quietly, 'and we'll be fine. What school do you go to?'

'The Katherine Price School for Girls in Sevenoaks,' she said, naming an upmarket commuter town in Kent.

'Nice.'

'It's boring,' she scoffed, placing the lipstick down next to the mirror.

'Boring is good,' Hooper told her. 'Believe me.'

Emma stubbed out her cigarette in an ashtray located by her feet, and immediately lit up another. 'You go and live there, then.'

'What can you tell me about Lottie's drugs operation?' he asked, standing up straight again.

'There was no "operation",' she said. 'Just Lottie and a few of the other girls making sure they had enough for their own needs and making a bit on the side as well.'

'Did you ever try any?'

'Once or twice, but it's not really my thing.' She waved the cigarette in front of her face. 'This is more my kind of poison.'

'So who else was involved?'

Emma gave him a dirty look before mentioning a few names that Hooper wasn't interested in.

'What about Rollo?'

'Have you seen the size of him?' Emma snorted. 'That fat queen never did *enough* drugs!'

'But did he deal?'

'Rollo? Nah. He's only ever been interested in a bit of recreational use.'

'So who else was knocking around the business who might have been involved?'

Emma stamped her foot in frustration. 'Come on!' she whined. 'I've been as helpful as I can. They're waiting for me downstairs.'

Hooper glanced at his watch. 'You've got plenty of time. I need a name.'

'I haven't got a bloody name!' She glared up at him.

'In that case,' Hooper said, 'things might just get a little complicated.' Taking a small cellophane packet of grey-white powder out of his jacket pocket, he placed it on top of her make-up bag.

'What's that?' she scowled.

'Pure heroin.' Hooper brought out his mobile and took three quick photographs. 'Enough for me to take you in for questioning.' Putting the phone back in his pocket, he scooped up the powder and waved it in front of her face. 'Bye-bye modelling career, hello job at the checkout in the Sevenoaks branch of Waitrose.'

'You couldn't,' Emma stammered, her bottom lip quivering.

This is just too easy, Hooper thought, as he took a pair of handcuffs from his back pocket. 'Just give me a name.'

'My dad's a lawyer,' she sobbed. 'He won't let you do this.'

'If your dad's so bloody smart,' he hissed, pulling her to her feet, 'why doesn't he make sure that you go to school?' Snapping on the cuffs, he gave her a gentle push towards the door. 'Let's go.'

'Okay, okay! Take them off,' she yelled. 'I'll give you a bloody name!'

'See?' he said. 'How difficult was that?'

'Just don't tell Rollo. I want to be able to work with him again.'

'No problem.' Undoing the cuffs, he slipped them back in his pocket.

'He's good for my portfolio,' she blubbed.

'I bet.'

Rubbing her wrists as if she'd been shackled for a week, Emma muttered, 'There's a guy . . .'

'Yes?'

'They say he's Rollo's backer. He's shown a lot of interest in Lottie over the last few months. One of his guys even asked me about her.'

'What's his name?'

'Dominic – Dominic Silver.'

'Good,' Hooper smiled. 'Now go and do your tampon advert –or, God knows, the world might stop turning.'

She looked at him doubtfully. 'Are we done?'

'If I need anything else, I'll be in touch.'

OUTSIDE THE PHOTOGRAPHER'S studio, Sam Hooper took the small packet of rat poison from his jacket pocket and dropped it down a nearby drain. 'Works every time,' he said to himself, grinning. Walking on down the street, he wondered if he should have made the stupid little bitch give him a blow job. Maybe next time. Pulling up a number on his mobile, he hit the Call button.

A gruff voice answered on the fifth ring. 'What do you need?'

'Give me everything you've got on a guy called Dominic Silver,' Hooper said. 'The full works, and I need it ASAP.'

Chapter Twenty-six

LESS THAN AN hour after her trip to the Foreign Office, Hilary Waxman was back in her office. The Israeli Embassy was located on Palace Green, less than five minutes' walk from the house at 17 Peel Street where Ryan Goya had gone missing. As she headed down the corridor leading to her office, she decided she couldn't wait any longer. Stopping under a picture of Golda Meir, she pulled a packet of Noblesse cigarettes from her bag. Back in the 1970s, when Waxman had been growing up, Meir – the fourth Prime Minister of Israel – had been seen as the personification of the true Zionist spirit: tough, austere and honest. Every now and again, Waxman liked to stand here, under her portrait, just to smoke a Noblesse and unburden herself. Checking that no one else was about, she looked up at the smiling granny in the portrait. 'What would *you* do about this bloody mess?' she asked.

Golda Meir, the Iron Lady of Israeli politics, once described as 'the only man in the Cabinet', decided to keep her own counsel.

'I know,' Waxman nodded sadly, 'I know. There's nothing *to* say, really.' Pulling a cigarette from the packet, she stuck it in her mouth and lit up.

'Aaahhh . . .'

The nicotine hit her bloodstream and Waxman felt herself relax ever so slightly.

'Shit!'

Out of nowhere the reptilian military attaché, Sid Lieberman, had appeared at her side. He was a small man – five foot five – with a head that was too big for his body. Buff, tanned and with his skull shaved army-style, Lieberman could easily have passed for forty-five although he was, in fact, almost fifty-eight. Dressed in a cream suit, blue polo shirt and brown loafers, he looked more suitably attired for the sunshine of the South of France, or maybe Barcelona, than for the cold and grey climate of London.

'Madam Ambassador.' Lieberman tipped an imaginary hat. He was the only person in the building who couldn't bring himself to call her Hilary. This was just one of the many ways in which he managed to annoy her.

'Sid.' Waxman tried for a smile, but couldn't quite hack it. She knew that the current Mossad operation in London wouldn't have gone ahead without some input from Lieberman, therefore she blamed him for the resulting fiasco. No shrinking violet herself, Waxman had no time for the spinelessness of her British hosts but, nevertheless, she believed that there were limits. Like not shooting down innocent people on London streets, for example. Men like Sid Lieberman and Ryan Goya not only crossed those limits regularly, they flipped the finger at anyone who tried to hold them to any kind of account. So, not only were they dangerous, they also destroyed any kind of moral authority that people like Waxman had spent their whole lives fighting for. She had hoped that this latest row would have seen Lieberman expelled from the country but, if anything, the British had appeared even more limp than usual. Waxman felt her heart sink at the thought. It was that kind of weakness which allowed people like Lieberman to flourish in the first place.

'What did they say?' Lieberman asked, as Waxman puffed furiously on her cigarette.

She sighed. 'It was the same old crap, basically. The Foreign Secretary nodded sagely while the Under-Secretary recited this little speech about how Britain recognizes that Israel is a responsible country and the fact that our security activity is conducted according to very clear, cautious and equally responsible rules. Therefore, they have no *underlying* long-term cause for concern.'

Looking like an emaciated Doberman, Lieberman tilted his head to one side and grinned. 'But . . . ?'

'But,' Waxman said, 'they would be really rather grateful if we could stop shooting people dead in their capital city.'

'Which,' Lieberman said blandly, 'of course, we do not admit to doing.'

'Of course.' Waxman killed off one cigarette and resisted the temptation to immediately light another. 'And we certainly don't care what our hosts think.'

Lieberman nodded sagely.

Did he miss the sourness in my tone? Waxman wondered. *Or did he just ignore it?*

Lieberman glanced up and down the corridor. 'Maybe we could talk in your office?'

Waxman checked her watch. 'I'm a bit busy at the moment. The trip to King Charles Street has blown a major hole in my schedule for the day.'

'I understand,' Lieberman said. 'The Brits,' he lowered his voice, 'are in a real mess with this one. MI6 and the Metropolitan Police are arguing over which of them should run the investigation.'

'Does it matter?' Waxman shrugged. 'From our point of view, I mean.'

'Not really. They are all amateurs. However, the distraction of their in-fighting makes it easier for us to do our job.'

Our job? Waxman didn't really want to know, but there was no way that she could credibly stay out of the loop. 'Any news about Goya?' she asked finally, helping herself to another cigarette.

'Nothing.'

Waxman raised her eyebrows. 'So what are you intending to do about it?'

'We are doing everything you would expect,' Lieberman replied stiffly.

Not wishing to aggravate the military attaché any more than was really necessary, she nodded in a manner that could perhaps have been mistaken for sympathetic. Sticking the cigarette in her mouth, she lit it with one of the many lighters that she always kept in her bag. 'Where are the rest of the team?'

'They've gone,' Lieberman said.

Waxman felt relieved and surprised at the same time. She took a long drag on her latest cigarette and pulled the smoke deep into her lungs. 'I thought they had one more guy still to get?'

Lieberman waited for her to exhale. Taking a half-step away from the cloud of smoke heading past him, he stared at his shoes.

Waiting for an answer, Waxman allowed herself the smallest of smiles. Part of Lieberman being an all-round asshole was his discomfort around women. When he had first arrived in London, Waxman had wondered if he was gay, but she had quickly concluded that he had no interest in sex at all; at least not any kind of sexual intercourse that involved another living human. The only thing that could possibly give Sid Lieberman a hard-on, she had decided, was a well-oiled Desert Eagle or a Micro-Uzi. An image of Lieberman, naked, rubbing a semi-automatic against his groin while groaning in ecstasy, popped into her head. Groaning in disgust, she fought to close down such a hellish vision.

'Anyway,' she said aloud, 'won't we need them if we're to get Goya back?'

Lieberman did another funny little dance step. 'I am going to sort things out,' he said finally.

Still troubled by persistent images in her head, Waxman half-turned away from him. 'Two things,' she began, trying to bring this conversation to a speedy conclusion.

He gave her a look that suggested he could not care less about the Ambassador's opinions on this matter or, indeed, any other. 'Yes?'

'First, be aware that the clock is ticking. Even the Brits might decide to take some action about this whole God-awful mess. To be honest, I'm surprised that they didn't expel you this morning. You could expect to be forced out of the country at any time.'

Lieberman held up a condescending hand, as if he was stopping the ramblings of a silly child. 'It's the same every time,' he said. 'As a military attaché you always run the risk that you could be sent packing without warning. I know how to handle this.'

'Okay, if you say so.'

'And the second thing?'

Waxman took another drag on her cigarette. This time she exhaled quickly. 'No more locals must get hurt. That is an absolute imperative.'

Lieberman looked impatient. 'You understand that this is not within my power and control. Anyway, the real absolute imperative is to complete the mission and recover Goya.'

'No man left behind . . .' Waxman mused, suddenly wearied by the endless supply of macho bullshit that she had been forced to endure over the years.

'The Americans may *talk* about this sort of thing,' Lieberman scoffed, 'but for us, it is a reality.' This time, ignoring the smoke, he stepped closer to the Ambassador. 'I will get Ryan Goya back – and if that means a few more collaterals, that will be a price well worth paying. We never leave our own in the hands of the enemy.'

Waxman struggled to retain a neutral expression. *Tell that to Itay Kayal*, she thought.

'A few more collaterals? But I said—'

'I know,' Lieberman replied, cutting her off, 'and we will be as . . . inconspicuous as possible. But I have to be allowed to do my job.' He gestured towards the heavens. 'So, if you would be so kind as to let me get on with it . . .'

Chapter Twenty-seven

On his way home, Carlyle bought four bottles of Peroni from his local newsagent on Drury Lane. Lager wasn't really his drink, but tonight he thought that a couple of beers would slip down nicely. He was tired of all the problems buzzing around his head with no solutions in sight. All he wanted to do was switch off for a couple of hours, maybe catch some rubbish on the TV, and then get to bed early. Tomorrow, after a good night's sleep, things might look more manageable.

It took an age for the lift to take him slowly up to the twelfth floor of Winter Garden House. Almost groaning with relief, he opened the door to his flat and stepped inside. Placing the plastic bag containing the beer on the floor, he took off his shoes and then his jacket. As he did so, he heard Alice's girlish laughter coming from the living room, and it suddenly struck him that he hadn't heard his daughter laugh like this for a long time. At least not with him. And certainly not with his wife. With a lump in his throat, he stood in the hallway listening to his own heartbeat. If Alice and Helen were sharing a moment, he didn't want to interrupt.

'Oh my God!' Alice let out another burst of giggles.

Carlyle felt stupid. How could he be embarrassed about standing in his own home? Picking up his stash of beer, he stepped into the lounge.

'Hi, Dad.' Alice looked up from the sofa. She seemed decidedly underwhelmed by his arrival, but for once she stayed where she was and didn't make an immediate dash for her bedroom.

'Hi, sweetheart.' Carlyle managed a half-smile but failed to make eye-contact. Instead, he nodded to her grandfather, who was sitting beside her on the sofa. 'Dad . . .' he said cautiously, almost as if seeking confirmation of the older man's identity. Carlyle hadn't spoken to his father in over a month, nor had he seen the old fella in more than two. And it had to be more than a year since Alexander's last visit to Covent Garden, despite the fact that he lived barely thirty minutes away, in West London.

Alexander Carlyle kept his hands clasped on his lap and gave his son a look that was even warier than Alice's. 'John,' he responded quietly.

Carlyle turned back to Alice. 'Where's your mum?'

'She's at work,' Alice said. 'There's some meeting tonight, don't you remember? She told you about it the other night.'

'Of course.' Carlyle vaguely remembered such a conversation. Or, at least, he thought that he did.

Alice glanced at her granddad in mock despair and raised her eyebrows.

Alexander smiled back at her and nodded.

What is it with the non-verbal communication? Carlyle thought, feeling slightly annoyed.

'Well,' Alice said, pecking her granddad on the cheek before sliding off the sofa, 'I'm off to do my homework.' A cheeky grin spread across her face. 'I'm sure that you two have a lot to talk about.' Body-swerving past her father, she disappeared into her bedroom before he had the chance to ask for a kiss of his own.

Sighing, Carlyle returned his attention to his father. The old man's smile had vanished and he now perched on the edge of the sofa, poised as if to make good his own escape at any moment. However, the son had to admit that, for a man going through a belated marital crisis, his father didn't look in too bad shape. Short and wiry, Alexander Carlyle was cleanshaven, with his white hair cut shorter than Carlyle remembered it. Wearing a black suit, black loafers and an open-neck navy shirt under a grey, V-neck jumper, he looked more than presentable. If not exactly *GQ* material, the overall impression was of someone alert and relaxed. In fact, he could easily pass for ten years younger than his seventy-odd years.

Carlyle felt his discomfort levels rising. What the hell was he going to say to the old bugger? Then he realized that he had a peace-offering to hand and could play for time. With some relief, he pulled a couple of bottles out of the bag and waved them at his father. 'Fancy a beer?'

'Sure,' his father replied, in a way that suggested he was very far from sure indeed.

Carlyle placed two bottles on the table and retreated into the kitchen to put the others in the fridge. When he returned with a bottle-opener and a couple of glasses, Alexander was looking more relaxed on the sofa. He had switched on the television, with the sound turned down low. There was a football match in progress and Carlyle too relaxed a little, there now being a good chance that they could get through this encounter without having to discuss anything important at all. If talking to his mother about her divorce was bad, then even the thought of talking to his father was excruciating. Carlyle couldn't think of one single 'important conversation' he'd had with his dad, ever. Also, as far as he was concerned, there was no need to start now. Their relationship was fine as it was: if his dad had dropped a monster bollock at home, it was up to him to deal with it. He was an adult, after all. If his parents couldn't sort it out among themselves, what the hell was Carlyle supposed to do about it?

Carlyle flipped the top off both the bottles and handed one to Alexander. 'There you go.'

'Thanks.'

'Want a glass?'

The old man shook his head and took a long mouthful straight from the bottle. Carlyle then did the same. His desire for a beer had evaporated, but it was cold and crisp, and he gave a gratified sigh after the first swallow. 'Who's playing?'

'United – and some foreign team.'

Carlyle couldn't make out the strip. 'Where are they from?' he asked.

'No idea – Poland or Romania, or somewhere like that. Wherever they're from,' Alexander sniffed, 'they're not very good.'

'Yeah.' Carlyle squinted at the small box in the top left-hand corner of the screen. Three-nil and barely thirty minutes played. 'Cannon-fodder. United always get an easy ride.'

Alexander nodded and took another mouthful of beer. He wasn't as keen on football as Carlyle himself, who had been a season-ticket holder at Fulham for almost thirty years, but usually he could just about keep up his end of a conversation about one of the top teams. This time, however, the old man kept his eyes firmly on the screen and said nothing. Taking the hint, Carlyle flopped into the armchair in the opposite corner and settled down to give this boring, one-sided game his full attention.

A minute before halftime, when the opposition defence stood still and allowed United's wretched ogre of a centre forward to make it four, Carlyle gave up even the pretence of being interested. He turned to his father. 'To what do we owe the honour of this visit?' he enquired, trying to keep it light and cheery. Surely it was up to his father to at least bring the matter pending into the conversation.

Alexander put the now empty bottle to his lips and pretended to take a final swig. 'Nice to see Alice so happy,' he said, completely ignoring the question.

'Yes,' Carlyle replied, confused by this opening gambit.

An evil twinkle appeared in the old man's eyes. 'Don't you think she's a bit young for a boyfriend, though?'

'Boyfriend?' Carlyle gripped his bottle so tightly that he thought it might shatter in his hand.

The twinkle grew brighter. 'Didn't you know?'

'Yes.' Carlyle tried to recover from his mistake. 'It's just that . . .'

The old man was grinning widely now, and Carlyle had a sudden urge to throw the bottle at his father's head. Instead, he breathed in deeply, waiting for the moment to pass. 'It's just that I think "boyfriend" is overstating it a bit.'

'I don't know about that, John.' The old man placed his empty bottle on the coffee table. 'She seems very fond of young Stuart.'

Bloody Stuart. He'd heard the name several times over the last few months. Whenever the little bugger seemed to have fallen off the radar, up popped the same name again. Carlyle took another deep breath. The last thing he wanted was his father to see how this issue worked him up. He was committed to playing the role of the relaxed parent, whatever he might feel inside.

'These things happen,' he said airily. 'It will pass in due course.' Jumping to his feet, he slouched into the kitchen to retrieve the remaining beers. By the time he returned, he had managed to put a grin on his face that was bigger than his father's. 'I just hope,' he said, sarcastically, 'that you haven't been offering her any tips on relationships.'

IT WAS AFTER eleven when Helen finally made it home. After a thirteen-hour working day she was in no mood to talk, but that didn't stop Carlyle pouncing on her as soon as she walked through the door.

'Who is bloody Stuart?' he asked, by way of hello.

Pulling off her coat, Helen stood on tiptoes to give him a peck on the forehead. 'Nice to see you, too.' Kicking off her shoes, she sighed with relief. 'A cup of tea would be lovely, thank you.'

'My father was here.'

'I know. Alice sent me a text. White tea, please. Bag in. I'm going to run a tub.'

Carlyle watched her disappear down the hall and heard the water as it began to fill the bath. Then he went off to make the tea.

Five minutes later, he sat on the lowered toilet seat, watching Helen sip her tea as she lay in the steaming bath. As Carlyle wondered about his chances of being invited to join her, Helen placed her mug carefully on the edge of the bath and gave him a stern look. 'Not a chance,' she said firmly. 'You're not getting in. There's not enough room. I'm trying to relax here.'

'But—'

'How was your dad?' His wife moved swiftly on. 'Did you have a good talk?'

'We talked about Alice mainly.'

'Ah, yes.'

'The two of them were laughing and joking on the sofa when I got in,' Carlyle said huffily. 'As soon as I appeared, Alice did a runner; claimed she had to do her homework. Dad said that they'd been talking about this guy Stuart. Apparently, our daughter reckons he's her boyfriend.'

'There's no "apparently" about it.' Helen made no effort to break it to him gently. 'She's very taken with Stuart.'

'And does this young Romeo have a surname?'

Helen thought about that for a moment. 'Wark . . . Stuart Wark.' She spelled it out. 'He goes to Central Foundation. He's a year older than her.'

'Great,' Carlyle muttered. 'Bloody great.'

Helen took another sip of tea. 'That's not such a big deal. If he was three or four years older, then we might have a *real* problem on our hands.'

'He's a boy,' Carlyle growled, exasperated at her inability to understand the most basic realities of life.

Helen looked at him blankly.

'A boy,' he repeated. 'Genetically programmed to try and fuck anything in a skirt.'

'From what I hear,' Helen said soothingly, 'he is a quiet lad who works hard and is very nice to her.'

'Because he wants something,' persisted Carlyle fretfully.

'You have to trust Alice to be able to look after herself. From what I hear, she keeps young Stuart on a fairly tight leash.'

'How do you know all this?' Carlyle asked.

'I did what any good police officer would do,' Helen grinned. 'I hung about outside the school and worked my contacts.'

Carlyle nodded. 'The mothers' network?'

'Yeah – and be thankful it still exists, just about. In another year or so, none of the parents will have a clue what their kids are up to, including us.'

Carlyle knew that she was right about that but, unable to bring himself to admit it, he changed tack. 'Why didn't you tell me all this earlier?'

'For God's sake, John,' she admonished him, 'when have you been around recently? And even when you have, it's not like you've exactly been focused on us.'

Carlyle bit back a reply. He didn't want a row – especially as he knew that she was right and he was in the wrong. 'What else did you find out about this boy? What do his parents do?'

'They're both bankers, apparently.'

Not exactly a character reference, Carlyle thought. 'And the kid himself?' he asked, finally getting to the nitty-gritty. 'What are his vices? Does he do drugs?'

'I don't know,' Helen said. 'No one has said definitively not, but there's no particular reason to suppose so.' She placed her mug back on the side of the bath again and stood up, gesturing for Carlyle to hand her a towel, which he did. 'Anyway, it's nothing serious. It never is at their age. The best thing we can do is just let her get on with it.'

'I suppose so,' said Carlyle unhappily.

Wrapping the towel around her chest, Helen carefully stepped out of the bath. 'Anyway, did you speak to your dad about their divorce?'

'Yes,' Carlyle replied. He didn't want to admit that the pair of them had sat and watched the whole of a totally meaningless football game, during which time they had spent barely a minute discussing the issue. As far as Carlyle was concerned, that had been more than enough. He had no interest in quizzing his father about some inappropriate shag that had happened decades ago. And, judging from his mumbled and indecipherable replies, it was clear that Alexander wasn't up for baring his soul either. 'He basically just reiterated what my mother had said. Clearly, she's driving the whole process, and I suspect he feels powerless to do much about it.' He leaned back against the cistern and folded his arms, feeling pleased at the comprehensive emptiness of his answer.

Helen gave him a dissatisfied look. 'So what are *you* going to do about it?'

'Me?'

'Yes, *you*.'

'Nothing,' Carlyle said ruefully. 'What *can* I do about it? The whole thing is a bit strange, but they have to sort it out themselves. They're grown-ups, after all. It's like you said about Alice and her young boyfriend, all we can do is let them get on with it.'

'You're simply abrogating your responsibility.'

'What responsibility?' Carlyle raised his eyes to the ceiling.

Ignoring the question, she opened the bathroom door and headed for bed.

Chapter Twenty-eight

HE WAS AWAKE after the first couple of slaps, making the bucket of freezing water hurled in his face seem rather gratuitous.

'Wake up!' a voice insisted.

Shaking his head, Ryan Goya slowly opened his eyes and looked up at the faces peering down at him. Either he was seeing double or this was a twin of the monster who had smacked him into the middle of next week as he had tried to flee through the garden of number 17 Peel Street. Ryan was so disconcerted by the sight that it took him a few moments to take in the rest of his surroundings. Sitting tied to a chair, in the middle of an empty room with only one door and no windows, it was the plastic sheeting covering the floor that sent a jolt of fear through his bowels. Taking a deep breath, he now focused his attention on the third man. Tall, dapper and white, he was considerably older than the other two and clearly the boss.

'They're coming for me,' Goya said defiantly.

Sol Abramyan smiled. 'Even if they are still looking for you,' he said, 'which I doubt, they have no idea where you are. I could have moved thousands of miles . . . or we could be back where we started. You could still be in the middle of London, or you could be in,' he waved an arm above his head, 'in Grozny, for all you know.'

'I wasn't out for that long,' reflected Goya, thinking out loud.

'How do you know?' Sol shrugged. 'It could have been hours, or it could have been days.'

Goya tried to manufacture a sneer. 'Everyone is tracked. No one is left behind.'

Abramyan looked at his two companions, who gave no indication of following the conversation. 'Hold onto that thought,' he said casually. 'It's all you've got.'

'What do you want?'

'Me?' Sol looked shocked by the question. '*Me?* I don't want anything – other than to be left in peace to get on with my business.' He looked at Goya. 'Don't you know who I am?'

'No idea,' Goya lied.

'I am a friend of Israel.'

Goya rolled his tongue round inside his mouth, trying to accumulate some spit. 'You are selling guns to the Palestinians!'

'Come on, soldier boy!' Sol shouted angrily. 'Get with the programme! They buy crap, shoot the odd round at your soldiers, then you have an excuse to mash them into the ground for the millionth time. Everyone's happy.' He shook his head in frustration at the stupidity of the man in front of him. Stepping closer, he bent down to stare into Goya's face. 'Then *you* come along . . .'

'So – what do you want?'

'What do I want?' Sol snorted. 'Coming from the man who tried to kill me . . .'

'I didn't try to—'

'From the man who would have shot me in my own home?' Sol thundered. 'From the man who tried to destroy my business?' He went red in the face, and Goya wondered if he might not be a little insane. 'I *should* want you dead. I *do* want you dead.' He paused, searching for the fear that Goya was fighting to keep from his expression. 'But,' he said, calming down, 'I am a businessman, above all. And a good businessman knows never to take things too personally, not even a bullet in the head.'

He is crazy, Goya decided.

'So,' Sol continued, 'if I can trade you, I will trade you. And if not, then you die.' He signalled to his bodyguards, who trooped out of the room. As he followed them, he stopped in the doorway. Turning round, he scratched his head. 'So, my friend, what you have to ask yourself now is "Does my life have any value?" Good luck in coming up with an answer to that one.' Switching out the light, he left Goya alone with his thoughts.

Chapter Twenty-nine

LYING NAKED ON a queen-size divan in the master bedroom of his Sloane Square duplex apartment, Rollo Kasabian wiped some of the Krug Rosé from his chin and let out a contented sigh. Holding the champagne flute in one hand, he lay back and scratched his more than ample belly. Somewhere below the curve of his gut, he felt his member stirring. Grunting with the effort, he leaned forward and gave it a gentle tug. He glanced over at the two young lads providing the world's worst floor-show at the far end of the bed. Both were stripped to the waist, but neither of them were showing any enthusiasm for following Rollo's order to 'fuck and suck with abandon'.

That's the problem with today's young people, Rollo thought, as he swigged down the last of the Krug. *The notion of taking pride in your work is now just an alien concept.*

Placing the glass on the bedside table, he forced himself up onto his knees and began pumping harder.

The rent boys eyed him blankly.

'Get on with it!' Rollo hissed, feeling the first beads of sweat forming on his brow. 'I've paid my money. Daddy is ready for the show!'

Finally one of them unbuttoned his jeans and, after some searching, pulled out a penis even limper than Rollo's. His mate began massaging it cautiously with one hand, without showing any desire to put it in his mouth.

Struggling to get hard but unwilling to give up, Rollo turned his attention to the porn video currently running on the 42-inch plasma screen fixed to the far wall. The sound was down, and it was hard to distinguish all the various body parts but, miraculously, it seemed to have the desired effect. As his member belatedly sprang into life, Rollo's priorities switched from avoiding a false start to avoiding a premature finish. He wondered if he shouldn't just get one of the boys to suck him off and have done with it. He now regretted not insisting that they brush their teeth and gargle with mouthwash beforehand but, for once, he could let his standards slip.

Lost in thought about such practicalities, Rollo barely heard the sound of the doorbell. He was more conscious of the second long, more insistent ring. A third blast followed it in quick succession. Disentangling themselves, the boys looked at each other and then at the bedroom door, hope of an early escape flowering in their breasts.

Saved by the bell, indeed.

'Go away!' Rollo croaked as he realized that his crucial moment had passed. With his rapidly softening member still clasped in his hand, he stalked over to the open window and stuck his head outside. On the street below were two seedy-looking men whom he didn't recognize. One of them stepped back up to the door and gave the bell another ring for good measure. Pushing his gut up against the windowframe, Rollo stuck his head out as far as possible. 'Fuck off!' he screamed, shivering in the cold. 'If you don't leave immediately, I will call the police.'

The two men looked at each other and laughed. Then the one who had been ringing the bell moved out onto the road where Rollo could see him, waving a badge above his head. 'My colleague and I *are* the police, Mr Kasabian,' he shouted up, with more than a hint of malice. 'So I suggest that you come down and open the door right now.'

AFTER SENDING THE rent boys packing, Sam Hooper told Rollo Kasabian to go and get dressed. Sitting down on the sofa, he then sent his sergeant to go and make some tea. Looking around, he was surprised to note that Rollo's living room had the nondescript, uncluttered look of a service flat, with no sign of the Shanghai-brothel chic that he had been expecting. The fat old queen clearly did not spend much time on interior decoration.

'So, how can I help you?' Rollo had reappeared in the doorway wearing a leopardprint kimono loosely tied at the waist. He had a glazed look in his eyes that suggested he was under the influence of something more than just alcohol. Casually scratching his groin, he let out a small fart. 'Oops!' he grinned, taking a step further into the room.

If it wasn't for the fact that Hooper had already been exposed to a full view of the naked Kasabian form, the inspector might very easily have lost his lunch at this point. Instead, he accepted the tea that the sergeant had just brought him from the kitchen. The fancy blue and white china mug had a gold band running round both the top and the bottom. Hooper turned it carefully in his hand until he found a legend in small script: *The Blue Drawing*

Room, Buckingham Palace. He looked up at Kasabian, who had at least stopped caressing himself. 'Nice crockery, Rollo,' he smiled.

Stifling a yawn, Rollo couldn't be bothered to muster a reply.

Hooper turned back to the sergeant, a permanently suspicious bloke from Bolton called Lawrie Kunesburg: 'One sugar?'

Kunesburg blinked and nodded twice, but said nothing.

'Thanks.' Eyeing Kasabian carefully, Hooper blew gently on the tea. He took a sip and grimaced. It was truly disgusting. 'Nice tea,' he said through gritted teeth, placing the mug on the coffee table next to the small transparent plastic packet, about the size of a matchbox, which was half-full of white power. Letting Rollo take notice of the packet, he sat back on the sofa and clasped his hands above his head.

'Mr Kasabian,' he said finally, 'do you know why we are here?'

Rollo moved his gaze slowly from the item on the table back to the inspector. 'That's not mine,' he protested feebly.

'That's what they all say,' Hooper grinned. 'Sergeant, if you could step outside for a moment, please.'

Kunesburg took his cue and headed past Kasabian, stepping out and closing the door behind him. Pulling his kimono closer, Rollo flopped into a nearby armchair. 'Are you arresting me?'

'Not yet.' Hooper sat forward and pulled a small, unsealed envelope from his jacket pocket. Turning it upside down, he tipped the contents onto the table.

Kasabian used an index finger to count the twelve identical packets of cocaine laid out in front of him. Then he counted them again, and looked up at Hooper. 'You bastard!' he hissed, going red in the face. 'You total . . . bastard!'

'Calm down, Rollo,' Hooper said evenly.

'Calm down?' the fashion designer squawked. 'Calm down? When here you are – Mr Bent Policeman – trying to do me up like a . . . like a kipper!'

Hooper jumped to his feet, jabbing an angry finger at the quivering blob in front of him. 'First,' he said forcefully, 'I am not "bent". Second, I am your new best friend.'

Kasabian pulled his feet up onto his chair, but said nothing.

'I am the only one who can help you here, Rollo,' Hooper continued quietly.

'I don't need any help!'

Hooper laughed. 'It's time to get real. One of your models was caught trafficking a large amount of Class-A drugs.'

'She wasn't *my* model.'

Hooper ignored the interjection. 'Charlotte Gondomar subsequently committed suicide.'

'I know.' Rollo buried his head in a cushion to stifle a sob. 'But how was that *my* fault?'

Hooper went in for the kill. 'How many more of your girls are dealing drugs, Rollo? And who is organizing them?'

Lifting his head, Kasabian grasped the pillow to his chest, and then threw it to the floor. 'I don't even take drugs,' he mumbled, 'apart from the odd line now and again.' He smiled weakly. 'My vices lie in other directions, as you saw.'

Hooper counted off the points on his fingers. 'You admit to being a regular user. You have employees who are chronic users, and some who are also dealers. You have a business which offers a classic front for laundering illegitimate profits. And,' he nodded to the powder on the table, 'you have more than enough here to classify as possession with intent to supply.'

'And you – the very person stitching me up – are my *friend*?' Rollo asked incredulously.

'Yes, I am,' Hooper smiled. 'I am the man who is going to get you out of this mess.'

Rollo sat up in his chair. He shifted as if to give his groin another scratch but quickly thought better of it and clasped his hands on his belly instead. Gazing at Hooper, his eyes narrowed suspiciously. 'And just how are you going to do that?'

Chapter Thirty

SITTING IN A meeting room on the top floor of Holborn police station, Carlyle gazed out, looking north past Great Ormond Street Children's Hospital, in the direction of Coram's Fields. Lost in thoughts of nothing, he watched a succession of grey-tinged clouds scud across the sharp blue sky.

'Hey!' Sitting on the other side of the desk, Alison Roche looked up from her BlackBerry. 'We've just had an email about Simpson.'

Carlyle turned his gaze from the view.

'Her husband has died.'

Joshua Hunt. Cancer of the colon. This was news that had been coming for a while but Carlyle still felt a sick sensation percolating in his gut. Hunt had been a good five years younger than he was. Sitting back in his chair, Carlyle closed his eyes and offered a silent prayer that shit like that would never happen to him. When he opened them again, Roche had returned to playing with her PDA. 'What does it say about Simpson?' he asked. 'Is she taking compassionate leave?'

'I don't think it said.' Roche scrolled down through the email to double-check. 'No, nothing. Just that he died at two thirty-seven this morning in a hospice in Sussex. Details of the funeral will be announced in due course.'

Another one I won't be going to, Carlyle reflected, with more than a smidgen of relief. His thoughts turned to Anita Szyszkowski, and the inspector wondered if now was the time to reach out and try to repair that broken relationship. The idea brought him up short and he let out a small laugh. Who was he trying to kid? He wouldn't know where to begin. He didn't even know if he wanted to begin. Probably the best he could do for Joe's widow and kids was to leave them well alone and let them move on. *Uncle John* most definitely he was not, and never would be.

Roche looked up from her BlackBerry. 'What's so funny?'

'Nothing,' Carlyle said, slightly embarrassed to have been caught contemplating such thoughts. Turning away from her gaze, he went back to staring at the clouds.

'SORRY TO KEEP you waiting!' Susan Phillips swept into the room in a cloud of citrus perfume. Taking a seat at one end of the desk, she dropped a slender file of papers on the surface. 'It took me a while to get cleaned up.' She smiled, knowing all about the squeamishness which prevented him from visiting her in the lab unless it was absolutely necessary. 'I had a customer on the slab downstairs – had to get in up to my elbows.'

'Nice,' Carlyle grimaced.

Roche, not wishing to play gooseberry to the two oldies in the room, tried to get right down to it. 'So,' she said with a faux cheeriness that did nothing to hide her impatience, 'you think we've identified our skeleton?'

Carlyle understood why Roche sounded a bit miffed. After all, identification of the skeleton had been her job. As far as he knew, she hadn't made much progress. But, given that it was really only of historical interest, he struggled to see why she should care. He smiled at Phillips. 'Branching out into detective work?'

'It was really quite random,' the pathologist replied modestly. 'My partner is something of an amateur historian. He's done a lot of research into the Special Operations Executive, Winston Churchill's sabotage unit in World War Two.' She pointed out of the window, waving her index finger vaguely in the direction of the BT Tower, rising to the north-west. 'The SOE were based over there, in Baker Street.'

'Known as the Baker Street Irregulars,' Carlyle put in. He had read a bit of modern history himself and liked to think that he knew a little about World War Two. Now that Phillips had given him the opportunity, he wasn't going to pass up a chance to show off.

Roche gave him a tight smile that said *Get on with it.*

Carlyle smiled back sweetly. 'The nickname came from Sherlock Holmes's fictional group of boy spies employed "*to go everywhere, see everything and overhear everyone*".'

'So?' Roche interjected, obviously not wanting to play along.

'They had lots of names,' Carlyle continued, now deliberately winding her up, 'such as Churchill's Secret Army – the Ministry of Ungentlemanly Warfare. Their job was simple: to set Europe ablaze.'

'Anyway,' Phillips said, 'Nick, my boyfriend, knew about three SOE guys who went missing just down the road from here in December 1940, in the middle of the Blitz. Only two of the bodies were ever found. I managed to dig out the pathology reports at the time – and guess what? They were shot with a Walther P38.'

'The same gun that was used on *our* guy,' said Roche, showing a bit more enthusiasm now.

'Indeed,' Phillips nodded.

'So,' Carlyle asked, 'he was killed by . . . ?'

'There was a group of German agents operating in London at that time, apparently,' Phillips said. 'They were blamed for almost twenty murders in total. In the end, they were finally tracked down to a house in Leytonstone in March 1941.'

'And?' Carlyle asked.

'They were all shot while resisting arrest.'

'Outstanding,' the inspector laughed. 'That's what we like to hear.'

Roche gave him a disapproving glance.

'So where were the other two found?' Carlyle asked.

'In an alleyway just behind Holborn tube,' Phillips said.

'And why was our guy buried in the park?' Roche wanted to know.

'No idea,' Phillips shrugged. 'What we do know, however, is his name: Julius Jubelitski.'

Roche started typing into her BlackBerry. 'How do you spell the surname?'

Phillips slowly enunciated each letter in turn.

'I'll see what I can find out about him,' Roche said. 'Maybe he still has family somewhere in the city.'

'Either way,' said Carlyle, his interest fast waning, 'we can put this one to bed. Thanks for chasing this down for us, Susan.'

She slid the file across the desk, towards Roche. 'No problem,' she said. 'It was nice to be able to help.'

'Well,' Carlyle stood up and made for the door, 'I need to get going. I'll see you next time.'

'One other thing, before you go.' Phillips sat back in her chair and yawned.

'Yes?' Carlyle turned to face her.

'Simpson – she left a message for you downstairs. She wants to see you in her office over at Paddington Green as soon as possible.'

Carlyle glanced at Roche and frowned. 'Why didn't she just call me on my mobile?' he asked.

'She did, apparently,' said Phillips. 'You didn't pick up.'

Carlyle rummaged through his jacket pockets until he found his phone. He looked at the screen and sighed – four missed calls. How could he have racked up four missed calls? He was sure the bloody thing hadn't rung once. He checked the missed-calls log and saw Simpson's number at the top. 'Okay,' he said, 'I'll head there now.'

'By the way,' said Roche, 'David wants to speak to you as well.'

'What is the news from Counter Terrorism Command?' the inspector asked.

'I don't know,' Roche said evenly. 'He just said it would be good for you two to have a catch-up.'

'Oh, what it is to be popular!' Carlyle said camply. He smiled at Roche. 'Consider it done. I'll see you back at the station.'

Chapter Thirty-one

CARLYLE SLOWLY SHIFTED his gaze from the bottle of Glenfiddich on the Commander's desk and looked his boss directly in the eye. *You look tired*, he thought. *Not surprising, really; but maybe it's not the best time to be hitting the single malt.*

'You're a hard man to get hold of,' Simpson observed.

'I'm sorry about that,' the inspector said. 'Problems with my phone.'

'Technology isn't your strong point, is it?' She smiled wanly.

'I've just seen Phillips,' he said, changing the subject. 'She's identified the guy that was dug up in Lincoln's Inn Fields.'

'Oh,' Simpson replied, clearly not that interested. 'What's the story?' Pulling a couple of small glasses from a drawer in her desk, she carefully poured a double measure into each of them.

'He was called Julius Jubelitski. We think he was killed in December 1940.' Carlyle filled her in on the remaining historical details.

Simpson played with her glass while he was speaking, but didn't yet take a sip. Once he'd finished, she said: 'Good. It sounds like Roche can put that one to bed. How's she getting along, by the way?'

'Fine.' Carlyle was beginning to feel uncomfortable, since Simpson usually got straight to the point. Whisky and small talk were rather out of character – at least where their relationship was concerned.

She finally took a small sip and gestured for him to do the same.

Carlyle let a tiny amount of the Glenfiddich coat his tongue, and he smiled appreciatively. 'Nice.'

'Your health,' said Simpson quietly, knocking back the rest of hers in one gulp.

Jesus, thought Carlyle, *what next? Dancing on the table?* He took another small sip and placed his glass on the floor beside him.

Simpson noticed the gesture and put her own glass to one side. 'Roche has a good reputation,' she said finally, 'and I think she will be good for you. Leyton are happy to let her stay on indefinitely, so I've agreed that's what she'll do.'

Carlyle wasn't sure what to make of that. Personally he thought that the jury would still be out on Sergeant Roche for a while. And he was put out that Simpson should agree to extend the officer's time at Charing Cross without consulting him first. But he could also see that this was not the time nor the place for nit-picking. He just had to go with the flow. 'Okay.'

She gave him a probing look. 'Make the most of her, John. Good coppers are few and far between, as we both know.'

'Very true.'

'And maybe she can help keep you out of trouble for a while?'

He pretended to look hurt. 'Me? I'm never in trouble.'

'You know exactly what I mean,' she chided. 'But there is some good news on that front, too. The IPCC investigation into the death of Charlotte Gondomar has been concluded. The report doesn't make great reading, but I've seen plenty worse. It seems that there may have to be some procedural changes at Charing Cross, but nothing that directly relates to you.'

That's because I did nothing wrong, Carlyle thought irritably. But he was happy nevertheless to be able to forget about the Independent Police Complaints Commission. 'Good,' he said. 'That's one less thing to worry about.'

'Quite,' Simpson replied. 'And how are things with the Joe situation?'

'I was hoping that you might be able to tell me,' Carlyle said. 'We know that a Mossad hit squad has been let loose in London. Meanwhile, Counter Terrorism Command and MI6 are fighting over who should be leading the investigation. I have to speak to the CTC guy, but it doesn't look like we're making much progress.'

Simpson refilled her glass with a smaller measure of Glenfiddich. She gestured with the bottle to Carlyle, who shook his head. Pushing it to one side again, she leaned forward in her chair. 'Keep at it, John, I know you won't give up on that one.'

'Of course not,' he said stiffly.

'The family know that you will look out for their interests.'

'The family?' Carlyle stared at her blankly. 'The family hate me. Anita wouldn't let me go to the funeral. And you were there yourself when one of her brothers thumped me at the hospital.'

'I know,' Simpson sighed, 'but you have to understand the truly terrible situation they are in right now.'

'Of course.'

'And whatever else they might feel, they know that you won't let Joe get forgotten amongst all of this.'

'No pressure then,' Carlyle smiled ruefully. Reaching down, he retrieved his glass and took a decent swallow. Feeling emboldened, he looked at Simpson. 'And what about you?' he asked, settling back into his chair.

Simpson clasped her hands together and glanced down at the desk. 'My situation's not great, it's true,' she said, 'but it's nowhere near as difficult as Anita Szyszkowski's. Joshua and I didn't have any kids, for a start. I think that's the most important thing. And he had been ill for quite some while, so I had plenty of time to prepare for what was coming.'

'Does that make it easier?' Carlyle emptied his glass and pushed it onto the desk. Simpson refilled it almost to the brim. Then she added another dash to her own glass. *Christ*, he thought, *they're going to have to carry us both out of here.*.

'I think that maybe it does,' she said, taking another mouthful of whisky. 'I was able to come to terms with things, and sort out all the practicalities.'

'Yes.' Carlyle slurped down some more Glenfiddich. The way this conversation was going, all he could do was to try and get pissed as quickly as possible.

Simpson let out a grim laugh. 'And anyway, it wasn't like I had seen a lot of him over the last couple of years, given that he was in prison.'

'No.' Carlyle was trying to stick his head as far into his glass as possible.

'The stupid bugger. I still don't understand how he could have done that to me.'

'When's the funeral?'

'Been and gone.'

'Oh.'

'Yes, thank God. It was a major relief to get that over with.'

'I can imagine.'

She tapped her desk and stifled a hiccup. 'His ashes are in the drawer here.'

'O-kay.' Carlyle nodded, as if bringing your husband's ashes to work with you was the obvious thing to do.

'Why I wanted to speak to you tonight . . .' Simpson deposited her glass on the desk and sat back in her chair. 'I wanted you to hear it directly from me. I've decided to quit.'

'What?' Carlyle reached over and grabbed the bottle, pouring himself another healthy measure. *That's it*, he said to himself. *No more after this one*. He could feel the effects of the alcohol now; if not exactly drunk, he was well under the influence. Looking at Simpson, he spoke slowly, being careful not to slur his words. 'So what are you going to do?'

'I don't know yet,' she replied, breaking off eye-contact.

'So why pack it in?'

'It just feels like the right thing to do.'

Carlyle watched her take another gulp of scotch. Either Simpson could hold her booze far better than him, or she was now three sheets to the wind.

Staring into her glass, she went on: 'I just want to draw a line under things. Ever since Joshua's . . . fall from grace, things haven't been too great for me here. Career-wise, it's over for me. I'll never get further than Commander.' Her voice started to waver and for a horrible moment Carlyle thought that she might start to cry. But she pulled herself together and eyed him with something approaching defiance. 'I'm just an embarrassment – "the fraudster's wife" – and the sooner I retire the better, as far as everyone's concerned.'

Bringing his glass to his lips, Carlyle exclaimed, 'Bollocks!'

'Well, thank you, John,' she sniffed. 'That's a very helpful insight.'

Carlyle put his glass on the desk-top. 'How old are you?'

'Well . . .' Simpson looked rather put out at the question.

'Whatever age you are,' Carlyle continued, 'you're certainly younger than me.'

Simpson nodded.

'And you're a copper, right?'

'Right.'

'That's who you are,' he pressed on, fuelled by the drink, 'and that's what you do. That business with your husband wasn't your fault, was it?'

'No.' She shook her head, eyes glazed and looking a little befuddled now.

'And, anyway, it's all in the past now. So why should anyone be pressuring you to retire?'

'Come on,' Simpson told him, 'you know what it's like here. No one comes out and *says anything*. But the way the Met *feels* is made clear.'

'Okay,' Carlyle pointed out, 'so you'll never make Commissioner, or even Deputy Commissioner, but so what? I'll never make Commander. If I was interested in a career, my parents were right: I chose badly in becoming a policeman. I don't have a career, I have a job. But it's *my* job. I chose it. It puts bread on the table and, sometimes, I can go home and say "I actually did something good today".'

Taken aback, Simpson let out a girlish giggle. 'In the words of Inspector John Carlyle,' she slurred, 'copper, philosopher and cynic, that's "bollocks".'

'It's not bollocks,' Carlyle protested. 'It's my choice, simple as that. I choose to do the job, despite all the bullshit, because it is what I do.' He beamed. 'Same as you.'

Simpson slumped back in her chair and studied him, unconvinced.

'Look,' Carlyle continued, 'when your old man was rolling in it and you lived in that multi-million-pound place in Highgate, did you ever think of packing in the day job?'

'*No.*' Simpson shook her head so vigorously that he thought it might suddenly fall off. 'I think Joshua would have liked me to, but he knew better than to push it. What else would I have done?'

'So what's changed? What will you do now?'

As Simpson thought about this question, her head dropped onto her chest. Then she started hiccupping. *Next, she'll be puking in her lap*, Carlyle thought. Standing up, he felt himself begin to sway slightly on his feet. Holding onto the edge of the desk for balance, he drained the last of his scotch. 'Carole?'

Simpson forced her head up and squinted at him. 'I'm okay,' she said quietly.

'I know you are,' Carlyle said. 'Now jump in a cab and go home. Get some rest. And, above all, don't do anything rash. Think about what I've just said. Not everyone here wants you to go.'

'Okay,' Simpson whispered.

'Good,' said Carlyle, as he slithered towards the door. 'We can talk again tomorrow.'

Chapter Thirty-two

Sitting in the Flat White café, Carlyle played with his phone. He was feeling annoyed that DI David Ronan hadn't returned any of his calls. With no idea what Counter Terrorism Command were up to, he felt completely out of the loop and totally useless. After a few moments, he hit Roche's number, but that call went straight to voicemail. Sighing, he hung up without leaving her a message. Looking across at Louisa Arbillot, he said, 'He's not coming, is he?'

Arbillot gave him a pained look. 'He promised me that he would.'

'Mm.' Carlyle was not in the mood to believe it. If he was not particularly surprised that Fadi Kashkesh had failed to appear at the appointed hour, he had not been expecting the man's estranged wife to show up, either. He wanted to conduct a serious interview, not a marriage guidance session.

Louisa saw the annoyance on his face. 'Fadi is usually fairly reliable,' she said unconvincingly.

The Grace Jones poster was still on the wall. It was incredible to think that the singer was now well into her sixties. *The original and the best*, Carlyle thought. *Lady Gaga, eat your heart out.* He glanced at his watch. Fadi was now more than half an hour late. 'I'm sorry,' he said, 'but I have to go.'

But Louisa ignored that statement. She was already struggling to her feet with a look on her face that contained hope and fear in equal measure. 'He's here!'

Carlyle waited while a small, wiry type pushed his way through the throng of customers and pulled up a stool at their table. While Louisa made the introductions, Carlyle sized the man up. Fadi Kashkesh was twenty-eight years old but, dressed in a faded denim jacket and white T-shirt, he could have passed for ten years younger. The youthful look was helped by the fact that his hair was neatly trimmed and he was cleanshaven. The dark rings around his eyes and the hollow cheeks suggested a boy in need of some looking after by his mother. Maybe that was where Louisa had come in.

Sitting there, his fists clenched tightly and a neutral expression on his face, it wasn't clear whether Fadi was more suspicious of Carlyle or of his wife. While Louisa jumped up to get him an espresso, Carlyle showed him some ID and explained what he wanted. 'What I need,' he concluded, 'are some leads.'

Fadi nodded but said nothing.

'Two members of Hamas have already been killed,' Carlyle continued, willing himself to show a degree of patience, 'and maybe that is the end of it. Maybe there will be no more.'

Still the Palestinian looked at him blankly.

'However, if there are still people here who are currently Mossad targets, I want to get to them first.'

Louisa returned with the espresso and placed it in front of her husband. He downed it in one, the coffee seeming to confer on him the power of speech. 'That is not something I would know anything about,' he said quietly. 'My life is very different now.'

His wife gave him a sharp look, but he ignored her.

'There can be no more bloodshed on our streets,' Carlyle told him. 'This city is not a war zone.'

Fadi gazed into his empty cup. 'Why are you telling me this?'

'You can help me,' Carlyle insisted.

The man shrugged. 'I am sorry, Inspector, but you are wrong.'

Carlyle glanced at Louisa, whose face was now a picture of helplessness. Time for a change of tack, he thought. He stuck out a hand. 'Show me your papers.'

The two of them stared at him.

'Your papers,' Carlyle repeated.

'But I told you,' Louisa whined. 'He is legal.'

Carlyle looked at her with contempt. 'I could spend a lot of time and effort making sure.'

'I am not a part of any of this . . . situation any more,' Fadi said, his lower lip trembling slightly.

'But you can help me,' Carlyle said again. He had no idea whether that was correct or not, but then again, he didn't have anything else to go on.

Fadi glanced at his wife and again lowered his head. 'Maybe I could talk to some people.'

'Good. Do it.' Carlyle got to his feet. 'Do it quickly.'

Clearly nervous at the prospect of being left alone with his wife, Fadi jumped up. 'Let me walk outside with you.'

Carlyle watched Arbillot's face crumple into a mess of hurt and resignation as they left.

Outside, a chill wind swept along Berwick Street. While Fadi buttoned up his jacket against the cold, Carlyle pulled a business card out of his pocket. 'Call me on this mobile number when you have something for me.'

Fadi took the card. As the policeman walked away, he shoved it into the pocket of his jacket. Picking a large red apple from one of the fruit and veg stalls standing in the street, he paid the stallholder and took a bite. His first inclination was to run, but he knew that was not a sensible option. *You have the right papers*, he told himself. *You have a right to be here*. Standing on the kerbside, deep in thought, he finished off the apple.

By the time he dropped the core in a waste-bin and began heading towards Oxford Street, he had something approaching a plan.

SHEILA SEKULIĆ SHIFTED uneasily on the bed. Her piles were playing up and the pink plastic bikini that she was wearing only added to her discomfort. She wondered how much longer she could bear to spend in this squalid room above a cut-price video store in Soho. For the millionth time she told herself that once she went home to Adelaide, that would be it: no more travelling. Europe was a dump and England was a total shithole; she wouldn't be coming back. Tossing a copy of yesterday's *Daily Star* newspaper onto the floor, she sat up and checked the clock sitting on the bedside table. The session was almost up. She glanced over at the shabby man who was still standing by the window. Her heart had sunk when he walked through the door, but he'd turned out to be the perfect punter – not really interested in her at all. All he seemed to want to do was stand by the window and take pictures of something out in the street below. As far as she was concerned, he could do that all day, as long as he paid her. She coughed politely. 'Your time's almost up.'

The man grunted and continued gazing out of the window.

'It'll be seventy-five,' she said optimistically, 'if you want to stay another half-hour.'

Sid Lieberman watched Fadi Kashkesh toss the remains of his apple into a bin and then disappear up the road. 'It's all right,' he said, dropping the Leica V-Lux 20 digital camera back into his pocket. 'I'm done.' He turned away from the window, feeling a stab of gratification as a look of disappointment swept across the whore's face. 'Nice to meet you, though,' he smiled as he moved towards the stairs.

Chapter Thirty-three

RECLINING ON THE sofa, Carlyle looked on nervously as Helen flicked rapidly through a succession of television channels, searching for some suitable crap to watch. His wife was clearly not happy about something and he knew that meant he was in for a stern talking-to. From past experience, it would not be long before she explained to him what he'd done wrong. Over the years, he'd become philosophical about it; after all, it was always best just to get the unhappiness over with as quickly as possible.

In the absence of finding anything better, Helen settled on one of the news channels. A British woman had killed her two young children in a Spanish hotel, for reasons that were not immediately apparent. It was just the kind of story that Carlyle found infinitely depressing. More than that, he resented being confronted by other people's tragedies in his own living room. He had to deal with more than enough of that kind of shit while he was at work.

Helen must have entertained a similar thought, because she quickly muted the sound. Finally turning to face Carlyle, she gave him a dirty look. 'Why did you do it?' she asked.

Carlyle tried his best to look innocent. 'Do what?'

'Don't play dumb with me, John Carlyle,' she replied, tapping him on the arm with the remote. 'Louisa Arbillot was in a terrible state when she got back to the office after your meeting.'

'She seemed all right to me when I left,' Carlyle lied.

'I very much doubt that,' Helen snapped. 'The strain has been building for months, and now you've pushed her over the edge.'

'Me?' He stifled a laugh. 'You were the one who put me on to her.'

'I think that she'll have to go on sick leave,' Helen said, refusing to acknowledge any possible involvement on her own part. 'Her doctor could be signing her off for months.'

'What a pain,' Carlyle said sympathetically. He knew what a problem that would cause Avalon. The charity's modest finances could not cope with members of staff taking extended absences on full pay.

Scowling, Helen shook her head at him.

'What can I do?' he protested. 'Other people's marriages are their own business. I don't work for Relate.'

'You could have persuaded him to talk to her,' she replied, folding her arms as she returned her gaze to the screen.

Carlyle shuffled along the sofa and slid his arm around his wife. 'For what it's worth,' he said, 'I don't think I could have done much to get Fadi talking to Louisa. Basically, I presume that it wasn't much more than a marriage of convenience as far as he was concerned.'

'I know, but for her . . .'

'Wasn't it a bit unprofessional of her, marrying a patient?'

'Yes, probably,' Helen agreed. 'But who are we to judge?'

'Quite. I suppose the poor woman deserves better. But realistically there's nothing that I can do to help. Anyway, I had enough problems getting him to talk to me, never mind to her.'

'Mm.' Stretching out on the sofa, she rested her head on his lap. 'Do you think he'll be able to help your investigation?'

'I don't really know,' Carlyle sighed, 'but it's not like I've got a lot else to go on. I *have* to find some way into this thing. It's the least that Joe deserves.'

Chapter Thirty-four

FABIO CAPELLO GAVE the inspector a hard stare as he entered Il Buffone. As previously agreed, AC Milan's '94 Champions League winning team had replaced Juve in the place of honour on the back wall of the café. *Well done, Roche*, Carlyle thought, as he greeted Marcello and ordered a double macchiato. Sliding into the back booth underneath Donadoni, Maldini and the rest, he shook hands with David Ronan nursing a mug of tea.

'How are things with SO15?' Carlyle asked, eyeing up the pretty girl in the next booth, who was shamelessly wolfing down a bacon roll.

Marcello appeared with his coffee. Placing it on the table, he saw Carlyle checking out the girl and smiled. '*Bella figura, sí?*'

Carlyle felt himself blush slightly. 'Thank you, Marcello,' he said, gesturing him away. He knocked back about half of the macchiato and looked at Ronan enquiringly. 'Have you made any progress?'

'Things are not great,' Ronan told him. 'Counter Terrorism Command has been given full authority to conduct its investigation, but no one seems able to tell MI6 to butt out.'

'So it's going swimmingly, then.'

'There is nothing to suggest that any arrest is imminent,' Ronan said stiffly. 'It seems likely that the Mossad crew have long since left the country.'

'Not necessarily,' said Carlyle. 'If they haven't completed their mission, they might possibly still be here.' Quickly he brought Ronan up to speed with selected highlights regarding his own enquiries, filling him in on his meeting with Fadi Kashkesh but leaving out any mention of either Sol Abramyan or Dominic Silver.

'Interesting,' was Ronan's only comment after Carlyle had finished.

'Up to a point.'

Both men knew that they were up shit creek without a paddle. In a boat that was sinking slowly but surely into the muck.

'Let's keep talking,' said Ronan, pulling some change out of his pocket.

'Sure,' said Carlyle, raising a hand. 'Don't worry, I'll get this.'

'Thanks.' Ronan slid out of the booth. 'How's Alison getting on, by the way?'

'Alison's doing great,' Carlyle said. 'Did she tell you about the skeleton that was dug up, just down the road?'

'Yes.'

'We've identified the body, so that's a result,' said Carlyle, happy to remind himself that there were still some things that could actually be resolved. He tapped the poster above his head. 'And she sorted this for Marcello, so she's basically considered one of the family already.'

At the mention of his name, Marcello popped up from behind the counter. 'The inspector needs all the help he can get now,' he joked, 'so I hope she's staying.'

'I think that she will be,' Carlyle said, 'which is fine by me.'

'That's good to know,' smiled Ronan. 'I'm sure she'll be happy to hear it.'

Watching the detective inspector leave, Carlyle finished the last of his coffee. Looking across, he was disappointed to see that the girl in the next booth had now gone.

Chapter Thirty-five

A LINGERING SENSE of unease sent Hilary Waxman down to the basement, in search of Sid Lieberman. For once, the military attaché was actually to be found in the gloomy, windowless closet that he called an office, sitting at his desk with a number of A5-sized black and white photographs spread out in front of him. Standing next to him was a guy wearing jeans and an Iron Maiden *Run for the Hills* T-shirt. The guy was extremely tall – maybe six foot five – and thin, with a shaven head and a tan that was in need of a top-up. Waxman had never set eyes on him before.

Standing in the open doorway, the Ambassador coughed politely. Both men looked up at her, but said nothing. After a moment's hesitation, Lieberman gestured to the empty chair filling up almost all of the empty floorspace in front of his desk. He didn't introduce the Iron Maiden fan and Waxman didn't bother to ask. Taking a seat, she picked up one of the prints. The photo was of two men conversing on a busy street.

Lieberman nodded to the other man, who stared at Waxman and left the room.

'The young guy in the picture is called Fadi Kashkesh. He's a Palestinian activist living in London. I believe he has been providing logistical support for the Hamas cell we have been . . . liquidating.'

The word made Waxman shudder, but not wanting to show any emotion that Lieberman might interpret as weakness, she simply said, 'And the other guy?'

'He's a London policeman,' Lieberman said. 'His name is Inspector John Carlyle. It was his partner that Goya accidentally shot outside the Ritz Hotel.'

Interesting use of the word 'accidental', Waxman thought, but again she said nothing. Instead she asked: 'So why has he hooked up with the Palestinian?'

'I presume,' Lieberman smirked, 'that, like us, he is trying to find Goya.'

'He is leading the investigation?'

'No, he is not officially involved at all, but clearly he is an interested party. Also, from what I am told, he is not the kind of police officer who cares too much about trampling all over other people's cases.'

'So what are you going to do?' Waxman asked.

Lieberman looked blank, as if confused by her question. Realizing that she was not going to get an answer, Waxman tossed the print back onto his desk and stood up. 'Just one thing,' she said, edging towards the door.

Lieberman barely lifted his gaze. 'Yes?'

'No more dead policemen, okay? There are limits, even for you.' Not waiting for an answer, she headed back upstairs.

'I'll do what I can,' Sid Lieberman muttered to himself, once she had gone, 'but no promises.'

Chapter Thirty-six

'How does it feel to be back?' Sol Abramyan smiled cautiously at Carlyle as he took a bite out of his miniature cucumber sandwich. The arms dealer was a tall, elegant-looking man of indeterminate age. Sitting across the table in an expensive-looking navy suit with a pale green shirt open at the neck, he finished the sandwich and carefully refilled his cup with some Earl Grey tea, which he preferred black. Looking him up and down, Carlyle was reminded of a more sinister version of the actor Stewart Granger, who starred in a version of *The Prisoner of Zenda* way back in the 1950s.

Carlyle slowly checked out the room, careful not to let his eyes linger on the two very large gentlemen sitting a couple of tables away. The duo looked more than a little out of place in the Palm Court of the Ritz; he presumed that they were Abramyan's famed Somalian retainers. 'It's fine,' he smiled.

The twinkle in Abramyan's eye grew brighter. 'I was wondering why you happened to be here in the first place?' He glanced at the third man at their table, Dominic Silver, whose expression was neutrality personified, then back to Carlyle. 'No offence, but I don't see you as a regular.'

'None taken.' Carlyle was just about to explain when Edwin Nyc, the hotel's Security Manager, appeared next to the table.

'Mr Abramyan,' Nyc gushed, over the din from the other tables. 'It's so nice to see you again.'

Abramyan nodded graciously, but made no effort to speak.

Dom gave Carlyle a questioning look and then took a nibble out of his pain au raisin.

'Are you staying with us at the hotel, sir?' Nyc continued.

Abramyan finally looked up. 'Not today, Edwin,' he replied. 'I am only in London on a brief visit and I thought that it would be nice to enjoy just a little of your excellent hospitality.'

Nyc bowed so low that Carlyle feared he might bang his forehead on the table.

'So I am just taking tea with some friends here.'

Nyc looked at the others, as if noticing Silver and Carlyle for the first time. Recognizing the inspector, he was unable to completely check the look of surprise that began creeping across his face. But, recovering well, he smiled obsequiously to all concerned, before beating a hasty retreat.

Abramyan supped a mouthful of tea. 'My apologies, Inspector. Some people are just too intrusive. What were you about to say?'

Ignoring Dom's amused expression, Carlyle explained about the annual ritual with his mother.

'I like that,' Abramyan said. 'Sadly, my own mother passed away some time ago – as did my father. But your mother must be very proud to have such a dutiful son. It is good that you still do things together, talk together . . .'

Carlyle looked down at his empty coffee cup. 'She told me she's getting a divorce,' he heard himself say.

'Why?' It was the first word Dom had spoken since he had made the introductions.

'She found out that my father had had an affair,' Carlyle explained, for some reason happy to discuss with an arms dealer and a drugs pusher certain things that he shied away from mentioning at home.

'Ach!' Abramyan objected. 'These things happen. How long have they been married?'

'Fifty years, give or take. The affair was thirty years ago, apparently.'

Dom failed to suppress a titter. Carlyle gave him a hard stare and he held up a hand. 'Sorry.'

Abramyan plucked a pastry from the cake-stand in the centre of the table. 'Your mother clearly is not one to forgive and forget,' he remarked, dropping the pastry on his plate and daintily wiping his mouth with a napkin, 'Normally, I like that robustness, especially in a woman. But in this case, well, what can she hope to achieve?'

Carlyle shrugged.

'Except keep everyone in a state of prolonged unhappiness,' Abramyan continued with a frown. 'And then they die.'

Carlyle nodded. 'That's basically my thinking. But it looks like that's the way it's going to be.'

Abramyan gave him a sly look. 'Maybe *I* could talk to her?'

Carlyle glanced at Dom, who now looked like he was going to piss himself with laughter. Aware that he'd let the conversation go too far off at a tangent, he held up a hand. 'That's okay. Thank you, though. They really need to sort it out among themselves. Anyway, it's not really what we're here to discuss.'

Abramyan's eyes narrowed. 'No, of course.' Reaching across, he patted Dom gently on the shoulder. 'Mr Silver here tells me that you're a very interesting man, for a policeman.'

Now it was Carlyle's turn to laugh. Catching Dom's eye, he said, 'Well, I do have some interesting friends.'

'But you have no interest in me?'

Carlyle sat up straight and looked Abramyan directly in the eye. 'No. My interest is in the man who murdered my sergeant in the street outside.'

Sol Abramyan folded his arms. 'And I am relevant to all of this because?'

Carlyle knew that Dom had already taken Abramyan through all of this in some detail. And he also knew that Abramyan wouldn't even be here if he hadn't become caught up in this whole sorry mess. But slowly, clearly, he took it all from the top.

'So you think I have this man, this Israeli killer?' Abramyan asked, when Carlyle had finished.

'He's disappeared,' Carlyle observed. 'That's all we know.'

Abramyan turned to Dominic and laughed. 'That's what these kind of people do. As I understand it, they disappear frequently.'

'His last known whereabouts were inside your house,' Carlyle persisted, leaning across the table and lowering his voice despite the background chatter, 'where he killed one of your customers.'

'All conjecture,' Abramyan said.

'The house was thoroughly searched, was it not?'

'Yes.'

'And what did you find?'

'Not a lot,' the inspector admitted.

'Quite. So, as I said, all you have is conjecture.'

Dropping his napkin on the table, Abramyam quickly stood up. The bodyguards at the nearby table appeared instantly by his side. After shaking Dominic's hand, he circled round the table to where Carlyle was now also on his feet. Abramyan offered his hand. When Carlyle accepted it, he pulled him closer and whispered in his ear: 'If there is anything that I can do to help you, I will let you know.'

'Thank you,' Carlyle murmured.

'And if I do help you, I expect to feel able to draw on your help in return sometime in the future. If I need it.'

'Understood.'

'Good.' Abramyan took half a step back and smiled. 'We have a deal.'

'We do.'

'Just remember,' Abramyan teased, 'I am a little bit like your mother.'

Slow on the uptake, Carlyle frowned.

Abramyan's smile grew wider. 'I am not one to forgive and forget. And if you break your word, if you make an enemy of me, you will have a lot more to worry about than a divorce in the family.'

Returning to his seat, Carlyle watched Sol Abramyan make his way through the lobby and head out onto the street. After checking that the pot was still hot, he poured himself a fresh cup of coffee and watched Dom demolish another Danish pastry. 'That went well,' he said, 'I think.'

Dom both nodded and swallowed at the same time. 'Yes. You made quite an impression there. I think Sol likes you.'

'How do you know?'

'If he didn't, the meeting would have been over in less than thirty seconds. Sol is not the kind of guy who has to put up with people if he doesn't want to.'

Carlyle thought about that statement for a moment. 'So what do we do now?'

'We wait,' said Dom cheerfully. 'Sol will be in touch pretty quickly, I'd imagine.'

'Do you think he really has got the guy who killed Joe?'

'How would I know?' Dom said. 'But I hope that he does.'

Carlyle took another mouthful of coffee. 'Why?'

'Because that's the only way there will be any justice for Joe.' Dom signalled to one of the waiters, who immediately brought over the bill, along with a hand-held card-reader.

Carlyle half-heartedly reached for his wallet.

'Don't worry,' said Dom, casually handing over a black credit card. 'I've already got it.'

Relieved, Carlyle put the wallet back in his jacket pocket. 'I thought you had to pay for this place in advance?'

'Not if you're Sol Abramyan you don't.' After entering his PIN, Dom took both the card and the receipt and stuffed them inside his coat.

'Thanks for that,' said Carlyle, getting back to his feet.

Dom held up a restraining hand. 'There's one more thing . . .'

'Oh?'

'Charlotte Gondomar.'

'That's all sorted. I spoke to Simpson last week. The IPCC investigation is basically a formality.'

'I'm not worried about the bloody IPCC,' Dom said quietly. 'That was never going to be my problem. What I *am* rather interested in, however, is the Middle Market Drugs Project.'

From the unhappy look on Dom's face, Carlyle realized that he'd made a mistake here. He should have raised the Middle Market Drugs Project with Dom before Dom raised it with him.

'I spoke to a guy called Sam Hooper at the same time as I was talking to the IPCC,' Carlyle said evenly. 'Hooper told me that he had been investigating Gondomar but was more interested in your fashion designer.'

'Rollo?'

Carlyle nodded. 'He reckoned that Kasabian was involved in Lottie's little scheme.'

The frown on Dom's face deepened. 'And you didn't think to tell me about this?'

'As far as I could see, it wasn't such a big deal,' Carlyle explained. 'Hooper was just fishing. Apart from anything else, your name didn't come up. To be honest, with everything else going on, I simply forgot about it.'

'What did you tell him?'

Now it was Carlyle's turn to frown. 'What do you think I told him?' he said, struggling to keep his annoyance in check. 'Absolutely nothing.'

The waiter reappeared and began clearing up, eager to get them moved on. Standing up, Dom chewed his lower lip for a moment as he stared into the middle distance. 'Maybe,' he said finally, 'Hooper thinks that you're bent.'

'He can think what he likes,' Carlyle snorted. 'The one thing I am *not* is bent.'

'But you *are* on his radar. Just be careful.'

'I always am,' Carlyle grinned, buttoning up his jacket. 'I always am.'

Chapter Thirty-seven

'OF COURSE, I never knew my grandfather.' Perched on a stool, on the far side of the central workbench, Ana Borochovsky blew on her camomile tea.

Sitting next to Carlyle, Roche gently nudged him in the ribs.

'Uh?' Carlyle finally stopped gawking at the size and opulence of Mrs Borochovsky's kitchen, which was almost as big as his entire flat, and smiled weakly. 'No, no, of course not.'

Neither woman was fooled into believing that he had been paying any attention to their conversation.

'Ana was just explaining,' Roche said, with a hint of exasperation in her tone, 'how Julius Jubelitski was the father of three children. One of them, Tom, was Ana's father.'

'I was born in 1960,' Ana Borochovsky explained.

Carlyle did the maths in his head. That made her . . . a very good-looking middle-aged woman. 'What do you know about your grandfather?' he asked.

'In terms of what he was doing during the war?' she asked. 'Not a lot really. It was deemed highly secret and my grandmother didn't ask. We knew – we assumed – that he had been killed by the Nazis, but it was the war, after all, and details were impossible to come by. In the end, he was just one of many who went missing, whose fate was never uncovered.'

How very stoical, Carlyle thought. On the other hand, it wasn't as if the family had been offered a lot of choice in the matter.

Mrs Borochovsky took a mouthful of tea. 'We were all very proud of him.'

'I can imagine,' Carlyle smiled.

'It's wonderful that you've finally found out what happened to him. My grandmother is dead now, of course, but my father is extremely grateful.'

'We're delighted to have been able to help,' Roche smiled. 'Your grandfather's remains will be handed over to the family in the next couple of days.'

'Thank you.' Ana Borochovsky gazed out through a set of French doors leading to her spacious Muswell Hill garden. A trampoline and a discarded football suggested the presence of small kids. *Maybe*, Carlyle thought, *she has grandkids of her own now.* He idly wondered if he would ever be a granddad, before sternly reminding himself that it was far too early to be thinking about things like that.

'It all seems such a long time ago,' the woman sighed.

'It *was* a long time ago,' Carlyle observed.

'We were always a political family,' Borochovsky mused, 'probably not the smartest thing to say to the police . . .'

Carlyle smiled but said nothing.

'But Granddad was just one of a long line of anti-fascist activists.' She sighed wistfully. 'Even in my day, I remember getting involved in things like the Anti-Nazi League and Rock Against Racism – anti-apartheid too.'

'I remember all that,' said Carlyle.

Borochovsky looked at Roche with a grin, before turning back to the inspector. 'You were probably busy trying to truncheon people like me on the head.'

'I'm not that old,' he said stiffly.

'Are you sure?' Roche asked, laughing.

'I was involved in the Miners' Strike when I first started out in the police,' Carlyle said, playing with his teacup, 'but that's the only major political issue I've really been involved in. There were the Poll Tax riots, of course, but that was just a few wasters pissing about.'

'There aren't really any big political issues to get worked up about any more, are there?' Borochovsky said. 'Not compared to my grandfather's time, or even the battles of the 1970s.'

'I don't know about that.' Carlyle gestured at their surroundings. 'Maybe not for the likes of us, at least. You know what it's like, you grow up, you have kids, responsibilities. Your priorities change.' He looked towards Roche, as a representative of a younger generation.

'People are more cynical these days,' Roche said. 'You might still want to campaign against globalization or global warming, or whatever, but basically it has become a lifestyle choice.'

'Not enough lefties around to thwack,' Carlyle grinned. 'Sometimes people try to blur the edges between political activity and crime but usually it's just as an attempt to justify what they've done.' He rubbed his face. 'I deal in crime, pure and simple.'

As he spoke his phone started ringing. 'Excuse me.' He pulled it out of his pocket. 'Hello?'

The connection was poor, but the voice was all business. 'It's Sam Hooper here.'

There was a pause.

Carlyle volunteered nothing.

'From the Middle Market Drugs Project.'

I know where you're from, Carlyle thought irritatedly, as he got out of his chair. 'Hold on one minute.' Opening one of the French doors, he stepped out into the back garden. The air was chilly, with the threat of rain. Carlyle waited until he was well out of earshot of the two women, before continuing. 'What can I do for you?' he asked as casually as he could manage.

'I wondered if we could meet up?'

Spit it out, Carlyle thought. 'Well,' he prevaricated, 'I am rather busy right now.'

'Tomorrow would be fine,' Hooper said firmly. 'Let's say ten a.m. at Charing Cross. I want to pick your brains about a guy called Dominic Silver.'

Chapter Thirty-eight

DOMINIC SILVER SAT in a chair on the second floor of his Soho townhouse, nursing the dregs of a Super Berry Smoothie. Yawning, he half-watched a rerun of an old Evander Holyfield–Mike Tyson fight that was playing on the 40-inch plasma screen in one corner of the room.

'Which one is this?'

'Ninety-six.' Gideon Spanner, Dom's senior lieutenant, shifted on the sofa and took another swig from his bottle of Sol. 'The first one.'

'So not the one where Tyson bites off his ear?'

'Nah, that was a year later. This ends with a TKO for Holyfield in the eleventh round.'

'Okay.' Finishing the last of his juice, Silver slowly got to his feet. 'I've got to get going.'

Gideon grunted an acknowledgement.

'Everything under control?'

'Yup.' Gideon placed his bottle on the floor and picked up the remote.

'Good.' Dom paused by the door. Starting to channel surf, Spanner looked up at his boss enquiringly.

'There are a couple of things we might need to deal with,' Dom said quietly. 'You might want to think about which of the guys we could use for a potentially tricky situation.'

'No problem,' Gideon told him, flicking through the TV channels with increasing speed. 'They're all reliable, but I know who my first choice would be.' Arriving at the Cartoon Channel, he found some vintage Tom & Jerry. 'Cool,' he grinned, tossing the remote onto the sofa and retrieving his beer.

'Fine,' said Dom as he slipped out of the door. 'I'll let you know how I want to proceed.'

Chapter Thirty-nine

SITTING IN THE Marquis pub, a couple of blocks from Charing Cross police station, Roche drank from a bottle of Peroni while Carlyle fiddled with his BlackBerry. Rather than reviewing his work emails, she could see that he was checking some football website. 'That's not exactly sociable behaviour, you know,' she huffed.

Carlyle looked up at her and replied, 'You sound just like my wife.' Logging off, he dropped the device on the table and took a swig of his beer.

Weighing up whether to have another, Roche played with her beer bottle, turning it this way and that. 'There's a couple of new things that Simpson wants us to take a look at,' she announced.

'Mm.' The inspector wondered if maybe his boss should take retirement after all. The last thing he wanted now was any more work. His desk was relatively clear at the moment, and he wanted to keep it that way. He eyed Roche with a pained expression, only to find that she was looking at someone behind him. Before he had time to turn around and check, a woman sat down next to him on the bench. Placing a large glass of white wine on the table, she deposited a red leather shoulder bag on the floor by her feet. Carlyle checked her out. Underneath a Burberry raincoat, she wore a pale blue V-neck sweater offering just the slightest hint of décolletage. At first glance, he'd say she was a foreigner, probably a tourist. A good-looking one too: slim, with long auburn hair and a pretty face, youthful-looking for someone Carlyle guessed to be somewhere in her mid-thirties.

Turning to face him, she smiled and offered her hand. 'Inspector Carlyle?' she enquired in a vaguely American accent.

'Yes,' he said reluctantly, before shaking her hand limply.

Roche waved her empty bottle at the new arrival. 'And I'm Sergeant Roche,' she said, not waiting to be introduced.

The woman smiled blandly and moved closer to Carlyle. 'I am Sylvia Swain,' she said, taking out a business card and placing it on the table in front of him. Then she produced a small tape recorder and placed it next to the card. 'I work for the *Globe and Mail* in Canada. I'm doing a piece on the current spate of political killings in London and their impact, both on people in the city and on the wider geopolitical situation.'

Good for you.

'And I wondered if I could possibly speak to you for a few moments about the murder of your partner?'

The inspector picked up the card and scanned it slowly. Swain bore the title of Senior Foreign Correspondent and she had an office address in Toronto. A mobile started ringing. He recognized the opening bars of U2's 'I Still Haven't Found What I'm Looking For' – as Roche began fumbling in the pocket of her jacket. Checking the number on the screen, she took the call, clamping the phone to one ear and sticking a finger in the other to block out the noise of the busy pub. 'Hi!' she shouted to the caller. 'Hold on a minute.' Giving him a crooked smile, she headed outside for the relative quiet of the street.

Annoyed at being abandoned by his colleague, he turned to face the journalist, who was waiting politely for him to respond to her question. 'I'm sorry,' he said, 'but this is an ongoing investigation. I am not at liberty to discuss it.'

Swain took a mouthful of wine and nodded. 'I completely understand.'

'Thank you.'

However, she went on: 'But you worked closely with Sergeant Sy . . .'

Carlyle glanced at the tape machine, double-checking that it was switched off. 'Szyszkowski. Joe Szyszkowski.'

'Interesting name. Where was he from?'

'He was English,' said Carlyle, not wishing to elaborate.

'Could you at least tell me what kind of an officer he was?' She noticed Carlyle again eyeing the machine on the table. 'Don't worry, Inspector,' she said, reaching over and tapping him gently on the arm. 'I am not recording this. This is all background. I will not quote you on anything.' Picking the machine up off the table, she dropped it into her bag, before pulling out a small Moleskine notebook and a cheap biro in its place.

Carlyle sighed. 'Joe Szyszkowski was an experienced officer,' he said quickly, 'a very dedicated officer who worked extremely hard on behalf of the people of London. He left a wife and two kids, and the very least that they deserve is that his killer should be brought to justice.' While the journalist scribbled down what he had just said, Carlyle glanced outside. Roche was standing on the far side of the road, still chatting away on her mobile. He felt weary and had developed an overwhelming need to go home.

Swain finished writing. Pen hovering over the page, she looked up expectantly, as if waiting for more.

'That's it,' said Carlyle, as he rose to his feet. 'I have to go now.'

'Thank you for your time, Inspector,' Swain told him. 'I appreciate it, and I will send you a copy of my story.'

'Good.'

'If you could let me have your email address?'

'Oh – right.' Carlyle dug out one of his cards. 'I look forward to reading it,' he lied, walking away.

Chapter Forty

'GET ON WITH it.'

Snivelling like a beaten child, Rollo Kasabian gingerly fingered the electrical cable looped around his neck. Clenching his buttocks tightly, he tried to swallow, but his mouth was too dry.

'Just take the photo and hit the Send button.' The voice behind him was calm but insistent. 'The sooner you do that, the sooner I can get you down.'

Rollo wobbled on the chair and felt the cable dig into the flesh underneath his chin. Regaining his balance, he carefully extended his arm, so as to position the camera on his phone directly in front of his face.

'Good man.'

Tears streaming down his cheeks, Rollo hesitated. A small voice in the depths of his brain was urging him not to take the picture. But he had been standing this way in the middle of his living room for almost an hour now, till his whole body ached with tiredness. He needed rest, lots of rest. All he wanted to do was to get down from here and crawl into bed. As his hand started to shake, he pressed the button. Flipping the camera round, he stared at the grotesque image of his bloated face on the screen. It looked like he was already dead.

'Send it.'

Fumbling with the handset, Rollo pulled up the number from his contacts book and pressed Send. The image disappeared from the screen and he let the handset slip from his fingers. Hitting the parquet floor hard, it disintegrated into a mess of plastic and metal components.

'Thank you.' The big man with the shaven head stepped in front of the fashion designer and smiled. 'That wasn't too difficult, was it?'

'Get me down!' Rollo gasped.

The man's smile grew wider. Stepping forward, he kicked away the chair, leaving the fat man clawing at thin air.

THIS TIME, SAM Hooper didn't bother to knock. A couple of swift kicks sent Rollo Kasabian's front door flying open, and the sudden stench led him straight to the living room, where the fashion designer was hanging from a noose that had been rigged from the light fitting in the centre of the ceiling.

Hooper didn't bother checking for a pulse. 'You useless fat fucker,' he hissed. 'You could have waited till I'd finished with you.' Pulling out his mobile, he hesitated before summoning an ambulance, knowing that he should give the flat a quick once-over first.

'Drop the phone,' a voice ordered.

Hooper heard the click of a safety-catch being released, and did just as he was told. The mobile bounced just once, then landed in the pool of urine that had collected beneath Rollo's corpse. Hooper raised his gaze to the ceiling. 'Shit!'

The muzzle of a semi-automatic was pushed firmly into the nape of his neck. 'Don't worry, you won't be needing that any more.'

Feeling relatively relaxed about his situation, Hooper didn't try to look round. He had been threatened before. The worst that was likely to happen to him would be a smack over the head. Drugs were one thing, but very few people indeed had the balls to off a copper. 'I'm a policeman,' he said confidently.

'I know,' said the man behind him, pulling the trigger.

Chapter Forty-one

CARLYLE WAS IN the middle of brushing his teeth when he heard the doorbell ring. Sitting on the toilet, Helen looked up at him expectantly. Carlyle shrugged and continued brushing. Alice was tucked up in bed and the rest of the world could look after itself. Whoever was buzzing them at eleven o'clock at night could sod off.

A second ring was quickly followed by a third. 'Go and answer it!' Helen snapped.

Grumbling to himself, Carlyle rinsed out his mouth, pulled on a moth-eaten SLF *Nobody's Hero* T-shirt and padded down the hallway. Pulling open the front door, he was genuinely shocked to see his boss, Carole Simpson, standing on his doorstep. The smell of whisky on her breath hit him immediately but her eyes looked sharp and focused. Not waiting to be invited in, she marched through the door and headed into the living room. Scratching his head in puzzlement, Carlyle closed the door and followed her.

'How did you get in the building?'

'I hit a few buttons. Someone buzzed me in.'

Typical, Carlyle thought. So much for having security. 'Can I get you a cup of tea?'

Simpson shook her head and lowered herself carefully into an armchair. 'Sit down, John.'

Doing as he was told, he waited patiently for her to explain precisely what was going on.

Simpson waited for several seconds. Finally she announced: 'Sam Hooper was murdered about two hours ago.'

Carlyle felt sick to his stomach but said nothing.

'He was killed execution-style, with a bullet to the back of the head.'

A million thoughts raced through Carlyle's mind, none of them good.

'Hooper had gone to the home of Rollo Kasabian,' Simpson continued flatly. 'It appears that Kasabian had hanged himself. Someone was waiting for Hooper when he found him.' She stopped, as if inviting Carlyle to speak, but still he said nothing. He knew that his next words would be crucial for his relationship with Simpson. It was vital that he stuck to the truth, but that was not the same as spilling your guts and revealing all of it.

'This will become very nasty,' Simpson sighed. 'Tomorrow, you and I will be having a very formal conversation.'

'But tonight?'

Simpson coughed. 'There will be no record of what is said now. That is why I came here. No one will ever know that we have even spoken. So, this is your chance to let me know what the hell you've been up to.'

'And then?' Carlyle was conscious of the adrenalin coursing round his body.

'And then we'll work out the best way to proceed.'

'Thank you.' He stood up and began to pace the room, his hands thrust into the pockets of his jeans. Helen appeared in the doorway and gave them an enquiring look. Simpson nodded to her but said nothing. Helen retreated, and a few seconds later Carlyle heard the familiar strains of Radio 4 coming from the bedroom. He was a long, long way from that BBC middle-class fantasy land now.

'Hooper called me earlier today,' he said, turning back to Simpson. 'We were due to meet at Charing Cross in the morning.'

'What did he want to talk about?'

Carlyle hesitated, but only for a fraction of a second. 'A guy called Dominic Silver.'

Simpson nodded. 'I've heard of him.'

Oh you have, have you? Carlyle thought. 'Hooper was trying to get to Silver through Kasabian.'

Simpson sat back in the armchair and closed her eyes. 'Maybe a cup of tea would be good. Do you have any peppermint?'

CARLYLE RETURNED FROM the kitchen with two mugs of peppermint tea. Handing one to Simpson, he took a sip from the other. Finding it too hot, he placed it on the coffee table to cool down.

Simpson waited for him to sit down. 'So Dominic Silver gave you Charlotte Gondomar?'

Carlyle knew that there was no point in trying to fudge it. 'Yes.'

She blew on her tea. 'Why?'

Carlyle shrugged. While waiting for the kettle to boil, he had been trying to get the answers straight in his head. 'He saw the chance to do me a favour,' he said. It was the best he had been able to come up with, at such short notice.

'You guys go back a long way?'

'Yes, all the way back to the beginning. We did our training at Hendon together.'

'Before he left the police force.'

Obviously, Carlyle thought. 'Yes.'

'And you have maintained a close relationship with a known drug dealer for years,' her voice hardened, 'indeed, for decades.'

'Silver has never been convicted of anything,' Carlyle mumbled.

Simpson sat up sharply, spilling tea over her coat. 'Christ!' She placed the mug on the carpet. 'For God's sake, John, do you have a professional death wish?'

Maybe, thought Carlyle glumly.

'Why did Silver want Gondomar arrested?'

Carlyle picked up his own mug and took a mouthful of tea. The truth couldn't carry him any further. 'We didn't discuss it.'

'Did you discuss Hooper with Silver?'

'No.'

Simpson stood up, looking pissed off. 'You'll need some rather better answers in the morning,' she hissed. 'What happens if it was your mate Silver who had Hooper killed?'

Good fucking question, Carlyle reckoned. He watched as Simpson let herself out, all hope of developing a credible strategy for the morning disappearing out of the door with her.

HELEN WAS ASLEEP by the time he went to bed, with thoughts racing endlessly round inside his head. In the darkness of the room, a woman on the radio was burbling away about religious imagery in India. Switching the set off, he crawled wearily into bed, managing to wake his wife as he tried to work his way under the duvet.

'John!' she complained, turning away from him, 'it's very late.'

'Sorry,' he whispered, giving the duvet another little tug.

'What was all that about, anyway?' she asked sleepily.

'Nothing really. Just something I need to sort out in the morning.'

Turning to face him, she draped one arm over his chest and cuddled up to him. 'If it's nothing, why the late-night visit?' Moving her hand to his chest, she noticed the rapid beating of his heart. 'That doesn't sound like *nothing* to me.'

'I'll sort it in the morning,' he repeated.

'Okay,' she yawned.

Wondering what the hell he was going to do, Carlyle stared up at the ceiling. After a short while, he felt his wife's warm hand move gently down his body. Slowly and expertly, she eased him towards sleep.

Chapter Forty-two

FEELING REMARKABLY REFRESHED after less than five hours' sleep, Carlyle jogged up the steps of Charing Cross police station just before eight-thirty the next morning, clutching a double espresso in one hand and one of Marcello's finest Danish pastries in the other. He still didn't have the remotest clue how he was going to handle the Hooper problem, but at least he had got laid last night, and that always made the world seem a better place.

Inside the main door, the desk sergeant – a new guy whom he didn't know but who seemed to recognize Carlyle – eyed the inspector carefully. 'There's someone to see you,' he announced, by way of introduction, 'down in room B2.' He gestured towards the stairs leading to the basement interview rooms.

Carlyle's heart sank. 'Who?'

'IIC,' the sergeant replied, before quickly looking down at his paperwork.

Internal Investigations Command: the perfect way to start the day.

'Great,' Carlyle said, heading for the stairs.

Arriving outside the room, he knocked on the door. There was no reply, so he stepped inside. Cold and damp, B2 was one of four essentially identical interview rooms occupying the basement of Charing Cross – a rectangular space, with a striplight on its low ceiling but no windows. Most of the floorspace was taken up by a table, with a couple of chairs on either side. He knew it well, having conducted many of his own interviews there over the years.

Apart from a briefcase on the table, next to a half-empty cup of steaming coffee, the room was empty. Resisting the urge to snoop inside the case, Carlyle took a seat and began eating his pastry. He was two-thirds of the way through it when the door opened and a large man wearing a grubby pinstripe suit bustled in. Carlyle put the remainder of his Danish down on the table, quickly finished chewing what was in his mouth and swallowed. Getting to his feet, he extended his hand. 'Ambrose . . .'

'Inspector.' Ambrose Watson looked at the hand suspiciously, gave it the briefest of shakes and quickly retreated to the opposite side of the table, behind the safety of his briefcase.

It was chilly in the interview room, but the IIC man was still sweating profusely as he lowered himself into the chair facing Carlyle, carefully checking its robustness before letting it take his full weight. If anything, Watson's waist had expanded further, and his hair gotten thinner, since their paths had previously crossed, a year or so earlier. On that occasion, the IIC man had been investigating the murder of a policewoman who had been burned alive while she was at home in bed with her girlfriend. Between them, the two officers had more or less worked out what had happened there.

God, Carlyle asked himself, *was that only a year ago?* More like eighteen months, he decided as he watched Ambrose pull an A3 pad out of his bag and place it on the desk. At least he had a relationship of sorts with the man, which meant something. He briefly wondered if Simpson had had a hand in Ambrose getting this case. Maybe she was still trying to help him despite her obvious and, he had to admit, well-founded doubts about his possible involvement in Hooper's murder.

Once he had finally located a suitable pen and checked that it was working, Ambrose Watson looked up at Carlyle and said, 'I assume that you know why I'm here?'

'In general.' Carlyle sat back and stuck the last of his pastry into his mouth. His game plan, such as it was, was to let Ambrose do as much of the talking as possible.

'Well,' Ambrose cleared his throat, 'you doubtless know that Sam Hooper was killed last night?'

'Yes,' Carlyle graciously admitted.

'Good,' Ambrose replied, relieved to have finally got the interview off the ground. 'I am interested in his connection with Rollo Kasabian, the fashion designer.'

'Okay,' Carlyle nodded. Normally, he had no patience with people going round the houses in such a way, but this morning he was quite happy for the IIC man to tiptoe round the main issue for as long as he liked.

'So . . .' Ambrose paused to scratch somewhere behind his left ear with his pen. 'What I want to know is . . .'

'Yes?' Carlyle smiled, helpfulness personified.

'The nature of *your* connection to Mr Kasabian. And also, what did you talk to Hooper about?'

Carlyle adopted a look of confusion. 'Isn't all that contained in Hooper's reports?'

A pained expression spread over Ambrose's face. 'There was a bit of a backlog in the inspector's paperwork, at the time of his death.'

That's a result, thought Carlyle. It was the first bit of good news he'd received about Sam bloody Hooper since he had first met the little bugger.

'In fact,' Ambrose grimaced, 'there are quite a few things regarding our ex-colleague that are in need of some . . . clarification.'

'Oh, are there?' Carlyle pulled his chair closer to the table, and sat up straighter. 'Tell me more.'

ONCE THEY HAD compared notes, Carlyle was feeling a lot happier about the current situation. Ambrose had unleashed upon him a tale of woe – missing drugs, questionable arrests, dodgy associates and expensive lifestyle choices – that clearly signalled that the IIC now thought it was Sam Hooper who was bent. Whatever Simpson had seemed to think the night before, Carlyle himself felt that he was merely being lined up as a witness to Hooper's various character defects. Under the circumstances, that was a role he would be more than happy to play.

However, none of this got him any closer to resolving the issue of Silver's possible involvement in Hooper's execution. Not for the first time recently, Dom had loomed large over a conversation in which his name had not even been mentioned. That didn't mean that he wouldn't end up on the IIC's radar sooner rather than later. What it did give him, though, was a bit of time.

As he left, Ambrose offered a more substantial handshake. 'Thank you for your time, Inspector,' he smiled. 'I'm sure that we will speak again on this.'

'My pleasure,' Carlyle smiled in return, striving to keep the relief from his voice. 'Let me know if I can be of any further assistance.'

'I will.' Ambrose dropped the notepad back into his briefcase and Carlyle was gratified to see that, apart from a single doodle in the top corner, it was as blank as it had been at the beginning of their conversation.

Just as Carlyle himself was about to get to his feet, there was a knock at the door. 'Come in,' he called.

It opened and a young black WPC popped her head round the door. 'There's someone to see you upstairs, Inspector,' she said.

'Who is it?' he asked warily.

'Tall bloke, didn't give a name,' she replied. 'He just said that it was very important and, quote, "that you were the most useless bugger he'd ever met when it came to answering your bloody phone" unquote.'

'Fuck!' Carlyle sighed, his good humour evaporating.

The WPC gave him a worried look.

'Don't worry,' he said, 'I'll be up in a minute.'

Carlyle made his way quickly up the stairs to find Dominic Silver leaning casually on the front desk, chatting away happily to the WPC and the desk sergeant. In no mood for small talk, Carlyle took Dom by the arm and guided him swiftly towards the front door of the police station.

'What the fuck are you doing here?' he hissed through gritted teeth.

'I needed to get hold of you,' Dom grinned, amused by the inspector's obvious embarrassment, 'and, of course, as always, you are not answering your phone.'

'I always answer,' Carlyle protested, 'eventually.' Dom was one of the very few people who knew the number for his private, pay-as-you-go phone: the one that Carlyle used for his more sensitive communications. The problem was that he forgot to answer it, more often than not. 'Let's go for a coffee,' he said, pushing open the door and heading outside.

'Let's not,' said Dom, following him down the steps. He pointed to the silver Porsche 911 Turbo parked across the street on a double yellow line. 'We're going for a drive. Sol Abramyan has called.'

'Could you contrive to be any more conspicuous?' Carlyle complained, staring at the hundred-grand motor with dismay.

Dom rolled his eyes to the heavens. 'God, you really are a moaner. Most people would kill for a chance to get a ride in a magnificent car like that.'

'When did you become such a flash bastard?' Carlyle sneered. Out of the corner of his eye, he saw a traffic warden approach the Porsche and begin typing the licence-plate number into his hand-held computer.

Dom gave Carlyle a gentle punch on the shoulder. 'Hey,' he cried, 'get him to stop that. I don't want a ticket!'

'Sorry, sunshine,' Carlyle chuckled, 'you're on your own. That's beyond my jurisdiction. Those guys are a law unto themselves.'

Dom gestured towards the police station. 'Do you really want a record of me being here?'

'Fair point,' Carlyle conceded. Stepping across the road, he flashed his warrant card at the warden and explained that the car was there on police business.

The traffic warden, a pale-looking man, doubtless a veteran of innumerable kerbside confrontations, listened patiently. 'I completely understand,' he smiled, tapping the screen of his computer as he spoke, 'but the car is illegally parked and you've got a ticket.' Moments later, he handed Carlyle an £80 fixed-penalty notice.

'Fuck!'

'There's no need for that, sir,' the warden said testily.

'But I'm a fucking policeman!'

'And this is a police car is it, *sir*?'

'Well, no,' Carlyle stammered, 'but . . .'

'I didn't think so.' The traffic warden's smile became more of a leer. 'And anyway, no one is above the law, you know.' His victory complete, he stalked off towards the Strand, in search of his next victim.

Biting his tongue, Carlyle turned to face Dom, who was standing by the driver's door.

'Good job!' Dom shook his head sadly. 'Well done.'

'At least I bloody tried,' Carlyle growled, tossing the fine notice at Dom and snatching open the passenger door.

Chapter Forty-three

Dominic Silver might be sitting behind the wheel of a deluxe driving machine with a top speed of more than 180 miles per hour, but that didn't mean he could do anything about the routine London traffic. As they edged their way round Trafalgar Square, Carlyle watched a woman on a bicycle wobble nervously past them and brooded on the statistic that traffic in Central London moved at an average speed of just 10 miles per hour, which was about the same speed as the horse-drawn carriages of a century earlier. Personally, he thought 10 miles per hour was an exaggeration, as most of the time it was quicker to walk.

Beside them, a taxi moved forward in the bus lane, squeezing the space left available for the woman on the bike. For a moment, it looked as if she would fall over onto the bonnet of the Porsche.

'Oi!' Dom shouted angrily. 'Watch the motor!'

Ignoring him, the woman gamely kept going. *I hope your life insurance is up to date, love*, Carlyle thought. Only an idiot with a death wish would get on a bike in London. There should be a law against it.

Yawning, he turned to Dom, who was still fretting about the possibility of someone crashing into his precious car. 'So, where are we going, then?'

'Where do you think, Mr Policeman?' Dom said, still keeping his eyes peeled for dangerous road-users. 'Back to the scene of the crime, of course.'

IT TOOK ALMOST exactly an hour for them to reach Peel Street, and then find somewhere to park. Getting out of the car, Carlyle estimated that the tube could have got them here in less than half the time. Keeping that thought to himself, though, he followed Dom along the road.

The police tape had gone from outside number 17 now and the house looked completely normal.

'They got the place back quickly,' Carlyle said, as much to himself as to Dom.

'The police had no reason to keep holding it,' Dom replied. 'Sol's lawyer – or rather a lawyer for the shell company that nominally owns the property – gave a statement saying that the place was not being occupied by the owners at the time of the murder, and that the corpse was inside illegally.'

'How convenient.' Standing on the pavement while Dom rang the doorbell, Carlyle hoped that their arrival would not be noticed by any of the neighbours. At this time of the day, however, there seemed little to worry about. The street looked deserted.

Dom smirked. 'Happily the rule of law still applies in this country – some of the time, anyway. Once Forensics had finished with the place, the police handed back the keys and Sol was free to move back in. He had the place thoroughly cleaned, of course, first.' The door was finally opened for them, and Dom slipped inside first. Carlyle quickly skipped up the steps and went after him.

In the hallway, as the front door closed behind him, Carlyle turned to be confronted by one of Sol Abramyan's Somalian bodyguards, a giant who was at least six inches taller than the inspector and almost as wide as the passage. In silence, he submitted to a thorough search of his clothing before being shown towards the back of the building.

Apart from an absence of blood on the floor, the kitchen looked the same as Carlyle remembered it. Sol Abramyan sat at the far side of the table, nibbling at a cheese sandwich, with an open can of Diet Coke standing next to his plate. Another massive bodyguard lounged beside the back door. Still chewing, Sol invited his visitors to sit. Swallowing, he took a long swig from his can. 'There's more Coke in the fridge,' he said. 'It's nice and cold. Help yourself.'

'Thanks.' Dom jumped up and fetched a couple of cans. He handed one to Carlyle, who pulled the ring and took a mouthful. It tasted good.

Sol dropped his sandwich back on the plate and looked up. 'You pair took your time?'

'The traffic,' Dom shrugged. 'It's terrible.'

'The traffic in London is always terrible,' Sol said. 'Even I know that. You live here. You should know better.'

Dom bowed his head. 'Yes, sorry.'

The inspector looked on, bemused. He wasn't used to Dom appearing so meek. Then, again, he didn't usually sit in on meetings with the guy's clients.

'So,' Sol eyed Carlyle, 'I have what you want.'

Jesus, Carlyle thought testily, *get to the point, why don't you?* He glanced at Dom, but his friend's expression gave nothing away. He turned back to Sol Abramyan and said, 'Okay. Good.'

Sol took another slug from his can and let out a small burp. 'So, if I hand it over, what do *I* get?'

Carlyle forced himself to maintain eye-contact. 'What might you want?'

'I have some business deals to conclude here.'

You now want me to sanction your arms sale? Carlyle thought. *You have to be fucking kidding.* 'What are you selling?' he asked, as if it made much of a difference.

'Just cheap crap that no one else wants,' Sol replied airily. 'These guys have no fucking money whatsoever. Even the Somalis can afford better stuff.' He grinned at the bodyguard, who gave no reaction.

Carlyle glanced again at Dom. This time, Porsche Man gave him a look that said, *It's nothing to do with me.*

Sol was watching Carlyle expectantly. 'Well?'

'Well . . .' Carlyle didn't have the remotest fucking clue what to say next. 'This puts me in a very delicate position,' he stammered.

'You've put yourself in this position,' Sol shot back. 'So what are you going to do?'

Carlyle took a deep breath. All he could do now was play for time. 'I need to check a couple of things first. I will get back to you, via Dominic, within the next six hours.'

Sol glanced at his Patek Philippe Aquanaut. 'You have three hours. After that, what you want is no longer available.'

Carlyle got straight to his feet. 'Thank you.'

Sol extended a hand and they shook. 'One other thing . . .'

'Yes?'

Sol picked at his sandwich. 'That man who died under my kitchen table.'

'The guy with a German passport . . .'

'He was travelling under the name of Lefter Sporel, but his real name was Jamal Al Amour. His family should be informed.'

Carlyle nodded. Taking a small piece of paper and a pen from his jacket pocket, he copied down the name as Sol spelled it out. 'I will make sure that the family are told,' he said. 'And we will get the body repatriated as soon as possible.'

'Good, good,' Sol nodded. 'That is as it should be.'

A thought popped into Carlyle's head. 'I am assuming that there are still members of the Hamas team here in London, in order to conclude your business?'

'Don't push your luck,' Sol grunted, returning to his sandwich. 'You have three hours.'

DECLINING DOM'S OFFER of the chance to fritter away his precious time sitting in another traffic jam, Carlyle headed for the tube. On the way, he phoned the number that he had for Fadi Kashkesh.

'Hello?'

Somewhat taken aback that the young man had answered on the first ring, Carlyle gave his name.

There was a pause while Fadi thought about hanging up. 'What do you want?' he asked finally.

'You were supposed to contact me,' said Carlyle brusquely, striding down the road and almost walking into a woman pushing a baby in a pram. Glaring at the poor woman, he hissed into the phone, 'So why didn't you give me a call?'

'I am still making my own investigations,' Fadi replied defensively.

'Time has run out, Fadi,' Carlyle almost shouted as he stepped off the pavement to avoid another pedestrian and landed straight in the path of a number 31 bus. 'Shit!' He jumped quickly back onto the pavement, and raised his voice another notch. 'I need something, and I need it now.'

'I am still trying,' the youth pleaded.

'Fuck that,' Carlyle snarled. 'I know where you live and I know where you work.' That wasn't technically true, but he could easily find out. 'You meet me in the next hour, with some useful information, or I will have you fucking deported by teatime.' As idle threats went, it was fairly lame, but he suddenly felt desperate.

'Louisa says that you cannot do that.' Fadi sounded like he was on the brink of tears.

'I'll have her fucking deported as well,' Carlyle told him, on a roll now and almost giddy with the nonsense he was talking. He named a café in Soho, near to where they had last met. 'Be there in one hour. *Don't* make me come and find you.'

Ending the call, he burst out laughing and disappeared into the depths of the tube station.

TWO HOURS AND three espressos later, Carlyle was feeling extremely wired but far less clever. Fadi Kashkesh hadn't showed up, his mobile was switched off, and the clock was well and truly ticking for Sol Abramyan's deadline. Looking at his own phone sitting in front of him on the table, Carlyle issued a slew of expletives, to the obvious dismay of a woman sitting nearby. Staring her down, he grabbed his mobile and stood up, cursing his own stupidity and wondering what the hell he should do next.

Just as he reached the door of the café, the phone started vibrating in his hand. Carlyle clamped it to his ear. 'Where the fucking hell are you?' he hissed.

'Inspector?' The woman on the end of the line was clearly disconcerted by his sophisticated opening gambit.

'Huh?'

'Is this Inspector Carlyle?'

Carlyle stopped under the shade of a tree at the north-east corner of Soho Square and took a deep breath. *Calm down*, he told himself. *Just calm down*. 'Yes, it is.'

'Inspector,' the voice purred, 'this is Sylvia Swain.'

Swain? The name didn't register. 'What can I do for you?' he said cautiously.

'We met in the pub,' she said, picking up on his confusion. 'I write for the Toronto *Globe and Mail*.'

'Yes, yes,' he said, annoyed now at having taken this call. 'I remember.'

'I'm still working on my story about your partner,' Swain said, 'and I was wondering if we could have another chat.'

Not a fucking chance. 'To be honest,' Carlyle told her, 'I don't really think I can add anything to what I said last time.'

It was not the kind of brush-off to deter an experienced journalist. 'I realize that you must be incredibly busy,' she replied evenly, 'but I have some information that you might find useful. I was wondering if maybe we could trade.'

'What kind of information?'

'Meet me at my hotel tonight and I can show you what I've got. I'm staying at the Garden on St Martin's Lane. Do you know it?'

'Yes,' Carlyle sighed, 'I know it well.' The Garden was near the police station, so if this was a wild-goose chase at least it wouldn't be wasting too much of his time. They agreed a time and he abruptly ended the call.

Walking down Frith Street, he tried Fadi's number again, gritting his teeth as once again it went straight to voicemail. Hanging up without leaving a message, he sidestepped a pile of desiccated dog shit and dropped the handset back in his pocket. Reaching into the other side of his jacket, he pulled out his private, pay-as-you-go mobile. Looking up the calls list, he hit the number at the top.

Dom answered on the third ring. 'What's happening?'

'Tell Sol that he's got a deal,' said Carlyle wearily. 'Let me know when I can pick up my package.'

Chapter Forty-four

THE INSPECTOR WAS almost an hour late by the time he walked into the Garden Hotel. Hurrying through the lobby, he nodded to Alex Miles, the chief concierge, who was talking to a stunning blonde in a silver dress, and headed for the Light Bar at the rear. The place was pretty full and it took several moments for his eyes to adjust to the gloom. He found Sylvia Swain sitting at a table in the corner. Peering over her reading glasses, she was looking through a draft of what was presumably her news story, typed neatly on several sheets of A4. As he approached, she crossed something out, then made a note in the margin with a pencil. On the table stood a very large martini.

'Sorry I'm late,' he lied, approaching her.

Swain made another mark on her copy before looking up. 'Inspector, how nice to see you again,' she smiled, slurring her words ever so slightly.

I wonder how many of those you've had already, he wondered, glancing at the three-quarters-empty glass.

'Would you like a drink?' she asked, waving to a waiter, who came skipping over to their table.

'A beer would be great, thanks,' Carlyle said, wondering how she managed to get such quick service. In smart places like this, it always took him forever to get served.

The waiter looked him up and down, making it clear that he was not impressed by what he saw. 'What kind would you like, sir?' he said threateningly, before reeling off a list of brand names, most of which meant nothing to Carlyle.

'Any of those will be fine,' Carlyle replied testily.

Sylvia ordered another cocktail and asked the waiter to put them on her tab. Nodding politely, he retreated behind the bar.

'How's your story going?' Carlyle asked, sinking into the soft leather armchair.

'We're getting there.' Swain gave him a crooked smile and dropped the sheets of paper into the shoulder bag resting at her feet. Unlike Carlyle, she was sitting on a regular wooden chair, giving her a height advantage of several inches. This allowed him an extremely good view of her legs, which were long and slim, and her skirt, which was exceedingly short.

The waiter quickly reappeared with their drinks and Carlyle took the opportunity to check out the rest of her. Her hair was kept in place with an Alice band and, along with the glasses, it added up to a rather stern librarian look. However, the flimsy-looking blouse suggested something else entirely. So too did the obvious absence of a brassière. Trying not to stare, Carlyle daintily sipped at his beer while Swain finished off her previous drink. Handing the empty glass back to the waiter, she immediately took a sip from the fresh one. She noticed him watching her. 'I know, I know,' she sighed, 'but it has been a long day. And this is only my fourth . . . so far.'

Perching on the edge of his seat, he focused on trying to maintain eye-contact. 'You said that you had something for me to look at?'

'Yes,' Swain murmured, eyeing him over the rim of her glass, 'but stupidly, I've left it up in my room.' Casually shifting in her seat, she opened her legs just wide enough to show Carlyle that she wasn't wearing any knickers either.

Taking another mouthful of beer, he lifted his gaze to the ceiling. For a moment, he was convinced that he could actually smell her sex and he inhaled deeply. *You are not following her upstairs*, his brain screamed. The message from his groin, however, was rather more ambivalent. Finishing his beer, he looked around for the waiter to rescue him. The guy was, of course, nowhere to be seen.

Swain drained her glass and, reaching over, she placed a hand on Carlyle's knee. 'Come on,' she purred, breathing alcohol fumes over him. 'I think you'll be *very* interested in what I've got to show you.'

As Carlyle struggled out of his armchair, one of the mobiles started ringing in the breast pocket of his jacket. He looked at the screen: *Helen. Saved by the bell*, he decided as the spell was broken. Turning to Swain, he held up a hand. 'Excuse me for a moment,' he said. 'I've got to take this.'

Swaying slightly, the journalist nodded.

Carlyle stepped back towards the lobby of the hotel.

'Where are you?' Helen asked by way of introduction.

'Work.'

'Sounds like you're in a bar.'

'I am in a bar. For work.'

'When will you be back?'

He exhaled deeply. 'I'm just leaving now. I'll be fifteen minutes, max.'

'Good,' she replied, 'we need to have a chat about Alice.'

'What's happened?' Carlyle asked, worried.

'It can wait till you get home. I'll see you soon.' She hung up before he had the chance to reply.

Seeing that he had finished his call, Swain veered across the lobby towards the lifts. He walked over as she hit the Call button.

'That was work,' he lied. 'I've got to go.'

She took him gently by the arm and whispered, 'I only need five minutes.'

Carlyle heard the lift arrive and the doors open. Walking her into the lift, he removed his arm and jumped back out. 'I really have to go,' he said firmly, 'but I will call you in the morning. Or maybe you could drop whatever you have off at the police station. It's just round the corner; the concierge will be able to point you in the right direction.' He nodded at the papers sticking out of the top of her bag. 'And don't forget to send me a copy of your story.'

'But—'

'Thanks for the beer, by the way.'

Before she could protest any further, Carlyle stepped aside to let another hotel guest enter the lift. Then he turned away and headed for the main door at a brisk pace.

Chapter Forty-five

ARRIVING HOME, CARLYLE looked in on Alice. Seeing his daughter sleeping the sleep of the just, a wave of serenity washed over him. Gently closing her bedroom door, he tiptoed back down the hallway. After making himself a cup of green tea in the kitchen, he wandered into the living room. Dropping onto the sofa, he kissed Helen on the cheek before stretching out with his head against her shoulder.

Helen muted the cookery programme she had been watching on TV and tapped him gently on the head with the remote control. 'Have you been drinking?'

'I had a beer,' he yawned. 'What's the story with Alice?'

'Well,' replied Helen, adopting the perky tone of one with special news to impart, 'I had a call today.'

Carlyle's heart sank. 'Oh, yes?' He took a slurp of tea.

'From Julie Wark, Stuart's mum.'

'Interesting.' Carlyle smiled at the thought of young love's worst nightmare: their respective mothers hooking up and meddling in their budding romance.

'She just wanted to introduce herself and tell me what a nice young lady they think Alice is.'

Carlyle took another mouthful of tea. 'And how do they know this?'

'Apparently she's been over there for tea a couple of times.'

'Oh, has she now?' exclaimed Carlyle in mock indignation. 'Did you know about this?'

'No,' Helen admitted, 'but it's not such a big deal.'

'I suppose not,' he said grudgingly.

'Anyway, I agreed to meet Julie for a coffee next week, so I'll doubtless find out more then.'

'Good idea.' Having Helen on the case made Carlyle instantly feel a lot better.

'And I've invited Stuart round here for tea, too.'

'When?' he asked warily.

'We haven't fixed a date yet, but I thought it was the least we should do, given that Alice has been round there twice already.'

'I suppose so,' Carlyle said, dreading the occasion already. He knew for sure that he was going to hate the little tosser. 'Maybe we could take them out somewhere?'

'That would be nice.'

'My treat,' he said, through gritted teeth.

'Thank you.' Helen leaned over and gave him a kiss on the back of the head. 'So,' she asked, 'how was your day?'

Knowing that full and frank disclosure was now the only sensible policy, Carlyle explained his run-in with Sylvia Swain at the Garden Hotel.

After he had finished, Helen struck him again with the remote, considerably harder this time. 'So, this woman flashed you her bits and then offered you a shag?'

'More or less.' Carlyle sat up straighter on the sofa in the hope of avoiding another thwack, but aware that he would have to accept some immediate grief before he got any longer-term benefit out of coming clean. 'She was drunk. As soon as I realized what was going on, I made my excuses and left. That's when you called.'

His wife gave him one of her stock pissed-off looks. 'So you were already on the way out of there when I rang you?'

'Um, yes.'

'And who was this woman?'

'Some Canadian journalist writing a piece about Joe. She claimed to have some useful information for me.'

'About what?'

'Dunno,' Carlyle shrugged. 'We didn't get that far.'

Helen pondered the information she had been given. 'So this journalist threw herself at you and you declined because you didn't want to, or because you were worried about getting caught?'

This was a conversation that they had reprised many times over the years, whenever The Job put temptation his way. It was always best to avoid temptation – which was the main reason why he had never worked in Vice, where temptation *was* The Job – but sometimes that was impossible. However, over the years, he had always been able to explain whatever had gone on with a clear conscience. 'I didn't do anything silly,' he declared, drinking the last of his tea, 'but it was a strange situation. I mean, how often do women actually throw themselves at me?'

'I wouldn't know,' Helen said huffily.

'Well, *you* certainly didn't,' he smiled, leaning over to kiss her tenderly. Even after all these years, it was still a standing joke between them that it had taken Carlyle such an inordinate amount of time to win her over.

'Don't try and butter me up.' She tried a scowl but ended up smiling, and he knew that he must have handled the situation well.

'The whole thing didn't seem right,' he continued. 'I'm fairly sure that I was being set up.'

Chapter Forty-six

Just as I am, thou wilt receive,
Wilt welcome, pardon, cleanse, relieve.
Because Thy promise I believe.
O Lamb of God, I come. Amen.

HELEN GLARED AT Carlyle as she shuffled further along the pew to make some room for him. 'You're late!' she hissed, as he took a seat beside her. Head bowed, he opened the Order of Service just as the Rector stood up to deliver the Bidding.

'We are here today to celebrate the life and honour the memory of Joseph Leon Szyszkowski, a father, husband and friend.'

Carlyle tried to remember the last time he'd been inside a church. He also tried to remember the last time he'd worn his full dress uniform. Hot and uncomfortable, he scanned the pews opposite, recognizing a number of familiar faces.

'We remember him with gratitude for his service in the Metropolitan Police, for his faithfulness and commitment to his colleagues, to his friends and his family.'

At the far end of the church, in the front pew, sat Anita Szyszkowski. Beside her were the kids, William and Sarah, and the rest of the family including the brother who had thumped Carlyle at the hospital. In the rows behind them were seated Carole Simpson and a number of the other top brass. Even from this distance, he could see how Anita looked pale and drawn. She glanced over towards where he was sitting, but Carlyle quickly looked away.

'We give thanks for his generous and hospitable character; his modesty, warmth and charm; his commitment to others; and for all that he meant to us as colleague, friend and father. And we pray that at the end of his life's voyage he may find a safe harbour and a firm anchorage within the loving mercy of Thee, our heavenly Father. May he rest in peace within the eternity of Thy Love.'

'Amen,' murmured Carlyle, along with the rest of the congregation. Taking Helen's hand, he gave it a tight squeeze. Leaning over, she gave him a gentle kiss on the cheek. She had been crying quietly and he felt sick to his stomach. Swallowing hard, he watched as Carole Simpson approached the pulpit. Should he have been giving a reading? It was too late to worry about that now. Simpson cleared her throat and scanned the audience. She looked frazzled and nervous, in a way he had never seen before.

'Sergeant Joe Szyszkowski,' she said, her voice beginning to crack almost immediately, 'made the ultimate sacrifice. His is a story of courage, and devotion to duty. Ours is a deep sense of loss: for the Metropolitan Police Service and, above all, for his family and friends. A career in policing has always been much more than just a job. A deep commitment to the notion of public service often leads our officers to put their own well-being at risk in order to help and protect others. This is undoubtedly one of our greatest strengths, but sometimes it means that we must pay a terrible price. Joe Szyszkowski was a first-rate policeman. We will miss him, but we will remember him with a smile. As the Scottish poet Thomas Campbell wrote, "to live in hearts we leave behind is not to die".'

As Simpson made her way back to her seat, the choir began to sing 'Guide Me, O Thou Great Redeemer'. Dropping his head to his chest, Carlyle had to fight back tears of his own. At that moment, he knew that redemption was a very long way off indeed.

Chapter Forty-seven

'YOU'VE CHECKED HER out?' Looking past Carlyle, Ronan scanned the lobby of the Garden Hotel. Sylvia Swain was now twenty minutes late and it was clear that he was getting fed up lounging about, even on an expensive sofa.

'Alison did a quick Google search,' Carlyle shrugged.

Sitting between the two of them, Roche handed a couple of sheets of A4 over to her boyfriend. 'She was a news anchor and reporter for a local TV station in Montreal before joining the newspaper,' she said, 'and before that she studied journalism at somewhere called Concordia University.'

'Never heard of it,' Carlyle grumbled.

Ronan shot him a look. 'At least *she* went to university.'

'Boys, boys.' Roche held up her hands. 'There's no need to bicker. She likes running, tennis, travelling and spending time with her dogs, Jerry and Libby.'

'No mention of a husband or any kids?' Ronan asked, scanning the print-offs.

'Not that I could see,' Roche said. 'But I only gave it two minutes. She has loads of recent articles online, stories from South Africa, Egypt, Turkey and so on. I even saw a couple of clips of her presenting the news. You can't fake all that, so she's got to be a genuine journalist.'

'On the other hand,' Ronan sniggered, 'she *did* try to make a pass at the inspector here, so there's got to be something strange going on.'

Carlyle felt himself redden. In the cold light of day, he could see that he was appearing just a little bit paranoid. Maybe getting Roche and Ronan to chaperone him to this rearranged meeting was rather over the top. He was just about to send them packing when Swain herself swept in through the front door. As she caught sight of the inspector with his companions, she checked her stride and a look of irritation crossed her face. Quickly regaining her composure, she headed briskly over to where the trio were seated.

'Inspector.' Swain smiled wanly, 'I didn't realize that you would be coming with full back-up.'

Getting to his feet, Carlyle shook her hand and introduced his colleagues.

'Pleased to meet you,' said Swain tonelessly. Wearing no makeup, she looked tired and hassled. In a shapeless trouser suit and navy blouse primly buttoned at the neck, she looked far from the femme fatale that the inspector remembered.

Carlyle noticed Ronan and Roche exchanging smirks, but knew that he had no alternative but to press on. He tried to smile back at the journalist. 'I'm sorry that I had to hurry off the other night.'

'These things happen.' Swain's accent seemed more pronounced than he remembered. 'So, to what do I owe this triple pleasure? How exactly can I be of assistance to you?'

'You said that you had some information for me to look at?'

Swain glanced at Ronan and Roche, and back to Carlyle. 'Of course,' she said. 'It's still in my room.' An amused grin spread across her face. 'Do you want to come up and collect it?'

'Sergeant Roche will accompany you,' Carlyle replied, 'if that's okay.'

Roche got to her feet and gestured towards the row of lifts. 'Shall we go?'

'Sure,' was all Swain could manage, glaring at Carlyle as she followed Roche across the lobby.

Watching them go, Ronan shook his head. 'All this just because you're worried about your wife.'

'You haven't met my wife,' Carlyle told him, settling back into the sofa.

AFTER ABOUT TEN minutes, Ronan frowned at Carlyle. 'Don't you think this is taking rather longer than it should?'

One of the lifts had just reached the ground floor, and Carlyle watched an elderly couple get out. 'Maybe they're having a girls' chat,' he yawned.

Ronan, however, was already on his feet. 'Let's check it out.'

'Hold on,' said Carlyle, as the other man headed for the lifts. 'We don't know the room number.'

It took another ten minutes for the girl at reception, a dumpy redhead with a bad perm and a name tag that said *Louise*, to finish dealing with the pensioners complaining about their bill, and to ring through to Swain's room. When she got no reply, it took a further five minutes for Carlyle to convince her that he was a genuine policeman, and for her to give him the room number. By the time she did so, he was sorely tempted to have her arrested on the grounds of threatening behaviour, i.e. behaviour that was threatening his mental health.

Once they were finally standing outside room 118, Ronan hammered on the door. 'Open up!' he shouted. 'This is the police!'

When there was no response, Ronan tried to kick the door in. As far as Carlyle could see, it didn't give an inch and he resigned himself to another argument downstairs with Louise, in order to gain a card key. However, just as he was heading back towards the lifts, a cleaner appeared round the corner hauling a cart filled with clean towels and replacement toiletries. Grabbing the startled woman by the arm, Carlyle waved his ID in her face and marched her to the door of 118. Snatching her pass key, Ronan thrust it in the slot, cursing when it failed to work. He tried it a second time, ramming the card in harder this time, but still without any joy.

'Slowly,' Carlyle advised. 'You've got to be gentle with it.'

'Fuck off!' Ronan muttered.

Shaking her head, the cleaner took the card out of his hand, carefully placed it in the door and slowly removed it again. As the door clicked open, Ronan pushed past her and rushed inside.

'Thank you,' said the inspector to the woman. 'Please wait here.'

Stepping through the door, he heard Ronan shout, 'Christ Almighty! Call an ambulance! Now!'

Carlyle fumbled in his pocket and pulled out his phone. As he waited for someone to pick up, he looked at Roche sitting up on the bed, clasping her head while Ronan looked on.

At least she's not dead, Carlyle thought, as he called in the details. The blood on the sergeant's hands and on her jacket, however, testified to a nasty head wound. Finishing the call, he stepped into the bathroom and stuck a towel under the hot water tap of the bath. Returning to the bedroom, he handed the damp towel to Roche.

'Thanks,' she said, giving Ronan a look that Carlyle could not decipher, before gingerly putting the towel to her head.

Carlyle located the mini-bar and tossed a couple of small bottles of mineral water on the bed. 'What happened?' he asked.

Roche picked up one of the bottles, unscrewed the cap and drank the contents in one go. 'What does it look like?' she snapped. 'That fucking bitch smacked me round the back of the head.'

Carlyle had never heard Roche swear before. He glanced at Ronan, who refused to make eye-contact.

'I need a fucking cigarette,' Roche declared.

'I'd wait until you've been to the hospital,' Ronan replied, turning away quickly when she shot him a dirty look.

There was a knock at the door and a paramedic entered the tiny vestibule. Glancing out into the corridor, Carlyle could see that the cleaner was still there, standing by her cart. *God bless you*, Carlyle thought, as he watched Roche being led away. People who did as they were told were as rare as hen's teeth. 'The woman in 118,' he asked, 'you haven't seen her this morning?'

The cleaner shook her head.

'Okay. Sorry for the hassle, but if you could wait a bit longer, we'll need to take a statement.'

The woman shrugged. It was no skin off her nose.

'Back in a minute.'

SURPRISINGLY, RONAN DID not offer to go along with Roche to the hospital. Leaning against the table with his arms folded, he watched Carlyle re-enter the room.

'Ali's gonna have a hell of a headache,' he reflected.

You could sound a bit more concerned, Carlyle thought. 'I'll take a look round in here,' he said. 'Why don't you see if you can track down Ms Swain?'

'All right,' said Ronan doubtfully, as if not sure he should be taking orders from Carlyle. 'I guess we're thinking she's not a journalist, after all.'

'Doesn't look like it,' Carlyle agreed. 'Most of the journalists I know do their violence with a pen.'

'Well, they do say that the pen is mightier than the sword,' Ronan quipped.

'Not in this case,' Carlyle said grimly, as he pulled open the doors of the wardrobe. 'Okay, let's get on with it. I'll let you know what I find.'

'If she's not a journalist,' Ronan wondered, 'what is she then?'

'God knows,' Carlyle sighed. 'Just another nutter who has arrived in our great city to cause us grief.' He gestured towards the corridor. 'On the way out, could you quickly check if the cleaning lady outside has anything useful to say, although I doubt it very much, then she can get back to work.'

'Okay.' Ronan grinned as he headed for the door. 'You know what this means, don't you?'

'What?'

'It looks like good old Sylvia wasn't trying to get into your pants, after all.'

'Yeah,' Carlyle laughed. 'Probably she just wanted to bash me over the head.'

Chapter Forty-eight

THE INSPECTOR PULLED a vinyl LP copy of *Strange Days* by The Doors out of a tattered cardboard box and peered around the cramped bedsit for a record-player.

'Do you have something to play this on?' he asked his father, who sat on the unmade bed, staring morosely out of the window at the cars speeding along the Westway.

'Er, no. I left the record-player at home. I'll fetch it later.'

Carlyle scratched his head in exasperation and dropped the record back in the box. 'So what did you bring the records for?'

His father just shrugged.

The room had only enough space for a single bed, a small wardrobe and a one-ring gas stove. On a chair in the corner sat a tiny TV. The wallpaper was peeling off the walls and the carpet didn't look like it had been cleaned in the last twenty years. All this for £165 a week. It was the most depressing place Carlyle had ever seen in his life.

'Come on,' he sighed, 'let's go and get a drink.'

THEY SAT IN the otherwise empty Queen and Artichoke pub, each nursing a pint of cold Grolsch lager. Carlyle wasn't in the mood for a drink, but drinking was easier than talking, so his glass was quickly empty. Getting to his feet, he gestured towards the bar. 'Fancy another one?'

His father nodded assent although his glass was still more than half-full. Crossing the room, Carlyle wondered why he had come at all and, more to the point, how quickly he could reasonably leave. As the barman poured their pints, he checked both of his phones in the hope that someone had called him. They hadn't. With a sigh, he paid for the drinks and returned to his father's table.

'So,' Carlyle said, after taking a sip, 'what are you going to do now?'

'I don't know, really,' said his father, keeping his eyes fixed on his drink. 'I suppose I never imagined that your mother would throw me out. The whole thing happened so long ago.'

You should have kept your mouth shut, Carlyle thought, *you bloody idiot*. 'Maybe she just needs a bit of time to calm down. Then you can put all this behind you.'

Alexander Carlyle laughed grimly. 'I don't think so. Not with your mother. Once she's got the bit between her teeth, that's it.' He looked up at his son and smiled sadly. 'Where do you think you got your own bloody-minded streak from?'

'Me?' Carlyle laughed in mock amazement. 'Bloody-minded?'

'Aye, you are, lad. And you know it fine well. Just like your mother.' Alexander took another swallow of his pint. 'I've seen that look in her eye before, many, many times. It means I won't be going back.'

Not wishing to think about the implications of that bald statement, Carlyle changed tack. 'What about the woman?'

His father looked at him sharply. 'The woman I had the affair with?'

'Yes.'

'Maureen Sullivan. You don't remember her?'

'No.' Carlyle shook his head. 'Not at all.'

'Well, it was a long time ago now. She was a perfectly nice woman, but it was just a passing thing. I only saw her for a couple of months, while your mother was up in Scotland. She was never a threat to our marriage, if you know what I mean.' He paused for a moment, reflecting on what he'd just said, before adding, 'At least, not as far as I was concerned.'

'I see,' Carlyle lied. He took a couple more mouthfuls of lager. What the fuck was the old fella on about?

Alexander finished off his first pint and started on the second. 'Anyway, she's dead.'

'Oh?' Carlyle mumbled into his glass.

'About fifteen years ago now. Cancer.'

'Bummer.'

'These things happen.' Alexander shrugged. 'Your mother and I went to her funeral. It was a horrible day, terrible weather. I remember it quite well, for some reason.'

Carlyle drained the last of his pint. *That's enough*, he told himself. *You shouldn't have another.*

'My round,' said his father, grabbing Carlyle's glass and heading for the bar.

HE WAS STARING into space when Roche appeared at his desk, sipping a mug of black coffee. Still recovering from her run-in with Sylvia Swain, she looked tired and a bit spaced.

'How's the head?' the inspector asked.

'Not too bad.' Roche carefully placed a hand on the tender spot behind her left ear, where she had been sandbagged. 'I got given a dozen stitches and as many painkillers as I can swallow. It'll be fine.'

'Shouldn't you take some time off? Go and let Ronan make a fuss of you?'

Roche grunted something into her coffee. 'Have you tracked that Canadian bitch down yet?'

'Not yet.' After four pints of lager with his father, Carlyle didn't really feel on top of his game. 'The hotel room was empty of her stuff. And I haven't heard anything from Dave – David. He's trying to track her down.'

'Good luck with that,' she scowled. 'Anyway, you've got a message from another woman.'

'Oh?'

'Yeah. Someone called Louisa says you need to give her a call. You have her number apparently.'

Louisa? It took Carlyle a moment to place the name.

'Turning into a right babe-magnet,' Roche grinned, 'aren't you, Inspector?'

'Hardly,' Carlyle sighed, picking up the phone.

Chapter Forty-nine

THE INSPECTOR HAD chosen Speakers' Corner in Hyde Park as the location for the meeting. It was a venue that he had used many times before – one of the few Central London locations where you could hide in plain sight, while also not having to worry about being overlooked by dozens of security cameras. Louisa had wanted to come straight to the station, but Carlyle, conscious of his 'deal' with Sol Abramyan, wished to keep his options open. He wanted to find out what Fadi Kashkesh was able to deliver before deciding how best to proceed. Assuming the little bugger turned up at all, of course.

At least on that score he was pleasantly surprised. When the inspector arrived, Fadi was already sitting on a bench next to a fast-food kiosk, staring at his trainers. Next to him sat an unshaven man in a Fila tracksuit. Standing over both of them was Louisa Arbillot, munching on a hotdog.

Leaning on a nearby fence, Carlyle studied the strange trio. He needed a piss but was reluctant to nip to the toilets next to the kiosk in case the two men decided to do a runner. He was fairly confident that he could be back in less than a minute, but still didn't want to risk it. Waiting for Louisa to finish her snack, he walked over to confront Fadi. 'So,' he said, placing a shoe on the bench, 'are you going to introduce me?'

Fadi looked up at his wife.

Louisa scowled at her estranged husband. 'For God's sake,' she said, 'how many times do I have to tell you? Here, in England, you help the police.'

Carlyle exchanged a glance with the guy in the tracksuit. The pair of them knew that they were thinking the same thing: Fadi was a very lucky man.

'Inspector . . .' Fadi began, as if every word was being torn from his throat, 'this is Adnan.'

About fucking time, Carlyle thought. He smiled and did a little bow. 'Good to meet you, Adnan.'

Adnan nodded, but did not say anything.

'He doesn't speak any English,' Louisa interjected, pulling the tab on a can of Coke and drinking down half of it in one go. 'Only German and Arabic.'

'Can you translate?' Carlyle asked her.

'No.' She shook her head. 'I've got a little Spanish but no German. But Fadi can.'

The two men on the bench mumbled something to each other.

'Adnan is the man you are looking for,' Fadi said quietly. 'He is the only one of them that the Israelis have not killed.'

Yet. 'So why is he still here?'

'Very good question,' Louisa interjected, before finishing off her Coke.

More mumbling, rather more animated this time, with some hand-waving and what sounded like cursing to Carlyle.

'He doesn't have a passport,' Fadi said. 'They took it off him when he arrived. He cannot leave. He is very scared.'

On cue, Adnan nodded and stuck a worried look on his face.

'He will need to come with me, then,' said Carlyle. His bladder was demanding that he take a slash right now, and he wanted to get this wrapped up as quickly as possible.

'What will happen to him?'

'Well, he won't get his guns,' Carlyle said, 'but he won't get killed either. So it's not all bad.'

This time, when Fadi translated, Adnan jumped to his feet. Jabbing Carlyle in the chest with a meaty finger, he began shouting angrily. Amazingly, Louisa had wandered off to buy herself something else to eat from the kiosk.

Carlyle took a step backwards and glanced at Fadi.

'He says he will be killed if he goes back with you. You will murder him.'

Carlyle held up his hands. 'I'm not going to kill anyone. I will help him apply for asylum.' He nodded towards Louisa, who was now returning with a pretzel. 'You and Louisa will be able to help him too.'

Fadi looked doubtful, even more so at the mention of his wife. But whatever he said had the effect of calming Adnan, who retreated to the bench and sat back down.

'Thanks for that,' said Carlyle, still desperate for a pee. Taking his mobile out of his pocket, he said, 'I just need to make a call, and then we're good to go.' Hopping from foot to foot, he watched the last of the pretzel disappear down Louisa's throat. 'Keep an eye on these two for a moment,' he began, striding quickly towards the toilets, 'while I take a quick leak.'

SHIELDED FROM ONLOOKERS by a massive oak tree, Richard Assulin slipped on a pair of latex gloves and casually attached the YHM Cobra suppressor to his Glock 19. Clicking off the safety, he turned to Sid Lieberman.

'Now?'

Lieberman nodded.

'And the policeman as well?'

Lieberman pulled a face. 'Up to you. If you can avoid it, fine. But if you have to . . .'

'Okay.'

Lieberman looked at his watch. 'You've got an hour and a half to get to the airport.'

'No problem.'

'See you in Tel Aviv.' Patting Assulin on the arm, Lieberman ambled away in the direction of the Park Lane underpass.

Running his hand across the top of his shaven head, Assulin counted to five as he watched the military attaché depart the scene. Then, standing up straight, he marched purposefully towards his targets.

STILL FEELING HUNGRY, Louisa Arbillot wondered about finishing her fast-food binge with a crêpe and a coffee. She jerked a thumb in the direction of the kiosk. 'Do you guys want anything?' Fadi gave her the briefest of glances, shaking his head. Adnan, however, happily overcame both his lack of English and his girth to spring quickly to his feet.

'Come on,' Louisa smiled, happy to be able to appeal to at least one man through his stomach. 'Let's see what you want.'

She had almost reached the kiosk when she heard a popping noise, followed closely by another. She turned in time to see Adnan hit the ground. Then, looking past him, she saw her husband lying on his back, staring expressionlessly at the sky. There was a bloody hole right in the centre of his forehead.

'No!' Louisa felt a warmth spread across her crotch and trickle down her legs as her bladder failed. 'Fadi!'. As she staggered towards him, Louisa saw a tall skinny man in a Nirvana T-shirt suddenly step between them. As she got closer, he raised the gun but Louisa kept advancing, with tears streaming down her face.

'*Fils de salope!*' she hissed, even as she took the third round right between the eyes.

'AAAHHH!' CARLYLE CAME to the end of a long, satisfying piss. After a quick shake, he zipped himself up. Not bothering to wash his hands, he headed back outside. As he stepped back onto the path, a constable and a WPC from Westminster's Cycling Squad rode slowly past on their mountain bikes, chatting away. Not the worst job in the world, Carlyle reckoned. He watched as the woman laughed at something her colleague said, then both of them stopped and were looking at something further down the path, hidden behind the kiosk. Almost instantly, the young woman's head snapped backwards, and she was thrown from her bike. As the PC reached for his radio, he was hit once, twice in the chest and collapsed on top of his bike.

It took Carlyle less than a second to understand what was going on. Another woman had been walking behind the downed police officers, ice cream in hand: as soon as she saw the blood spreading across the concrete, she started screaming her head off. Racing round to the rear of the kiosk, Carlyle almost tripped over the bodies of Louisa Arbillot and Adnan. Kneeling, he quickly confirmed that they were both dead. Not even needing to check on Fadi, he rushed back to inspect the two coppers.

Someone started retching. Looking up, the inspector saw that a crowd was quickly growing. Waving his badge above his head, he screamed at the gawkers to stay back. As the sirens approached from the direction of Oxford Street, he wondered just how the fuck he was going to explain this latest fiasco.

Chapter Fifty

'Do you want a drink?' Alison Roche asked.

'Got any whisky?'

'Of course not.'

'In that case, a coffee would be great. The stronger the better.'

He watched Roche disappear inside the empty kiosk and start banging about, trying to work the complicated-looking coffee machine.

'What happened to the guy serving here?' Carlyle asked no one in particular.

'He took two in the head as well,' David Ronan replied, matter-of-factly.

'Ah.' With a terrible sick feeling gnawing at his intestines, Carlyle scanned the scene. A forty-yard stretch of the park on either side of the kiosk had been sealed off. Beyond the police tape, a crowd of maybe 100 people had gathered, swelled by half-a-dozen or so TV crews and a deal more reporters. The satellite trucks illegally parked all along Park Lane had attracted a swarm of traffic wardens, who were happily writing ticket after ticket as excited television producers equally happily ignored them. Somewhere amid the scrum, Commander Simpson was doing a round of interviews, dispensing the usual platitudes, promising that the perpetrators would be brought to justice. As if.

'Makes a grand total of six,' Ronan remarked. 'Four men and two women.'

I can fucking count, Carlyle thought angrily, but he knew that all of his frustration should rightly be directed at himself.

'Both women and two of the men were taken out with one shot each.' Ronan gestured over his shoulder. 'The PC on the bike and the guy in the kiosk were both shot twice.'

'Eight shots, six bodies. Professional job.'

'Extremely professional,' Ronan agreed.

With his hands resting on his hips, Carlyle closed his eyes. Pushing his head back and then down, he tried to halt the progress of the monster migraine relentlessly building at the base of his skull.

'You were fucking lucky. That was a very good time to go for a leak.'

'Yeah.' *What was it with him and toilets?* Carlyle wondered. Not so long ago he'd survived a bomb blast by going for a timely dump. *I must be the only bloke in the world who's escaped death twice by answering the call of nature.* Struck by the stupidity of it all, he started laughing.

'What's so funny?' the detective inspector demanded.

'Nothing.' Carlyle opened his eyes and quickly composed himself. 'I was taking a piss over there,' he explained, gesturing towards the toilets. 'I came out, saw the guys on the bikes, saw them get shot . . .'

'Did you see who did it?'

'No,' Carlyle said, 'the kiosk blocked my line of sight. I came round the back and saw the other three bodies.'

'And the gunman was already gone?'

I wouldn't know, Carlyle thought, *because I didn't bloody look*. 'Yes.'

'We found the gun dumped amongst the rubbish over there.' Ronan pointed to a waste-bin about five feet away from where Fadi's corpse lay under a blue plastic sheet.

'If he dumped it, it will be clean,' Carlyle sighed.

'Of course.'

After a short while, Roche returned with three small paper cups, each filled near to the brim with a steaming black oily liquid.

Carlyle took a mouthful and almost had the back of his throat burned off. Once he'd finished coughing, he turned to Roche and smiled grimly. 'Perfect.'

Ronan sipped his coffee more carefully. 'Could you maybe have kept us more in the loop on this?' he asked, raising his eyes from his plastic cup.

They were both studying him. Carlyle took a deep breath and slowly explained the connection to Fadi, via Louisa Arbillot, taking time to work out how he was going to spin himself being the catalyst for a massacre in Hyde bloody Park. 'I didn't know for sure that Fadi would turn up,' he said by way of a conclusion. 'And I had no idea that he would bring the other guy. Mossad must have already had them under surveillance.'

'We've already identified the guy in the tracksuit as Adnan Al Bzoor,' said Ronan. 'A relatively low-level Hamas fixer.'

Carlyle nodded. 'Fadi told me that he was the last of the cell left in London.' He aimlessly scanned the middle distance. 'Job now done for the Israelis. At least that should be the end of it.'

'Maybe,' said Ronan doubtfully.

'We still have to bloody catch them,' said Roche. 'Three dead officers . . .'

'Of course,' Carlyle nodded. 'Absolutely.' The adrenalin was wearing off and he felt a huge weariness descend on his shoulders. He drank the rest of his oily coffee and crushed the cup in his fist. 'We have to catch them.' It wasn't the same as saying they *would* catch them, but it was the best he could manage.

'You've got a long night ahead of you, then,' Ronan declared. 'At this rate, you'll get your own IPCC team.'

'IIC too,' Roche laughed.

'Great,' Carlyle replied. Over Roche's shoulder, he saw Simpson duck under the police tape and head towards them. As she got closer, he could make out the look on her face and knew that he had more immediate things to worry about than any internal investigations.

CARLYLE WATCHED ROCHE and Ronan melt away as the Commander approached. At first, Simpson seemed too angry to speak.

'You haven't resigned, then?' Despite everything, Carlyle couldn't resist the quip.

'The way the bodies are piling up,' she said brusquely, 'it has been rather hard to find the time.'

Together they turned to watch a trio of ambulances slowly roll up to the police tape, in preparation for the removal of the bodies.

Suddenly solicitous, Simpson eyed Carlyle. 'Are you okay?'

'I'm fine,' he said earnestly, before breaking into a grin. 'It was certainly one of the most memorable pit stops of my life.'

She gently took hold of his arm. 'Can you try and be serious for just one minute?'

Hating this kind of lecture, Carlyle took half a step away from her.

'You have been incredibly, *incredibly* lucky here today. You can joke about it all you like but no one, least of all you, knows what the psychiatric impact might be.'

Carlyle sighed theatrically, lowering his gaze to the ground.

'You can continue to work with Ronan,' Simpson said, 'but you will have to see a police psychiatrist as a matter of routine.'

'But last time—'

Simpson raised her hand and cut him off. 'By "last time", I presume you are referring to when young Horatio Mosman got blown to kingdom come.'

'When, once again, I was in the bog, taking a—'

'Yes, yes,' she said irritably. 'I would assume there are shorter odds on winning the lottery. Anyway, the point is I should have sent you to get some help back then. The Federation were very unhappy about the way things were handled. This time, they will insist on counselling for every officer who attends this crime scene, even me. Apart from anything else, it will be necessary for any compensation claim that might be forthcoming.'

'Compensation?'

'If you end up wanting to make a claim for stress or emotional damage or something.'

'Me?' Carlyle snorted. 'So you're worried that I might sue the Met because I *didn't* get shot dead?'

'No, I know that you wouldn't,' said Simpson crossly. 'You are not that kind of officer. But for once, please, just go by the book.'

Carlyle watched as the first of the corpses, the policewoman, was lifted onto a trolley and loaded into the back of an ambulance. 'Who was she?' he asked.

'WPC Karen Abbot,' said Simpson grimly. 'Twenty-five. No kids thankfully, but she was engaged. The wedding was due—'

Now it was Carlyle's turn to raise his hand. 'Okay, okay. I get the picture.'

Simpson gave him a hard stare.

'And, yes, I'll go and see the shrink.'

'Good,' said Simpson. 'I'll have one turn up at Charing Cross at nine a.m.'

He was about to protest but thought better of it.

'Now go home and see your family. Give Alice a big kiss.'

Surprised that Simpson remembered his daughter's name, Carlyle said nothing. After a moment's pause, he began walking slowly in the direction of Hyde Park Corner, away from the crowds and the journalists.

'And, John,' Simpson shouted after him, 'you're right. I have decided to stay. I'm not retiring – not yet anyway.'

'Never doubted it for a minute,' he yelled back over his shoulder, quickly lengthening his stride.

Chapter Fifty-one

'DAD'S HOME!'

When Alice rushed into the hallway and jumped into his arms, almost knocking him over, he felt an overwhelming urge to burst into tears. After Helen appeared a moment later, he buried his head in her shoulder as he fought for control.

'We saw you on the TV!' Alice proclaimed.

'You could have bloody called,' Helen scolded, embracing him tightly.

'Yes,' he said, and cleared his throat. 'Sorry.' Composing himself, he stepped back to close the door.

'What happened?' Alice asked.

Carlyle smiled wanly. 'Just a bad day at the office.' Slipping off his shoes, he headed for the kitchen.

Helen appeared in the doorway as he filled the kettle. 'Was it the same people that killed Joe?'

'Yeah,' Carlyle replied, closing the lid and switching the kettle on. 'I think so.'

Alice squeezed past her mother, her brow creased with concern. 'Is someone trying to get you, Dad?'

'No, sweetheart.' He bent over, kissing her hard on the top of her forehead. 'I'm trying to get *them*.' He ignored Helen, who was rolling her eyes to the ceiling, and changed the subject. 'Your mum tells me that we're having your friend Stuart round to tea.'

Alice's cheeks went a shade of bright pink. 'Dad!' She folded her arms and gave him a fierce look. 'I haven't even asked him, or anything.'

'Well,' said Carlyle, grinning at Helen, 'we're looking forward to meeting him.'

'Yeah, whatever.' Still blushing furiously, Alice turned and fled to the safety of her bedroom.

'That was well handled,' said Helen sarkily, dropping a couple of teabags – white for her, green for Carlyle – into two mugs and adding boiling water from the kettle.

'Thanks.' Using the very tips of his fingers, Carlyle carefully dunked the bag a couple of times, before lifting it out and dropping it on a saucer waiting on the draining board.

Leaving her own teabag in the mug, Helen took a cautious sip of her tea. 'There was no need for you to embarrass her like that.'

'Come on,' Carlyle protested, 'it's not a big deal.'

'It is to her.'

'Would you prefer me to talk about how six people got shot in the park today?' he asked angrily. 'Including your friend Louisa – who was despatched to the great hotdog-stand in the sky.' He regretted the words as soon as they were out of his mouth, but at least Helen was used to his potential for crassness.

She blanched. 'They're not saying a lot on the news. What exactly happened?'

Carlyle quickly ran through some heavily edited highlights.

'Fucking hell, John,' was her only response.

Putting down his tea, he gave her a hug. 'The important thing to realize is that it's over now. Everybody who the Israelis wanted dead is now dead. To them, Joe was only collateral damage. No one is coming after me either.'

'What about you going after them, like you told Alice?' she asked, pulling away from him.

He shook his head. 'Never going to happen. The people responsible for this will be long gone by now. Even if they were still in London, which they're not, the Met doesn't have any jurisdiction. These guys are soldiers and I'm just a cop – a British cop at that. Not much use to anyone when the shooting starts.'

'Jesus, John.'

For a moment, they stood silently sipping their tea, each keeping any doubts and fears unspoken.

Chapter Fifty-two

THE PSYCHIATRIST THAT Simpson had sent him was a short, wizened gent with long grey hair, a complete inability to maintain eye-contact, and an accent that Carlyle couldn't place. Every time he spoke, the shrink would end up staring at his shoes as if lost in his own thoughts. Carlyle simply nodded and watched the minute hand of the clock on the wall tick round increasingly slowly.

After twenty minutes, there was a knock and Alison Roche stuck her head round the door. The shrink looked up, bemused.

'I'm very sorry, Inspector,' Roche said, trying her best to look disconcerted, 'but I need to speak to you.'

Just about managing to keep a straight face, Carlyle nodded towards the psychiatrist. 'Can it wait?' he asked. 'I'm in a meeting right now.'

Roche dropped her gaze to the floor. 'I'm afraid that it's really quite urgent, sir.'

'Okay,' Carlyle sighed, slowly getting to his feet. He turned to the shrink. 'Apologies, but I need to confer with my sergeant.'

The man shrugged but said nothing.

Trying not to break into a run, Carlyle shuffled out of the door, pushing Roche in front of him.

'You took your time,' he said in mock annoyance once they had retreated further along the corridor.

'You said twenty minutes,' Roche smiled, 'so I gave you precisely twenty minutes. Was he any use?'

'Of course not,' Carlyle snorted. 'Now let's go and get a coffee.'

THEY CELEBRATED HIS escape from the forces of psychobabble with a trip to Carluccio's on Rose Street. Sitting in one of the red leather booths, Carlyle sipped a double macchiato and nibbled on an almond croissant, while Roche had a glass of herbal tea. Waiting until he had finished his pastry, she reached into her bag and took out a copy of a grainy black-and-white photo. Placing it on the table, she pushed it over to Carlyle, who gave the image a careful once-over. It was clearly a still taken from a security camera positioned in the entrance to a tube station. Various people were entering and exiting through the barriers, but it wasn't clear which one he should be interested in.

'What am I looking at?' he asked.

Roche leaned across the table and tapped a finger next to the head of the man nearest the camera, who was passing through a barrier and into the station. Carlyle noticed that Alison was wearing green nail polish. *Green*, he thought, *I've never seen that before.* Somehow it seemed out of character, although, if pushed, he would have to admit that he didn't have the first clue about Roche's character.

'Who is he?'

'That is Sid Lieberman. He's a military attaché at the Israeli Embassy.' She moved her finger to the time and date stamp in the top right-hand corner of the image. 'This shows him entering Marble Arch underground station just after the shooting started at Hyde Park Corner.'

Carlyle did the maths. The tube was a walk of only two or three minutes from the spot where Fadi, Louisa and the others had been murdered.

'David sent this over this morning.'

'Does he really think this guy is the killer?'

'No.' Roche shook her head. 'Too senior. More likely a handler. But David thinks he was definitely involved.'

Carlyle tried to recall noticing anyone who might have been Lieberman hanging around the park before he had gone to take a piss, but his mind remained a blank. Still, this constituted progress. 'How did SO15 manage to dig out this image?' he asked.

'Dunno,' Roche said. 'Luck, I guess.'

'Well, it's about bloody time we had some of that.' Carlyle jumped to his feet. 'Let's go and see your boyfriend and find out what he's intending to do next.'

RONAN'S HECKLER & Koch P30 didn't set off the metal detector. Carlyle's house keys did. Shaking his head, he allowed the guard to pat him down before he was buzzed through the turnstile that led to a further set of security doors. Having been buzzed through those, they headed down a long hallway before eventually turning into the reception area.

Standing between Ronan and Roche, Carlyle patiently waited for the woman behind the desk to finish her phone call. A small badge above her left breast said that her name was Shahar. Looking her up and down, he guessed she was in her early twenties. Her jet-black hair was cut short; her face was pinched and unsympathetic. She was wearing a sleeveless white T-shirt, revealing stick-like arms which reinforced the sense that what the woman needed above all else was a good feed. Having already worked himself into a foul mood, Carlyle took an instant dislike to young Shahar.

Finishing her call, the receptionist looked up at Roche and flashed a fake smile. 'Good morning,' she trilled. 'How can I help you?'

'We are here to see Mr Lieberman,' Roche replied primly.

Shahar looked down a list of internal numbers and picked up the phone. 'Where are you from?'

'The Metropolitan Police,' Roche told her.

A scowl crossed the woman's face but she dialled the number and listened to it ring for several seconds. 'I'm afraid there's no reply,' she said, holding the receiver away from her ear.

Fuck this, thought Carlyle, declaring, 'Then we'll see the Ambassador.' In a previous case a few years earlier, he'd been helped hugely by the Chilean Ambassador after coming across a similar problem with a rogue employee. The experience had reinforced the maxim: *If in doubt, go straight to the top.* It suddenly struck him how the perpetrator in that particular case, a scumbag called Matias Gori, had been a military attaché as well. *Why do we let all these fuckers into the country?* he wondered.

'You need to have an appointment,' Shahar said curtly, 'if you wish to see the Ambassador.'

Carlyle pulled a pair of Hiatt Speedcuffs out of his back pocket and waved them in front of the receptionist's face. 'Do you know what obstruction of justice means?'

'Inspector.' Roche put a restraining hand on his shoulder, but he shrugged it off.

'You have to have an appointment,' the woman repeated defiantly.

'Right!' Carlyle marched round the desk, hauled the woman to her feet, pulled her hands behind her back and roughly snapped on the cuffs, making them tight so that they wouldn't slip off her skinny wrists. Ignoring the amused look in Ronan's eyes, he pushed Shahar back into the chair. 'You are now under arrest,' he hissed as the receptionist burst into tears. 'You do not have to say anything, but it may harm your defence if you do not mention when questioned, something which you may later rely on in court. Anything that you do say may be given in evidence.'

'What is going on here?'

The three of them turned away from the unfortunate Shahar to find themselves facing a middle-aged woman carrying a stack of papers, with a young male flunky in tow.

'Police,' said Ronan firmly as he flashed his ID.

'What have you done to Shahar?' the woman snapped. 'You understand that you have no authority here.'

'First things first,' Carlyle snapped back. 'Who are you?'

Shocked at the way his boss was being spoken to, the lackey looked as if his eyes were going to pop out. Her own eyes blazing, the woman took a step forward. If her hands weren't already full, Carlyle reckoned that he would have been odds on to receive a good hard slap.

'I'm Hilary Waxman, the Israeli Ambassador to London.'

'Shall I call Security?' the lackey squeaked.

Joining in the fun, Ronan pulled back his jacket to give everyone a glimpse of his P30.

Waxman eyed the gun carefully. 'It's okay, Daniel,' she said. 'Let's all just calm down, shall we? I'm sure that these officers can explain what is going on here.'

'We have an arrest warrant for one Sidney David Lieberman,' said Ronan, tapping his jacket pocket.

'As I said before,' Waxman stated patiently, 'you do not have any authority here in my Embassy.'

Roche smiled maliciously. 'We are perfectly aware of the situation,' she said. 'However, given your extremely good relationship with our country *and* your obvious desire to see the rule of law upheld, we feel sure that you will wish to offer us every possible assistance in this matter.'

Tapping her foot on the carpet, Waxman gave Roche a look that screamed *Go fuck yourself.* After a moment, she thrust the papers at her aide. 'Daniel, deal with these as we discussed.' As the lackey scurried off, she turned back to the police officers. 'Let's talk about this in my office.' She nodded towards Shahar, who was sitting, head bowed, mumbling to herself in a slightly hysterical manner. '*After* you've uncuffed our receptionist.'

SITTING IN WAXMAN'S office, Carlyle wasn't going to pass up on the chance to further wind up their host. 'Any chance of a cup of tea?' he grinned.

Settling herself behind her desk, the Ambassador simply ignored this impudent request. 'You are in deep trouble, all of you, as a result of this outrageous and *criminal* behaviour. Apart from anything else, if I hadn't turned up when I did, Security could have shot you.' The tiniest of grins tickled the corners of her mouth. 'And I think that the London Police Service has lost enough officers recently, don't you?'

Gritting his teeth, Carlyle said nothing.

'So,' Waxman continued, 'let's see what we can do to try and avoid a diplomatic incident, and perhaps even save your jobs along the way.' She paused, directing her gaze at DI Ronan before asking, 'What precisely do you want with Mr Lieberman?'

'The nature of the investigation is confidential,' Ronan answered stiffly, 'and also the investigation is ongoing, so I am afraid that we cannot go into details.'

Waxman shook her head sadly, as if every last ounce of her patience had already been wasted by these state-sanctioned idiots in front of her. 'So how can I help you,' she enquired, 'if I don't know what you need?'

'What we need,' Roche chipped in, 'is to speak to Mr Lieberman.'

Waxman inspected each of them in turn. 'I'm afraid that he is not here.'

'Where is he?' Carlyle demanded.

'I have no idea,' she shot back. 'Sid Lieberman is a very senior colleague. I am not his keeper.'

'Has he left the country?' Roche probed.

Waxman shrugged. 'It is possible. Travel, after all, is an integral part of a diplomat's job.'

'He's hardly a diplomat,' Carlyle snorted, 'is he?'

Waxman drummed her fingers angrily on the table-top. 'If you cannot be polite, Inspector,' she said sharply, 'I do not see the point of continuing with this meeting.'

'Fine.' Carlyle quickly got to his feet, followed by Roche and Ronan. 'We will need Mr Lieberman's home address in London, along with any contact details you have for him in Israel and elsewhere.'

'Of course,' Waxman said, lowering her gaze. 'If you make a formal request, through the proper channels – that is to say the

Foreign Office – I am sure that we will be able to do what we can to help you.'

Fuck you, thought Carlyle.

Screw you, too, thought Waxman. 'Thank you for coming.' She reached for the phone on her desk. 'I will get my assistant to see you out.'

Chapter Fifty-three

'In his assessment, Dr Wolf thought that you were both engaged and responsive,' Simpson said, sounding suitably surprised. 'He used the phrase "mentally robust." '

Carlyle sat back in his chair and casually lifted his feet onto his desk. 'Good,' he said, happy that Simpson, on the other end of the line, could not witness the dismissive gesture he made with his hand.

'He thinks that there will be no need to make any note in your file . . .'

'Excellent.'

'. . . once you've completed an agreed number of sessions.'

Typical, Carlyle thought. *Everyone is on the make, even the shrinks. Especially the shrinks.* Now, however, wasn't the time to antagonize his boss by complaining. 'Fine,' he said, trying to keep the total lack of enthusiasm out of his voice.

'I will get the doctor's office to arrange some times,' said Simpson briskly, knowing that she had to press home her advantage immediately, before the inspector tried to wriggle off his hook.

'Okay. So, where are we on the other things?'

'I've heard no more about the Hooper investigation,' Simpson sighed, 'but you should get the chance to speak to Ambrose Watson about that soon enough.'

'Oh?'

'Yes. He will be part of the ICC investigation into Hyde Park.' She let out a small chuckle. 'They clearly seem to think that old Ambrose is becoming a bit of an expert on you. You could become the first officer in the Met to have his own dedicated Internal Investigations Command handler.'

Ha, bloody ha. 'I'm sure I wouldn't be the first,' Carlyle said tartly.

'I expect to be speaking to both the IIC and the IPCC during the next couple of days,' Simpson continued, 'so we'll see where things stand after that. I should imagine that both investigations should be relatively straightforward.'

Compared to the Hooper case, Carlyle thought, anything would be straightforward.

'You are building up quite a track record, though, John.'

The inspector merely grunted.

'Every time your name appears in regard to another investigation, it becomes more likely that someone is going to discern a pattern emerging.'

'What pattern?' Carlyle frowned.

'I didn't say that there actually *was* a pattern,' Simpson told him, 'but that isn't going to stop someone at IIC from looking for one. That's what they do. It's what *we* do, for that matter.'

'Mm.'

'You may think he's a bit of a loser, but good old Ambrose is very fair. Some of his colleagues might turn out to be less so if they come to believe that you are in some way dodgy, and then decide to go after you.'

'Everyone gets investigated,' Carlyle shrugged, 'even you.'

'Yes, they do,' Simpson agreed, 'but not with regard to two separate cases involving multiple homicide, at the same time – including the multiple homicide of fellow officers.'

'Point taken. I will be on my best behaviour from now on.'

'No, John,' Simpson said, '*your* best behaviour isn't going to be good enough in a situation like this. You'll need to raise your game beyond that.'

'Yes, sir!' Carlyle laughed.

'And be professional with Ambrose. He could be an important ally for you in all of this – assuming, of course, that you have nothing to hide.'

'Why,' Carlyle wondered aloud, 'would I have anything to hide?'

Chapter Fifty-four

SITTING IN THE kitchen of his parents' flat – correction, his *mother's* flat – in Fulham, Carlyle sipped his tea as he scanned the room. The place looked absolutely the same as he remembered from his previous visits in recent years. There was nothing to suggest that his father was no longer living here. On the other hand, there was nothing to suggest that he had ever been here at all. Pulling his private, pay-as-you-go mobile out of his pocket, he switched it on and dialled 901, only to be told that he had no new messages. He checked the call log and saw that he had three missed calls from an unknown number. Assuming that these were from Dominic Silver, he rang him.

Dom picked up on the third ring. 'You always reply in the end, don't you?' he laughed.

'I've been kind of busy,' Carlyle said.

'I can see that,' Dom replied, the laughter gone. 'You've been all over the bloody TV. You need to be more careful.'

'Tell me about it.'

'Sol is not happy now that his deal has gone completely tits up.'

'I can imagine,' Carlyle said, 'but there's not a lot I could have done about it.'

'You had a deal.'

'I know we had a bloody deal,' Carlyle snapped, nodding to his mother who had reappeared in the kitchen to make herself a cup of tea, 'but what happened wasn't entirely within my power and control, was it?'

'I suppose not,' said Dom grudgingly.

'So, if the fu—' glancing at his mother, he lowered his voice. 'So, if the deal is off, I completely understand.'

'How very generous of you,' Dom sneered. 'Don't forget that this also involves my relationship with my client.'

Taking a seat at the table, Lorna Gordon daintily sipped tea while shamelessly eavesdropping on her son's conversation. Opening a packet of biscuits, she offered Carlyle a chocolate digestive. When he declined, she took one, broke it in two and stuck one half in her mouth.

'So what do you suggest that I do?' Carlyle hissed down the phone.

'THAT ALL SOUNDED very interesting,' said Lorna drily, once Carlyle had ended his call.

'Just work.' Carlyle dropped the phone into an inside pocket. Changing his mind, he extracted a biscuit from the packet and began munching it noisily.

She gave him one of her stern looks. 'Your work seems very dangerous at the moment. It must be incredibly stressful for Helen – and Alice too.'

'It comes with the job,' Carlyle mumbled through a mouthful of crumbs. He reached over to the packet for another, but his mother slapped his hand away.

'Well,' she said, 'if that's what the job involves, perhaps it's time to think about doing something else.'

Carlyle stared at her, shocked. Originally, neither of his parents had wanted him to be a policeman but, after a couple of arguments, they had accepted his decision. Once he had started his training, it had never again been a topic of discussion. As far as he was concerned, his career was none of their business.

'Surely now, as a parent yourself, you can understand how hard it is for me to see you getting shot at?'

'Ma . . .'

'What about your friend? What about *his* mother?'

Carlyle didn't have the heart to tell her that Joe Szyszkowski's mother had died ten years ago. Sipping more tea, he waited for her to finish saying her piece.

'It was never like this in the beginning. Now it seems that it's just a matter of time before it's you yourself that goes and gets shot. This is all just too dangerous. Your family shouldn't have to put up with this. That's not right.'

An idea popped into his head and a large grin spread across his face.

'What's so funny?'

Carlyle stuck up a hand. 'Nothing, nothing.'

'People might start thinking that you like causing all this upset.'

'Not at all.' He finished his tea. 'It's just the job.'

'Pah! That's such an easy thing to say.'

'Ma, enough! I understand what you're saying.'

'So why don't you do something about it?'

This time he held up both hands. 'Okay, okay, I will pack the job in . . .'

She eyed him suspiciously.

'. . . if you and Dad get back together.'

Lorna put her mug down on the table and folded her arms. 'This is nothing to do with your father and me.'

Mimicking her body language, Carlyle took a deep breath. 'You talk about being stressed out by my job – well, what stresses *me* out is you two behaving like children.' Ignoring the shock on her face, he ploughed on. 'Whatever happened years – *decades* – ago, you should be able to sort it out. Whatever mistakes the old fella made, he should be able to make amends without being condemned to some shitty bedsit in Hammersmith for the rest of his life. For God's sake, what good does this do anyone?'

'This is something that your father and I have to deal with ourselves,' she replied quietly.

'He wants to come back.'

'I'm sure he does.'

'So,' he smiled, 'I'm offering you a deal.'

She tried to smile back but couldn't quite manage it. 'John,' she said eventually, 'I don't think that there's any chance of your father and me getting back together.'

'Why not?' he asked, exasperated beyond belief by her stubbornness.

Her gaze drifted towards the window. 'Because I've started seeing someone else.'

'What the fuck?' he stammered.

'John Carlyle! I will not have that kind of language in my house. Swearing is the sign of a poor education and a limited vocabulary.'

Don't try and bullshit your way out of this, Mother, Carlyle thought, gritting his teeth. 'Does Dad know about this?'

'It's none of his business,' she said tartly. 'And, for that matter, it's none of your business either.'

'Spoken by the woman who just told me I had to pack in my job because she didn't care for it.'

'That is something completely different,' she harrumphed. 'Don't you want me to enjoy some happiness?'

'I want you to grow up.'

'My conscience is clear.'

'It's not your conscience that I'm worried about.'

'Look,' she said firmly, pointing a bony index finger at his chest, 'we only get one shot at this life – all of us.'

Jesus, thought Carlyle. *She's turning into a fucking life coach.*

'How many years have I got left?' she wondered.

'All the more reason not to waste them on pissing about in this vendetta against Dad.'

'This is no vendetta. We only get a few years, then we die . . .'

Carlyle was reminded of the similar sentiments expressed by Sol Abramyan in the Palm Court of the Ritz Hotel. The idea of his mum being on the same philosophical wavelength as the arms dealer made him smile.

'What's so funny?'

'Nothing, Ma, nothing.' Getting to his feet, Carlyle leaned over the table and kissed his mother on the forehead. 'Thanks for the tea. I need to get going.' Without waiting for a reply, he fled before she could start telling him anything about this new man in her life.

Chapter Fifty-five

'GOOD TO SEE you again.' Ambrose Watson held out a meaty paw and Carlyle shook it. He was beginning to warm to this corpulent Internal Investigations Command man, which was just as well, given the increasing regularity of their meetings. For his part, Ambrose seemed to be relatively at ease with the taciturn inspector. Maybe they were getting used to each other.

Not wishing to endure another session in the basement at Charing Cross, Carlyle had suggested a meeting on neutral ground, a café called Madigan's, just off Golden Square, on the west side of Soho. Sipping his second macchiato, he watched queasily as Ambrose demolished a Full English Breakfast, followed, rather improbably, by a huge slice of chocolate cake.

'Best meal of the day,' said Ambrose, as he stacked his empty plates, then he signalled to the waitress behind the counter that he would very much like another mug of milky tea.

'Absolutely.' *It'll be a miracle if you don't drop down dead with a coronary before this investigation is over,* Carlyle thought. With Ambrose's gluttony effectively killing off his own appetite, he was sticking to coffee alone. He now felt happily wired as the caffeine raced through his bloodstream.

After the waitress brought the fresh tea and had cleared the table, Ambrose reached into his battered briefcase and pulled out a sheaf of papers. 'First things first,' he said, slapping them down and returning to his bag for a pen. 'The Hooper business has been closed.'

'Commander Simpson already told me,' Carlyle said, nodding. Even so, he still felt a surge of relief at the further confirmation of this happy news.

'She's a good woman, Carole Simpson,' Ambrose grunted, finally pulling out a red biro. 'You are very lucky to have her on your side.'

'So people keep telling me,' Carlyle said, in a tone that sounded rather more sarcastic than he intended.

Ambrose shot him a quizzical look.

'How do you know her?' Carlyle asked.

'Our paths have crossed several times,' Ambrose replied cautiously, realizing that he could now be boxing himself into a corner.

'Were you involved in the investigation regarding her husband?'

Ambrose gave his head a little shake, as he added a heaped teaspoon of sugar to his tea. 'I cannot comment on any of that,' he said, lifting the mug to his lips. 'But it was, as you can imagine, a very difficult situation for the Commander. I think everyone agrees that she handled it with great dignity and professionalism.'

'It can't have been easy, having your husband exposed as a crook like that.'

'Of course not.' Ambrose slurped a mouthful of tea. 'A lesser woman – a lesser officer – would have crumbled under the strain.'

'And she knew nothing about his whole scam?'

'Husbands deceive wives all the time.' Ambrose raised his eyes to the heavens. 'Stranger things have happened.'

'Yes, they have,' Carlyle agreed. Finishing his coffee, he moved on. 'And regarding Hooper, will they ever find out who killed him?'

'That is a very good question,' said Ambrose, lowering his voice and glancing around theatrically. 'However, it doesn't look like it at the moment.'

'Oh?'

'Well,' said the big man, 'things have been left on the back-burner since we found almost two hundred and fifty grams of heroin and almost twelve grand, in used fifties, in the man's flat. Everyone just wants to forget that Inspector Sam Hooper ever existed. There's a major investigation going on into the Middle Market Drugs Project – I'd say it's very likely that the operation will be wound up sooner rather than later.'

Dominic will piss himself, Carlyle thought. 'Really?'

'The whole thing is a real mess,' Ambrose sighed. 'Nobody wants to touch it with a barge-pole.'

'Jesus.'

'Anyway,' Ambrose said cheerily, 'back to the matter in hand. I hear that you're undergoing counselling for what happened in Hyde Park.'

Carlyle almost fell off his chair. '*What?*'

Ambrose blushed furiously. 'It's not a big deal,' he stammered. 'Completely standard in these type of situations, in fact.'

'And supposed to be completely confidential,' Carlyle snapped.

'Yes, yes, absolutely.'

The inspector leaned across the table, all the better to give Ambrose the hard word. 'So it's not something that should appear in any IIC report.'

'No, no, of course not.'

'And if my rights are breached in any way,' Carlyle went on, 'the Union will come down on those responsible like a ton of bricks.' Carlyle didn't have much time for the Police Federation. As far as he was concerned, they were the worst kind of nit-picking, jobsworth bureaucrats. But, at the same time, he was more than happy to make use of their services when it suited him.

'Don't worry, Inspector,' Ambrose spluttered, 'that will never happen. My apologies for even mentioning it.'

'Don't worry about it.' Carlyle scratched his chin. 'Maybe it's better that we have this conversation now; get it out of the way.' He sat back in his chair and crossed his arms. 'So, how can I help?'

'Well,' Ambrose lifted a sheet of paper from the top of his pile of documents and squinted at it. 'I've read through your statement regarding Hyde Park, which seems thorough enough.'

'Thank you.'

'I just wondered if now, on reflection, you had anything that you wanted to add?'

Carlyle made a show of thinking about the question for a few moments. 'No,' he said finally.

Ambrose gave him a slightly pained look. 'It's just that I can't seem to get my head round what you were doing there in the first place.'

Good bloody question, Carlyle thought. 'I was meeting with Fadi Kashkesh,' he explained. 'I didn't know that the other two victims were going to be there.'

'Yes, but why meet in the park?'

'It was his suggestion,' Carlyle lied. 'He said he felt safer out in the open.'

Ambrose sighed. 'And how wrong that belief proved to be.'

'Quite.'

'And you, Inspector . . .'

'Yes?'

'How are you coping? Any flashbacks? Survivor's guilt? Trouble sleeping at night?'

'That,' Carlyle grinned, 'is between me and my shrink.'

'Fair point,' Ambrose laughed. Scooping up his papers, he dropped them back in his briefcase, along with the unused biro. 'Well, I think we can leave it at that for now. I know where to find you.'

'Of course.'

'Frankly, it's going to take months to wade through all the witness statements and reports. Then there's the IPCC and God knows what other investigations that will have to take place.' Ambrose gave Carlyle a weak smile. 'I can see my whole life disappearing in front of me.'

Your choice, thought Carlyle.

'But it's great that you've managed to take it all in your stride.' Struggling to his feet, he again offered Carlyle his hand. 'Good luck, Inspector. I'll be in touch.'

'Okay.'

Out on the street, Ambrose hailed a black cab and hoisted himself into the back seat. It was only after the taxi had disappeared off into the traffic that Carlyle realized he'd been left with the bill for breakfast.

Chapter Fifty-six

'I'M GOING TO kill the little bastard!'

'Calm down.'

'I'm going to fucking kill him!'

'Look, just calm DOWN!' Standing in the middle of the kitchen, Carlyle put an arm round Helen and pulled her close. She tried to squirm away from him but he held on tight. He could feel her rapid heartbeat as she dug her fingernails into his back. 'We will sort this out,' he said quietly. 'I promise.'

'Okay,' she said doubtfully, finally pulling away.

'Where is Alice now?'

'She's in her bedroom, pretending to be asleep.'

'I see.' Carlyle leaned against the fridge and blew out a breath. 'So tell me again what happened.'

'I already told you,' Helen said. 'The school rang me at work to say that Alice had been sent home and suspended for three days. They had found what they said was a small amount of cannabis in her locker. We have to go in for a meeting at the school the day after tomorrow.'

Great, thought Carlyle, *that's just what I need: my first trip to the Headmaster's office in more than thirty years.* 'What did she have to say for herself?'

'When I asked her about it, she got very annoyed and started screaming at me to mind my own business,' Helen said. 'I asked her if it was Stuart's dope and she told me to fuck off.'

Jesus, Carlyle thought.

'That's your fault.' Helen gave him a scowl. 'You've never watched your language around the house.'

Carlyle was feeling too tired to get into an argument. 'Let me talk to her,' he said, trying to sound as conciliatory as possible.

'Now?'

'No. Let's leave her be for tonight. I'll speak to her tomorrow, and then we'll go to the school.'

Helen stepped over and gave him a hug. 'Okay.'

'These things happen. We'll get it sorted out.'

'This could kill her chances of an award.' Helen sounded stressed.

Don't I know it, thought Carlyle bitterly. After struggling for several years to meet the costs of Alice's private school, they had been hoping that she could finally win a scholarship. 'Let's worry about that later.' He took his wife's face in his hands and gave her a kiss on the lips. 'Don't raise it as an issue at the meeting, though.' Before she could protest, he continued, 'I will speak with her and then we will decide what we're going to say.'

'You mean how much grovelling we're going to do?'

'Yeah,' he laughed, 'exactly.'

'The stupid thing is,' Helen wiped her eyes, 'it's not even her dope.' She tried to laugh but couldn't quite manage it.

'How do you mean?'

'Well, it's not like she's using it herself. At least I'm fairly sure that she's not. It's not even like she's ever tried smoking a cigarette.'

'As far as we know,' Carlyle pointed out.

'As far as we know,' Helen reluctantly agreed. 'But the only time she could have done anything like that is when she was with that bloody Stuart.'

'You were the one who said he was a nice boy.'

She gave him a punch on the arm for being such a smug bastard.

'I guess young Stuart won't be coming round to dinner until this is all sorted out, then?'

Helen gave him a sheepish look. 'I think dinner is off for the foreseeable future. I spoke to his mother . . .'

Uh, oh, Carlyle thought.

'The stupid bitch wouldn't have anything to do with it,' Helen told him. 'She just didn't want to know.'

Carlyle's heart sank. 'What did you say to her?'

'I told her that Alice had been caught with her son's dope and had been suspended from school.'

'But you don't know that it was his dope.'

'Where else could she have got it from?'

Carlyle closed his eyes and began rubbing his temples.

'To listen to Julie Wark, you'd think Stuart was training for the priesthood.' Helen adopted a whiny, girly voice. '"My son wouldn't do that kind of thing. He doesn't know anything about drugs."'

'I'm going to run a bath,' said Carlyle. 'Let me talk to Alice in the morning, then we can worry about what to say to the school. *Then* we can worry about Mrs Wark.'

BY THE TIME he finished his bath, Helen was sitting in bed, doing a Sudoku puzzle in the evening paper. He slipped under the duvet and gave her a kiss on the cheek.

'I went to see my mother,' he told her. 'She only reckons she's got a new boyfriend.'

'Bloody hell, that was quick!' Helen tentatively wrote a number in one of the boxes.

'She's driving me round the bend.'

His wife smiled at him over her reading glasses. 'That's what mothers do. Who is he?'

'Who?'

'The boyfriend.'

Carlyle stretched out. 'Dunno.'

'What?' Helen gave him a gentle thwack with the paper. 'Did you even ask?'

'No.'

'For God's sake, John,' she sighed. 'Sometimes you are just so clueless it's not true.'

'Dad'll be beside himself.'

'He should have thought about that before he shagged the woman next door.'

'That was thirty years ago! Jesus.'

Helen tossed the paper onto the floor and put her pen on the bedside table. 'Well, they're having to deal with it now.'

'I suppose so.'

She carefully removed her glasses and placed them next to the pen. 'I wonder what Lorna's new man is like?'

'I don't want to bloody know,' Carlyle said grumpily.

'Come on,' she said kindly, '*you* have to be grown up about this.'

I don't know about that, Carlyle thought.

'Anyway,' said Helen, switching out the light, 'if your mother's happy, that's got to be a good thing.'

'But what about my dad?'

'Well, we'll just have to find someone for him, too.'

Chapter Fifty-seven

ALICE SLID INTO the back booth at Il Buffone and gave Carlyle a cheeky grin. 'So is this me getting a monster bollocking?'

Marcello, hovering in front of the Gaggia coffee machine, laughed out loud.

God give me strength, Carlyle thought. Glancing at the AC Milan team on the wall above Alice's head, searching for inspiration, he was disappointed to see that the new poster was already grubby and torn. Someone had even scribbled over Fabio Capello's face.

'I know,' said Marcello, arriving at the table with a double macchiato for Carlyle and a hot chocolate for Alice. He gestured at the poster with his chin. 'It's a bloody shame.'

'I'll speak to Alison,' Carlyle replied, 'see if she can get a new one.'

'Who's Alison?' Alice asked.

'Sergeant Roche. She's working with me at the station.'

'Is she Joe's replacement?'

Carlyle looked at Marcello, who just shrugged. 'Yes.'

Alice bent down and took a slurp of her hot chocolate. 'It must be a real bummer, getting shot like that.'

Carlyle was stunned by her apparent insouciance.

'What would you like to eat?' Marcello said quickly.

'I'll have some toast with honey, please, Marcello,' she said brightly.

'The usual,' said Carlyle.

'Coming right up.' Marcello shuffled back behind the counter.

'So,' said Alice, taking another sip from her glass, 'let's get it over with.'

'Don't give me that attitude,' Carlyle growled. He lifted the demitasse to his lips and drained the coffee in one. 'Just tell me what happened.'

'It was a fair cop,' Alice sniggered.

'I know that,' Carlyle grinned, 'but where did the dope come from?'

'It wasn't mine,' she said hastily, stirring the remains of her hot chocolate with a spoon. 'I don't *do* drugs.'

'Glad to hear it,' Carlyle observed testily.

'I was just holding it for someone.'

'Who?' he asked a bit too eagerly. 'Stuart?'

'No,' she frowned. 'It's got nothing to do with him.'

'Well, you'd better explain that to your mother. She's got him firmly in her sights.'

'She should mind her own bloody business!' Alice complained.

'She's your mother,' Carlyle responded, 'so this *is* her business. Mine too.'

All he got by way of reply was a pout. As the silence started to lengthen, Marcello appeared with Alice's toast and a huge raisin Danish for Carlyle, along with a second macchiato. For a couple of minutes, they focused on eating.

'You know,' said Carlyle, after swallowing the last of his pastry, 'this is a serious business.'

Munching her toast, Alice eyed him doubtfully.

Carlyle grinned. 'I have to go and see the bloody Headmaster tomorrow!'

'Really?' Alice giggled, propelling a mouthful of crumbs across the table.

'It's the first time I've been called in to see the Head since . . . oh, I dunno, something like 1979.' He gave her a wink. 'I was busted for drugs, too.'

Alice's eyes grew wide. 'Really?'

''Fraid so,' Carlyle said. 'I was a bit older than you, but not much. I got done for selling half a gram of speed to Kenny Morris from 5C.' Carlyle tutted in mock amusement. 'I was suspended for a fortnight.'

'Wow!'

Carlyle shook his head at the memory. 'And then the little bastard never paid me.'

'Ha!'

He leaned over and kissed his daughter on the forehead. 'There's nothing new under the sun, sweetheart.' While that last statement may well have been true, the rest of his story was a complete fabrication. The young Carlyle had never been a playground dope dealer. Kenny Morris did exist though; he had had his nose broken and his head held down a flushing toilet after stealing a tenner from Carlyle's school bag. After the subsequent investigation, Carlyle was sent home for a week.

'You did drugs?'

'A little – for a while. Speed mainly. Dope wasn't my thing.'

'And Mum?'

'Not as far as I know.'

'Did you like it?'

Carlyle shrugged. 'Speed was okay. It wasn't that big a deal. It's like most things, you grow out of it.'

Alice finished her toast. 'I don't do drugs.'

'So where did the cannabis come from?'

'Skunk.'

'What?'

'It was skunk.'

'Whatever,' Carlyle persisted, 'where did it come from?'

Alice gave him a long hard look. In that moment, she looked so like her mother that he found it impossible not to smile.

'Patricia Fine,' she said finally.

Carlyle affected insouciance. 'Who's she?'

Alice sighed. 'She's two years above me. I just did it as a favour.'

'Why did she want you to look after it for her?'

'I don't know,' Alice hissed. 'Stop being such a bloody policeman.' She tried to slide out of the booth, but Carlyle put a hand on her arm.

'Okay, okay,' he said, 'no more questions. I will go and take my punishment from the Headmaster. *And* I'll get your mother to apologize to Stuart and his mum.'

'I wouldn't worry about that,' Alice told him. 'His mum can be a bit stuck-up. Stuart thought it was funny that they'd been arguing about it.'

'Anyway,' Carlyle said wearily, 'I'll get it sorted. Just don't do anything like this again.'

Chapter Fifty-eight

FOLLOWING ALL THE domestic dramas, it was a blessed relief to get back to the station. After arriving at Charing Cross, Carlyle spent a happy hour reading the newspaper and surfing the internet for football gossip and other such chat. He was on his second cup of coffee by the time Roche arrived, grim-faced.

'What's the matter?' Carlyle asked.

'Nothing,' she replied unconvincingly.

Suit yourself, Carlyle thought. 'I need to speak to Ronan. What's he up to this morning?'

'No idea,' she said sharply, before stalking off in the direction of the coffee machine.

'I'll have an espresso,' Carlyle shouted after her.

'Get it yourself,' was the terse reply.

Okay, he shrugged, *I will*. Putting on the cheeriest expression he could manage, Carlyle followed her across the room. When he was halfway there, he stopped and watched in amusement as she jabbed a succession of buttons, then gave the machine a good slap.

'For fuck's sake!' She gave the machine another slap, then a kick for good measure. As he reached her side, Carlyle saw the *Out of Order* notice flash across the small display screen.

'Come on,' he said, 'let's go out somewhere. That stuff's shit anyway.'

SITTING IN STARBUCKS on St Martin's Lane, Carlyle sipped a double espresso and was happy to watch the world go by. He ignored his colleague as she gloomily drank her latte and picked at an orange and lemon muffin. Across the road, he noticed a pretty girl walk into the Garden Hotel and wondered what had happened to Sylvia Swain. The Canadian journalist appeared to have vanished off the face of the earth: there was no record of her having left the country, and a phone call to her editor had simply elicited a gruff response that she was 'on assignment and not contactable'. *Fucking Canadians*, Carlyle thought. *What a Mickey Mouse country.* However, he realized that it wasn't worth starting an international row to try and track her down. What with his confrontation with the Israeli Ambassador, he was doing enough for the UK's international relations already.

Swain, whoever she was, was a minor player in this little drama. The inspector would be perfectly happy if she never resurfaced.

'The fucking bastard!'

Carlyle was shaken out of his thoughts by Roche's sudden outburst.

'Pardon?'

'The bastard was shagging his sister-in-law.'

Carlyle frowned. Had he missed something? What the hell was she talking about?

She looked at him like he was terminally stupid. 'DI fucking Ronan. I caught him fucking his bastard sister-in-law – in our bed.'

Ronan, Carlyle thought, *you dirty dog.* Returning his gaze to the window, he tried not to grin and said nothing.

'He's been banging her for months, apparently. The little bitch is only nineteen.'

'I see,' was all Carlyle could think of by way of reply.

'I could have killed the little shit.'

'But you didn't?'

'What?' Roche gave him a funny look. 'No, no.' She laughed. 'I did put the P30 to his head, though.'

'A measured response,' Carlyle acknowledged. He casually wondered if brandishing a Heckler & Koch P30 in front of his parents might help bring them to their senses. Somehow, he doubted it.

'His skinny little girlfriend pissed herself when I flicked the safety.'

'Literally?'

'Yeah.' Roche was grinning widely now.

And they send me *to the shrink*, Carlyle thought to himself.

'I thought Dave was going to shit himself.'

'David,' Carlyle corrected her.

'What?'

'Nothing. Do you need some time off?'

'Nah.' She shook her head. 'I've already moved out.'

'Okay.'

'I'm staying with a friend until I find somewhere permanent. In the meantime, I just want to get on with things.'

'Very sensible.'

'I'm not the kind to mope about.'

'Good,' Carlyle smiled. He realized that he was beginning to really like Alison Roche. She was shaping up to be a worthy successor to Joe Szyszkowski. Just as long as he never gave her cause to pull a gun on him. Draining the final drops from his cup, he stood up. 'Come on.'

Roche grabbed her bag and got to her feet. 'Where are we going?'

'You'll see.'

HILARY WAXMAN GRITTED her teeth and forced something approaching a smile onto her lips.

'Inspector . . .'

'Carlyle.'

'Inspector Carlyle, this is harassment. I have already lodged an official protest with the Foreign Office and I will be pressing them to take this up with your superiors at the earliest opportunity.'

Sitting forward in his chair, Carlyle smiled at Roche and Waxman in turn. 'This is hardly harassment, Ambassador,' he said evenly. 'We are pursuing our legitimate enquiries and we are respectfully requesting your assistance.'

'Mr Lieberman is not here,' Waxman snapped. 'As I told you, I am not apprised of his movements and you have no jurisdiction inside my Embassy.'

Bowing his head, Carlyle pressed his hands together, as if in prayer. 'On this occasion, we are not here in connection with Mr Lieberman.' Pulling a small brown envelope out of the inside pocket of his jacket, he dropped it on the table.

'What is that?' Waxman asked, making no effort to pick it up.

'It's a warrant for your arrest,' Roche said quietly.

Waxman snorted with laughter as she stared at the two police officers in front of her. 'Don't be preposterous.'

'Hilary Waxman,' Carlyle said tonelessly, 'you are under arrest for the non-payment of fines totalling one million, two hundred and fifty-six thousand, three hundred and twelve pounds and forty-seven pence.'

'That,' Roche chipped in, 'accounts for the unpaid parking tickets run up by diplomatic staff working here at the Embassy, additional penalties and accumulated interest. The figure is only up to date as of last month, so it may have edged up a little.'

Waxman smacked a fist down on her desk. 'You have got to be kidding.'

'We'll take a cheque,' Carlyle smirked.

'Get out of my office this instant.' Waxman pounded a buzzer on her desk.

'Have it your way,' Carlyle sighed. Getting to his feet, he pulled a pair of handcuffs from his pocket and quickly moved round behind the desk.

'Get your hands off me!' Waxman shrieked, as Carlyle tried to pull her to her feet. Grunting with the effort, he signalled to Roche to give him a hand. Together, they finally managed to wrestle her far enough out of the chair for Carlyle to snap on the cuffs.

'Where are you taking her?' Daniel, the lackey, had appeared in the doorway. Unable to make sense of the scene in front of him, he looked like he was about to cry.

'I don't know yet,' Carlyle lied. 'She'll be allowed her phone call in due course.'

'You know what to do,' Waxman hissed to her aide, as she was hustled away. 'Get this sorted immediately!'

Chapter Fifty-nine

STANDING AT THE bar of the Stern Arms, David Ronan started on his second bottle of Estrella Damm and idly watched one of the club's strippers mechanically going through her routine for the benefit of a scanty, post-lunch crowd.

'Hey, there.'

Ronan turned to meet the gaze of Suzie Perrin, aka 'Starburst', one of the Stern's regular performers. Young-looking, with a page-boy haircut and cheeky grin, Ronan knew that Suzie could easily clear a couple of hundred quid in one lunchtime session. Most of it, however, immediately disappeared up her nose, just like the cash he gave her from the 'confidential informer' budget, in exchange for a regular bunk-up in one of the pub's private rooms.

'How's it going?' he asked.

'It's going,' she sighed. 'Wanna buy me a drink?'

Ronan peeked at the sheer black basque visible under her barely tied robe. 'Yeah, okay.'

Almost instantly, the barman placed a bottle of Spanish beer in her hand. 'Cheers,' she smiled, taking a long drink.

Ronan watched the other stripper complete her act. 'Who's she?'

'New girl,' Suzie said, finishing her beer and smacking the empty bottle down on the table. 'Don't know her name. Why? D'ya fancy her?'

'Nah,' said Ronan, shaking his head. 'Just wondering.'

'She won't last,' Suzie said, without malice. 'She just hasn't got what it takes.'

And what would that be, Ronan wondered ironically; the ability to stay coked out of your head twenty-four hours a day while flashing your arsehole at the world? 'Are you on next?' he asked.

Suzie scanned the room. 'For this lot? Nah, not worth it. I'd barely make a tenner.' She gave him her trademark impish smile. 'Tell you what, though, come upstairs and I'll give you a special show.'

Ronan thought about that for perhaps a nanosecond, trying to conceal the fact that his crotch had already decided for him. 'Oh, all right then,' he grinned, 'you've talked me into it.'

On the second floor, Ronan nodded to Steve, one of the club's bouncers, as he walked past the *No physical contact allowed* sign and down a corridor which had three doors on each side.

'Take the left on the end,' Suzie directed him.

'Okay,' said Ronan, as he started stroking himself through his trousers.

It was a room he'd been in several times before and he knew the drill. Throwing his jacket over the back of a chair, he took a seat on a low sofa that had been pushed up against the rear wall. Without any ceremony, Suzie slipped off her robe and switched on a CD player that rested on the floor, beside the door.

'You know the rules,' she said giggling, as 50 Cent's 'In Da Club' started thumping out of the tinny speakers. 'No touching me, no touching yourself . . .'

Ronan grunted as he unzipped his fly.

'And if I have to hit this panic button,' Suzie continued, now speaking for some reason in a fake American drawl, 'Steve will be in here immediately to stomp on your ass.'

'Just get on with it,' Ronan shouted.

Two and a half minutes later, having broken every house rule he could think of, Ronan sat content, his aussieBum Wonderjock trunks around his ankles as he finished his beer.

Dropping a wad of tissues in a bin next to the CD player, Suzie turned to him and smiled. 'Fancy another beer?'

Ronan gave himself a good scratch. 'Yeah, why not?'

She slipped her robe back on, then opened the door. 'Same again?'

'Perfect.'

'Okay, I'll be back in a minute.'

'Great.' Yawning, Ronan dropped his empty beer bottle on the floor, closing his eyes as Fiddy faded into the background.

'HEY, BIG BOY, wake up.'

Ronan slowly brought the room into focus. Still in a state of undress, he had been placed in a chair. Pushing himself up in his seat, he looked at the woman in front of him. It took him a moment or two to realize that it wasn't Suzie. He was fairly sure he hadn't seen her before. She looked quite old, in her forties maybe, but not in bad shape. And she was caressing his scrotum. At least the gun in her hand was.

'What the fuck?' Completely startled, Ronan reared up, tipped over backwards on his chair and went sprawling across the floor.

'Much as I like looking at your ass,' said the woman, in an accent not unlike Suzie's earlier, 'I need you to put your underwear on. You're coming with me.'

Chapter Sixty

ARMS CROSSED, SIMPSON paced the room with a look of constipated fury plastered all over her face. 'Where did all those bloody journalists come from?'

Carlyle bit his tongue and tried not to look at Roche, who was perched on the edge of his desk desperately trying not to laugh. *At least I've managed to cheer her up a bit*, he thought.

'Where is she?' Simpson demanded.

'Downstairs,' Carlyle admitted.

'Well, I hope you're ready to grovel when you go back down. She is to be released immediately.'

'But I've got a warrant,' Carlyle protested.

Simpson stepped forward and jabbed him in the chest with her index finger. 'John, do not try my patience one second longer. How in the name of Jesus Christ you ever managed to convince a judge to grant you such an arrest warrant is beyond me. What kind of idiot would let you try and arrest someone with diplomatic immunity?'

Carlyle decided now was not the time to share the story of Judge Brian Cosby and his unfortunate relationship with cocaine, something which the inspector was happy to overlook in return for the odd favour, however outrageous.

'As you well know, only the Foreign Office can request a waiver of a person's diplomatic immunity,' Simpson stormed, 'and even then it is up to the sending state – in this case Israel – to decide if they wish to comply.'

'But they never do,' Carlyle said huffily.

'No.'

'So fuck them.'

'John . . .'

'The judge signed the warrant,' Carlyle shrugged.

'Did he even bother to read it?' Simpson screamed.

No. 'Of course.'

'Then why did he fucking sign it, then?'

Because we didn't explain to him precisely who she was. Carlyle raised a calming hand. 'We can put it down as a bureaucratic error. Under the circumstances, I'm sure that the Ambassador will be,' he stifled a chuckle, '*diplomatic* and not make too much of a fuss.'

Taking a step backwards, the Commander fought to get her anger under control.

'I'll go down and release the prisoner,' said Roche, slipping off the desk.

'You stay where you are,' Simpson ordered. 'I can't believe that you could have picked up so many of the inspector's appalling habits already.' Roche started to reply, but Simpson cut her off. 'One more word from you and you'll be back in East London before the end of the day – if not in jail yourself.'

Silenced, the sergeant stared at the floor.

'Have they paid the fines?' the inspector asked.

Simpson's face turned puce, until he thought that she might explode. 'Carlyle!'

Keep your bloody hair on. Moving towards the stairs, he held up both his hands, trying not to grin like a naughty schoolboy. 'Okay, don't worry. I'm going.'

'And make sure she gets taken out the back way,' Simpson shouted after him. 'There's a car already waiting.'

IGNORING BOTH SIMPSON and the protests of Waxman's lawyer, Carlyle marched the Ambassador though the reception area, pausing at the front entrance to undo her handcuffs.

'Your career is over,' she hissed as he pulled open the door. 'You've got a serious problem.'

'That's right, I've got a problem. My problem is that one of your psycho goons killed my sergeant.'

'You're talking crap.'

'You can always give up Lieberman.'

'He knows nothing about your guy.'

'My guy had a name: Joe Szyszkowski. He had a wife and two kids. He was shot dead in the street.' Grabbing Waxman by the arm, he shoved her out onto the steps to confront the waiting press.

Immediately, the cameras started flashing and the journalists surged forward.

'Ambassador!'

'Over here!'

'Do you have a comment on your arrest?'

'Did you pay the fine?' someone shouted, to the general amusement of his colleagues.

Feeling empty and deflated, Carlyle slipped back inside.

'HOLY SHIT!' ROCHE laughed as he reappeared on the third floor. 'Did you see what happened?'

'What?' Carlyle said dully.

'Waxman just smacked a journalist in the face!' She pointed to the TV monitor hanging from the ceiling. 'They just ran it live on Sky. Some guy asked her if she was going to pay her parking tickets, the rest of them started laughing and she just hit him with a left hook. The bloke went down like a sack of potatoes.'

'She's a big woman,' Carlyle mused. 'I expect she packs a fair old punch.'

'That'll take the heat off us, though.'

Us? 'Where's Simpson?'

'Dunno. She pranced off somewhere. She might have left. Anyway, the issue now is the Ambassador clocking the hack. We're old news already. The world has moved on.'

'I don't know about that,' Carlyle said. 'I'm sure there will still be hell to pay.' He placed a hand on her shoulder. 'But that's my problem. It was my decision to give Waxman this grief, and I have to take full responsibility.'

'But—'

'It was down to me. You will be kept out of it.'

'I don't think so.' Roche patted his hand and gently eased it from her shoulder, giving it a small squeeze before letting go.

'There's no point in us both taking the flak.'

'Hey,' she smiled, 'we're in this together. After all, I wouldn't even be here if these fuckers didn't think they could shoot up our streets like it was the Wild West.'

'The Wild West of Beirut,' Carlyle grinned. Could this woman rise any higher in his estimation in just one day?

'Anyway, even if there is any comeback, we can both claim posttraumatic stress disorder.'

Carlyle gave her a funny look. 'How do you reckon?'

'Well, you've had to deal with more deaths in the last week than the average copper faces in a lifetime.'

'I suppose.'

'And I've had to deal with my boyfriend's dick in some bimbo's mouth in front of my very eyes.'

Too much information, Carlyle thought. 'I'm sure that Dr Wolf will be delighted to make your acquaintance,' he said. The mobile on his desk vibrated with a message. It was from Ronan: *Urgent! Have found our man. Meet me at the stern arms shoreditch asap.* Carlyle thought about that for a second, then rang him back. He listened to Ronan's phone finish ringing and go to voicemail. Without leaving a message, he hung up and looked at Roche. 'Do you know a pub called the Stern Arms?'

'David likes to go there now and again.' She sighed theatrically. 'Strippers downstairs, private dances on the first floor.'

'And on the second floor?'

'I don't want to think about what might happen upstairs. Why do you ask?'

'He's asked me to meet him there.' *Helen will be delighted*, Carlyle thought. 'How do I get there?'

'Come out of Liverpool Street tube, walk up Shoreditch High Street for a couple of minutes and it's on your left.'

'Okay.' Carlyle got to his feet. 'Don't suppose you want to come?'

Stalking away, she didn't bother to reply.

Chapter Sixty-one

Wearing raincoats over their stage outfits, a couple of strippers were standing on the pavement outside the Stern Arms, enjoying a fag and a chat. One of them gave the inspector a wan smile as he shuffled past them and headed inside. At the bar, he ordered a bottle of Budweiser and looked around. Dark and grimy, the place was almost empty save for a handful of men, each sitting at a table facing the space at the far end of the room, which had been cleared for the performers. A girl with badly bleached blonde hair wearing high heels and what looked like an Indian squaw outfit, was going round each customer in turn, collecting pound coins in a pint glass before starting her act. When she had done the various tables, she tottered over to the bar and thrust the glass under Carlyle's nose.

'It's a pound,' she explained flatly, 'but you can give more if you want.'

Embarrassed, Carlyle dug into his trouser pocket and dropped a two-pound coin into the glass.

The girl brightened at this accidental show of generosity. 'Thanks,' she smiled, stepping in front of him. 'If you fancy a special show upstairs afterwards, it's twenty quid.' Handing her pint pot to the barman for safekeeping, she then wandered off. Finishing his beer, Carlyle rang Ronan's number again. Again the voicemail kicked in. Sighing, he watched the barman shove a CD in the stereo behind the bar and then hit Play. Kylie Minogue's 'Go Hard or Go Home' started blaring from a couple of speakers as the squaw began slowly gyrating like a wounded buffalo.

Where the hell was Ronan? Should he stay? Or should he go? Carlyle was feeling paralysed by indecision when he suddenly felt a hand on his shoulder.

'About bloody time!' he hissed, turning to face the detective inspector.

'Enjoying the show?'

It took him a moment to realize that it was Sylvia Swain – or at least the woman he knew as Sylvia Swain – who was standing next to him. Her hair had been cut short and she was dressed in cowboy boots, jeans and a Foo Fighters T-shirt. The overall effect was to make her look older.

'I didn't know you worked here,' he grinned, after getting over his initial surprise.

'I'm not sure I could live with the competition,' she replied, gesturing at the stripper, who had just managed to struggle out of her bra.

'So what can I do for you?'

Swain slipped her arm through his and led him away from the bar. 'We have to take a little walk.'

'And if I don't want to do that?' Carlyle asked.

She gave his arm a gentle squeeze. 'That's fine by me, but it means your colleague Dave will be dead within the next ten minutes.'

'I think he prefers to be called David,' Carlyle said, falling in step with her as she headed for the door.

SWAIN LED CARLYLE down an alley that ran alongside the pub, and past a couple of dilapidated apartment buildings. A young girl who looked like she was walking home from school stared at them as they passed, otherwise the street was empty. Stopping outside a boarded-up newsagents, Swain rapped firmly on the door. After a few moments, it opened and he was ushered inside.

'Inspector Carlyle, how very good of you to join us.'

Carlyle forced out the thinnest of smiles. 'My pleasure, Mr Lieberman.'

The room had been completely gutted. Everything that might have been of any value had been stripped out, including the electrical wiring from the walls and even some of the floorboards. 'Over there.' Lieberman gestured towards a door at the rear with the Browning Hi-Power semi-automatic held in his right hand. 'Head right to the back. The room on your left. Be careful where you put your feet.'

Carlyle followed Swain down the corridor, with Lieberman bringing up the rear. The room at the back was maybe fifteen feet by twelve. It had also been stripped bare. In one corner, handcuffed to a narrow metal pipe protruding from the wall, about two feet off the floor, Ronan looked in bad shape. With a nasty gash on his forehead and his left eye closed up, it was clear that he'd taken a severe beating. There was blood-spatter on the wall behind his head and the DI looked barely conscious. When Carlyle gave him a gentle nudge with his boot, he got no response.

'Not a great advert for your people, is he?' Lieberman gestured for Carlyle to sit down next to the SO15 man.

'Fuck off,' Carlyle snorted. 'You're not doing that to me.'

'Sit down,' ordered Lieberman quietly. 'Take out your cuffs and attach yourself to that pipe.' Kneeling down, he aimed the barrel of the Browning directly into Ronan's face. 'Otherwise your friend dies now.'

Well done, excellent effort, Carlyle said to himself. *You've got yourself into a really great situation here.* Slowly lowering himself to the floor, he attached one cuff to the pipe and clicked the other around his left wrist.

'Good,' Lieberman approved.

'What do you want?' Carlyle asked.

'We want our man back,' Swain said. Standing over Carlyle, she gently massaged his crotch with the toe of her boot. 'It would have been easier if you'd let me just fuck it out of you, but there you go.' She gave him another prod. 'Or maybe you'd like to fuck now?'

'Why not?' Carlyle smiled. 'Just take these cuffs off and I'll see what I can do.'

'But, Inspector,' she mocked, 'there's nothing happening down there.' Swain glanced at Lieberman in mock disappointment. 'Maybe he's a faggot.'

If Helen could see me now, Carlyle thought.

Sid shrugged. 'That doesn't stop him from telling us what we want to know.'

'I've been looking for your guy,' Carlyle told him, 'but I haven't found him.'

Swain kicked him hard in the groin with her heel. 'Don't be such a fag!'

Grunting, Carlyle took a deep breath. Beside him, Ronan groaned in apparent sympathy.

'Hey!' Sid said, placing a hand on Swain's arm. 'There's no need for any of that rough stuff.' He turned to Carlyle. 'It's very simple now. You have two more chances to answer the question.'

'I don't know.'

Lieberman waved the Browning at Ronan. 'If you fail to answer, he dies.'

'I don't—'

'If he dies and you still don't answer, we will leave you here while we go and get your wife.'

'Or maybe his daughter,' Swain chipped in. 'Don't you think that would have more impact?'

'Maybe.' Lieberman stroked his chin in apparent thought. 'But no, let's bring them both. Then we'll let you sit around together a while, a happy family, before we kill you all.'

'Fuck you,' Carlyle hissed. *Jesus Christ Almighty*, his brain complained, *how the hell did I get into this fucking mess?*

Lieberman stepped to the far side of the room and gestured Swain out of the line of fire. 'Last chance . . .'

Oh shit, Carlyle thought. 'Sol Abramyan.'

'Who?' Swain asked.

'Sol Abramyan is the arms trader who set up the London deal for Hamas. He has your guy and I've been trying to get him back.'

'Well done – *Mazel tov*,' Lieberman said. 'You got there in the end.' Then, raising the Browning, he put two shots into the middle of Ronan's chest. 'At last, we're making some progress.'

Chapter Sixty-two

'AT LEAST HE won't be banging the sister-in-law any more,' Carlyle quipped, as they watched Ronan's body being placed in the back of an ambulance and driven slowly away.

'I'm sure that the skanky little bitch will be heartbroken,' Roche said.

'Are you sure you're okay?'

'Me? Oh yes.' She gave him a shaky grin. 'And before you ask, I have an alibi.'

'Just as well,' he replied. 'But I'm sure that the shrink will still have a field day with you.'

'That poor sod has got more than enough on his plate dealing with *you*.'

'I have got to be one of the most straightforward cases he's ever come across,' Carlyle deadpanned. 'There's nothing wrong with me at all.'

'Yeah, right.'

Out of the corner of his eye, he saw Simpson emerge from the building where Ronan had been shot. Directly behind her was a senior-looking guy in uniform whom the inspector didn't recognize. He flicked again through his story. The key thing was to sprinkle the lies sparingly among the facts. Carlyle knew he was quite good at that, but there was no room for complacency.

'What happened?' Simpson asked.

Ignoring the question, Carlyle held out a hand to her companion. 'Inspector John Carlyle. And this is my colleague, Sergeant Alison Roche.'

Overcoming an obvious reluctance, the man shook Carlyle's hand. 'Commander Gavin Dugdale. I'm Simpson's opposite number at SO15, and Ronan's boss.'

Carlyle nodded. 'We were working with Ronan on this investigation. Sergeant Roche here was also his partner.' While Simpson and Dugdale exchanged bemused looks, Roche gave him a sly kick. Undeterred, he ploughed on. 'His girlfriend.'

An angry look passed over Dugdale's face. There were so many things wrong about this situation that he clearly didn't know what to complain about first. In the end, all he said was, 'I'm sorry for your loss.'

It sounded hollow and insincere but, with head bowed, Roche managed to mumble something that might just about have been construed as a 'Thank you'.

'So, what actually happened?' Simpson repeated.

'Ronan was shot twice by Sid Lieberman,' Carlyle said matter-of-factly. 'It appears that he was severely beaten in advance of his murder. Lieberman was being assisted by a woman who'd previously approached me claiming to be a journalist called Sylvia Swain.'

Simpson waited for him to go on. When he didn't, she asked, 'And how did you happen upon the scene?'

Carlyle gave both of his superiors some good eye-contact as he took his mobile from his jacket pocket. 'I received a text from Ronan's phone,' he said, pulling up the message and handing the phone to Simpson, 'asking me to come to the pub down the road.'

Simpson read the message and showed it to Dugdale. 'What does *have found our man* mean?' she asked.

'I presume that he was referring to Lieberman,' Carlyle lied. 'However, I can only speculate. When I got to the pub, Swain led me here. She told me that if I didn't go with her, Ronan would be killed. When we arrived, Ronan was still alive but in a bad way. He did not seem conscious. Lieberman seemed to believe that Ronan or I could help him find a missing member of the Mossad hit squad that killed Joe. Neither of us were able to give him what he wanted, so he shot Ronan. He was going to shoot me, but then his gun jammed – so they just left.'

'Why didn't they stab you,' Simpson mused, 'or strangle you?'

'I don't know,' Carlyle replied, ignoring the wistfulness in her tone. 'Maybe you can ask him yourself, if we catch him.'

'Don't worry,' said Dugdale, 'we'll get them both.'

I've heard that before, Carlyle thought. 'They seemed extremely stressed and in a considerable hurry. They left me with my phone and the keys to my handcuffs. Once I was sure that they were gone, I was able to call you straight away.'

Dugdale glanced doubtfully at Simpson, but her expression was giving nothing away. 'Very well, Inspector,' he said, 'go and get yourself cleaned up. We'll deal with this from now on.'

RETURNING TO THE bar in the Stern Arms, the inspector downed a triple measure of Jameson's and a couple of Budweisers in less than five minutes. The barman gave him a funny look, but said nothing as Carlyle ordered another round.

'I haven't finished the first one yet,' Roche protested.

'Don't worry,' Carlyle told her, 'I can always drink it for you.'

'I think you should slow down a bit.'

'You didn't have someone just point a gun on you and pull the fucking trigger.' Across the room, a lithe black girl with an outsized Afro swayed unconvincingly to 'Wonderwall' by Oasis. She was a lot prettier than the earlier stripper, so Carlyle reached into his pocket and pulled out a couple of pound coins.

Roche followed his gaze and smiled.

'Just don't bloody tell my wife I was in here,' he joked.

Roche sipped at her beer in a rather amateurish fashion. 'Why did you tell them that I was David's girlfriend?'

Mm, that was a good question. The alcohol was quickly pickling his brain and Carlyle had to stop and think about it for a moment. 'Two reasons,' he said finally.

'Yes?'

'First, and most important, they are going to find out anyway. Everything he's ever done will now come out in the wash, so you might as well be upfront with them.' Taking a large mouthful of the whiskey, he gently clinked his glass against her beer bottle. 'And, second, there might be some compo in it for you.'

'What?'

'Compensation. We live in a compensation culture these days, especially in the Met. You can get awarded thousands for mental distress if someone says they don't like your bloody haircut. Having your boyfriend brutally slain in the line of duty must be worth a few bob, even if he was playing away.'

Laughing, Roche almost choked on her beer. 'I don't think so.'

'You never know.'

'Anyway, I wouldn't want their bloody money.'

Carlyle looked aghast. 'You can always give it to me.' Oasis had finally stopped their racket and he watched as the black girl did the rounds with her pint pot, trying to catch any punters she hadn't tapped up before starting her act. Disappointed that she had put her clothes back on, he waited patiently to hand over his contribution.

Chapter Sixty-three

HELEN SMACKED HIM hard on the arm. 'Put the paper down!'

Reluctantly, Carlyle did what he was told. They were waiting outside the Headmaster's office, sitting side by side like two sixth-formers who had been caught smoking in the bogs. Ahead of his telling-off, he wasn't feeling in the mood for conversation.

'I thought you said that it was all over,' Helen whispered as one of the office secretaries walked past, giving them a stern look.

'It was,' Carlyle said, trying not to let his exasperation show. 'And then it wasn't.' He shrugged. 'These things happen. You know what it's like.'

'No.' Helen shook her head. 'I don't know what it's like. You are running around like a big kid, trying to get yourself killed. It's almost as if you feel guilty because Joe got shot and you didn't.'

'You sound like the shrink,' Carlyle snorted.

Helen folded her arms and stared into the middle distance. 'Well, maybe you should go back and see him again.'

'I will,' Carlyle said, happy to concede something. 'Simpson has already set it up.' He took her hand and gave it a squeeze. 'But there is nothing to worry about. A, I'm not going loopy and B, this issue really is under control now. There will be no more bloodshed.'

She reciprocated the squeeze. 'I'm not convinced about either of those things,' she said. 'We both know that the Met isn't likely to do much to protect you, mentally or physically.'

He leaned over and gave her a gentle peck on the cheek. 'And so far, I've never relied on them to do either, have I?'

She turned to look at him. 'What does that mean?'

It means that we're going to deploy the skills and resources of Dominic Silver and his boys, Carlyle thought. He shot Helen the best smile he could manage. 'It means that we'll be fine.'

THE DOOR TO the Headmaster's office opened and out popped the bald head of Dr Terence Myers. 'Mr and Mrs Carlyle? Please come in.' He held the door open while the condemned parents shuffled inside. 'Please take a seat.'

Once he had resumed residence behind the massive desk, Myers gave them the smallest of smiles. 'Thank you for coming in at such short notice. I realize that this is a difficult issue, but let me tell you that I have to deal with situations like this on a fairly regular basis, and I am sure that we can get it sorted out.'

'Thank you,' said Carlyle.

'It's good that you have spoken to Alice about it,' Myers continued, 'and we will, of course, look into what she has said. But, remember, this is not a blame game that we are playing here. Everyone makes mistakes. The important thing is that there is no repeat of this incident on Alice's part.'

'Yes,' both parents chirruped in unison.

Myers tapped a thin file resting on his desk. 'Your daughter is doing very well here, both academically and socially. She is very much a valued member of our community.'

Carlyle glanced over at Helen. Despite the circumstances, his wife was bursting with pride at the praise being handed out to their daughter. He had to resist the urge to smile.

'However,' said Myers, 'we cannot tolerate a repeat performance. The school, as you know, has had its share of problems with drugs over recent years, and we have to show that we deal with such things firmly. So Alice will have to complete her suspension, I'm afraid.'

Pride well and truly burst, Helen hung her head in shame. 'Yes.'

'Good.' Placing his hands on his ample belly, Myers sat back in his chair and told them, 'That's all. Do you have any questions?'

Bloody hell, Carlyle thought, *we've got a result. Let's get out of here.* Looking at Helen, he jumped to his feet.

'I was just wondering,' Helen said, 'will this affect Alice's chances of winning a scholarship?'

No, no, no! Don't start begging for money. Let's just get going. Struggling to hide his annoyance, Carlyle slowly sank back into his chair.

'I understand the considerable financial commitment that you have made to send your daughter to our school,' Myers smiled, 'but that is true of many parents. As you know, there is a lot of competition for our scholarships. All I can really say is that this incident will not prevent Alice from taking the scholarship exams. However, we do take a wide range of factors into consideration before making any award.'

So Alice being a drugs mule means we're screwed, Carlyle thought morosely. *I am going to be broke for the rest of my life paying your bloody school's fees.* 'That's very helpful guidance,' he said politely, getting to his feet a second time. 'Thank you for your time today. We will make sure we impress upon Alice the seriousness of the situation.'

'Good,' said Myers.

As Helen rose too, Carlyle took her by the arm and gently but firmly steered her towards the door.

'Inspector?' Myers had bounced out from behind his desk and made to open the door for them.

'Yes?' said Carlyle, wary at this belated use of his title.

'I was wondering if there was something that you might be able to do for us regarding the drugs issue.'

Bollocks. 'Of course.'

'We occasionally organize outside speakers for the older girls – fifth- and sixth-formers mainly. I was wondering if you might give them a talk on drugs?'

'Well . . .'

'He would be delighted to,' said Helen cheerily. 'Just let us know when.'

'I THINK THAT went okay,' said Helen as they walked slowly, hand-inhand, across the empty playground.

'Yes,' Carlyle sighed, 'as well as could be expected.' He glanced at the phone in his free hand: it was his private, pay-as-you-go mobile, the one he usually forgot to answer. Tomorrow, this phone would be history – the handset thrown in the bin and the SIM card tossed down a drain in some distant part of London. Now, however, he desperately needed it to ring.

'Do you think we can afford to keep paying the school fees?'

'Absolutely.'

'Are you sure, John?'

'Look,' he snapped, 'if I say we can afford it, we can afford it, all right?' She gave him a dirty look and dropped his hand. Immediately he regretted being so sharp. 'I'm sorry,' he said, planting a kiss on the top of her head. 'I didn't mean to shout at you.'

'There's no need to be so mean,' she pouted.

'I said I'm sorry.' Trying to avoid compounding his mistake, he took a deep breath. 'You know how our finances stack up as well as I do. We'll be fine.'

Before she could answer, the phone started vibrating in Carlyle's hand. He stepped away from his wife. 'Hello?'

'Have you got what we need?'

Carlyle cleared his throat. 'Yes, I have,' he said. 'Let me give you the details . . .'

Chapter Sixty-four

LOOKING UP FROM his mug of steaming black coffee, Sol Abramyan invited them to sit down.

'Want some?'

'Thanks.' Under the watchful gaze of Sol's bodyguards, Carlyle stood up from his chair and stepped over to the counter. Reaching for the coffee pot, he lined up a couple of mugs, filling one for himself and one for Dominic Silver. Placing Dom's mug on the table in front of him, the inspector returned to his seat. He took a sip and savoured the distinct chocolate flavour.

'Nice coffee.'

'Elephant Arabica beans from Guatemala,' Sol explained. 'I always pick up a couple of kilos when I'm in London.'

'You should try some Monsoon Malabar,' said Dom, gripping his mug nervously. 'It's very nice. Just a little smoother.' He tried to smile but didn't quite manage it. Carlyle didn't think he'd ever seen his friend looking so wired. Maybe more caffeine wasn't such a good idea.

Sol took another sip. 'So,' he eyed the inspector carefully, 'here you are sitting in my kitchen once again.'

Carlyle nodded.

'Only this time, as far as I can judge, you have nothing to trade.' He glanced at the Somalis who stood impassively by the back door, giving no impression of understanding any of what was being said. 'In fact, it seems like the only thing you've managed to do is derail my current business plans, costing me a lot of money in the process.'

Taking another mouthful of coffee, Carlyle shook his head. 'That was not my fault.'

Sol held up a hand. 'Look, to be honest, I don't really care who did what to whom or when or how and least of all, why. Regarding the politics of it all, I couldn't give a damn. Apart from anything else, my Israeli clients are far more lucrative than my Arab ones. Money is no object to those boys; they can afford any shit they want, and they always want the best.'

'The best kind of clients,' Dom quipped. Sol gave him a sharp look and he quickly returned his gaze to his cup.

'I have no problem with Mossad, or whoever the fuck it was, nailing whoever they like. My only wish is that they wouldn't liquidate clients before they've settled their accounts.' Sol shrugged. 'It's a simple business principle: you gotta get paid.'

Carlyle nodded, happy to let Sol continue spouting off for as long as he liked.

'I've got nothing against the Israelis – apart from the little shit downstairs,' he nodded to a small door in the far corner of the kitchen, 'but then he tried to fucking kill me. They are great people to deal with, hard but fair.' He grinned at Carlyle. 'If I may be so bold as to give you a word of advice, I think that you have been rather too aggressive in your dealings with them. They will fuck you royally in the end.'

Carlyle gave him a *what's-done-is-done* type of a shrug.

'So, what have you got for me?'

'Well,' Carlyle smiled, 'I'm going to let you walk away . . . live to fight another day, as it were.'

Sol looked at Silver and frowned. 'Excuse me?'

Silver just stared into his mug.

'I need you to hand over the captive downstairs,' said Carlyle evenly. 'He needs to be taken into custody and processed.'

'Oh yes?' said Sol, a mixture of amusement and annoyance in his voice. 'He's going to be *processed* all right. He's going to be processed all the way to Hell. And if you don't start talking some sense, you'll be going with him.'

Carlyle ignored the threat. 'I'm sure that if I were to have you arrested,' he continued, 'that would prove to be only a temporary inconvenience. Anyway, I assured Dominic here that I would respect you, being his client. Like I said, you can walk away. Sure, the deal fell through, but these things happen. It certainly wasn't my fault and I am doing you the very great favour of overlooking the fact that what you are doing is completely fucking illegal.'

'How very kind of you.'

'That's a more than fair exchange for a man you don't really have any use for anyway.'

Sol sat back and crossed his arms. 'And if I say no?' Behind him, the two bodyguards, sensing the meeting had taken a downward turn, swayed forwards on the balls of their feet, ready for action. As they did so, there was a gentle tinkle of breaking glass, and the kitchen window disintegrated.

'What the fuck?' Before Sol could get out of his chair, the Somalis were both lying face down, blood leaking out of almost identical head wounds, brain matter splattered over the wooden floor and the fridge door. Reaching over to the nearest one, he tried to retrieve the Uzi pistol sticking out of the dead man's Wrangler jeans.

'Step away from the body!' Sid Lieberman edged his way through the door, the Browning Hi-Power that had killed DI David Ronan – now with an outsized suppressor attached to the end of its barrel – pointing at Sol Abramyan's head.

Carlyle looked over at Dom, who was gripping the table in order to stop himself shaking. The inspector gave him a gentle pat on the arm, and Dom almost jumped out of his skin. 'Just stay calm,' Carlyle murmured, 'and we'll walk out of this.'

Dom let out a constipated grunt that suggested he wasn't entirely reassured, in view of the evidence in front of him.

Sol moved away from Lieberman, until he was standing next to Carlyle. 'You are one fucked-up policeman,' he hissed, just before a .40 S&W round punched straight through his skull and sent him flying backwards.

'That was neat!' Sylvia Swain stepped from behind Lieberman and trained a second silenced Browning on Carlyle. She had that glazed expression on her face that suggested she was high on either drink or drugs. 'Can I do the copper as well?'

'First things first,' Lieberman scowled. He turned to Silver. 'Who are you?'

'A civilian,' explained Carlyle quickly.

'There *are* no fucking civilians,' Lieberman snarled. 'He dies here with you.'

'Kill him and you get nothing,' Carlyle said quietly.

'Give me my man right now,' Lieberman screamed, 'or I will fucking kill you both right this second. Then I will go straight to your home and kill your fucking family.'

'Cool!' trilled Swain.

Carlyle glanced at Dom, who was staring at a spot somewhere out in the darkness beyond the shattered window. There was something that might have been a smile on his face, and Carlyle realized that he was thinking about his kids and his wife, and all the things that made his life worthwhile. Fighting back a tear, he felt a flood of overwhelming gratitude towards the man who was at his side. If he was going to die, at least he wouldn't die alone.

'Where's Goya?' Lieberman demanded.

Carlyle gestured at the door in the corner. 'In the basement.'

'Well, what are we waiting for?' Swain demanded, pointing the way with her semi-automatic. 'Let's get down there.' Rising from his chair, Carlyle hauled Dom after him. 'Hurry up,' Swain shouted. 'Open it!'

The small wooden door, only about five feet by two feet, looked like it should give access to a cupboard or pantry. Grabbing the handle, Carlyle tried pulling and then pushing. 'It's locked.'

'No problem,' Swain grinned. 'Step aside.'

Carlyle barely had time to jump out of the way before she blasted the lock three times. The door disintegrated and they were left looking at a steep set of narrow wooden stairs, leading down into darkness.

'On you go,' the military attaché said. 'Both of you.'

Carefully taking one step at a time, Carlyle led the way, followed by Dom. When he reached the bottom, he groped for a light switch. Flicking it on, the space was illuminated by a single bare bulb hanging from the middle of the ceiling itself. A couple of large flies buzzed around it before settling for the view from the ceiling. The large, windowless room smelled of damp and decay. The walls were whitewashed brick, and the floor of rough, untreated concrete was covered in plastic sheeting. In the centre, a man sat tied to a chair. Slumped forward, he did not respond in any way to Carlyle's presence. Naked to the waist and barefoot, the smell coming from his jeans suggested he had been left alone there for a long time. The blood on his head and chest were evidence of multiple beatings, presumably at the hands of the Somalis.

Breathing through his mouth, Carlyle stepped over to the chair and placed a hand on the man's neck until he found a pulse. What had Lieberman called him? Goya? Carlyle gingerly pulled back the man's head by the matted hair. Even through the blood, it was easy to recognize the face. He glanced at Dom. 'That's the guy who shot Joe.'

'Result,' Dom grunted without enthusiasm.

'Is he alive?' Swain pushed Dom further into the room and stepped away from the stairs, allowing Lieberman to follow her down.

'Yes,' Carlyle nodded, 'but he's in a bad way.'

'Let's get him upstairs,' Swain commanded. 'Quickly.'

Carlyle grabbed the front legs of the chair and signalled for Dom to get hold of the back.

'When you reach the top,' Lieberman barked, 'untie him and put him on the kitchen table.' Turning, he disappeared back up the stairs.

'Then the pair of you get yourselves back down here,' Swain added, 'and we'll have some fun.'

Carlyle let Dom take the lead and they shuffled awkwardly towards the stairs. With his front foot on the bottom step, Carlyle thought he heard a noise upstairs. Pushing forward, he knocked Dom off-balance.

'Hey!' Dom half-tripped on the stairs but didn't lose his grip on the chair.

'Sorry.'

'Get on with it!' Swain pushed the muzzle of the Browning's silencer into the nape of Carlyle's neck.

'I'm trying,' the inspector protested, 'but he's heavy.' With another large grunt, he began the climb.

At the top of the stairs, Carlyle quickly dropped the chair and skipped away from the door, leaving Goya blocking Swain's view into the kitchen. Stepping round the table, he saw Sid Lieberman lying face down between the two dead Somalis, his hands tied tightly behind his back with plastic cuffs. The size-ten boot of Gideon Spanner was placed firmly in the small of the military attaché's back. Spanner had a SIG Sauer P226 pointed at Lieberman's head and a bored expression on his face.

Pulling a couple of cans of Stella Artois out of the fridge, Dom handed one to Carlyle and swiftly downed most of the other. 'What about the bitch in the basement?' he asked.

'She'll be up in a moment,' said Carlyle, cracking open his can. 'No need to go and get her.'

Dom looked over at Spanner, who gave the impression of being less than impressed with their drinking on the job but said nothing. Instead, he signalled to another of Dom's boys loitering in the hallway. Immediately, the man took up position to one side of the stairwell, P226 at the ready.

Dom finished his beer and dived into the fridge for another. 'She's got thirty seconds or we just go down and shoot her.'

'I want all of them alive,' said Carlyle firmly.

'No, you bloody don't.' Dom defiantly killed the second beer. 'You let them walk out of here, they get sent on a plane straight home and that's the end of that. No justice for Joe Szyszkowski's family.'

Or David Ronan's for that matter. Frowning, Carlyle finished his beer.

'Anyway, we're not standing around all night, arguing the toss about it.' Dom chucked his empty cans into a plastic bag lying by the sink and gestured for Carlyle to do the same. 'We need to clean up and get going.' Picking up a dishcloth from the draining board, Dom wiped down the handle of the fridge. 'I've kept to my end of the deal, now we need to vamoose.'

'I know.'

'So why don't we just whack them?'

'Like you did with Sam Hooper?'

Dom gave him a dirty look. 'Careful, Johnny boy.'

'Sid? What's going on?' Sylvia Swain's head popped out through the doorway at the top of the stairs, to be greeted with an unceremonious smack in the face with the P226. There was a half-shriek, followed by the sound of her tumbling back down the stairs.

'Told you she'd be right up,' Carlyle grinned.

Dom gestured at his man to go and get her. 'Can't we at least just shoot the fucking psycho bitch?' he pleaded.

It took a couple of minutes to finally retrieve Swain from the basement and place her next to Lieberman and Goya. Lost in thought, Silver gazed at the three of them, sullen and brooding, trussed up on the kitchen floor. After a few moments Gideon cleared his throat, breaking the silence. He looked at his boss, who gestured to the back door. Nodding, Gideon and his colleague slipped out into the night. 'At last,' Dom sighed as he watched them go. 'Now we can go and really get pissed. Or at least I can.' He looked at his watch. 'The call to the police will be made in five minutes. Let's see what they make of this mess.' Stepping round the bodies, he stood at the kitchen table, on which had been piled the Somalis' Uzis and the Israelis' Browning semi-automatics. Using the kitchen cloth, he carefully picked up one of the Uzis and tossed it down the stairs into the basement. Then he did the same with the second Uzi and one of the Brownings. The final gun he took in his hand and stepped over behind the three Israelis, shooting each one in the back of the head.

'Dom!'

Carlyle slumped against the kitchen wall as a wave of nausea washed over him. 'For fuck's sake,' he whimpered.

'Don't be such a fucking pussy,' Dom scowled. 'How can we leave any witnesses?'

'But – we've . . . you've . . .' Tears welled in the inspector's eyes. He felt as if he was ten years old again, on the receiving end of a monster shoeing from some fat bully in the school playground.

Ignoring his sobs, Dom calmly wiped down the grip of the gun and tossed it into the basement with the others. 'That was for Joe.'

Chapter Sixty-five

THEY REPAIRED TO the Old Swan pub. Only a couple of blocks from the horrors of Peel Street, life was proceeding pretty much as normal. Stepping into the saloon bar, Carlyle let Dom order him a double of Jameson's while he himself went to the gents to clean himself up. Before returning to the bar, the inspector took his private mobile out of his pocket and removed the SIM card. Dropping it down the toilet, he flushed and watched it disappear into London's crumbling sewerage system. Then he smashed the handset against the porcelain and dropped it in the waste-bin by the door.

Dom was sitting at a table when he returned. On a TV fixed to the wall, Chelsea was playing some foreign team that Carlyle didn't immediately recognize. Squinting at the screen, he could see that the chavs were winning 1-0. 'Wankers,' he hissed.

'Too right,' said Dom, who was a West Ham man.

'I'm changing my phone number,' Carlyle said as he took a seat. 'The old one isn't working any longer.'

'Okay.' Dom took a mouthful of his Theakston's Paradise Ale and nodded. He was already three-quarters of the way through his pint, with a second one waiting on the table.

Carlyle swallowed about half of his whiskey. 'I'll let you have the new number in the next couple of days.'

'Fine.'

For a few minutes, they watched the game in silence. It was extremely one-sided, and it was no surprise when Chelsea quickly scored a second goal. Carlyle shook his head in disgust.

In the distance, they heard a succession of sirens.

'Gideon obviously made the call,' Carlyle smiled.

'Gideon is very reliable,' Dom replied, now well into his second pint. 'How long are you going to give it before you put in an appearance?'

'I'll wait for them to call me.' Carlyle drained his glass. Taking his work mobile out of his jacket pocket, he placed it on the table. 'Meantime,' he said, getting to his feet, 'it's my round.'

Chapter Sixty-six

IT STARTED TO rain as the inspector stood on the pavement waiting for Anita Szyszkowski to buy her post school-run latte from Caffè Nero. Despite the poor weather, the widow decided that she wanted to drink her coffee while sitting under the awning outside. After giving her time to settle, he braced himself and waited for a break in the traffic, so that he could cross the road.

By the time he approached her table, Anita had been joined by a miserable-looking blonde, sucking an orange and mango smoothie through a straw while chatting away through the other side of her mouth.

'So I told him that I wasn't prepared to do that sort of thing,' she trilled indignantly.

With her back to Carlyle, Anita nodded while sipping on her coffee.

'It just can't be hygienic,' the woman continued, 'can it?'

Carlyle tried to tune out of the discussion and yet catch a pause in their conversation at the same time.

'I mean . . .' The woman caught Carlyle's eye and stopped in mid-flow. Following her gaze, Anita turned in her chair. A look of surprise and anger swept across her face.

'Hello, Anita.' Carlyle moved around to where she could see him more easily.

'What do *you* want?' She looked pale and drawn, but her eyes sparkled with hatred.

When she didn't offer him a seat, Carlyle rocked back on his heels. He had rehearsed what he wanted to say, but the words suddenly stuck in his throat. 'I'm sorry that I didn't get the chance to speak to you earlier, but—'

'You have nothing to say to me,' Anita said bitterly. The blonde, unsure what was going on, pulled a phone from her pocket and began playing with it nervously.

'I just wanted to let you know,' Carlyle continued, keeping his voice deliberately calm, 'that we got the man who did it.' The rain was coming down more heavily now. He could feel the dampness seeping through his jacket but made no effort to find cover. 'He's dead.'

'Is that supposed to make me feel better?' Anita demanded.

'I just wanted to let you know,' Carlyle told her.

Anita gripped her cup tightly, spilling coffee over the table. 'Why should I care?'

'Because it's important,' he said gently. 'The kids can know that the man who killed their dad didn't get away with it.'

'Important? The only thing that's important,' she said, tears welling in her eyes, 'is that their dad is gone.'

'I know,' said Carlyle, head bowed.

'And the only thing that would make me feel better was if it had been you rather than him.'

'I just wanted to let you know,' he repeated.

'Fuck off, John,' she sobbed. 'Just fuck off. Leave me alone – and leave the kids alone, too.'

The blonde bashed at several keys on her handset and lifted it to her ear. 'If you don't bugger off,' she squawked, 'I'll call the police.'

'Okay. I'm going.' Carlyle held up both his hands and watched a solitary tear roll down Anita Szyszkowski's cheek and fall into her lap. Turning away from the weeping woman, he walked off down the road, relieved that – for him at least – it was finally over.

Chapter Sixty-seven

WAS ANA BOROCHOVSKY giving him the eye? Or was he just imagining it? Either way, after his run-in with Sylvia Swain, Carlyle had vowed that he would never gawp at another woman again. Carlyle quickly broke off eye-contact with Julius Jubelitski's granddaughter and lifted his gaze to the heavens. He shuffled from foot to foot and stifled a yawn. Turning to Roche, he whispered, 'Why can't they just bloody get on with it?'

'Be patient,' she replied, giving him a gentle smack on the arm. 'It won't take long.'

Carlyle looked at his watch and sighed. 'It has already been almost forty-five minutes.'

'Don't be so grumpy.' She pointed to a large black limousine that had just pulled up outside the northern gate of Lincoln's Inn Field. They watched as the back door opened and a small silverhaired man climbed out. Accompanied by a young female aide, he walked briskly over to the small group of friends and family standing close to the spot in the park where the skeleton of Julius Jubelitski had been dug up a few months earlier. After shaking hands with the

Council Services manager, he stepped over to the piece of ground where what looked like a large navy towel was lying on the ground. Lifting a hand for quiet, he pulled a piece of card from his pocket.

'Ladies and gentlemen,' he began, after quickly checking with his notes, 'this is my first official engagement as Israel's new Ambassador to London. And it gives me great pleasure to be unveiling this memorial to Julius Jubelitski, who was a great Jewish freedom-fighter.' He nodded to the aide, who knelt down and whisked away the towel to reveal a small round plaque fixed on a granite plinth. The legend, in white text on a blue background, read: *In memory of Julius Jubelitski, victim of fascists in this park during WWII. RIP.*

There was a small ripple of applause, and a couple of photographers stepped forward to take pictures.

After a few minutes, the Ambassador's aide started to escort him back towards his car.

'Sir!'

The Ambassador stopped at the open door.

Ignoring the aide's scowl, Carlyle approached, hand extended. 'Inspector John Carlyle, Metropolitan Police.'

'Ah, yes.' The Ambassador reluctantly gave the hand a weak shake. 'I believe that I've heard of you,' he said, lowering himself to slide into the limousine.

'I had some dealings with your predecessor,' Carlyle smiled, holding firmly on to the car door.

'Yes, you did,' the Ambassador agreed wearily.

'I was just wondering, what happened to her?'

'After a life devoted to public service, Ms Waxman resigned in order to take up a very lucrative job with a technology company in Tel Aviv. It will make her very rich.'

'Lucky her,' Carlyle said.

'Luck has nothing to do with it, Inspector. I have known Hilary for many years. She is a very talented and hard working woman.'

'That's one way of looking at it.'

'That is the way most people look at it.' The Ambassador looked up at Carlyle and added: 'I will let her know that you were asking after her.'

'You keep in regular touch?'

'Of course. You will not be surprised to hear that Hilary is keeping a close eye on the police investigation into the horrendous murders of our citizens in Peel Street. Like me, she is disappointed and frustrated by the complete and utter lack of progress you are making in finding the killers.'

'Not my case,' Carlyle shrugged, releasing his hold on the door and stepping away from the car. Keeping his thoughts to himself, the Ambassador pulled the door closed and signalled to his driver that he was ready to go.

Stepping into Il Buffone, Roche was disappointed to see that her AC Milan poster was no longer displayed on the wall.

'What happened, Marcello?' she asked, pointing to the empty space.

'Kids,' Marcello sighed. 'They graffiti all over it. Write disgusting things. Nasty pictures. In the end, I had to take it down.'

'Don't worry,' Roche told him. 'I'll get another one.'

'Maybe we should go for a different team this time,' Carlyle said.

Each of them brooded on that for a few moments, but no one could come up with a decent suggestion. Leaving the matter in abeyance, Marcello headed behind the counter to fetch their drinks.

Carlyle joined Roche at the small table by the window.

'They've asked me to go back to Leyton,' she announced.

'Asked you or told you?' Carlyle enquired, sitting down.

'I dunno.'

'I thought that the Commander had sorted it out that you would stay at Charing Cross.'

'She did,' Roche agreed, 'but Leyton's got some kind of staffing problem and they're pressing to have me back.'

Carlyle looked at her carefully. 'What do you want to do?'

Staring out of the window, she shrugged.

He thought about it for a minute. 'I want you to stay.'

She looked at him and smiled. 'Okay.'

'It's not always as . . . dramatic as this, but it's never dull.' He paused, letting Marcello place their drinks on the table. 'And I think we get on okay.'

'Yes,' she said, 'I think we do.'

'Good,' he smiled, 'that's settled, then. I'll have another word with Simpson.'

For several minutes they sat together in companionable silence, enjoying their coffee. Finally, Carlyle asked, 'How about Ronan? Do you think you'll be able to deal with that okay?'

She gave him a melancholy smile. 'I was so mad with David for what he did – playing away – that for the first few days I actually felt that he deserved to get whacked. Since then, my sense of perspective has returned.'

'Glad to hear it.'

'The whole thing is very sad, but I'll get over it.'

Which is more than you can say for Ronan himself, Carlyle thought, stifling a giggle.

'The funeral was last week.'

'Sorry,' he said, pulling himself together. 'I didn't realize.'

'Don't worry about it. You've had a lot on your plate. The funny thing was, I was there with David's mum and she was the one consoling me. I don't think she knew about the sister-in-law.'

'Was the sister-in-law there?' Carlyle asked, prurience getting the better of him.

'She was,' Roche grinned, 'but I kept my distance. She looked pretty upset about the whole thing.'

Marcello appeared from behind the counter. 'Hey, you two, it's time for me to close up. Haven't you got any work to do?'

'Yes, unfortunately.' Getting to his feet, Carlyle dug a fiver out of his pocket and slapped it down by the tin. 'I'll see you tomorrow.'

'I'll be here, as always.'

'Good to know,' Carlyle said sincerely, as he ushered Roche out of the door and back towards the police station.

Chapter Sixty-eight

FEELING ON LESS than top form, Carlyle was not best pleased to get home and find Helen also in a foul mood. After listening to her banging around angrily in the kitchen for several minutes, he couldn't take any more.

'Bad day at the office?' he asked.

'Totally shit,' she confirmed, racking a selection of dirty plates into the dishwasher.

He waited for her to explain, but she declined to elaborate. 'Anything in particular?' he asked finally.

'Four of our medical staff were arrested today,' she said, slamming shut the dishwasher door. 'A doctor and three nurses. They had been working in Gaza and took some time off in Tel Aviv. We got a call this morning to say that they had been arrested by the Israeli police . . . two bloody days ago.'

Knowing where this was going, Carlyle felt his heart sink.

'*Then*,' she continued, 'we got a call from some snotty little bureaucrat in the Israeli Foreign Ministry, informing us that what he called "the so-called medical aid charity" Avalon had seventy-two hours to close down all of its operations in Gaza or our people will be charged with espionage offences carrying a jail term of up to twenty-five years' imprisonment each.' She kicked a cupboard door in frustration. 'It's just such total fucking crap!'

He slung a comforting arm round her shoulder and pulled her close even as she tried to wriggle free. 'Can you do it?'

'Do what?'

'Close everything down in three days.'

This time he let her push him away. 'What are you suggesting?' she demanded, eyes blazing. 'That we should just give in?'

Carlyle shrugged. 'Don't fight battles you can't win.'

She gave him a firm punch on the chest. 'That's not advice I remember you yourself ever sticking to.'

'And look what happened.' Carlyle flung his arms wide in frustration. 'People got killed. The Israelis basically got what they wanted. It was all a bit messy, and they had a few casualities of their own, but they don't really care about that. They sit there, doing their American TV interviews, smugly refusing to confirm or deny ever doing anything to anyone. Meanwhile, I saw two kids in the piazza today walking around wearing *Don't mess with the Mossad* T-shirts, like those guys are some kind of rock stars. The whole thing might be totally fucked up, but there's nothing you can do about it. Trying to fight against it will just drive you mad.'

'So you think you got it wrong?'

He let out a terrible sigh. 'What did we achieve in the end?'

'Oh, John.' Stepping towards him, Helen buried her face in his chest.

'Look,' he said quietly, 'you are a small charity. You do great work all over the world. There is never going to be any shortage of places for your people to go and things for you to do. You have to live to fight another day.'

'I suppose so,' she sniffed.

'The other thing to remember is that it won't be you who's sitting in some shitty jail, wondering if you'll ever get home again. You can't play politics with other people's lives.'

She looked up at him. 'Haven't I heard that somewhere before?'

'Probably,' he grinned.

'There's an emergency board meeting at nine a.m. tomorrow to discuss what to do,' she said. 'I think that there will be a fairly energetic debate.'

'I bet there will.'

'But we will make a decision.'

'Good.'

'Then I have to leave at lunchtime, to go to Louisa's funeral in Reims.'

Carlyle had completely forgotten about that commitment.

'I catch the Eurostar at two-fifteen. The funeral is at eleven the next morning. I'll be back around seven in the evening.'

'Okay.'

'Alice has promised to look after you while I'm away.'

'Great. How are things with her boyfriend?'

Helen raised her eyes to the ceiling. 'Don't ask.'

'Like that, eh?'

'All part of growing up,' Helen sighed.

A thought popped into his head. 'Is Louisa being buried with Fadi?'

'No. Her parents didn't approve of the marriage, so that was a non-starter. I was told that he was cremated.'

'And will his ashes be returned to his family?'

She shrugged. 'I hope so, but that will be a matter for the Foreign Office.'

Carlyle shook his head. 'Poor bugger.'

'That's exactly why we have to fight for these people,' Helen reminded him.

'Fight and lose,' he said sadly. 'Fight and lose.'

Chapter Sixty-nine

SITTING IN THE same basement interview room where they had met previously, Carlyle watched Ambrose Watson happily polish off a jumbo croissant before picking up a sheet of IIC-headed paper and then passing it across the desk.

The inspector quickly scanned the tiny font. 'What's this?'

Ambrose said, as if it should be blindingly obvious, 'It's the form you need to sign to say that you have voluntarily agreed to take part in this investigation, that you understand its conclusions and that you agree to undertake any suggested remedial actions relevant to yourself. There's a copy for us and a copy for you.'

'What remedial actions?'

'Nothing really.' Ambrose scratched his nose. 'Just that you agree to continue seeing the psychiatrist that Commander Simpson has arranged for you.'

'For how long?' So far, Carlyle had endured three follow-up visits to Dr Wolf, and the novelty had long since worn off.

'That's hardly for me to say, now, is it?' Ambrose chided. 'That is something you will have to agree with the good doctor in due course. The Met is by no means prescriptive in these things. It just wants what is best for you.'

'Right.'

Ambrose handed Carlyle a biro and pointed at the two small *x*s pencilled at the foot of the page. 'Just sign here and here.'

Carlyle frowned. 'And if I don't?'

'Inspector,' Ambrose sighed, 'you really can get too suspicious sometimes. Normally when I hand over an X 37/C, people can't sign it quickly enough.'

'What's an X37/ C?'

'It's the form that you've now got in front of you,' Ambrose replied tartly. 'It's our standard investigation-completed form. In this case, it's a bit of a miracle that it's ever got to see the light of day. With so many bloody corpses, I would have expected the investigation to run for years, if not decades.'

'So what happened?' Carlyle asked innocently.

'It was dealt with at a higher level,' was all Ambrose would say.

'Okay.' Carlyle scribbled something approaching his signature in the appropriate places and returned the form to Ambrose

'Thank you.' Ambrose took back his pen and gave Carlyle his personal copy of the document. 'If you don't mind me saying so, I think you've been more than a little lucky in all of this.'

Carlyle grunted.

'It could have hung over your career like a big black cloud for a very long time.'

Tell me something I don't know, Carlyle thought.

Stuffing his papers back into his briefcase, Ambrose got to his feet. 'Well, Inspector,' he said, 'that concludes our business on this occasion. Please don't take it the wrong way if I say that I hope our paths don't cross again for a while.'

'Amen to that,' said Carlyle, smiling.

After Ambrose had left, he sat for a while with his mind empty, simply enjoying the silence.

Chapter Seventy

CARLYLE TOOK HIS seat by the side of the runway, rather disappointed that he hadn't been invited backstage to get another chance to gawp at the naked models getting ready to showcase the final collection from the late, lamented Rollo Kasabian, whose giant portrait now hung above the entrance to the runway. All the talk this evening was of Rollo and his genius, but Dominic Silver had decreed that tonight's show, being held in a disused railway station, would be a benefit for the family of Lottie Gondomar, the model who had hanged herself in the police cells at Charing Cross. Closing his eyes, Carlyle spent several minutes trying to recall the girl's face, but his mind remained blank.

The business was now being run by one of Rollo's erstwhile assistants, a dour fellow by the name of Karl Auclair. Before putting him in charge, Dom had Auclair checked out by a firm of private investigators, who had given the young man a clean bill of health, or had at least reported that his drug use was within socially acceptable limits and that his sexual appetites were modest and dull. Noting that they were now almost thirty minutes late in getting started, Carlyle presumed that good timekeeping had not been a key part of the job description.

It was decidedly chilly on the station platform and Carlyle wished that he had brought along a coat. He idly watched the seats around him fill up till finally the lights dimmed and a bombastic rock track that he didn't recognize began blaring out of the speakers positioned beside the runaway. Moments later, the first model sauntered into view, wearing what looked to Carlyle suspiciously like a bog-standard kaftan.

Dom slipped into the seat beside him. 'What do you think so far?'

Carlyle shrugged. 'It's only just started.'

Dom punched him gently on the shoulder. 'Don't sound too excited, will you.'

'Would you wear that?' Carlyle grunted, pointing to the kaftan.

'You've got to broaden your horizons, Johnny boy,' said Dom, waving a hand in the air. 'You've got to broaden your horizons.'

AT LEAST THE show was mercifully brief. Passing on Auclair's afterparty, the pair of them headed for a quiet bar half a block away.

'Do people actually buy that stuff?' Carlyle stared into his glass of Jameson whiskey.

'There's no accounting for taste.' Dom took a swig from his bottle of Peroni beer. 'And don't forget this is Rollo's swansong; the last ever Kasabian collection. The fashion editors can't get enough of it. The fat, rent-boy-loving, drug-snorting fuck-up has been offi-cially rebranded a genius.'

Carlyle laughed.

'Now, you know and I know that *genius*,' Dom continued, 'is almost certainly the most over-used word in the English language. But the point is that his legend has already been written. Anything with his name on it will now sell like hot cakes.'

'Was he really any good?' Carlyle asked. 'I mean, how difficult can it be to design a shirt? Or a pair of jeans? It's not like it's never been done before.'

'I know, I know,' Dom agreed. 'I don't understand it either. But I'm not complaining. Rollo did me a big favour by shuffling off this mortal coil so quickly. The business might even move into profit this year.'

Carlyle let a mouthful of whiskey lie on his tongue before swallowing it. 'Of course,' he said casually, 'that would have given you a pretty good motive for having him killed.'

Dom took another gulp of his beer. 'Is that a question or an observation?'

'No one has ever been charged with the murders of Kasabian or Sam Hooper,' Carlyle observed matter-of-factly.

'These things happen.'

Carlyle emptied his glass and said, lowering his voice, even though there was no one else within earshot: 'We have an unusual relationship.'

Dom smiled, knowing where the conversation was going. 'Yes,' he said, 'we do.'

'But we can only stretch things so far.'

'That is understood.'

Carlyle exhaled slowly. 'So – there are certain lines that cannot be crossed.'

Dom nodded. 'That has always been not only understood but respected.'

'So, I need to know . . .'

'What do you need to know, John?'

'Were you responsible for the deaths of Kasabian and Hooper?'

'Responsible?'

'Did you have them killed?'

'Bloody hell!' Dom laughed. 'What kind of a question is that?'

'I need to know,' Carlyle said grimly.

Dom's eyes narrowed. 'Do you *really* want to know?'

No, screamed a voice in the inspector's head. *Absolutely not. Never in a million fucking years.* 'Yes.'

'Okay, suit yourself.' Grabbing Carlyle's empty glass, Dom got to his feet. 'Let me just nip to the bar and I'll be right back with an answer. Same again?'

Feeling sick to his stomach, Carlyle merely nodded.

DOM HANDED CARLYLE the double whiskey and sat down with a fresh bottle of beer. 'Cheers!'

'Cheers,' Carlyle repeated, without enthusiasm.

'Remember the night you arrested Lottie?'

'Yeah.' That seemed a hell of a long time ago now, but even if he couldn't remember her face, he could recall what the rest of her looked like, standing naked, backstage.

'And remember I told you about Marina and Cockayne Syndrome.'

'Yup,' Carlyle said.

'Well, since then, there have been more tests and the news isn't getting any better. The other day, the child even asked me "When am I going to die, Dad?" ' He shook his head. 'Five years old. What kind of a fucking question is that?'

'What did you say?' Carlyle asked, wondering where Dom was going with this.

'What *could* I say?' Dom cleared his throat. 'I told her that we loved her and we would look after her and that we wouldn't lie to her, but that we didn't know the answer to everything.'

'How did she react to that?'

'She went off to play with her dolls.' Dom said in a low voice, 'It drives me insane, worrying about what's going on inside her head.'

'It must be tough.'

'That's the understatement of this or any other fucking lifetime.' Dom waved his beer bottle in the direction of Carlyle's face. 'But *you* are doubtless wondering what this has to do with your question.'

Carlyle shrugged.

'It means that Marina is a brutal reminder to me of which way is up,' Dom said forcefully. 'Of what's important.'

'Certainly,' Carlyle agreed.

'Family is the most important thing. That's true for you, just as it is for me. That's why we have managed to work together so well over the years. Both of us have our priorities right. We do our jobs and we go home to our families. We do what we have to do in order to make sure, as far as we can, that they are safe and sound.'

'Maybe so.' Carlyle rubbed his temples. 'However, that does not mean that you can operate outside of the law.'

'John, just listen to yourself! You were standing next to me when I took down those crazies in Sol Abramyan's house.'

'There's a difference between that and killing a copper, for fuck's sake,' Carlyle argued.

'Hooper was bent.'

'And Rollo, what was he? Just collateral damage?'

Dom raised his eyebrows.

Carlyle knocked back the rest of his whiskey. 'I knew it, I fucking knew it. Have you gone crazy?'

Dom gave him a hard stare. 'I was crazy enough to stand shoulder-to-shoulder with you when that Browning was being waved in my face,' he hissed. 'You can't have it both ways.'

'Fuck . . . fuck, fuck, fuck, fuck, fuck.'

Dom reached over and gave Carlyle's shoulder a squeeze. 'Don't worry,' he said soothingly, 'it'll be fine. After all, we're in this together.'

Chapter Seventy-one

SIMPSON'S OFFICE AT Paddington Green still looked as if no one had occupied it for many months, if not years. There was not one thing – book, file, photo or piece of office stationery – to suggest that it was in use. Staring at the grime on the window, Carlyle did a mental inventory of his current workload: there were a couple of expensive car thefts from a garage in Drury Lane; a home invasion in Bloomsbury; and a couple of cases of ID theft – all in all, nothing very exciting. That made for a nice change. Roche, now happily ensconced in Charing Cross for the foreseeable future, could take the lead in most if not all of them. Meanwhile, he himself could enjoy some downtime, get home at a reasonable hour every evening and put the horrors of recent weeks behind him. Maybe he could even persuade his mother-in-law to come up to London and look after Alice, allowing Carlyle and Helen a couple of days by the sea.

Carlyle smiled at the prospect of having a more 'normal' existence. That would be fine, for a while. But he knew perfectly well that, after a fortnight or maybe a month at the most, he would need to find something to occupy both his brain and his time. Otherwise he would start feeling restless and grumpy. Helen and Alice would start to find him annoying, and would be relieved to get him out from under their feet. Not for the first time, it struck him that he needed the bloody criminals to help keep him sane. Well, some of them, anyway. Did that make him a bit mad? Maybe it was something that he should be discussing with the shrink?

'Anything interesting?'

'Eh?' Carlyle looked up at Simpson, who had suddenly materialized behind her desk.

'You seemed deep in thought,' she said, placing a mug of steaming coffee on the blotter in front of her, and then slipping into her seat.

'I was just looking forward to things being a bit quieter for a while.'

'Aren't we all,' she grinned.

'I thought I might take Helen to Brighton.' Immediately the words were out, he cursed himself. Being recently widowed, Simpson wouldn't want to be hearing about his domestic plans.

If the remark caused her any upset, however, she didn't show it. 'I think that's a great idea,' she said warmly, taking a sip of coffee.

'There's nothing hugely pressing to deal with back at the station,' he added, keen to get back onto matters of work, 'and Sergeant Roche is very much on top of things.'

Simpson nodded. 'I'm glad that it's working out so well with her. It's good that you have been able to deal with that aspect of the Joe situation so . . . professionally.'

'It's difficult to get the balance right,' Carlyle explained. 'You can't go to pieces, but you don't want to appear a heartless bastard either. I did try to reach out to Anita, but, well, you know what happened there.'

'Yes,' Simpson sighed, 'you just have to leave it for now. At least, you were able to tell her that Joe's killer had been . . . dealt with. Even if she doesn't seem particularly grateful for that now, you have to hope that it will provide some succour in the future.'

'Yes.'

'Maybe things will change over time.' She looked at him hesitantly. 'There is one thing, though.'

'What?'

'The case on Joe's murder isn't going to be officially closed.' She quickly held up a hand before he could begin his protest. 'The bodies of the Israelis were repatriated yesterday. The Foreign Office is not going to further annoy Tel Aviv by publicly naming one of its people as being the man responsible for shooting a policeman on a London street.'

Carlyle made a noise of disgust.

'It's better than the other way round,' Simpson went on, 'with a situation where the case was closed and the killer was still running around flipping us the finger.'

'Fair point,' Carlyle reflected.

'I'm told that Lieberman, Ryan Goya and Maude Kleinman will be buried in a military ceremony with full honours.'

'Maude Kleinman?'

'That was the name on the ID they presented for the woman you knew as Sylvia Swain.'

Carlyle shook his head. 'All this cloak and dagger shit is just so wearisome.'

'Did you speak to Ambrose Watson?' Simpson asked, moving the conversation on.

'Yeah. He told me that his various investigations are now closed, so I signed the necessary bits of paper.'

'Ambrose is very fair.'

'Yes.'

'Did he ever mention a man called Dominic Silver?'

Carlyle looked her squarely in the eye. 'No.'

'Okay.' Simpson paused, then went on: 'You do understand just how terribly *problematic* your relationship with Mr Silver is, don't you?'

'I do not have a *relationship* with Silver,' Carlyle said stiffly.

'Don't get all mealy-mouthed with me, John,' Simpson shot back. 'It just doesn't suit you. What is he? A CI? I haven't seen him on any list.'

Confidential informant? Carlyle thought. *Hardly. The whole bloody world seems to know about me and Dom.* 'Dom is not a CI,' he said evenly. 'I wouldn't describe him as an informant at all.'

Simpson grimaced in exasperation. 'So what would you describe him as?'

'I would describe him as a former colleague who is still keen to help the police whenever the opportunity presents itself.'

'Oh? So you wouldn't describe him as a drug dealer who gets you to do some of his dirty work for him?'

That's a pretty fair summary of our relationship, Carlyle conceded. 'No,' he said firmly. 'I wouldn't.'

Sitting up in her chair, Simpson gave him a long, hard look.

A terrible thought suddenly hit him. 'Are you suggesting *I* killed Hooper?'

'No, no,' she said irritably. 'Of course not.'

'Good.'

'I don't think even you could be that stupid.'

'That's good to know,' he said humourlessly.

'Look,' she jabbed an angry finger at the space between them, 'never forget how bloody lucky you were here. This whole thing became such a terrible nightmare that in the end no one wanted to touch it. Everything has been buried and any paperwork beyond the absolute bare minimum will be destroyed. Under a different set of circumstances, you could have been hauled over the coals. You could easily have got the sack – and ended up in jail.'

Carlyle held her gaze but said nothing.

'If the Sam Hooper killing hadn't got lost in this total mess – if he wasn't just one body among so bloody many – the investigation into his death would doubtless have been a lot more detailed,' she persisted.

'Ambrose told me that Hooper was bent,' Carlyle commented.

'I still don't think that is sufficient justification for someone executing him,' Simpson said tartly.

'No,' Carlyle agreed.

'It is a very, very serious crime indeed and I would expect anyone with information relating to his murder to come forward immediately, regardless of the status of the investigation.'

'Absolutely.'

Simpson stared at him for several more moments. When Carlyle said nothing, she warned him, 'If this comes back to haunt you, somewhere down the line, there's nothing I can do to protect you. More to the point, there is nothing I would want to do to protect you.'

'I will keep my eyes and ears open,' Carlyle promised. 'If I discover anything, I will let you know immediately.'

Simpson glared at him.

'But,' he went on, unable to resist the dig, 'there are always grey areas. Things are never black and white, as you know from your own personal experience.' The message was clear: *I supported you when your husband was arrested and people wanted to believe that you were his accomplice, so get off my fucking back now.*

For a heartbeat, it looked like Simpson was going to hurl her mug of coffee at him. Carlyle sat, unflinching, as he watched her slowly bring her anger under control.

'I understand what you are saying, Inspector,' she said finally.

Nodding, he got to his feet.

'There's one other thing . . .'

'Oh?' Slowly, he sat back down again. A sly grin appeared on Simpson's face, making him brace himself.

'You've been put forward for a Commendation.' Simpson dropped her gaze to the desk. 'I assume it will be a formality. You should get written confirmation in the next couple of weeks.'

Carlyle waited for her to restore eye-contact, daring her not to laugh. 'Are you joking?' he asked, trying to recall her ever having done so in the past.

Keeping a straight face, Simpson said, 'No. The citation will read: *For bravery in attempting to apprehend armed criminals and showing unflinching courage in the line of duty.* Or something like that. You know the kind of thing.'

'Unflinching courage.' Carlyle smiled. 'I like that.'

'It relates to the incident at the Ritz.'

Carlyle had already garnered a number of Commendations during the course of his career. Another one was of little interest. 'Do I get a pay rise?' he asked cheekily.

This time Simpson did laugh. 'Don't push your luck. And don't think that this in any way invalidates what I've said. IIC could have buried you after this business here. Having decided not to do that, you're being made something of a hero.'

'To better put a lid on the whole bloody thing,' Carlyle mused.

'Yes, indeed,' Simpson said, 'and I suggest, for once, you just act bloody grateful and go along with it.'

'I think I will,' Carlyle told her.

Chapter Seventy-two

ONE IMPORTANT THING that Carlyle had learned from his sessions with Dr Wolf was that the coffee in the doctor's office was truly dreadful. To get round this problem, he quickly developed a routine whereby, on the way to each session, he would drop into the Starbucks next to Wolf's office. This morning, he sat happily drinking the last of his Venti Latte, wondering if the doctor, head bowed, was contemplating their earlier exchange or had simply fallen asleep. Draining his cup, he reached forward and dropped it in the bin at the side of the shrink's desk. The noise seemed to rouse Wolf from his slumber. He looked up at Carlyle, who smiled blandly.

'I was wondering,' said the psychiatrist, 'if we could maybe spend some time talking about your parents . . .'

Chapter Seventy-three

HELEN ASSUMED HER best smile as she handed a plate of snacks round the table. 'It's so nice to meet you.'

'Thank you,' said Ken Walton, happily dropping a couple of cucumber sandwiches onto his plate. 'Lorna has told me so much about you all. It's a pleasure to meet you at last.'

Refusing to look at her son, Lorna Gordon nodded sagely as she sipped her peppermint tea.

Looking Walton up and down, the inspector wondered what his dad was doing right now – probably sitting in his shitty little bedsit, looking through the record collection he couldn't play. Seated in the Palm Court with his mother and her new boyfriend, he felt a mixture of guilt and embarrassment. At least Helen had been pressganged into coming along, too. She had been in a foul mood since Avalon's board had decided to pull out of Gaza, and Carlyle hoped that this little outing would help take her mind off work troubles for a short while.

He glanced at his wife for some moral and spiritual support, but in return simply got a look that said *For God's sake, say something.*

'So,' Carlyle mumbled, 'how did you two meet?' Grabbing a slice of lemon cake from his plate, he took a large bite.

'Lorna and I have known each other for a long time,' Walton replied vaguely.

Carlyle gave his mother an enquiring look. 'Oh, is that right?'

Lorna put her cup back on the saucer and placed a gentle hand on Helen's forearm. 'And how is Alice?' she asked, changing the subject with a lack of subtlety for which the Carlyle family had long been famous.

Helen looked at Carlyle and grinned. 'She's not on the best form, to be honest. She's just split with her boyfriend and things are a bit – well, tense.'

'It's just part of the *growing up* process,' Carlyle remarked.

Head down, Ken Walton gave the cucumber sandwiches his full attention.

'These things are always hard to take,' said Lorna, effortlessly ignoring her son's churlishness. 'She will snap out of it soon enough.'

Helen smiled sadly. 'I'm afraid I didn't help things by getting into a row with the boy's mother.'

'Ach,' said the older woman, 'the child's still very young. It's right that you are still getting involved.' She glanced at Carlyle with amusement. 'There will be plenty of time for her to make mistakes all on her own.'

Gritting his teeth, Carlyle said nothing. Instead he scanned the restaurant, hoping to spy some outrageous criminal activity in progress that might serve to rescue him from this latest domestic nightmare. Sadly, this time round, there was none to be found.

About the Author

JAMES CRAIG has worked in London as a journalist and consultant for almost thirty years. He lives in Covent Garden with his family.

www.james-craig.co.uk